WAKING THE TIGER

D1513793

WAKING THE TIGER

MARK WIGHTMAN

This edition produced in Great Britain in 2021

by Hobeck Books Limited, Unit 14, Sugnall Business Centre, Sugnall, Stafford, Staffordshire, ST21 6NF

www.hobeck.net

A CIP catalogue for this book is available from the British Library.

ISBN 978-1-913-793-33-3 (pbk)

ISBN 978-1-913-793-32-6 (ebook)

Cover design by Jem Butcher

www.jembutcherdesign.co.uk

Printed and bound in Great Britain

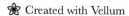 Created with Vellum

For Lillian

Singapore 1939

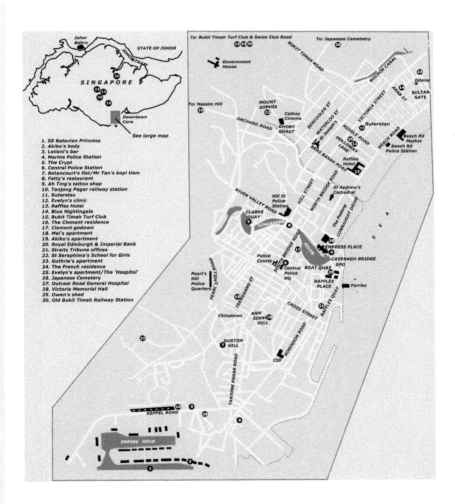

1. SS Batavian Princess
2. Akiko's body
3. Leilani's bar
4. Marine Police Station
5. The Crypt
6. Central Police Station
7. Betancourt's flat/Mr Tan's kopi tiam
8. Fatty's restaurant
9. Ah Ting's tattoo shop
10. Tanjong Pagar railway station
11. Suteretsu
12. Evelyn's clinic
13. Raffles Hotel
14. Blue Nightingale
15. Bukit Timah Turf Club
16. The Clement residence
17. Clement godown
18. Mei's apartment
19. Akiko's apartment
20. Royal Edinburgh & Imperial Bank
21. Straits Tribune offices
22. St Seraphima's School for Girls
23. Guthrie's apartment
24. The French residence
25. Evelyn's apartment/The 'Hospital'
26. Japanese Cemetery
27. Outram Road General Hospital
28. Victoria Memorial Hall
29. Owen's shed
30. Old Bukit Timah Railway Station

Chapter One

The driver, a stout Malay named Awang, brought the long-nosed police car to a halt. He parked alongside the dockyard wall where a dilapidated outbuilding, cobbled together from corrugated asbestos sheets and salt-rusted iron straps, provided shade from the equatorial sun.

Whenever Inspector Maximo Betancourt − late of the Singapore CID and now the lone member of the recently formed Special Investigations Unit of the Marine Branch − had reason to commandeer a pool car, he travelled in the front with the driver. This was no grand gesture of solidarity; it was simply that sitting in the back made him carsick. But to his European colleagues, his habit was one more piece of evidence that, despite his marriage, he wasn't, and never would be, one of them. Not that they paid him much attention any longer. His Detective Branch days belonged to a fast-receding past and his work, such as it was, was now to be found here, on the Singapore waterfront.

He threw open the door, a little too exuberantly as it turned out, and a crunch of metal on stone told him he'd hit the wall. He squirmed through the gap until enough of his body protruded from the car that he could free his hands and haul himself the rest of the way out. He examined the door. The damage to His Majesty's property could have been worse, but the scratches to the paint meant yet more paper-work. He sighed and leaned in through the window.

'Nicely parked.'

Awang nodded, accepting the compliment as his due. Not for the first time, Betancourt reflected with regret on how his command of the Malay language didn't lend itself well to sarcasm. At least his English had that going for it.

Ahead of him, a ship swayed lazily in the tide that lapped up against the sea wall. Her name was the *Batavian Princess* and the hawsers, thick as a man's arm, that held her fast to the dock, creaked in protest.

Free me! she seemed to cry. *I don't belong here. I should be out there at sea, not tied to this Godforsaken piece of land.*

He knew how she felt.

He dragged his attention back to the reason for his visit. A noisy crowd of men carrying crudely painted placards and shouting slogans had gathered by the bow of the ship.

Half an hour previously, he'd received a call to alert him that another confrontation had broken out. Protests like this had become commonplace in the six months Betancourt had been working the docks. Earlier that year, the Colonial Government had placed an embargo on the export to Japan of strategically important goods, such as rubber, oil, or anything else that could be deemed useful to the Japanese Imperial Army in furthering its designs on Asia. Ever since, Chinese dockworkers had taken to protesting against any trade with Japan, legitimate or otherwise. The *Batavian Princess* had arrived that morning from Kobe, by way of Shanghai, with a cargo of silk, tea, rice – all perfectly legal – and now the rabble were calling upon their brethren who were busy emptying the ship, to set down their burdens.

Ranks of rickety flat-bed trucks queued back along the harbour front as far as the main gate. There was no breeze down here to sweep away the exhaust fumes and the air was thick with the smell of their diesel. Unloading of the ship's holds should have been in full flow, but the caterpillar of cargo had ground to a halt and the truck drivers were sounding their horns in unison, drowning out the shouts of the protesters. Betancourt understood their impatience. The shipping agents paid the drivers by the load. The quicker they got in, loaded up, and got away again, the quicker they could be back for their next load. The drivers were becoming fractious; the great god Trade was hungry, and it was Betancourt's job to make sure its hunger was sated before things got ugly.

An elderly Malay man approached, taking care to keep Betancourt between himself and the mob. His name was Abu Bakar. He worked as a tally clerk for the owners of the ship, overseeing the loading and unloading of cargo, and he was one of several wharf-side workers Betancourt was cultivating as a personal informant. As usual, Abu Bakar was wreathed in clove-perfumed smoke from the *kretek* that never left his mouth. The month before, on a tip-off, Betancourt had searched a Buginese fishing boat from South Sulawesi and confiscated a crate of smuggled cigarettes. He'd never been a stickler for procedure, so, instead of handing them over to Customs as the rules required, he'd stashed the contraband under his desk and had been steadily redistributing the contents to Abu Bakar and a few select others as an inducement. When he'd first started with the Marine Branch, he'd found it nigh-on impossible to get any cooperation from the dockers, but his discreet bribery was paying dividends as it was Abu Bakar who'd called him earlier.

'How long have you been here?'

'The ship docked around nine o'clock and I've been here since. Everything was normal at first. A few protesters – no more than usual. We just ignored them and got on with emptying the holds. Then this lot turned up.' He pointed to the men with the placards.

'Ever see any of them before?'

'Never.'

When he'd received Abu Bakar's call earlier, Betancourt thought he'd known what to expect. It tended to be the same faces every time, and he usually recognised at least some of the demonstrators, but this lot were unfamiliar. Betancourt studied the group of men. They were an odd lot. For one thing, no one seemed to be in charge and what's more their efforts at admonishing their colleagues for working were decidedly half-hearted, as though they were just going through the motions. If trouble-making was their aim, they weren't doing a very good job of it. Hopefully, this was a one-off.

A shrill cry cut through the chants of the strikers and interrupted his thoughts.

'Oi, you!'

A tall, dark-haired European emerged from one of the godowns and pointed a finger in Betancourt's face.

'What the bloody hell do you think you're playing at, standing around watching? Get this lot rounded up. A month in the cells will remind them which side their bread is buttered on. Well? What are you waiting for? Get on with it.' He looked to be in his early twenties with the hard, taut body of an athlete. Betancourt felt no warmth towards the man or his like, but he knew from experience that the quickest way to get rid of him was to pour oil on troubled waters.

'Soon have this sorted out, sir. Just a bit of high spirits.'

'High spirits? Why isn't there a proper English policeman seeing to this? What's the bloody point in sending one of your lot down here? You're as bad as them. Probably take their side. Do as you're told or I'm calling the Assistant Commissioner.'

Betancourt had tried the reasonable approach and it hadn't worked. He'd neither the energy nor the inclination to reason with this pompous fool any longer.

'Get back inside your office now or I'll arrest you for interfering with police activities. And you won't need to telephone Assistant Commissioner Bonham. I'll let him know which cell he can find you in, if he wants to speak to you.'

The man's face turned a deep crimson, but he shut up and retreated with bad grace back to the godown.

Before leaving his office, Betancourt had placed a precautionary call to Police Headquarters asking for backup, and at that moment a van sped into the yard, its bell ringing. The influx of uniformed reinforcements was enough to divert the attention of the mob, and there was a momentary lull.

The new arrivals tumbled from the van and gathered before him. Betancourt surveyed them. Raw recruits. He hoped they'd at least completed their basic training. A young sergeant was doing his best to sort them out and had assembled them into a ragged line. Betancourt called him over. The sergeant pulled a notebook and pencil from his shirt pocket as he scurried across. He started to introduce himself, but Betancourt pre-empted him with a raised hand.

'Don't tell me. Sergeant Quek.'

Quek seemed baffled by this display of perspicacity. 'How did you know?'

'I'm a detective, I work things out.' Betancourt tapped the man's chest. 'And your name is on your badge. Come on, I want your men split into two groups.'

'Two groups...' Quek repeated, nodding as he scribbled away furiously in his notebook.

'You take three of them and sort that lot out.' Betancourt pointed to the protesters, so there would be no misunderstanding. 'Tell them to pack it in and get back to work. The other three can come with me and we'll get the cargo moving again.'

'Pack it in and get back to work... cargo moving again...' More scribbles.

Betancourt laid a hand on the frenetic pencil. 'You don't have to write down everything I say.'

'Yes, Inspector,' Quek agreed, copying down what Betancourt had just said.

He shook his head. 'And you don't have to keep calling me Inspector, either.'

Quek looked perplexed. 'What should I call you then?'

What should he call him? Betancourt had become unused to anyone calling him anything.

'Boss is fine.'

'Yes, Insp—. Yes, boss.'

Quek gave the men their instructions and after a minor squabble about relative seniority and who would rather be in which group, they stood in two lines. They were a ragtag bunch and made for an uninspiring sight. It was as well, Betancourt reflected, that he wasn't expecting any serious opposition from the strikers.

'Right, listen up. You three with Sergeant Quek here, the rest of you come with me. We need to break this up as quietly as we can. Diplomacy and tact, got it?'

One constable apparently had his own idea of what constituted diplomacy and tact. He reached to his side to unclip the holster that held his blackwood baton.

Betancourt walked over to him. 'What did I just say? No

weapons.' He'd a feeling this might be a long day.

Breaking up the protesters proved easier than expected. The strangers turned out to be nothing more than a bunch of labourers from a nearby construction site. A man had come to the site and offered them a day's wages to go down to the docks and join the protest. Their daily rate was a pitiful amount, but to these men the money was a gift from heaven. A truck had been waiting to take them to the dockyard.

Protests usually attracted a decent turnout, and it puzzled Betancourt that someone had seen fit to hire additional agitators. He'd questioned the men afterwards. They said they'd been given no special instructions and none of them knew the man who'd hired them. Asked if they could describe him, they were, unsurprisingly, overcome with collective amnesia.

When he'd tried to relieve one of the men of a placard fixed to a broken stick, they'd got into a tangle and the jagged point had sliced through the thin linen sleeve of his suit jacket. Could a tailor fix such a hole? He'd no idea. Anna, his wife, would have known what to do. He was picking at the loose threads that fringed the hole when an anguished shout pierced the air.

'Inspector! Come quickly!'

Abu Bakar, greatly excited, pounded across the tarmac as fast as his old legs could carry him. Betancourt encouraged him to take a breath and slow down. A few wheezes later control was regained.

'She's dead.'

'Who's dead?'

'The woman.'

'Which woman?'

'The dead woman.'

'Let me get this straight. The dead woman, the one who's dead, is dead?'

'Exactly.'

Betancourt sighed. Dead women were a matter for Detective Branch. Six months previously, that would have meant him, but no longer. He'd call CID and get them to take care of it, but in the meantime, someone needed to be here to keep an eye on the body and that someone would have to be him.

Fifty yards away, in the angle between the wall of a godown and the dockyard perimeter, lay a mound covered by a battered green tarpaulin. Nearby, the branches of a jacaranda tree in glorious full bloom provided cover for a group of workers who'd gathered in the shade of its purple canopy, jostling and straining to catch a glimpse of whatever lay beneath the canvas.

He took in the surrounding buildings. His earlier portentous feeling about the day ahead had been correct. Of all the places a dead body could have been found on the expanse of land that comprised the Keppel Docks, it had to be here, outside the godown that belonged to Louis Clément, his erstwhile father-in-law.

Medra.

When they were first married, Anna had commented on how amusing she found it that when faced with any situation that merited profanity, it was Kristang, the barely remembered Portuguese-Malaccan creole of his childhood, that he reached for first. She'd been right. She usually was.

A clerk stuck his head round the jamb of the door of the Clément godown. Seeing Betancourt, he gave an exaggerated shrug, palms raised upwards and to the side: the universal signal for *What's going on?*

Betancourt waved a languid hand. *Later.*

He pulled away the cover. Working like a camera, his detective's eyes took in everything. The woman was young, probably early twenties. Pretty. The tight-fitting *cheongsam*-style sheath she wore had been ripped open and pulled apart to leave her exposed from the waist down. Her shoes matched her dress and one had become dislodged and now lay close beside her body. A blue jewelled necklace and matching earrings glinted as the gems caught the afternoon sun. She lay on her back, arms folded across her chest. The tips of the fingers of one of her hands were missing, the wounds fresh. The other hand was clasped tight shut, as though she'd been clutching at something in the moment of her death. He broke off a low-hanging twig from the jacaranda tree and prised the hand open. Inside was a fragment of yellow parchment. It appeared to be torn from the top left-hand corner of a larger document and bore the letters REGI in an ornate script. Regina? That meant queen, didn't it?

Abu Bakar leaned over his shoulder. 'I knew a man called Reggie once. Purser with the Blue Funnel Line. He said his name was Reginald, but he didn't like it. Strange people, the English.'

Betancourt continued his examination. The woman's knees were cinched together with a length of gold and black cord. A regular line of bloody marks ran from the dark triangle between her legs to the tops of her stockings, the blood dried brown, emphasising the pallor of her skin. It was as though she'd been prepared for death and laid out for some bizarre shamanistic ritual. Her head twisted away at an unnatural angle, towards the trunk of the tree, as if she was trying to decipher something scratched in the bark. A snail had left a glittering trail across the ashen skin, from one eye to her throat, where it had halted at the edge of three parallel cuts to her neck, encrusted with dried blood. As a boy growing up, he'd seen plenty of goats being slaughtered at a never-ending string of celebrations of the lives of saints whose names he'd long since forgotten, but he'd never seen cuts as perfectly executed as these.

'How did you find her?'

Abu Bakar pulled the packet of *kretek* from his pocket, struck a match, and let it flare before cupping his hands around the flame. He offered the pack to Betancourt, who took one and accepted a light. The rough mix of cloves and tobacco hissed and crackled as it burned. Through plumes of scented smoke, Abu Bakar recounted his story. He'd gone to find one of the ship's officers to sign off the manifests. No, he wasn't exactly sure of the time as he didn't wear a wristwatch himself, but he recalled the officer had written two o'clock on the lading document. He'd then left the ship to take the documents to the shipping agent further down the waterfront for filing. On his way, he was overcome by the need to relieve himself. It happened more and more frequently these days. Perhaps Betancourt was the same? No? Anyway, he was looking for somewhere to go when he saw the rat.

'The rat?'

'That's how I found her. I saw a rat.'

That would explain the damage to the woman's fingertips. Rats were a common enough sight around the godowns on the river to the north, where rice was stored, but it was rarer to see them down here, next to the sea.

'A big one.' Abu Bakar spread his hands apart to show how big. Judging by his estimate, this thing could have taken on a tiger cub with one leg tied behind its back. 'I looked for a stone to throw at it and I stepped in that.' He pointed to a rivulet of blood, now baked dark and all but congealed. 'I followed the blood, and that's when I found her. I thought maybe someone had killed a cat and covered it up. Sometimes you see a truck hit one when it doesn't get out of the way quickly enough. I tell them to slow down, but you know how it is. But this was much too big for a cat. Then I thought maybe a dog. Or a pig. But who would kill a pig here, in the middle of the dockyard, and leave it to bleed? And then I saw the shoe.'

News travelled fast round here and the crowd of onlookers had swelled. The sheer weight of numbers propelled the throng forward.

'Stop!'

The men were mostly Chinese or Indian and he'd no idea how many of them understood Malay, but the raised hand and the tone of authority had the desired effect. Betancourt pulled at the woman's dress in a vain attempt to give her back some modesty and recovered her with the green tarpaulin before wiping his hands on a tuft of sea grass that sprouted from a crack in the tarmacadam.

He looked again towards the Clément godown. He could use the phone in there, but he didn't want to run into anyone he knew. When he spoke to the Cléments these days, he preferred it to be on his own terms.

'I need to call CID. When you spoke to me earlier, which telephone did you use?'

Abu Bakar pointed across the road, to a wooden building trimmed with fluorescent lights advertising Tiger beer and Player's Capstan cigarettes.

'Try to keep this lot back, will you, while I make the call?' Abu Bakar had to be at least sixty, but a lifetime of hard, physical work around the docks had kept him wiry and strong. If any of the coolies tried anything, it would be at their peril. Without waiting for a reply, Betancourt jogged away through the gates guarding the entrance to the dockyard and across dusty Keppel Road to Leilani's Bar.

Chapter Two

M ama Leilani's Tropical Tavern was a waterfront bar-cum-nightspot occupying a prime location yards from the dockyard entrance. It had always been a popular joint, perfectly placed to welcome sailors of all creeds and colours off the boats. With the recent influx of British servicemen, Leilani had never had it so good, and she'd taken to staying open round the clock.

The early afternoon was the graveyard shift in the bar trade, and only the hardiest of drinkers were in. A sailor in soiled Navy whites slouched against the bar, muttering to himself, a folded newspaper acting as an impromptu bar mat for a half-drunk bottle of Tiger beer. Men like this were the bread and butter of Leilani's business: dedicated souls who hung around long enough to drink themselves sober again.

The bar smelled of spilled beer and tobacco laced with a faint trace of A Night in Hong Kong perfume. The perfume-wearers, with the exception of Leilani herself, were nowhere to be seen. Resting, presumably, before another evening fending off, or perhaps welcoming, the attentions of a drunken clientele.

Leilani was a sizeable woman who wore bright florid *muu-muus* and who'd never be seen without a frangipani blossom tucked into her long black hair. She claimed to be a Polynesian princess, the daughter of an island chief, and played the role with aplomb. She'd once told Betancourt her name meant "voice of heaven" in Tahitian and after a few gins of an evening she didn't take much convincing to entertain her patrons with a risqué music hall number or two. He'd long known her origins lay nearer to Bangkok than Bora-Bora, but she kept an orderly house, and she didn't stand any nonsense when the sailors had too much grog, so he was happy to keep her secret.

She put down the glass she was polishing and came over to greet him.

'Things must be slow, Inspector. What brings you in at this time of the day – business or pleasure?'

'Business, I'm afraid. I need your telephone.'

'Ten cents.' She always asked, he never paid.

'Put it on my tab.'

'You don't have a tab. There's no point. You'd never settle it.' She lifted the telephone from behind the bar and placed it on the counter.

The operator picked up and asked for the name of the other party.

'Police. CID. Robinson Road.'

'Putting you through now.'

The voice that answered introduced itself as Sergeant Heng. Betancourt knew him slightly. He was a conscientious sort who kept himself away from CID politics. As much as a man ever could, anyway. Betancourt identified himself, and Heng sounded surprised.

'Inspector. Long time. Gone to Marine Branch, I heard.'

'That's right.' Betancourt didn't feel the need to elaborate. 'Listen, I'm at the docks. One of the workers has found a body. A woman.'

'Local?' Heng sounded like he was willing it to be so. If the woman was a European, he'd have to get his men to drop everything. If she was Asian, it could take as long as it took.

'Japanese, by the look of her.'

An audible sigh of relief came down the line. 'A *karayuki-san?*'

He used the colloquial term for a Japanese prostitute. Premise: a Japanese woman had been found at the docks. Conclusion: she must have been a prostitute. Heng might have been right, but the lazy thinking irked Betancourt.

'Not for me to say. I'll need a detective, the doctor, and a photographer. As quick as you can.'

Heng sounded doubtful. They were busy, but he'd do his best.

Busy? At this time of the day? It was CID code for *not a priority*. Betancourt handed the telephone back to Leilani and thanked her. She'd been watching him speak as she'd continued to polish glasses.

'Trouble?' She was asking if she needed to be careful.

'I doubt it. Probably just an unfortunate incident. CID will be along to tidy up. Eventually.'

The sailor dragged himself to his feet, let forth a beery eructation, and staggered off to whatever the rest of his day held, leaving the damp newspaper behind.

'Mind if I take this?'

'Be my guest.' Leilani cleared away the sailor's abandoned glass and bottle. 'You know you're always welcome here, Inspector.' And then with a coquettish pout, she added, 'Don't wait for someone to be killed next time.'

A police car, horn blaring and tyres screeching, swung into the yard and pulled up twenty feet from the jacaranda tree. Whoever was driving didn't appear to understand that the woman was dead, and no amount of automotive histrionics would bring her back.

Two men emerged. From the rear, a slight, dapper European alighted carrying a leather case. It was Dr Gemmill, the police surgeon. Betancourt was surprised to see him. Gemmill was selective about which cases he attended and was more likely to be spotted ministering to the grieving widow of an expired colonial, plying her with solace and patting her arm soothingly, explaining in a respectful *sotto voce* that: 'It was his heart, my dear. None of us lasts forever.'

The doctor flapped a hand at him in acknowledgement and called out, 'Won't be a moment,' before heading towards a group of uniformed ship's officers who'd gathered near the stern of the *Batavian Princess*. Strange. What was he playing at?

The second passenger, a local, eased himself out from the front seat. It was the perpetually glum Yung, the crime-scene photographer. That was it, just the two of them. No detective. It looked like Betancourt would have to take care of this one himself, at least for now.

He pushed through the gawking crowd huddled under the jacaranda tree. When he reached the front, the flash of a bulb burned a starry image on his retina. He raised one arm in an involuntary gesture of defence.

'Sorry, didn't see you.'

Yung didn't sound sorry. Betancourt shook his head to clear away the stars.

'Long time.' He extended a hand. Yung and he had worked together when he was still *persona grata* at the Detective

Branch. Yung returned the gesture without apparent interest, as though they'd seen each other only the previous day and nothing had happened in the interim that required any comment. He scowled as he circled the body, snapping photographs from every angle. For as long as they'd known each other, Yung had scowled like this when going about his work. Betancourt wondered if he cast off his morose expression when he went home to his wife and children. Somehow, he couldn't imagine it.

'When can you have the photographs developed?'

Yung shrugged. 'Day after tomorrow? Maybe.'

'I need them on my desk tomorrow morning. First thing.'

'Busy, *lah*.' Yung used the universal emphasiser to show just how difficult the request would be. He wasn't merely busy, he was *lah* busy.

'Tomorrow morning. Understood?'

Yung nodded sullenly and continued with his gloomy photo-study.

Dr Gemmill had returned from his conversation with the ship's officers. 'Ah, Betancourt. They told me I might run into you down here. How long has it been? A year?'

'Give or take.' Betancourt shook the proffered hand and nodded towards the officers. 'Friends of yours?'

'Napier's men.' As if that was all the explanation required for why he had needed to speak to them first before attending to the body of the dead woman. Betancourt groaned inwardly at the mention of the name. Napier & Campbell, or Napier's as it was universally known, was the richest and most powerful of the British mercantile companies in Singapore and wasn't shy about wielding its considerable power if it saw the need. He'd better tread carefully.

Gemmill bent to examine the body. There was even less breeze here in the lee of the godown, and the sun glinted off the tiny balls of perspiration beading his bald head. This sun, European skin… he should wear a hat. As if hearing Betancourt's thoughts, Gemmill produced a bright red handkerchief from the pocket of his jacket and with an exaggerated flourish mopped away the moisture.

His lips moved soundlessly as he continued his examination. Finally, he nodded to himself in apparent satisfaction, made a note in a small, embossed leather notebook with a tiny silver pencil, and stood. 'Well, I'd say it's just what you'd expect it to be.'

'I make a point of not expecting too much. That way I'm not disappointed. Can you be more specific?'

'Just a tart who ran out of luck, from the looks of her.'

Betancourt looked again at the dead woman and suppressed anger at Gemmill's blasé dismissal of her as "just a tart". Whatever she may have done for a living, she'd been someone. A daughter, perhaps a sister, a friend.

Gemmill pointed to the wounds on her throat. 'Suicide. It would have been quick. The cause of death, at least, looks cut and dried.'

Betancourt raised an eyebrow at the pun, and the doctor gave an apologetic shrug.

'Suicide? And then, presumably ashamed of what she'd done, she crawled under a tarpaulin to die?'

Gemmill either missed the irony in Betancourt's tone or chose to ignore it. 'More likely someone discovered her and covered her up.'

'Or brought her here and dumped her.'

'It's a possibility, I suppose, but if she'd died elsewhere, it wouldn't explain the blood.' Gemmill pointed to the trail Abu Bakar had stepped in earlier and frowned. 'Mind you, it's odd…'

'What is?'

'Human body holds about eight pints of blood. There's nothing like that amount here.'

'Meaning?'

Gemmill shook his head firmly, unwilling to commit himself to anything. 'Too early to say.'

'Is there anything to identify her?'

'Not that I can see. There's no sign of a handbag and there's nothing engraved on the jewellery that might tell us who she was.'

So, whoever covered her up had taken her bag, assuming she'd carried one, but left her jewellery.

'When are we talking about?'

The doctor crouched and pointed to what looked like light bruising on the woman's arm, where the skin touched the tarmac. 'Livor mortis has begun, but discolouration is still faint. My guess would be less than twelve hours. I'll know better when I've taken her back to the Crypt and completed the post-mortem.'

The mere mention of the police morgue tunnelled under the Singapore River caused Betancourt to break out in an anxious sweat. He slackened his collar and circled the body, looking for anything else that might shed light on what had happened to the woman. He poked at the dockyard detritus with his foot: an empty Spam can, already rusting in the salt air; a chipped and scuffed beer bottle; a banana leaf containing the remains of a hastily taken meal, chicken rice by the looks of it; a discarded playing card. Nothing of any interest. It would just have to wait for the post-mortem and by then, with luck, it would be someone else's problem.

An elbow nudged him in the back. The crowd was pressing in close again, ogling the dead woman.

'Let's get her covered up and out of here. And can you let the station know when the post-mortem is complete?'

Gemmill nodded. An ambulance had arrived, and the doctor set about organising the moving of the body.

Betancourt turned to the sea of faces behind him. 'Back up!' He waved his arms at them, shepherding them towards the wall, as if shooing away a flock of seabirds.

Down here there were always those who'd rather not attract undue attention from the authorities, and several of the coolies were already peeling off from the main group, making their way back into the anonymous recesses of the docks, casting wary glances over their shoulders. He let them go. There was no point taking statements from them as none of them would have seen anything. Nobody ever saw anything down here. In any case, he wanted to have a word with the ship's officers whom Gemmill had considered so important.

———

A nervous-looking, sparse little man broke away from his colleagues and hurried forwards, half walking and half running, legs protruding like two bowed sticks from his starched white shorts. He reminded Betancourt of the jockeys who rode at the Bukit Timah Turf Club. The man gave his name as Newton and said he was captain of the *Batavian Princess*. He wrung his hands repeatedly as he spoke, as though trying to expunge a stubborn stain.

'Dr Gemmill said you're the local police.'

Betancourt introduced himself. 'Marine. Special Investigations.'

Newton looked surprised. 'And is this a "special investigation"? I was told it was just a dead Japanese girl.'

Just. Betancourt resisted rising to the comment. 'Technically, this should be one for the Detective Branch, but it appears CID are thin on the ground at the moment.'

Newton sounded doubtful. 'When will the proper police be here?'

Betancourt held his gaze. 'I am the proper police.'

'Yes, well, if you say so. It's a bad business, Inspector. We have passengers due back on board, so I'd be grateful if you'd hurry things along.' Newton gave his hands an extra-hard wrench.

'The sooner I can interview you and your colleagues, the sooner I can let you be on your way.' It did no harm to remind them who was in charge.

Newton introduced the other two men, also dressed in the white uniform of the shipping line. 'This is Mr Harvey, my first officer. He was on watch when the... when she was found.' Harvey was tall – well over six feet – and wore the smug expression born of privilege: a look that said, *I'll humour you until I'm bored*. The third man, a boy really, was Stevens, the ship's deck cadet. He stood, wide-eyed and fidgety, caught between anxiety and excitement.

'What time did you berth?'

Newton looked to the ship, as if for inspiration. 'Around nine o'clock. We were due in at first light but there was a fire on board a palm-oil lighter in the Straits off St John's Island. We had to sit offshore until they could tow her to safety.'

'And the passengers all disembarked as soon as you arrived?'

'More or less. There were the usual formalities to complete. Your chaps checking papers and such like.'

'How many on board?'

'About twenty passengers, give or take, and two dozen crew. I've released the other men for shore leave. We keep a skeleton crew on board when we're berthed. I was just about to depart myself.'

Betancourt looked up at the *Batavian Princess*. She was small compared to the passenger ships that arrived daily. Two dozen crew members for twenty passengers seemed a lot. Newton must have read his thoughts. 'The crew have other duties. We're mainly a cargo ship.'

'You said: "About twenty passengers, *give or take*." Don't you know how many passengers were in your charge?'

Newton looked to his first officer for corroboration. 'Does twenty sound about right to you?'

Harvey nodded. 'Yes, sounds about right.'

Betancourt let this slide. 'You mentioned passengers returning this evening. Is it common for them to remain on board when the ship is in port?'

'It's not exactly common, as you put it, but it's not unknown. Some of the passengers are down to celebrate New Year before returning up-country when we sail on the fourth. As the company is paying, I suppose they thought they might save a bit of money by staying on board.'

'When you say "the company", you mean Napier's?'

'Yes, we're a Napier's ship and the passengers were mostly Napier's men.'

'Was there anyone else travelling?'

Betancourt caught the merest shake of the head from Newton to Harvey. It was the latter who answered. 'It's just… they're mostly single men, plantation managers and the like. It can be a lonely life out in the middle of the jungle, so I'm told – happily married myself – and sometime the passengers like to travel with… companions.'

'I understand. I'll need to see the passenger manifest.'

This time there was a sharp look between the two men that they didn't even try to mask. He'd touched a nerve. Harvey took a step forward. He was a good head taller than

Betancourt and made a point of standing close, so that he was looking down. He drew himself up to the full extent of his height. He must have decided it was time he reminded this Serani of his place. 'Is that really necessary? As the captain explained, the passengers were all Europeans, down for the New Year festivities. There's no need to trouble them with this surely. I mean, it's obvious the woman was just a tart who pushed her luck too far.'

What was it Gemmill had said? *Just a tart who ran out of luck.* Harvey had used almost the exact same words. Was that why Gemmill had gone straight to talk to them earlier before even examining the body? Had he been briefing them? If so, at whose behest?

'Obvious is it, Mr Harvey? It's not at all obvious to me. Unless you know something that you're not telling me.'

'That's enough, Harvey.' Newton stifled any response the first officer might have been about to give with a glare at his subordinate. He instructed Stevens to fetch the passenger list, and the deck cadet ambled away.

Betancourt continued as though the exchange between the two senior men hadn't happened. 'How did you find out there had been a death?'

Newton's rebuke seemed to have cowed Harvey. When he replied his voice had lost some of its earlier truculence. 'From the Malay.' He pointed across the yard to where Abu Bakar sat smoking. 'It was around two. He'd come up to the bridge to let me know the unloading of his portion of the cargo was complete. I checked the time when I signed the dispatch note. It can't have been more than a quarter of an hour after that he came back. He'd found the woman.'

This all seemed to tie in with what Abu Bakar had told Betancourt

'Did you see or hear anything unusual?'

'Not a thing. Other than those damned malcontents protesting. Should sack the lot of them. See how happy they are then.'

Stevens arrived back, puffing a little from his run. He held out an envelope. Betancourt took it and pulled out a single piece of foolscap containing a handwritten list. He scanned this quickly. There were more than twenty names, and they weren't all European as they would have been if Harvey's earlier assertion had been true. The additional names must have been the companions. Betancourt skewered Harvey with a stare but said nothing. Harvey's sheepish countenance told him the message had hit home.

The lack of transparency from the two men was annoying, but they were still well-connected Europeans, and it wouldn't be productive to annoy them too much. Not yet anyway. He'd check the names later. If he came across anything untoward, he'd pay Messrs Newton and Harvey another visit. He handed Newton a business card and told him to call the Marine Branch station if anything else came to mind.

Abu Bakar sat patiently astride a bollard that years of chafing ropes had polished as smooth as glass. Betancourt apologised for keeping him from his wife for so long and gave him a few dollars so he could hire a taxicab to take him home. Abu Bakar thanked him for the money but didn't seem in the slightest put out by the delay. If anything, he walked away looking a little deflated that the excitement was drawing to a close.

The crowds had all dispersed and the docks lay quiet again. There wasn't much else he could usefully do here. Off to the west, towards Sumatra, sheets of lightning arced across the sky in an electrical extravaganza, promise of a storm to come. He shivered and turned up the collar of his jacket – futile protection against the forces of nature – and headed back towards the lights of the city.

Chapter Three

The air in the small office was as still as a dead cat in a gutter. Betancourt lifted the rattan chicks that covered the windows in a fruitless attempt to take advantage of what little breeze there was, but all that wafted in was a mixture of diesel oil, human detritus, and the sea. The unique smell of the Singapore River that Anna used to refer to as the "stench of commerce".

He watched as a large, grey-backed gull bobbed past, navigating the river atop an upturned orange crate. The bird cocked its head and held his gaze with its black eyes, as if enquiring about the day's news. It seemed oblivious to the buzz of the bumboats criss-crossing the river like so many water beetles, the boatmen shouting at one another and cursing as they vied for prime position on the riverbank.

Although it was still early and the temperature had yet to reach its mid-day high, Betancourt's shirt was already damp with sweat and clung to his back. The Europeans who came out to Singapore assumed the locals had an inbred immunity to the heat. He was born here and he'd never got used to it.

After nigh on forty years he didn't expect he ever would. Peeling off his jacket, he turned up the ceiling fan as high as it would go, but the blades turned slowly, as if lacking either the wherewithal or the will to stir themselves into anything more energetic. He reached for a broom he kept specifically for the purpose and gave the mechanism three hard raps with the handle. The fan woke from its slumber and began to rotate with renewed zest while Betancourt stood underneath, arms outstretched. When the fan had chilled him a little, he pulled up the old cane-backed mahogany chair he'd scrounged from an empty office on an upper floor and sat down.

A silver-framed photograph took permanent pride of place on the otherwise cluttered table that served as his desk. Looking out at him was Anna, face frozen in laughter while sharing a secret joke with their daughter, Lucia. The picture had been taken at a garden party a year before, shortly after Lucia's fourteenth birthday and a month before his wife went missing. What the joke was, he'd no idea, but he'd often wondered. He couldn't even remember where the photograph was taken. He hadn't been there. He never was. As usual, work had come first. The image gave him the same stabbing sensation of guilt it always did. That's why he kept it here, on this table, where he couldn't avoid seeing it. Having to look at this photograph every day was his penance.

Untended piles of documents faced him. They were an indicator less of a man with too much work to do as of one with little regard for the work he'd been given, and even less desire to do anything about it. Months of rubber-stamping documentation, trapping smugglers with paltry amounts of minor contraband, and breaking up dockyard brawls had taken their toll. Lately he'd lapsed into a semi-permanent haze of distraction.

The desk sergeant thrust his head around the door. 'Message.' He handed Betancourt a pink slip. His immediate superior, the Assistant Commissioner, wanted to see him. Urgently. Betancourt screwed the piece of paper into a ball and lobbed it into the wastebasket next to his desk, where it joined several others.

Pushing aside a stack of manifests, he picked up the copy of the *Straits Tribune* he'd taken from Leilani's counter the previous afternoon and fanned himself idly with it. A mosquito circled, too small to see at first but audible over the noise coming from the river. He rolled up the newspaper, squinted, and took aim.

Missed.

As usual, the front page of the *Tribune* was filled with the News from Home. In amongst gloomy reports on the progress of the war in Europe, a more light-hearted piece provided an update on Harrods' preparations for the coming festive season and the likelihood of a white Christmas in the capital. He studied the image that accompanied the article. Crowds of people huddled in greatcoats, heads down, not showing any indication of acknowledging one another. The caption beneath read: *A Happy Time of Year.* He wondered if the irony was intentional. To him, London looked like a sad place. Big and grey and cold and sad. He'd never been there – he'd never been further than Georgetown on the island of Penang – and harboured no desire to do so. To him, London wasn't a place you went to, it was a place the British escaped from.

To be fair to them, he reflected, the British weren't the only ones happy to come here and take what Singapore offered while constantly harking back to what they'd left behind. The Chinese who'd come here to seek their fortunes, and stayed, still owed their allegiances more to Fukien or Hainan than to Singapore; the gangs of Indians who worked the docks dreamed of Madras; and the Malays pledged their loyalties to sultans most of them had never seen. It amused him, although he never understood quite why, that his people, the Serani – descendants of distant unions between Portuguese seafarers and local Malaccans – were the ones who would most often refer to Singapore as "home" and mean it.

Another article further down the page touched on the growing spectre of fascism. The news agency cited the example of the "handsome and charismatic" Oswald Mosley who had, apparently, toured the country addressing gatherings of the British Union of Fascists. Mosley, it was reported, had been calling upon "noisy and enthusiastic" crowds to extent the hand of friendship to Herr Hitler and Signor Mussolini. In a commentary accompanying the article, the editor of the *Tribune* appeared to disagree with Mr Mosley's point of view and urged the good citizens of Singapore to do their bit to help keep the home fires burning by purchasing war bonds, application forms available at all post offices and banks.

The fascist leader's name rang a bell, and Betancourt searched through the papers on his desk until he found a memo from headquarters. He'd been right. Mosley was due to visit the colony shortly. The name had meant nothing at the time he'd received the briefing, so he'd ignored it. In his previous life, he might have been tasked with keeping the peace at such an event, but no longer.

The local news occupied page four, sandwiched between the births and deaths and classified advertisements for motor oil and radiograms. In amongst an account of an expatriate society wedding and the minutes of the Annual General Meeting of the Singapore Tennis Club, nestled a piece by a local reporter, George Elias. According to him, the city fathers were outraged by the recent increase in the numbers of

Japanese prostitutes on the streets. Why the city fathers were frequenting the same streets as those patrolled by the *karayuki-san*, and therefore putting themselves in the way of being outraged, he neglected to mention.

Elias could be prone to hyperbole at times, but he was a decent journalist and wasn't afraid to ruffle feathers when they needed ruffling. Legalised prostitution had been outlawed by the British a few years earlier. Before, when it was still legal, they'd been able to police the red-light districts and enforce rules. Now it had been chased underground and back into the hands of the secret societies. If George Elias had convinced his editor to run the piece, chances were there was some truth in it. If there was an increase in the number of Japanese women illegally entering the country, they were probably arriving by sea. And if they were being smuggled in onboard ships, then it was on Betancourt's watch and he needed to do something about it before Bonham, the Assistant Commissioner, told him to. The fewer reasons he gave his superior for taking an interest in him the better. Betancourt found the chewed butt of a pencil on the floor and scribbled a note on his desk jotter to double the checks on incoming vessels.

He finished reading. There was no mention of the dead woman found at the docks. Had he been hoping there would be? As Elias' article pointed out, *karayuki-san* weren't exactly a commodity in short supply, so why would there have been? Still, it bothered Betancourt. She didn't deserve to be dismissed as just another dead prostitute. She'd been someone. Whatever she'd done in life, her death should still matter.

He stretched and yawned and continued to leaf through the newspaper until he came to the Comings and Goings section. A lethargy had seeped into his bones these past months, and he approached the task with the same heartfelt lack of enthusiasm with which he'd approached everything else since Anna had gone.

The list of ships that had recently entered or were due to leave Singapore waters was short. The *Batavian Princess* – the ship Abu Bakar and his men had been emptying the day before – was the last arrival due before Christmas and, like many of her sister ships, she'd remain in port until after the New Year's festivities were over. The British *tuans* and their *mems* didn't like to sail with hangovers.

He was finishing marking off the names of the vessels he planned to inspect when the discordant jangle of the telephone reverberated through the room. He scowled at the receiver and lifted the handset.

'Betancourt. Marine Branch.'

A woman's voice replied. English. She was brief and to the point. 'I was instructed to call you when my examination of the body found at the docks yesterday was complete.'

'And?'

'And nothing. The post-mortem is finished, I've notified you. If you want anything else, you'll have to come down here.'

"Here" was presumably the Crypt. Gemmill normally carried out autopsies alone. This woman hadn't explained what her involvement was.

'Who am I talking to?'

It was too late. A click indicated she'd ended the call. He sighed. He could count on the fingers of one hand the things he enjoyed less than visiting the police morgue, but there was nothing else for it. He picked up his jacket from the floor where he'd dropped it, dusted it off, and relocked the office door.

A familiar churning gnawed at his gut as he descended the steps to the cavernous subterranean room below the river on Clarke Quay. He glanced nervously at the curve of the tiled roof and blenched at a mental image of the massive body of water flowing over his head. Reaching for the damp wall of the dark corridor for reassurance, he reminded himself his fear was irrational. An engineer friend at the Public Works Department had once explained how the building was constructed, but the knowledge did nothing to help quell his unease. Neither did the smell of formaldehyde that penetrated every crevice.

The door to the examination room creaked as he pushed it open and the electric lights, brighter here than in the tunnel, caused him to blink. Inside, a stout Indian woman wearing a nurse's uniform was busying herself by piling instruments into an autoclave at a long stainless-steel bench placed against the far wall. In the centre of the room, another woman, a European aged about thirty, stooped over a shroud-covered cadaver, pulling at a lengthy piece of catgut. She wore a blue apron, below which a brightly coloured print skirt peeked out. Her hands were hidden by rubber gloves, flecked with blood. On her nose, which was longer than might be considered classically beautiful, perched a pair of circular wire-framed glasses, and her copper hair was pulled back into a severe bun. She looked up and wiped a stray lock from her eyes with the back of one wrist.

'Yes?'

'I'm looking for Dr Gemmill.'

She resumed her task. 'Not here. Apparently, he and Mrs Gemmill were on the reserve list for a garden party at the Governor's Istana.' Her tone was one of barely concealed disdain. 'A place came available, which means you've got me instead. I'm Dr Trevose. I take it you're here about the body of the poor woman found at the dockyard.'

Betancourt introduced himself. 'I'm the investigating detective from the Marine Branch and I need the post-mortem results.' When he gave his name, she seemed taken aback, as though he'd momentarily wrong-footed her.

'I'm just finishing up now.' She peeled off the gloves and dropped them into a bin. 'This isn't official, you understand, as I've still to write up the report.' She turned to the Indian woman, who was watching their exchange with apparent interest. 'Martha, pass me the notes, will you?' Martha handed over a thin buff file, which the doctor held to her chest.

'I don't believe I've seen you around here before.' She extended a hand, palm upwards.

'It's been a while.' Misreading her intentions and thinking she wanted to formalise the introductions, he put out his own hand in response. She made no move to take it, arching an eyebrow instead.

'Identification?'

He placed his wallet in her hand, warrant card upper-most. She scrutinised it, back and front, and made a note in the file before returning it. She then extracted a single foolscap page from the folder and began to read.

'Female. Twenty to twenty-five years of age. Not Chinese. Judging by her features, she could be Korean, but I would say Japanese was more likely. She was pregnant when she was killed – I'd estimate about twelve weeks. She was well nourished and there was no sign of any recent sexual activity.'

So much for the prostitute assumption. Betancourt thought back to his own examination of the body, the previous day.

'When I examined her yesterday, there was blood on her legs. Have you ruled out rape?'

'There's nothing at all to suggest it. But I'll come back to those marks.'

Betancourt nodded. 'When did it happen?'

'From lividity and temperature... I'd say sometime between six in the morning and noon.'

He cast his mind back to the dockyard. Gemmill had seemed convinced the woman had killed herself. What was it he'd said? *Suicide. It would have been quick. The cause of death, at least, looks cut and dried.*

'You said "when she was killed". So you don't believe she took her own life?'

There was no answer at first as the doctor considered her response. 'I suppose it's possible, but no, I don't believe so.' It was Betancourt's turn to raise an eyebrow. She pointed to the three parallel cuts on the woman's neck he'd noticed at the dockyard. 'This pattern is fairly typical of *seppuku*: ritual suicide.' She looked at him for a sign he'd understood. He had. 'Any of these wounds would have done enough damage to kill her: her carotid artery was severed. But the cuts are clean and there's very little blood. I don't believe she was killed where she was discovered. The body had been all but exsanguinated prior to being moved.'

'Dr Gemmill mentioned the lack of blood.'

'But there's something else. I missed it at first.' Dr Trevose took an instrument that looked like a pair of cake tongs and placed it in the centremost cut. Using the tongs, she gently pried open the laceration. 'See?'

He circled the table to get a better view. 'Not really. What is it I'm supposed to be looking at?'

She made a small impatient noise. 'Look. There.' She pointed. 'At the base of the cut.'

There was a dark hole beneath the slash in the woman's neck.

'Imagine: for this woman to have killed herself, she'd have to have used something that cut and stabbed simultaneously to inflict this pattern of wounds.' She punctuated the words *cut* and *stabbed* with expansive hand gestures, jabbing with the tongs. He took an involuntary step back.

Dr Trevose apologised. 'Sorry. I get carried away sometimes.' She placed the tongs in a kidney dish. 'I've never seen a weapon like that, have you?'

He hadn't, and he was confused. 'So, what are you suggesting?'

'Judging by the coagulation of the blood in the puncture wound, my guess would be that whatever caused that was what killed her.'

'And the other cuts?'

'Done later?' She sounded as if she was unsure herself whether her hypothesis made any sense.

But why? If the woman was already dead, what would be the point? He continued to stare at the wounds while gathering his thoughts. 'You said you missed it at first. What did you mean?'

She picked up the tongs again. 'See how the deep wound runs sideways, in the same direction as the lateral cuts? It wasn't until I opened up the cuts to look for foreign matter that I saw it.'

'It's almost like it was hidden... Perhaps that's what happened.'

'How do you mean?'

'Just what I said. She was stabbed and then she was cut, but the cuts were intended to obscure the first wound.'

'I suppose it's a possibility.' The doctor sounded intrigued.

If the woman had committed *seppuku*, then someone could

have moved her body from wherever she had died to the docks, to avoid any scandal or embarrassment, though that seemed unlikely. On the other hand, if she'd been murdered, then moving the body made a lot more sense.

'It's an odd one.'

'And it keeps getting odder. Did you notice the blood next to the body?'

Betancourt nodded. 'The man who found her stepped in it.'

'Well, get this: it was pig's blood.'

He stared at her for a second. 'Are you sure?'

'Quite sure, Inspector.'

He hoped he looked as though he was taking all this in, but the truth was none of it was making much sense.

'There's something else you should see.' She pulled back the green surgical sheet and called to Martha, the nurse, for help. Together they turned the body on its side. He leaned over to get a better view of whatever it was she was about to show him. They were close and he could smell the soap she'd used that morning. He forced himself to concentrate.

Running the full length of the dead woman's upper rear body was a magnificent tattoo of a tiger, its body drawn in exquisite detail, finely etched in golds and browns and blacks. The creature faced away from the observer, as though ascending the woman's back. On the left shoulder blade was a rocky outcrop upon which a paw had been depicted, the animal's head turned outwards towards the viewer, teeth bared in warning: *She's mine. Stay away!*

Betancourt whistled. 'Have you ever come across anything like this before?'

She hesitated before speaking. 'I've heard stories about such things, but not here. In Shanghai.' There was a hesitancy in her voice that suggested she was holding something back.

Martha broke in. 'Show him the marks.' She nodded vigorously.

Dr Trevose rested the body on its back again and peeled back the rest of the shroud to uncover the dead woman's legs. She pointed to the marks he'd seen the previous day. 'The blood on her legs is human, and it's the same type as traces from the body cavity. I'd need to do more tests to be certain, but I'm confident this is her own blood.' She picked up a long, thin surgical knife and used it as a pointer. 'See here. At first glance, these marks seemed random, but the extent bothered me. I could understand an assailant getting blood on his hands, and some of that blood being transferred to the body, but there's too much of it and it's too regularly distributed. Look closely.' She pulled down a magnifying glass attached to an extendable arm. 'You see how the marks are thinner at the edges than in the centres?'

He found himself fascinated, and wasn't at all sure what to make of the feeling.

'The thinner edges are where the blood has run and settled. Watch.' She took a piece of damp gauze and wiped gently around the edges of the marks. 'See?'

'It's as though someone painted stripes on her. But why would stripes, in blood, be put on a dead woman's body? We don't have voodoo in Singapore.'

Again, the doctor was slow to answer, and when she spoke it seemed to be with reluctance. 'I've heard rumours about this. The secret societies do it to women who attempt to escape from their control. As a warning to others: try to get away from us and this is what will happen to you.'

He was rarely speechless, but he'd no idea what to make of all this. He was so engrossed it didn't occur to him to ask how a pretty young English doctor knew so much about Asian gang rituals.

'I'll need photographs. I'll get them to send Yung down. He's a miserable so-and-so, but he'll do a good job.'

She nodded and recovered the woman's body with the shroud. 'I'll have to keep her here for a few days until the coroner gets around to completing the inquest.'

By law, any death in or around a brothel, be it of madam, prostitute or client, required a coroner's inquiry. Although this woman had been found at the docks, Gemmill's initial report would have been enough to deem her a *karayuki-san*, and therefore subject to the coroner's scrutiny, even if any such inquiry was bound to be fleeting.

The inspector placed his card on the steel examination table. 'I'd like a copy of the full report as soon as it's ready.'

She picked up the card and studied it. 'Betancourt.' She seemed to savour the word, as though tasting an exotic fruit for the first time.

'It's Portuguese. My family were originally from Malacca.'

'Yes, I know.' She looked him in the eye and her gaze softened. 'I recognised it earlier, when you introduced yourself. There can't be too many Betancourts, I thought. You're Anna's husband, aren't you?'

He nodded slowly. 'How…'

'The orphanage. The Holy Infant.'

When Lucia was old enough to start school, Anna had found herself alone at home a lot in the cramped married quarters provided by the force. The other women in the compound were friendly enough, but language was always an issue, and she became used to spending long hours alone. More and more of the social invitations from her former circle dried up, and she missed her old lifestyle and longed for something to do. A friend had told her the orphanage was short-handed, and so she volunteered. She'd found her calling and was happy again.

'I drop in a couple of times a week to check up on the children and I met her there. She was lovely. I was shocked when I heard the news of her disappearance. I'm very sorry.'

He'd received many words of condolence since Anna disappeared. Some were carefully chosen and sincere, others perfunctory and little more than a matter of polite form. He'd become adept at distinguishing one from the other. Dr Trevose's words were genuine, and he was touched by the sincerity in her voice. He never knew what to say in situations like this. What *was* there to say when his life had disintegrated, leaving him alone, empty and raw?

He simply nodded and thanked her before letting himself out.

Emerging from the bowels of the morgue, he stretched out his arms and turned his face to the sun, and stood like that for a few moments, letting the heat recharge him. It wasn't an unusual occurrence, meeting people who'd known Anna and were sorry for his loss, but this was the first time her name had come up in the course of an investigation. In a flash of clarity, he realised he'd probably been waiting for this moment. After all, that was how it had all started.

Chapter Four

Betancourt called back into the office, to check if there had been any messages in his absence. There was nothing. Until he received the autopsy report and the photographs from Yung, there was little he could usefully do. And by the time all that arrived, it probably wouldn't be his case anymore. The summons from Bonham wasn't going to go away and the more he ignored it, the more irate the Englishman would become, so he decided to beard the lion in his den.

He crossed the broad plaza that separated the Government Buildings on Empress Place, home to the Marine Branch, from the Singapore River, which glided lazily past on its way to emptying into the Singapore Straits. In the centre of the plaza that fronted the Victoria Memorial Hall stood a bronze statue of Sir Stamford Raffles, arms crossed, one leg in front of the other, haughtily surveying his subjects as they scuttled about their business of administering the colony that he'd established over a hundred years before.

Joining the foot traffic streaming across Cavenagh Bridge, Betancourt bore right to follow the course of the river along Boat Quay where the riches of the orient – palm oil, rubber, copra, tin, and spices – awaited shipment to an expectant world. Normally, the noise and bustle of the godowns engrossed Betancourt, but today his thoughts were occupied by the results of the post-mortem. And, he was a little perplexed to realise, by the English doctor who'd performed it.

He turned left into South Bridge Road and approached the Central Police Station with more resignation than enthusiasm as he anticipated the conversation to follow. There was one bonus: at least he'd get to see Marjorie again.

Marjorie French, personal secretary to the Assistant Commissioner, sat back in her chair and surveyed him like an exhibit at a show.

Always a slim woman, he thought she had now taken that slenderness too far, her cheeks pale and hollow. She was tall, taller than him by at least an inch, even when she wasn't wearing high heels. When she was young, a rogue monkey had sprung from the canopy of a tree and clung on to the horse she was riding, pulling at its ears. The horse had reared up, causing Marjorie to collide with a sharply pointed branch that tore open one side of her face. She'd remained self-conscious about the resultant scar and always wore her fair hair pulled forward, framing her face into a distinct oval. He used to tease her she looked more like a local than he did.

Marjorie had grown up in a grand bungalow on Nassim Hill where her neighbours were a family of timber merchants named Clément. Anna Clément and Marjorie were the same age and had hit it off immediately, quickly becoming inseparable. They'd attended the same schools, formed a nigh-invincible doubles partnership at the tennis club, and argued over the attentions of the same boys at garden parties. It was Marjorie who'd introduced him to Anna, and later she was their automatic choice, first to be Anna's bridesmaid and then godmother to Lucia. And when he lost everything – Anna, Lucia, his career – it was Marjorie who'd first provided solace and then intervened to help him secure the job at Marine.

'Well, well, well, look what the cat's dragged in. Should I feel honoured, Inspector?'

'The honour is all mine, Mrs French.' He perched on the side of her desk and pilfered a date from a box that lay open beside her typewriter. She slapped his wrist.

'Hands off. Those were a gift.'

When she moved the box out of his reach, a shaft of sunlight caught the metal of her new wedding ring and reflected a burst of yellow onto the wall opposite. It had always been assumed Marjorie wouldn't marry. It wasn't for want of offers – she'd had plenty of suitors from among the colonial set – but she'd steadfastly rejected them all. She just hadn't seen the need, Anna had explained. So, it was a surprise to everyone when she'd returned from a recent trip to England with a husband in tow. When she'd told Betancourt her news, he'd assumed the role of her self-appointed protector-in-chief and taken it upon himself to do a bit of digging into Raymond French, her new spouse. It was with a mild sense of disappointment that he wasn't able to turn up anything untoward. Postings all over Asia during a solid if not exactly stellar career in the Colonial Office; loyal and dependable colleague; confirmed bachelor, or so everyone had thought; no vices that anyone knew of. According to a clerk in the titles office at the Public Works Department, French owned his house on Swiss Club Road outright with no mortgage or lien or any other debts. A paragon, in other words. He now did something important up at Government House where he was rumoured to be a trusted confidante of the Governor, Sir Shenton Thomas. Betancourt had no idea what they all got up to at Government House and cared even less, but when Marjorie spoke about her husband, Betancourt did his best to seem interested, out of loyalty to her.

She inspected him. 'You look awful. When was the last time this was cleaned and pressed?' She picked at the sleeve of his suit jacket, torn during the scuffle at the dockyard the previous day. 'Or mended?' Taking a clothes brush from a hat stand in the corner, she set about trying to minimise the effects of his encounter with the strikers. She stood back and appraised her handiwork. 'A bit better, I suppose.' She didn't sound convinced.

She sat back at her desk. 'I'm fine, thank you for asking. Which you would know if you came to visit occasionally. Why don't you come for lunch? Ray was saying just the other evening how he'd like to get to know you better. How about this Saturday? We're having a few people over. You could stay the weekend. Bring Lucia.' She brightened at the prospect of seeing her goddaughter again.

For the first few months after Anna – his entire perception of time was now divided into Before Anna and After Anna – weekends would have seen him taking his daughter out to the cinema or a show or just for a walk in one of the parks followed by an ice cream. Initially, they'd been united in their grief, their mutual bond seemingly stronger than ever in the face of their loss, but as Lucia's acceptance of her mother's departure had grown, so too had her resentment towards him and gradually he saw her less and less, and now, since she had gone to live with her grandparents, not at all.

'Sorry, I've something on.'

It was a lie, and from Marjorie's look of resigned disappointment, she knew it was.

The intercom on her desk squawked. 'Is he here yet?'

She replied to the disembodied voice in the affirmative.

'Send him in then.'

Betancourt looked towards the panelled mahogany double doors leading to Bonham's inner sanctum.

'What sort of mood is he in?'

'Grumpy. When isn't he?'

Her tolerance of the pompous ass in the next room was one of the many things about Marjorie that Betancourt marvelled at.

'Why do you put up with him?'

She shrugged good-naturedly. 'If I got rid of this one, they'd only send another in his place. Besides, I've just got him house-trained and I've no intention of putting myself through all that again.'

Betancourt, not for the first time, wondered how Anthony Bonham, Assistant Commissioner of the Straits Settlements Police, always managed to appear so flawlessly identical whenever they met. As ever, his khaki uniform was pressed to within an inch of its life; his Sam Browne belt gleamed like a newly minted coin; his moustache was trimmed so straight and so level that it surely must have involved the use of spirit level and ruler; and his hair parted and oiled, every strand immaculately aligned beside its neighbour such that the whole effect was of one created by an artist's brush rather than a valet's comb. In a flight of fancy, Betancourt had speculated on the possibility that Bonham had arranged for someone to fabricate a hermetically sealed cupboard, which, when he returned home in the evening, Mrs Bonham simply popped him into, and where he could rest, unsullied, until it was once again time to face the day.

Betancourt waited patiently while Bonham shuffled a pile of papers, doing his best to give the impression of being busy. Eventually, the papers were cast aside and Bonham looked up, as though he'd only just become aware that Betancourt had entered the room.

'Oh, it's you. Sit.' The Assistant Commissioner pointed to a large, overstuffed chair, and Betancourt sat. 'You look bloody awful.'

'That seems to be the sentiment of the day, sir.'

'And would it really be so damned difficult for you to wear a uniform? That's the meaning of the word you know. Uniform. So that the entire force looks the same.'

'Sir.'

They'd had this conversation before. Several times. Crumpled linen suit, white shirt, black tie – this was Betancourt's idea of uniform, even if it could do with a bit of sprucing up. He'd explained to Bonham about his need to blend in around the docks and how a standard issue police uniform only put the denizens of the wharves on edge. They both knew it was an excuse. No one else wore a suit around the waterfront, but Betancourt had so far won their skirmishes.

Bonham was in the habit of carrying a pigskin-covered swagger stick with which he slapped his leg when making a point. Betancourt had often wondered if it hurt, but if it did, it didn't seem to deter the AC from using it. Today, the stick lay on his desk, weighing down a pile of reports. Bonham picked it up and prodded at a newspaper.

'Seen this? Streets flooded with Japanese women. Bloody disgrace.'

Betancourt leaned over to see what was being pointed at. It was the piece by George Elias that he'd read that morning, so he admitted he'd seen it.

'Government House isn't happy. Not happy at all. And if Government House isn't happy, then I'm not happy.'

This was exactly what Betancourt had hoped to avoid. 'I'll look into it, sir. George is usually reliable. I'll speak to him and see if I can find out where he's getting his information from.'

'Be sure that you do. This is your territory, Betancourt. If these women are coming in by boat, I expect you to put a stop to it. Do I make myself clear?'

'Crystal. Sir.'

Bonham rifled through his papers again until his fingers alighted on a folder. He scanned the document within and raised his eyebrows, as though he was seeing the contents for the first time and what he read surprised him.

'And this is why. This prostitute.' He tapped the folder. 'The one that killed herself at the docks.'

'Prostitute, sir?'

'Why, are you suggesting she wasn't?'

'I'm not suggesting anything. Not yet. I've no idea if she was a prostitute or not, but there seem to be plenty of people who've made up their minds that she was. As for the killed herself bit, the post-mortem suggests otherwise.'

Bonham consulted the details of the report again. 'Young woman hanging around the docks on her own, dressed for business… Sounds like a tart to me.'

There was that word again. Tart. First Gemmill, then Harvey, and now Bonham. Someone had primed him. Gemmill, perhaps? Or if not Gemmill, who else?

'May I ask, sir, why the special interest in this woman's death?'

Bonham paused for a moment before speaking. 'I gather she was found next to a Napier's ship. I received a call from Sir Archibald Napier himself earlier this morning. He's concerned about his ship and his people being dragged into this nonsense.'

Things fell into place. So it hadn't been Gemmill then, or at least not only Gemmill. Old Archie Napier wasn't shy about wielding his considerable power and influence. It was widely assumed, if never actually mentioned in polite company, that the Governor took his instructions from Archie, rather than the other way around.

'Napier's owns a lot of properties in Selangor – rubber, tin, palm oil. The usual. Apparently, the company thinks it's good for the estate managers to let off a bit of steam occasionally. Consequently, a group of their men boarded the *Batavian Princess* at Port Swettenham and sailed down to Singapore for the New Year. Napier's pays their passage, food, bar bills and whatnot.' He hesitated. 'And, occasionally, they lay on a few women. I don't have to explain to you how this all works, do I? You're a man of the world.'

Not of Bonham's world, he wasn't, and not of the world he'd just described either.

'Are you suggesting the dead woman may have been a passenger on the ship?'

Bonham looked wildly from side to side, as though an interloper might have sneaked in while they'd been talking and overheard this scurrilous suggestion. 'For Christ's sake, man! No, I'm not saying that at all. Quite the opposite. It will have been a complete coincidence she turned up next to the boat the Napier's men travelled on. There'll be some simple explanation. She'll have picked up a travelling salesman or the like. He was taking her back to consummate the deal, they quarrelled, perhaps she asked him for more money, he was drunk, they fought...' His voice trailed off.

'And she slipped and inadvertently cut her throat, three times?'

Bonham flushed. 'Less of the attitude, Betancourt. Decent people arrive at and depart from that part of the docks, and it's your job to make sure they aren't confronted with women like this. If common tarts are going to get themselves killed, they can bloody well do it somewhere else. Do I make myself clear? Who's taking care of the paperwork?'

'I am.'

It just came out. Betancourt wasn't sure if it was the *decent people* comment or the one about *common tarts* or just Bonham's generally insufferable attitude, but whatever it was, he resolved to find out what had happened to the woman and bring whoever had done it to justice. 'Or at least, I will be once I've completed my investigation.'

'You? Absolutely not.' None of this exchange appeared to be doing Bonham's blood pressure any good. 'I want someone from Detective Branch seeing to this so I can assure Sir Archibald that things have been properly taken care of.'

Swept under the carpet, you mean. Betancourt studied Bonham before replying and then raised his hands, palms facing away, as if in reluctant acquiescence. 'Well, I suppose we *could* stretch the rules, if you think it best.'

Bonham squinted, suddenly suspicious.

'What do you mean?'

Betancourt adopted his blandest, most innocent tone. 'I was just thinking... the woman's body was found within the confines of the Port of Singapore and, as we both know, per the Maritime and Port Authority Act, jurisdiction therefore lies with Marine Branch.' He was enjoying Bonham's growing discomfort. 'But if you insist on Detective Branch picking it up…'

He had Bonham in a cleft stick. The one thing that would worry the Assistant Commissioner more than getting on the wrong side of Archie Napier, was any suggestion that he hadn't played the game strictly by the rules. The room was perfectly still, the only sound the *swoop, swoop, swoop* of the electric ceiling fan above. When Bonham spoke again, there was an unmistakable edge to his tone.

'Very well then, you take care of it, but I want your report on my desk tomorrow. Do we understand each other? And I want to see you highlighting the fact that there is nothing – I repeat, nothing – to link the death of this woman to the Napier's ship, her crew or her passengers.'

Betancourt knew he should leave it there, but this was Bonham after all. He couldn't resist another dig. 'And if I find evidence to the contrary?'

By this time, his superior's face had turned an unhealthy-looking shade of puce. 'Are you happy where you are, Betancourt? Because I suggest that unless you want to spend the next twenty years picking through tea chests and issuing fines for wrongly completed shipping manifests, you learn to play the bloody game.'

The word *game* hung in the air between them.

'A woman is dead. I fail to see how this is a game.'

Bonham sat forward in his chair. He had the look of a man who'd been pushed too far and had run out of patience. 'I'm never sure if it's naivety or plain stupidity with you, but you just don't seem to get it. Your lot are all the same.'

'And what lot would that be?' He paused. 'Sir?'

'Serani, Eurasians… whatever the hell you're calling yourselves these days. You know what your problem is, don't you? You're neither one thing nor the other. You're not one of us and you're not one of them. It's time to decide which side you're on, Betancourt. She was just a prostitute. Treat her death accordingly and then get back to doing what the Force pays you for. Savvy?'

He returned to the mound of papers on his desk. Apparently, the discussion was over.

Chapter Five

By the time Betancourt had finished with the last of the demands of the day's paperwork and departed Empress Place, it had already gone six o'clock, and the first shadows of the equatorial night crept across the pavement in front of him. When he was a child, an old lady who'd looked after him from time to time when his aunt couldn't, told him shadows were the souls of people who were stuck between heaven and hell and if he were to stand on them, those souls would be condemned to wander in limbo for all time. Although a schoolteacher had later assured him that this was most definitely not the case, he'd seen no advantage to be gained from risking it, and so his walk home that evening was a meandering one.

The small flat he occupied above the shophouse on Chinatown's Duxton Hill smelled of fried noodles, reminding him he hadn't eaten since breakfast. He tried the refrigerator. A square of hard cheese, green mould crawling across its surface. A potato, sprouting shoots from all of its eyes. A half-empty bottle of milk. He sniffed. Rancid. He washed the curdled milk down the sink and descended the wooden steps to the shop below.

Someone at work had recommended he try the *char kuay teow* at Mr Tan's *kopi tiam* on Duxton Hill, so, when he found himself passing one day, he stopped to put the endorsement to the test. The food was as good as he'd been told, and he was just finishing up when the owner of the shop received a visit from two members of the local branch of the Lucky Seven Provident Society. The men suggested it would be in Mr Tan's interests if he were to make a small donation to their welfare association. In return, they'd ensure he need never again worry about the safety of his premises or, heaven forbid, the well-being of his family. Fortunately for Mr Tan, Betancourt overheard the whole exchange. He drew his warrant card from his wallet and placed it casually on the countertop where it could be seen, so there could be no confusion. After he'd made conciliatory murmurings about being happy to look after Mr Tan's well-being himself, the men left, apologising for any misunderstanding. Mr Tan was duly grateful and when it arose that Betancourt was in the market for accommodation, they quickly came to an agreement for him to rent the vacant space above the shop. The going rate was higher than Betancourt paid, but Mr Tan was happy to make a reduction in return for having a policeman as a tenant.

'I'm not too late, I hope, Mr Tan?'

'Never too late for you, Inspector. What can I get you?'

It had always been like this: "Mr Tan" and "Inspector", mutual respect the hallmark of their relationship.

'Just whatever you have left. Don't go to any trouble.'

'Never any trouble for you, Inspector.'

Mr Tan lit the gas ring beneath a vast wok and when the lard smoked, he threw in handfuls of rice noodles, bean shoots, pieces of soybean curd, slices of preserved sausage, and several different condiments.

'You have post. Over there behind the till.'

Betancourt pocketed the letters without looking at them. A newspaper lay on the counter, open at the sports page. Notes in pencil were scribbled next to the runners and riders for the weekend's races. Mr Tan pulled a sheaf of astrological charts from his back pocket and threw them down next to the newspaper. He'd consulted his personal astrologer that very afternoon and was now in possession of all the lucky numbers.

'Race four, number four.' He pointed to one of the scribbles with his spatula.

Circus Top. Trainer W. Allenby. Betancourt knew Bill Allenby and was a regular visitor to his stables at the Bukit Timah Turf Club. He realised with a stab of regret he hadn't spoken to the old Australian for a while and made a mental note to remedy that soon.

'This astrologer of yours. Is he any good?'

'The best.'

If Allenby was readying a touch, he'd have let Betancourt know. The fact he'd heard nothing about Circus Top's chances meant the horse had none.

'Thanks for the advice, but I think I'll keep my money. If there's one thing that'll slow a horse down, it's me betting on it.'

Mr Tan laughed, as if to say: *your choice, your loss.* The food was ready, and he piled a steaming, fragrant pile of noodles onto a banana leaf, parcelled the whole lot up, and secured it with rattan twine. As usual, he dismissed the offer to pay for the food and Betancourt felt bad for not steering him clear of Circus Top. But everything Allenby told him, or just as importantly didn't tell him, was sacrosanct. He'd find another way of repaying the shopkeeper's kindness.

He unlocked the door of his flat and stooped to pick up a strand of cotton from the ground. When he was still a raw young sergeant, he'd shared a flat in the single men's quarters at the Hill Street station. One day, he'd arrived home to find a man walking out of the flat carrying the radio he and his roommate had pooled their meagre wages to buy. He'd lunged at the thief, but the man had covered himself in grease, a favoured trick at the time, and had squirmed free, dropping the radio in the process and smashing it to pieces. Ever since, Betancourt had placed a piece of thread in the door jamb whenever he left home. If he found it dislodged when he returned, he'd know someone had been in.

He pulled the sheaf of letters from his pocket. A small envelope bore a Georgetown postmark, posted from Penang. His name and address were printed in precise cursive handwriting, the bottom of each letter flat and straight – written using a ruler. He sniffed the envelope and was greeted by the familiar scent of violets. Theresa always dabbed her letters with a drop of toilet water. He'd never thought to ask her why.

Theresa was the aunt who'd taken him in and cared for him when his own mother had left. She wasn't his real aunt. She'd had the fortune – good or bad, he wouldn't like to say – to be the cousin of a young woman named Maria Monteiro whose family in Malacca had sent her to Singapore in the hope that it might help to tame some of her wilder tendencies. They'd asked Theresa if Maria could board with her and Theresa, good-natured soul that she was, agreed the girl could come and live with her in her bungalow on Waterloo Street. Maria was what the people of the neighbourhood had delicately referred to as a free spirit. "Flighty" Theresa had called her. When Maria's friends were busy doing their homework or learning to cook or sew, she would be out dancing the night away in the jazz halls and night clubs of the city. It was in one such place she met Julius Betancourt. Julius played jazz piano, music was his life, and it was no surprise to anyone, except possibly Maria, and then only briefly, when he abandoned her, child at her breast, to follow his star. A few months later, undaunted by the apparent rejection, she pinned a note to her baby son's blanket and left him outside Theresa's bedroom door. *Gone to find my beautiful man*, it read. No one, Betancourt included, heard from her again. He wondered from time to time if she ever found what she was looking for. Wondered if she was happy. Hoped she was. But he'd never stopped loathing the sound of the piano.

Theresa had long since married and moved with her husband to Penang. She wrote to him regularly: brief letters asking after his health and happiness and that of Lucia. Rather than explain to her he'd become all but estranged from his daughter, he'd just stopped replying, but Theresa never alluded to his negligence and kept on writing. He propped the letter up behind the telephone – a visible reminder to find her number and call her.

He glanced at the two remaining letters. The first one had the words FINAL DEMAND stamped in red on it, and the second URGENT – DO NOT IGNORE. He added them, unopened, to a growing collection in the kitchen drawer. Correspondence taken care of, he picked up his two serviceable plates from the draining board and compared them. He tipped the food, still warm from its banana-leaf cocoon, onto the less chipped of the two.

An army of bullfrogs had taken up residence in a nearby storm drain. After he'd eaten, he sat next to the window, listening to their *a cappella* chorus. Across the road, a blinking neon sign reminding passers-by of the pleasures of a Tiger beer provided a lambent backdrop to the street below.

As he chewed, he went over his earlier conversation with Bonham. The remarks about his race were nothing new. He was used to Europeans looking down their superior colonial noses at him and his people. It was the man's anxiety about the affair that interested him more. Napier must really have put the frighteners on him. The woman's body had turned up next to a Napier's ship and the old man wanted the investigation taken care of quickly, and above all quietly, with no muck being seen to stick. And what Napier wanted, Napier usually got. It was said that if he wanted a white Christmas in Singapore, you wouldn't want to bet long odds against it happening. But why did the death of an unknown Asian woman have people so riled?

Betancourt considered turning in for the night, but he found sleep difficult enough at the best of times and with all that had happened the last two days, it would be impossible tonight. He threw on his jacket and headed out.

The noise of evening endeavour pierced the air as he criss-crossed the lanes and alleyways of Chinatown: restaurants and fortune tellers, herbalists and loan sharks, massage parlours and opium sellers. Every aspect of life-as-normal could be found in these back lanes. He liked that he was considered enough of a local that he could talk to people on these streets and find things out, where Europeans would have met a wall of silence. Inevitably, though, his presence caused heads to turn. Whispered warnings suggested some recognised him as a policeman. To others, he was simply not one of them and therefore of no particular interest.

Eventually, as though steered there by an unseen hand, he reached the river and sat at a rickety metal table outside a restaurant frequented by godown workers. The place was owned and run by a Hakka named Chiang, but no one ever referred to him by his proper name. The man was inordinately fond of his own food and, as a result, was known to all and sundry as Fatty. Apparently, he'd taken no offence at this as he'd named the restaurant Fatty's too.

The sultry night air was filled with cigarette smoke and the clash of mahjong tiles. The coolies stopped playing and looked at the new arrival curiously. He knew what they were thinking. What do we make of this one? With his burnt-honey-coloured skin and black, softly-curled hair – perhaps a little longer than was strictly fashionable – he clearly wasn't a *gweilo* – a ghost man – but nor was he Chinese, like them, nor Malay, nor Indian. He was used to it: treated as a local when it suited the locals, and as a sort of European when it suited the Europeans. When it didn't suit either of them, he was treated as neither. The lot of the Serani was nothing new.

Fatty came over to his table. An oil-spattered singlet barely stretched around his pendulous gut and a cigarette hung from one corner of his mouth. His appearance wasn't the best advertisement for the eatery, but Betancourt knew he needn't worry. Fatty's traditional Hakka food was legend. He ordered a coffee. Fatty asked him if he was sure he didn't want a beer. He was sure. The restauranteur went away to make the coffee, muttering under his breath. Profit margins were better on beer.

As was so often the case when he was alone, Betancourt's thoughts turned to Anna's disappearance. CID had received intelligence that a new secret society *tong* was smuggling opium across the causeway from Johor, and he was assigned to the case. One day, a letter addressed to Anna arrived at their home. It said that if Betancourt didn't back off from the investigation, they'd both regret it. She was scared and begged him to heed the threat, for the sake of their daughter, Lucia, if not hers. Threats like that were commonplace, and most of the men in the Detective Branch had received something similar at one time or other. They rarely came to anything, so he told her to ignore it. A few days later, her car was found near the docks. There was no trace of her. She was gone, and it was his fault, and he'd have to live with that until the day he died.

For months he'd looked for her, ignoring his work in the process. He'd leaned on, intimidated, cajoled, and threatened every contact he knew, looking for any information he could get about the secret society that had taken her. Two of his Detective Branch colleagues – the ones he hadn't completely alienated – covered for him and, for a while, even took on his case load, but eventually they too had had enough and his absence from duty was noted. He was warned, then reprimanded, and eventually dismissed. He had to give up the family home in Pearl's Hill, and with it, his daughter, Lucia, who went to stay with her grandparents. He pressed on with his search, spending every cent of their savings and more, until he was forced to borrow from moneylenders just to keep going. But so powerful was the grip grief held him in, he barely noticed the depths to which he'd descended.

Eventually, gradually, his sanity returned, and he had to face the fact that she was gone and most likely wasn't coming back. He tried reconnecting with his daughter, but by then it was too late. Lucia blamed him for his part in her mother's loss. That was when he dragged himself back together and sought Marjorie's help. She had put in a good word with Inspector General Onraet, a family friend. It seemed that Onraet was in a long-running disagreement with the Comptroller of Customs and Excise over who, exactly, should police Singapore's shores, and how. His off-the-record brief to Betancourt was "to keep his eyes and ears open". It was clear the IG wanted his own man on the ground around the docks and a grateful Betancourt was, it seemed, to be that man. And now here he was, sitting at a riverside bar at midnight, wondering what to do about a dead woman found abandoned at the docks.

His thoughts turned to her, this woman no one seemed to think deserving of even common justice. Anna was gone and he couldn't bring her back, but he could find out what had happened to this mystery woman and make someone pay for what they'd done to her. It was the very least his wife would have expected of him.

Chapter Six

B etancourt woke early the next morning. He set a pot of coffee on the gas ring to boil, before picking up a long knife from the draining board. He realised he no longer had any idea how much he actually owed, so he fished out the pile of red-lettered envelopes – it was thicker than he'd remembered – and one by one, sliced them open. Laying out the letters by category, like columns in a game of solitaire, he scribbled down the totals. School fees: $480; grocery bills: $45; laundry bills: $35; petrol station: $50; a final, final demand from the Public Utilities Board for power and light: $65. He owed Mr Tan $170 for back rent and he'd lost count of the IOUs he'd handed out. There must be at least ten of them; call it a hundred each: another thousand. The total came to nearly two thousand dollars. How could he have let it get this far?

Scorched coffee, bitter as sin, cauterised his mouth. He examined the knife he'd used to open the letters. The blade was bowed thin in the middle from too many whettings on the stoop of the house below. He turned it over in his hand, weighed it, felt the heft. He thought of the dead woman and those blood-encrusted lines trisecting her neck. He laid the knife against the side of his own neck and was surprised by how pleasant the cool steel felt. Shaking himself out of his morbid reverie, he stuffed the letters back into the drawer. Out of sight, out of mind.

He descended the stairs to the small lot behind the shop-house. The rain had slackened a little, but he eased his arms out of his jacket and pulled it over his head, pressing it into service as an impromptu gabardine. He crossed the courtyard on the tips of his toes to avoid the worst of the puddles, until he reached a dilapidated wooden shed, half-covered by rampant climbing plants. Propping open the doors, he peeled back the waxed canvas sheet that hid its contents. He swept away silken filaments laid by spiders during the night and wheeled Alex out into the daylight.

Alex was a 1926 Scott Flying Squirrel motorcycle. He'd lovingly restored her with a not insignificant amount of assistance from a mechanic who ran a repair shop near the dockyard whom he'd helped by recovering a stolen generator from a barge bound for Sibu, on the island of Borneo. The generator had been an expensive one that the man, in a moment of ill-advised frugality, had neglected to insure. He'd been very grateful for its return.

The motorcycle itself had been seized from an American-owned freighter flying a flag of convenience. When Betancourt was still in the CID, an informer had tipped him off that a load of Bourbon whiskey for which excise duty had not been paid was due to arrive in port. The whiskey was easily enough found but the real prize lay beneath the crates of spirit: straw-filled crates containing Egyptian relics, smuggled out through the port of Alexandria, from where the ship had sailed a week earlier.

Alex, named for her port of embarkation, had been a bonus. The captain of the ship, a garrulous, red-faced Mississippian, was only too happy to dish the dirt on his erstwhile employers. He'd won the motorcycle in a game of cards with an Englishman named Armitage, the shipping agent who'd arranged the illegal transport of the artefacts. Betancourt made a pre-emptive bid prior to the motorcycle being sent from the police impoundment yard to be sold at auction.

It was Anna who'd come up with the name Alex. She'd refer to the motorcycle, only semi-jokingly, as his "other woman". At the time he'd thought naming a machine a silly affectation, but he was now glad of having the connection to his wife when so many others were fading.

He reversed his jacket and put it on back to front, local style, so his white shirt wouldn't catch the dirt and debris kicking up from the road. He tightened the chin strap of the hemispherical steel helmet Anna had insisted he wore, and engaged gear before easing out into the traffic on South Bridge Road.

Evidence of the late monsoon rain was everywhere. Even at this time, the streets were alive and pedestrians played out a carefully choreographed dance, taking care to avoid not only each other but also the puddles dotting the pavements. Some covered their heads with sheets of newspaper to protect themselves from the fat, bulbous drips falling from the awnings shielding the shopfronts. Clouds of dank-smelling steam rose from the street, reminding him that, at its heart, Singapore was little more than a patch of cleared jungle.

'Delivery for you.' The desk sergeant handed over two thick brown manila envelopes. 'The photographer left them.'

Betancourt took the envelopes and thanked him. 'Anything else?'

The man shook his head. 'Just the usual demonstrations at the docks. I've sent a couple of men down to sort it out.'

Betancourt nodded his approval and gave instructions he wasn't to be disturbed – no phone calls and no interruptions.

He closed the door to the small office behind him and, settling himself at the cluttered desk, untied the first envelope. It contained the pictures taken at the docks. Yung might not be the cheeriest man alive, but he took a good photograph. The images were crisp and clear and there was a good selection of shots taken from every angle with a range of focal lengths. Betancourt scrutinised them closely. A full-length study of the woman showed her exactly as he'd first seen her when he'd peeled back the tarpaulin. He held up the print. He studied her face and wondered what she'd thought as her life ebbed away. Had she even been aware of what was happening to her?

He opened the second envelope and went through the pictures taken at the Crypt. Dr Trevose and Martha, her nurse, had been busy after he left. The first photograph was a headshot of the woman, the shroud pulled up to cover the wounds on her neck. She looked so peaceful she could easily have been asleep. Her hair had been neatly brushed and a touch of make-up applied to her face. Who had done that? he wondered. It was a touch of humanity that wouldn't have happened if Gemmill had done the post-mortem. The photograph was the closest thing he had to presenting the woman as she'd been in life, so he put it to one side.

His first task was to identify her. Once he knew who she was, he could start finding out who had borne her sufficient ill will to want her dead. He leafed through the rest of the photographs and added a second picture – one that showed the tiger tattoo in its full glory. If anything, Yung's photography made the animal appear even more impressive than it had in the artificial light of the morgue. Isolated like this, it was hard to imagine an image so striking could have been made with a needle. Most of the local tattoo artists catered for the passing maritime trade and their repertoire didn't stretch much beyond anchors and ropes, or hearts and arrows, or brief, unimaginative messages recalling distant sweethearts. This one must have taken a rare talent. Pocketing the photographs, Betancourt locked the door behind him and set off for the docks.

There was a coffee shop near the railway station on Keppel Road, opposite the dockyard, that he occasionally frequented. He parked Alex outside and waved through the window, to catch the attention of the owner of the shop. He pointed to the motorcycle, to indicate he was leaving it there, and the man waved back. No problem.

The ink shops were clustered around the bars used by sailors, and in a narrow alleyway that ran between Patani Street and Selangor Street he found the door he'd been looking for. A small slat opened and an almond-shaped eye peered out. He held up his warrant card. The slat slammed shut. He heard the scraping of furniture being hastily rearranged. Eventually, the door cracked open and a skinny, sallow face with a long thin moustache like two rat's tails peered out at him.

The owner of the face was a man named Ah Ting. He had the reputation of being one of the better tattoo artists and knew everyone in the trade. Betancourt held the photograph of the tiger up to his face.

'Thinking of getting something like this done. I was wondering if it was the kind of thing you could help me with.'

Ah Ting shook his head. 'Sorry. Closed.'

Betancourt leaned forward and looked into the small front room where four anxious-looking men sat at a bare table. It was an old trick. The tabletop was hinged so that when the police came calling, a quick flip would deposit cards, chips, money, scorecards, and IOUs into a false bottom beneath, safe from inquisitive eyes.

Betancourt smiled at them and gave a wave, before returning his gaze to Ah Ting who relented and opened the door. 'Upstairs.'

In the small room above, a woman, presumably Ah Ting's wife, stirred a pot on top of a portable cooker. She paid Betancourt no attention, as though visits from strange Serani in suits were a regular occurrence. They sat at a table and Betancourt passed across the photo.

'Who could do this kind of work?'

Ah Ting took a pair of spectacles from the pocket of his shorts and placed them on the end of his nose. He held the photograph close to his face, tilting it first away and then back towards him, squinting at the detail as it caught the light.

'Where did you get this?'

'Never mind that. Could it have been done by someone round here?'

'I can't tell you anything about this. You need to go.'

'But I've only just arrived. Perhaps I should have a look downstairs. What do you suppose I'd find inside that table?'

The man swore under his breath. He considered the threat for a moment and then barked an order at the woman. She gave as good as she got, waving a ladle and arguing back. After a few more rallies, she switched off the gas ring and clumped down the stairs, muttering a string of insults as she did so.

'You don't understand.'

'You're right. That's why I'm here, speaking to you.'

'No, no. If I tell you, they'll kill me.'

It sounded a little melodramatic, killing someone for recommending a tattooist.

'Who'll kill you?'

Ah Ting shook his head firmly.

'All right, at least tell me who could do this kind of work.'

There was a silence as Ah Ting chewed over his options. It was either give up some information or face a fine and possibly jail time for running an illegal gambling den. It seemed he'd decided information was the lesser of two evils.

'*Horishi.*'

'Who?'

'No. Not who. *Horishi.* Japanese *irezumi* master. Traditional full-body tattoo. Like this.' He reached behind him and picked up a magazine. 'See?' He folded over a page and showed Betancourt a photograph of a man, taken from the back. A twisting, writhing dragon-like creature ran from the man's neck, over his back and down his legs. Every other inch of his skin was marked with some aspect of a scene that looked like it had come straight from a horror film. It was a work of art.

'These *horishi*, where would I find them?'

Ah Ting shook his head again. 'Not here, not in Singapore. Japan. Maybe Shanghai. I can't say any more. You must go now. Try the *suteretsu.*'

Betancourt had intended to go there next anyway. He watched the man carefully. If the tattoo hadn't been done here, what was he so worried about? When they reached the front door, he took out a business card. 'Call me if you change your mind.'

Ah Ting declined the offer and fixed Betancourt with sad eyes. 'I hope you know what you're doing, Inspector.' He closed the door, leaving Betancourt with the feeling a cold wind had just blown right through him.

He returned to find Alex scattered with papery-winged seed pods that had fluttered down from a nearby angsana tree. He swept away the worst of them from the seat and was donning his helmet when a voice called to him from the shade of a godown across the road. A man waved an arm, suggesting he wished to speak. He wore the usual dockside coolie attire of dirty white singlet, black cotton shorts, and a woven rattan minaret-shaped *topi* to protect his head from the unrelenting sun.

Betancourt waited for a gap in the traffic and sprinted across the road.

'What is it?'

The man launched into an animated monologue. Whichever dialect he was speaking, it was beyond Betancourt's grasp. The coolie gesticulated first towards the *Batavian Princess*, and then to a godown. Apparently, there was something Betancourt needed to see.

He tried Malay, but the man just shook his head. 'Wait.' He held up his hands, palms outwards, to indicate to the man he should stay where he was, and then a single finger. '*Sebentar.* One minute.'

He scanned the yard. By a bollard at the stern of the *Batavian Princess*, poring over a sheaf of papers, were Abu Bakar and the young sergeant he'd spoken to the previous day.

'What dialect do you speak?'

Sergeant Quek broke off from his perusal of the bills of lading. 'Hokkien, boss. And a bit of Cantonese. My mother was from Canton.'

'I don't need your life history – I just need you to translate. Come with me. See if you can make out what this fellow wants.'

The coolie spoke rapidly while Quek listened, interjecting occasionally, head cocked to one side so he could catch everything the man was saying. He held up one hand to bring the explanation to a halt.

'My Cantonese is rusty, but I can understand most of what he says. His name is Leung. He's from Hong Kong. He works for one of the stevedores, carrying cargo. He saw you yesterday, with the dead woman.'

'What does he want?'

Quek turned back to the man and questioned him. 'Yesterday morning, about ten o'clock, his wife was working on one of the boats and she saw something.'

The man spoke a few agitated words and Quek hushed him gently, as one might reassure a child who had awoken in the night, frightened of monsters.

'He's afraid. He can't afford to get in trouble. He and his wife, they only have these jobs, and they owe money.'

It was a common enough situation on the dockside. Destitute families from China who scrimped and saved to pay for their passage hoping to find work on the gold-paved streets of Singapore. Their agents would take every *yuan* and then charge exorbitant finder's fees, couched as loans, for arranging jobs as menial labour around the docks, and yet more to arrange accommodation: ten to a room in rat-infested wooden tinder boxes. They even charged ridiculous amounts for clothing, which could be purchased anywhere, but which the traffickers asserted only they could provide, insisting the clothes the workers had brought with them were "not permissible". The men and women, now penniless, had no option but to stay and do as they were told, condemned to a life of servitude until they grew too old and feeble to carry their burdens, at which point they would be cast out, onto the streets, to fend for themselves.

'Tell him he can speak in confidence.'

Quek relayed the message. After a few more exchanges the man seemed to relax, or at least became resigned to inevitability, and indicated they should follow him back to the godown.

Deep in the gloom cast by the rusted corrugated sheeting enclosing the building stood a woman, her eyes cast down. She was streaked from head to foot with oil and grime. A *long sai*, one of the band of women who clung like limpets to the sides of ships, suspended by sisal ropes from daybreak to sunset, scrubbing away the rust and other visible imperfections from the merchant fleet. Her head was bound with a torn piece of dirty grey cotton and she wore the de facto *long sai* uniform of grey cotton tunic and black trousers. She was small and frail, the result, Betancourt guessed, of malnourishment in her youth. The skin of her gaunt face was like tanned leather, and her mouth, when it eventually opened, held only a few long, yellowed teeth. She stooped, with shoulders hunched, and on appearance alone could easily have passed for fifty or sixty years old, but Betancourt had seen enough women like her to know the toll exacted by the combination of backbreaking work and raising a family in penury. In reality, she was probably no older than thirty-five.

The man barked a command and she acknowledged him with an obedient '*Hai*'. Satisfied she would do his bidding the man turned again to Quek and spoke at length. The sergeant listened intently, constantly watching the man's lips as he spoke, interrupting occasionally for clarification or encouraging him to slow down. Eventually, he raised a palm and the man stopped talking.

'He said she's his wife. The one who saw something.'

'I'd rather guessed that. Any chance of finding out what it was she's supposed to have seen?'

'She was working on the ship.' He pointed towards the *Batavian Princess*. 'There was a commotion. He says all the *long sai* stopped working to see what was going on—'

Betancourt interrupted. 'I'd like to hear it in her own words.'

Quek explained to the man, who argued until Betancourt silenced him with a stern look. Quek then addressed the woman directly, speaking slowly and deliberately. At first there was silence. Eventually she began to speak, hesitantly to begin with, but as her story unfolded, gaining in confidence until the words came more easily.

'They heard cries from the area by the dockyard gates.' Quek asked the woman something, and she nodded. 'A man was arguing with a well-dressed woman.'

'Well-dressed? What was she wearing?'

'A blue *cheongsam.*'

The woman added something.

'Very pretty.'

'What did she mean by "arguing"?'

Another exchange.

'The woman had a bag. The man tried to take it, but she fought back and pulled away. Then he grabbed her by the hair and pushed her out the gates, towards the road. Two *gwei lo* were walking towards the rickshaw rank. They saw what was happening and intervened.'

Gwei lo. Ghosts. The Cantonese epithet for Europeans, and not one used with any fondness. They were probably just passers-by, but it was worth checking.

'When we're finished here, have a word with the rickshaw

pullers outside the gate and see if anyone remembers seeing anything. What happened next?'

'The man tried one more time to take the bag and then he gave up and the woman ran away.'

'This woman, was she a local?'

'She says Asian, but the woman was pale.'

'Could she have been Japanese?'

Quek asked the question. 'Maybe. She said she doesn't know what Japanese look like.'

'And what about the man? Local or European?'

There was another interchange between Quek and the woman, this time lengthier, and her husband seemed to have an opinion on the matter as well.

'Well?'

'She says neither.'

'What do you mean, neither? He had to be one or the other.'

Quek asked another question, as if to check he'd heard correctly. Then he frowned and seemed unwilling to pass on the answer. 'She said he was like you.'

The woman pointed at Betancourt with a bony finger, as if to emphasise her assessment. He held her gaze for a second. There was no malice or disaffection in her eyes, only an amiable curiosity.

'Anything else?'

'Nothing. The foreman scolded them, and they went back to work. Later, when she heard about the death of the woman, she told her husband what she'd seen.'

The conversation had run its course and they were all quiet. For a moment, the only sound was the scrabbling of fruit bats' claws in the eaves of the godown, disturbed from their diurnal slumbers by the noisy humans below.

The man asked something of Quek.

'He wants to know if this information is useful.'

'Very useful. Thank them both from me.'

The man removed the rattan *topi* from his head and stood fidgeting. When he spoke again, it was with an air of deference and humility.

Quek cleared his throat. 'He asks, if they have been of use, would the boss consider a reward?'

Betancourt pulled a few crumpled dollar notes from his pocket and handed them over. The man's face broke into a crooked grin and he gave a small bow before summoning his wife, to depart back to wherever it was they lived.

Chapter Seven

He parked Alex in an alley beside an apothecary's shop on North Bridge Road. Thick, pungent aromas assaulted his nose. The shop was packed to the ceiling with jars of roots and herbs, deer antlers and other animal parts, now too dry and deformed to decipher their origin with any certainty. Signs promised the proprietor could cure any ailment.

Lazy liver? We have the answer!
Slippery pulse? No problem!

He wondered if there was a potion that could cure a broken heart.

A storm drain ran the length of the road. Following the recent rains, it was full and fast-moving. The head of a small boy, no more than six or seven years old, popped up from the swirling brown water and the child clambered up the side of the concrete gulley, like a mud crab fleeing the incoming tide, much to the delight of his friends who clapped and shrieked from the bank above.

'Money, mister,' one of the urchins shouted. His friends

joined in. 'Mister, you throw money!'

He considered cautioning the boys about the perils of playing in the storm water, but decided it wouldn't make any difference, and anyway, hadn't he done exactly the same thing when he was their age? He rummaged in his pocket. He came up with a five-cent coin which he laid across the side of his index finger. The boys readied themselves, one foot in front of the other, like tournament swimmers preparing to start a race.

'Three... two... one...'

He gave the coin a sharp flip and it spun away through the air, arcing out beyond the reach of the boys. No sooner had the coin hit the water than they leaped as one. For a few moments they disappeared below the roiling foam before a hand appeared above the surface of the water, clasping Betancourt's coin. A shock of black hair above a toothy grin followed, and the triumphant diver shouted: 'Money, mister, you throw more money!'

Betancourt held up another coin. 'Watch the motorcycle for me and I'll give you fifty cents.'

The boy scrambled up the side of the drain and scampered over, wide-eyed at the promise of such riches. 'Very good, mister. Anybody comes, I'll fight them.' Betancourt left him, still dripping, as he took up his sentry position on the stoop outside the apothecary's shop.

It was a while since he'd last had reason to visit Bugis Street. Since the services peddled here had been outlawed, the practitioners had retreated from view a little, but the brightly coloured lanterns that hung above the ornate wooden doorframes lining the street were a clue to the business still thriving behind these walls. An occasional plate bore a name such as Miss Heavenly or Madam Pleasure, showing houses where a prospective client would find European company. The English nameplates were a calculated conceit, intending to imply the occupant was in fact English. The workers of the different races who frequented these streets considered English women to be a forbidden fruit, and to spend an hour with one was to indulge in a delicacy well worth the additional premium. The truth was the colonial administration unequivocally forbade English prostitutes and Miss Heavenly would invariably be one of a band of poor émigrées from Eastern Europe – Russian Jewesses, minor Polish countesses down on their luck, Hungarians, or, occasionally, a Frenchwoman who had got on the wrong boat and never bothered to retrace her steps.

But mostly, the *suteretsu* area was home to hundreds of *karayuki-san*: women, many of them no more than girls, who had fled the poverty of their homelands in southern Japan in search of a better life and who had ended up here, in the brothels of the red-light district that butted up against the central business district.

He only ever came here on police business, but he felt a genuine fondness for the area. To him, the *suteretsu*, although Japan in microcosm, was typical Singapore. These people, most of them impoverished, had arrived in the colony and immediately set to work establishing a community. Dotted amongst the houses were small shops providing everything the residents required. Tea shops provided Japanese food, tailors made silk kimonos, and a funeral parlour tended to the traditional customs of those who were no longer in need of any other service.

A pretty girl in a silver kimono stepped out from the shadows of a doorway and smiled encouragingly at him. The most fetching-looking girls in each house were the lucky ones: they were put outside on procurement duty, where they used their charms to lure passing trade inside for their sisters to service. She took Betancourt's polite rebuff with practised good grace.

He stopped outside a red lacquered door and rapped three times. A giant of a man wearing an ill-fitting jacket about three sizes too small for him opened the door. Betancourt pulled himself to his full height, but his head still only came up to the man's chest.

'What?'

'Tell Madame Belle there's someone here who wants to speak to her.' He produced his warrant card and held in front of the man's face.

'Wait.' It seemed he had trouble using more than one word at a time.

The door closed firmly in Betancourt's face. A few of the nearby shopkeepers and their customers had ceased their activities and were watching the exchange with interest. There hadn't been so much as a flicker to show if the man had read his card and, if he had, what he'd made of its contents. Betancourt wasn't sure what to do next. Should he knock again? Any further deliberation was cut short as the door swung open. 'Busy.' A flick of the colossal head in the direction of the street was enough for Betancourt to get the message he was being dismissed. He debated whether there was any point in trying to force his way past. The man filled the doorway, thick arms folded across his belly, an impassable barrier. Probably not.

The inspector removed a business card from his wallet. 'Tell Madame Belle to call me. When she's less busy.' He walked away to the sound of paper being torn to shreds.

* * *

At a Japanese tea house, a few doors down from the brothel, a young servant girl dressed in a pink kimono poured tea for two elderly customers. She bowed repeatedly at the curt commands of the women, steadfastly avoiding meeting their eyes as she did so. Even here, in the heart of the red-light district, there were the rulers and those who were ruled.

He was pondering his next move when the sound of running feet snapped him from his musing. A girl dressed in a simple undyed *yukata* stopped before him, bowed, and handed him a note. She waited, so he opened the note, reading: *Tea shop. Two o'clock. Don't be late.*

'From Madame Belle?'

The girl nodded.

'That tea shop?' He pointed to where the pink-kimono-ed waitress was clearing a newly vacated table. The girl nodded again, smiling now, before turning and running back down the street, her mission successfully accomplished. Betancourt tucked the note into his pocket and set off to retrieve Alex.

Up ahead, a familiar figure crossed the road. Dr Trevose darted between the trucks rumbling down Victoria Street while burdened with bales of latex bound for the godowns which lined the Singapore River to the South. She moved with a practised ease that suggested she was familiar with these streets and their hazards.

A vehicle veered towards the tiled five-foot way on which she was walking, tyres throwing up a cloud of red dust. She was momentarily engulfed and when he could make her out again, she was coughing and waving an agitated hand, as though able to spirit the billowing dirt away on command. Driven by a desire to speak to her again that he barely understood, he set off in pursuit.

Although he'd visited the *suteretsu* many times over the years in the pursuit of his enquiries, he realised he'd rarely strayed away from its main thoroughfares. Ignoring the heated epithets of disgruntled passers-by as he cannoned off them, he pushed his way through the crowds, all the time keeping the doctor just about in his line of sight.

The crowds thinned and he turned into a dark, narrow lane lined with a ramshackle collection of wooden buildings. Up ahead, Dr Trevose hurried, head down, as though deep in thought. In his eagerness not to lose sight of her he failed to notice an old woman appear from the topmost window of a tenement, nor did he see the long bamboo pole she held, snake its way out over the street below. When he realised what was happening, he stepped smartly off the footpath onto the road, but it was too late to avoid being soaked by drips from the newly washed clothes that decorated the pole. Shaking off the water, he stepped back onto the walkway and continued his pursuit, but Dr Trevose had disappeared. He kept going, peering into each of the shops as he passed, to see if he could spot her.

He was forced to cover his nose and mouth as he was assailed by the smell emanating from a teetering stack of wire cages crammed with fowl waiting to be slaughtered and made into pressed duck or chicken rice. A glassless window framed a Chinese man in a filthy singlet wrestling with a large wok. Flames lapped the sides of the pan and fat sizzled as he threw in handfuls of an unidentifiable meat.

Beyond the restaurant was a tailor's shop filled with sewing machines at which rows of women of all ages sat hunched, stitching brightly coloured fabric. His presence drew a few questioning glances from the seamstresses, but they either didn't care who he was or why he was outside their shop, or they had guessed what he represented and had no desire to attract his interest.

He followed the lane until he found he could go no further. A group of young women had gathered outside an open shopfront, smoking and talking. At the head of the queue, he spotted Dr Trevose, surrounded by a circle of girls chattering in Japanese, Hokkien, Cantonese, and a few odd words of broken English. They were all begging to be seen first, so they could get back to work.

'Please, Doctor, please? I'm already late and my boss will beat me with a *rotan*.'

This last plea came from a tiny sparrow of a girl. He'd seen the damage a stiff bamboo cane could do and with this one being so small and frail, he feared for her.

'Yes, all right. Come along. Martha will see to you first.'

There was a half-hearted chorus of protests from the other girls, but the doctor shushed them and entered the shop.

As Betancourt edged his way past the queue, the babble of conversation dropped and the girls stepped back, watching him with suspicion. By the time he reached the front of the shop, there was silence.

Inside, sitting at a desk in a tiny room, sat Dr Trevose. She spooned a dose of yellow powder into an envelope made from folded waxed paper and gave the girl some instructions. The girl took the paper, smiled, and placed her hands together in thanks before leaving.

The doctor looked up. 'Inspector. What are you doing here?' It was more of a demand for information than an expression of interest.

He explained he'd been in the area, spotted her crossing the road and, brilliant detective that he was, had followed the trail to the clinic.

She looked past him at the now-silent group of girls outside. 'Let's go for a walk. You're making them nervous.'

She was right. The queue was already shorter than when he'd arrived and he could see a few of the girls drifting away down the lane, looking over their shoulders as they went.

Giving Martha instructions to take care of the remainder,

she led him away from the shop and back towards the main thoroughfare.

'Have you eaten?'

A sudden pang gnawed at his stomach, reminding him he'd had nothing since the previous evening. 'Is that an invitation, Doctor?' It came out sounding far too flippant, and he regretted it the moment the words had left his mouth.

'Take it however you want. I need to eat something. You're welcome to join me.'

They found a coffee shop on Victoria Street where the owner greeted Dr Trevose like a long-lost family member and ushered them to a quiet table at the back of the room. She ordered for them both without waiting for him to express a preference. Coffee and banana cake slathered in *kaya* – thick, sticky coconut jam.

'Sorry, I haven't eaten a thing all day.' She helped herself to a third slice of the cake, licking stray jam from her fingers. 'I'm always telling my girls they need to eat better. If they saw me now, they'd never listen to me again.'

He cocked an eyebrow. 'Your girls?'

'I think of them as my girls. I've had the clinic for a year now. It was originally owned by an old German named Baum. He'd stitch up the soldiers and sailors who got into fights when they'd had too much to drink and generally act as the local neighbourhood medico. When he retired, I took over the practice.'

'And the girls?'

Dr Trevose sat back in her chair, brushed crumbs from her blouse, and folded her arms. 'Do you have a cigarette? Only I don't carry them.' After she'd lit it, she looked away, studying the traffic and the people and the dust outside, and then looked back at him. 'The thing is, I'm wondering how much I can trust a man – a *policeman* – whom I only met yesterday.'

'Why don't you try me?'

She thought about it for a moment. 'Very well. They're local girls.' She waved a hand to indicate local meant the surrounding streets. 'I give them check-ups. Prescribe sulphanilamide when they catch infections.' She hesitated. 'Arrange anything else that needs taking care of.'

By arrange, he took her to mean perform.

'Business must be good, if the queue earlier is anything to go by.'

A flash of annoyance crossed her face. 'Business? These girls don't have any money, Inspector. This isn't a business, it's a...' She looked away for a moment. 'Well, never mind what it is. That's why I stand in for Dr Gemmill when he's lunching with high society. Even a lady doctor has to eat.'

'Why don't the girls have money to pay? Aren't their services much in demand?'

A sardonic smile suggested she'd seen more than a woman of her breeding or station should have. 'Oh, yes, their services are in demand all right.' She appeared to think about what she'd just said and then ground out her cigarette. 'Come with me. I'd like to show you something.'

He left his last few notes and coins on the table and hoped it was enough to cover the bill. The doctor had walked on ahead and he had to run to catch up with her as she turned back into the lane.

Between the restaurant kitchen and the tailor's shop was a narrow wooden staircase that he hadn't noticed earlier. When they reached the first floor of the house, she led him into a tiny windowless room which contained four cots, closely abutted, each equipped with an old mattress and a single bedsheet. Under each bed was a porcelain chamber pot, and the furnishings were completed by a chest of drawers topped by a pitted mirror. A tattered old magazine lay beside a tin ashtray. On each of the beds sat a girl. None of them was any older than his own daughter. Their obvious pleasure at seeing Dr Trevose turned quickly to distrust when they saw him.

One girl sat up and looked at her, pleading in her eyes, and spoke in rapid Hokkien. To his surprise, Dr Trevose answered the girl in her own language.

'She wants to know if you're here to take her away. What should I tell her, Inspector?'

'Tell her she's safe here.'

Dr Trevose gave a small nod, apparently satisfied he'd said the right thing this time. She spoke again and the girl relaxed back on to her bed, reassured.

'If the girls need anything more than simple medicine or a bit of advice, I bring them here. They call it the Hospital. Most of the time I admit them just to give them a rest and then invent a contagious ailment so their owners will let them stay a day or two. But eventually they all have to go back. These girls...' Her jaw stiffened and she paused while she collected herself. 'Where they come from, it's so poor they'll do anything to get away. They hear about this mythical Lion City with all its bounties and they or their families somehow scrape together the money to pay the traffickers for their passage. But when they arrive, they are in so much debt they must do whatever their captors want. So, they end up working here, in the brothels of the *suteretsu*, serving eight, nine, ten men a night – more on a Friday or Saturday. But they don't see a single cent of the money they earn. They're owned, like animals.'

His earlier question about the girls' earning capacity had

offended her, and Betancourt was annoyed with himself. He was well aware of the plight of the women in the *suteretsu*. Dr Trevose bade the girls goodbye and promised to stop in and see them again later.

They descended the stairs in silence. When they reached the sunlight of the street outside, she took an outsize pair of sunglasses from her bag.

'I seem to have killed the conversation.'

'Not at all. You just got me thinking.' He held out his hand and, on impulse, gave her a shallow bow. She responded with a small curtsey, struggling to hide her amusement. It had been so long since he'd spoken to a woman, socially, like this, and here he was, bowing to a virtual stranger like a schoolboy at his first school dance.

The blood coursed to his cheeks. She seemed to sense his discomfort and turned to go. 'Goodbye, Inspector.'

Her figure receded into the throng of humanity. He called after her: 'My name is Max.' But she carried on walking, giving no sign she'd heard him, and he was left alone, wondering again just exactly what the hell he thought he'd been playing at.

Chapter Eight

By the time Betancourt left Dr Trevose it was well after two and he hoped Belle had had the patience to wait for him. He was met at the tea shop by the girl in the pink kimono who seemed pleased to see him. She smiled and bowed and pressed her hands together in a mixture of welcome and deference. Without a word, she beckoned him to follow, and turned away with that peculiar shuffling, running walk so many of the Japanese women affected. Joss smouldered somewhere, and the building was infused with the smell of sandalwood. The girl pushed aside a beaded curtain hiding a back room that contained sacks of tea of various types and flavours and stacked cardboard boxes of condensed milk and sugar and signalled for him to enter.

Beneath a slatted window a woman sat at a small table, dealing cards to columns assembled in front of her. She was dressed in an emerald green raw silk *cheongsam* and her bright crimson lipstick gave the impression of a bloody gash across her heavily powdered ghost-white face. Ornate jade earrings stretched almost to her shoulders. When she opened her mouth to speak gold teeth glinted in the soft light.

There were lots of theories about Belle. The most popular one, being the one she told the most people, was that she was a white Russian émigrée: the daughter of a Romanoff prince and a Tatar princess, hence her oriental features, but Betancourt knew different.

She carried on playing cards, ignoring him, so he waited. When she finally spoke, her voice was accusatory. 'You're late. You're lucky I didn't leave.'

Her pupils were little more than pinpricks. She was using opium again.

She swept the cards to one side and inserted a Black Russian cigarette into a long gold holder. She waited for him to light it for her and, when he'd obliged, sat back, one arm folded across the other, and blew out a long plume of smoke.

'You went away.'

It was simultaneously a statement of fact and an indictment. In his days in the Detective Branch, Belle had been one his most trusted informants. What she didn't know about the goings on in the *suteretsu* and the surrounding streets was hardly worth knowing. They'd formed a pact: she would tell him what she heard and he, through discreet intervention, would discourage any unwanted attention from the protection gangs that plagued the area. The system had worked well for both of them.

'I had things to do. Anyway, I was – I am – a policeman. You make it sound like I was your personal security service.'

'What things?'

She'd have heard the news about Anna and his subsequent fall from grace, but it seemed she wanted to hear him say it.

'My wife. She disappeared. I had to find her. I was given an ultimatum: either concentrate on the job or leave.'

'So, you left?'

He nodded.

'And did you find her?

'No.'

Her eyes never left his.

'And now you're back.'

'Now I'm back. But it's not the same. I'm with Marine now. This isn't my patch anymore.'

'Marine.' She appeared to think about this development. 'You want to know what happened to the woman who was killed at the docks.'

'I don't think she was killed at the docks. I think she was killed somewhere else and her body was dumped there. Why, I've no idea yet.' He took the photograph from his pocket and placed it on the table. 'Do you recognise her?'

Belle stared at the picture intently for a long moment. She seemed to wrestle with some internal conflict.

'I knew her. Not well. She used to work round here. It was a while ago. She was Japanese, but I'm sure your new lady friend, the doctor, told you that.'

'My lady friend? I hardly know the woman. I only met her for the first time yesterday.'

'You were seen dining together.'

He'd forgotten what this place was like for gossip. It was worse than the local *kampong* for private business becoming public knowledge.

'Christ, Belle! It wasn't even half an hour ago. Anyway, we weren't dining, it was only a piece of cake.'

'Village gossip can be very useful, Max. Anyway, I like her. She looks after the girls, the ones who can't afford to look after themselves.'

'Can we talk about the dead woman instead of my lunchtime activities?' He tapped the photograph. 'How did you know her?'

'She used to work here. Her name was Akiko. Akiko Sakai. She told me Akiko meant *superior child*. Her mother must have had high hopes for her.' Belle appeared to derive amusement from this idea. 'She arrived a few years ago, but she was never going to stay a *karayuki-san* for long. You learn to spot the type. They find themselves a special man and then they're gone. Last I heard, she was working at the Blue Nightingale.'

He couldn't remember the last time he'd been inside the Blue Nightingale. The owner, Ruby De Souza, had been an old friend of his Aunt Theresa and had always been kind to him, bringing him sweets and comic books whenever she visited. She must be in her sixties now, he thought, and felt a momentary stab of guilt for neglecting her.

'So, you've not seen Akiko for a few years?'

'I didn't say that. I said she worked here a few years ago. She turned up again about six months ago. I used to see her visiting some of the houses, calling on the girls. Don't ask me what about because I don't know. Sometimes she was with a man, sometimes she was on her own. I always liked Akiko – she could be headstrong, but underneath she had a good heart. I asked one or two of the other *mama-sans* if they knew what she was up to, but they seemed scared to talk. It was like she held some sort of power. I'm pretty sure she was connected.'

'To the gangs?'

Belle nodded.

'Was that who answered the door to me earlier? Your protection?'

She exhaled a long plume of smoke through her nose and

ground out her cigarette. She shrugged. 'It's your fault – they wouldn't have tried it when you were here.' He bit his tongue. There was nothing to be gained by allowing her taunts to get to him. 'Things have changed around here, Max. We've always had gangs – you know the ones – but this new lot are different.'

'Different how?'

'Secretive. Dangerous. And they're Japanese. About a year ago, more and more Japanese girls started arriving. Their owners are setting up new houses all over town.' She looked at him with one eyebrow raised, ironically. He didn't need another reminder that as an officer in the Marine Police he was specifically tasked with stemming the flow of illegally trafficked women into the colony. 'Just last week, one of my girls received a letter from her home village, saying her parents had arranged for her sister to come and join her.'

Betancourt shook his head with a mixture of dismay and disgust. The parents of these girls thought they were doing a good thing by sending their daughters to Singapore. At first, he hadn't been able to understand why the families kept sending their girls away when they found out what happened to them once they'd been sold. He soon learned they never did find out. Quite the opposite. The traffickers employed scribes who would write letters to the parents and families on behalf of the girls, stating how wonderful everything was and how happy the girls were with their new life. They were forced to sign these letters. They were even charged postage for sending the lies back home.

'Some of the other *mama-sans* had heard the same sort of stories and we talked about where these new girls would go. None of us had space. But that was never the intention. The gangs just set up new houses and put their own *mama-sans* in. They're not like our girls. We pay ours and look after them.

These girls are kept like slaves and, from what I hear, they don't see a cent of the money they earn. Their owners send everything back to Japan.' She lowered her voice. 'To fund the Japanese war effort. It's happening all over Asia.'

'What? That's ridiculous. Surely it can't be worth it?'

Belle laughed. It was a mirthless, mocking sound. 'You've been away too long, Inspector Betancourt. You're out of touch.' She explained the economics to him, and he sat quietly for a moment, digesting what he'd just heard. If what Belle had said was correct, and after her explanation he no longer had any reason to doubt her, millions of dollars were being siphoned out of Singapore and were going to Japan every year.

'You said you saw Akiko with a man.'

'I said sometimes she was with a man. Sharp dresser.'

'Local?'

She shook her head. 'Not local. Not quite Chinese but not Japanese either. A bit of a mixture. Maybe one of those northern places. Manchuria or somewhere like that.'

Betancourt had intercepted a fishing boat out of Harbin the previous month. It had little fish on board, but he'd found plenty of opium. The crew had the same sort of features as Belle had just described.

'Do you know the name of this sharp dresser?'

She shook her head. 'None of my business.'

'What about the gang? And any idea what they're called?'

'Only rumours. The girls aren't my girls, so I stay out of it and don't ask too many questions.' The way these gangs worked, Betancourt doubted Belle could stay out of their clutches for too much longer, but he said nothing. 'I heard a name being mentioned, but you didn't get this from me. They call themselves the Sleeping Tigers.'

Back at Empress Place, the piles of outstanding manifests faced him, accusingly, from across the desk. He pushed them away. Out of sight, out of mind. He should visit Ruby and see what she had to say about her former employee. Did she even know Akiko was dead? He decided he'd go that night.

On a whim he couldn't have explained even if he'd tried, he called the morgue, hoping to find Dr Trevose there. He was in luck. He'd just caught her. She was finishing up some paperwork and was leaving shortly. Was his call a quick one?

He cited some small matter of procedure to do with the coroner's report for Akiko's death and asked a few other questions. Her responses suggested she was perfectly well aware he already knew the answers. Their conversation quickly reached its natural conclusion, and he hesitated.

'Was there anything else, Inspector?'

He'd shouted his name to her in the street earlier and yet he was still "Inspector" to her. He supposed this could be classed as an official call, which might explain her formality.

'I found out that the dead woman – her name was Akiko, by the way – worked at a nightclub called the Blue Nightingale.'

'Congratulations. That sounds like a fine piece of detective work.'

This wasn't going well.

'I know the owner, so I thought I'd go there this evening. See what I can find out.'

'Good for you.'

Oh, God. What on earth had he been thinking about? It was all very well regretting starting this, but he was committed now so he ploughed on.

'Do you like jazz?'

There was silence while she processed this sudden shift in the conversation. 'I beg your pardon?'

'Jazz. I was wondering if you enjoyed listening to it.' If a large hole had opened at that precise moment and swallowed him up, he'd have welcomed it cheerfully.

'I'm sorry, but I'm struggling to understand what my taste in music has to do with the death of your woman.' Her words were blunt, but he thought he detected a vein of humour lacing her voice. It was probably just wishful thinking.

'They have a trumpeter there. He's very good. Or he used to be. I haven't heard him play for a while.'

'Inspector, let me get this clear. Are you asking me to accompany you to a nightclub?'

She was taking this the wrong way. Could he blame her? How was she supposed to take it?

'Not exactly. At least, not in that sense. I need to ask some questions... About the dead wo— About Miss Sakai. I thought...' What exactly did he think? 'I thought perhaps your analytical skills might come in handy.'

'I see. I suppose I could take that as a backhanded compliment.'

'With the investigation, I meant.'

'Naturally.'

There was another silence, which he prayed she would break.

'Very well, Inspector. I'll help you analyse your trumpeter.'

After the previous awkwardness of the conversation, he was taken aback by her decisiveness. 'Right... well... I can collect you...' He waited, wondering if she would give him her address.

'There's no need. Where is this place?

'Arab Street.'

'I'll meet you in the Raffles lobby at eight. We can walk from there.'

'Until eight o'clock, Dr Trevose.'

'Until eight, Inspector Betancourt. And by the way – my name's Evelyn.' With that, she hung up.

He was just about to switch off the light when the telephone rang. His first thought was that Dr Trevose – Evelyn – was calling back to say she'd reconsidered, but it was his father-in-law, Louis. There was no introduction, no pleasantries. There was no longer even a pretence of civility between them.

'We need to speak to you. It's about Lucia.'

'Is she all right?'

'It depends on what you mean by "all right". She's not ill, and she hasn't hurt herself.'

'What is it, then?'

'Come to the house tomorrow morning. Nine o'clock. Of course, that's if you've nothing more important to do, Inspector.' Louis almost spat out the word *Inspector*. Before Betancourt had a chance to reply, there was a click, and the line went dead. Tomorrow then.

Chapter Nine

R affles had started life as a beach house and had been transformed into the luxurious bastion of European social life that it was today by two Armenian Persians named Sarkie. Betancourt reflected on the irony that, if the brothers were to step into their own hotel these days, their presence would attract disapproving looks. On the occasions he'd visited himself it was always with Anna, which had bought him a pass for the evening. This was the first time he'd set foot in the place since and if it hadn't been for Evelyn's suggestion to meet here, he'd have happily given the place a wide berth.

He was late and had run the last half-mile, so stepped behind a potted palm to get his breath back. A hotel employee in a white tailcoat and bow tie ghosted up and cleared his throat in a pointed fashion.

'Is there anything with which I can assist, sir?'

Betancourt flashed his warrant card and raised a finger to his lips. 'Keep the noise down, man. I'm here on a matter of national security. See that woman over there? She's a spy. Whatever you do, don't mention this to anyone.'

The man swallowed and then nodded and shuffled away, doubtless to do precisely the opposite of what Betancourt had told him to. Either way, he was left in peace to continue his study of Evelyn Trevose.

He was taken aback by the difference in her from their previous meeting. Gone was the severe bun, her hair now brushed out into a copper cascade. Pale shoulders peeked out from beneath a lace shawl and a short cream silk evening dress revealed a pair of elegant calves. Gone too were the spectacles, leaving a face that was surprisingly beautiful. Why he was surprised, he was unsure. She'd made considerably more effort with her appearance than he had, and he tugged at his suit in an attempt to remove some of the creases.

He stepped out from behind the palm tree and crossed the foyer. Was it his imagination or did her face light up a little when she saw him? She extended a long arm, the back of her hand facing upwards. What was the correct protocol? He'd no idea and, for the second time that day, felt like a clumsy schoolboy. He quickly weighed up the options. He took her hand in his and shook it firmly. Her free hand went to her mouth as she tried to suppress a giggle. He was left once again with a suspicion he might have misjudged things.

The tailcoat and bow tie combo returned looking unconvinced that this tryst qualified as a matter of national security.

'Cocktails, sir?'

There was just enough of a pause before the *sir* to leave Betancourt in no doubt about the waiter's lack of sincerity. He picked up the cocktail menu and nearly choked when he read the prices. Some quick mental arithmetic told him he could afford two Singapore Slings if he stuck to water for the rest of the evening and somehow convinced Evelyn to do the same.

She must have read his mind and he gave an inward sigh

of relief when he heard her say, 'Do you know what? I don't think I will. The cocktails here haven't been up to their usual standard recently.' She gave the waiter a withering glance. 'Let's just go.'

They walked up Beach Road towards the Arab Quarter. The kerosene lamps that lit the five-foot way hissed and spluttered, punctuating the sound of the traffic bustling past. The night air had cooled a few degrees and Evelyn pulled her shawl closer. He offered her the jacket he carried over his arm, but she shook her head.

They turned up a side alley where the light was dimmer, and Betancourt stopped outside a pair of ornate carved wooden doors. In their original unretouched state, they might have adorned a fine home in Malacca. Now, painted a lurid shade of azure, they guarded the entrance to the Blue Nightingale. Muffled sounds of horns and snare drums spilled out. The light from the lamp suspended above the door washed over Betancourt's face and the doorman stood back and swept out one arm in a welcoming gesture.

Even though it was still early the club was filled with revellers. A hostess with a tired smile introduced herself as Hedy and showed them to an empty table on the mezzanine, looking down on the dance floor below. Evelyn ordered a whisky and water. Betancourt nodded. 'Same.'

The table Hedy had chosen for them was off to the side, where it was a little quieter. The walls were covered with red flock, the fibres of the material carved into dragons, lanterns, and other propitious symbols. Rows of photographs in ebony frames embellished with gold leaf contained pictures of smiling patrons taken with a man dressed in evening wear and holding a trumpet. The pictures were signed with messages like 'To my good friend, Leo' and 'You're the best, Leo!' Betancourt recognised a few of the faces. Some were minor local celebrities: here a playboy, there a boxer, but there were a few better-known figures too. In one photograph, a bleary-eyed Noël Coward toasted the camera. The message read: 'To Leo and his music, the cheapest poison of all.'

Ruby De Souza, his Aunt Theresa's friend, had been a popular singer in the nightspots around town when she was younger. Quite a few men had tried and failed to woo her, and eventually she'd settled for Leo, a trumpeter of some renown before the fame and adulation went to his head.

The band was in full swing, blasting out popular favourites like 'In the Mood' and 'Woodchopper's Ball'. At the next table, a woman kept the beat with a chopstick on an empty beer bottle while her companion tapped his feet. Elsewhere, couples sat with heads touching as they tried to make conversation over the sound of the music. The more energetic swung back and forth on a small parquet dance floor.

Leo took pride of place at the front of the stage, trumpet to his lips, his eyes closed, lost in the music. The years had taken their toll on him, but he could still play. Behind him, flanked by two backing singers, her face partly obscured by a box microphone, Ruby crooned soulfully, her singing voice as fine as it had always been.

Their drinks arrived. Evelyn stirred hers. 'So, Inspector, are you going to tell me what this is about?'

'I'm sorry for dragging you along like this. It's police business and I don't know what I was thinking.'

'Don't apologise. Consider me officially intrigued. It beats dining at the Cricket Club, listening to some company man who only wants to talk about how big his bonus is, which was my other option for the evening. How did you find out our woman was connected to this place?'

Earlier, when they'd spoken on the telephone, she'd been *his* woman. Now she was *our* woman. He told her about his visit to Belle. 'Akiko had worked as a *karayuki-san* before a man bought out her contract and found her a job here.'

'You know Belle? How interesting.' She studied him, thoughtfully, but didn't explain what was so interesting about him knowing a *mama-san*.

Their conversation was interrupted as the music stopped. Leo stood in front of Ruby at the microphone. When the applause had died away, he announced an intermission and promised the band would return 'damn' soon.

Betancourt rose as Ruby and Leo headed straight for their table. Ruby hugged him so hard he wanted to gasp for air and he was surprised when Leo too gave him an expansive embrace and told him it was 'damn' good to see him again.

He introduced Evelyn. Leo lifted her hand and caressed it with his lips before complimenting her on how fine she looked. Betancourt remembered the earnest shake of the hand he himself had given her back at the Raffles Hotel and reflected again on his own lack of social abilities.

Leo called for another round of drinks. 'On the house.' He watched the hostess, Hedy, walk away, his eyes fixed on her bottom. There was an awkward silence, which Evelyn broke.

'This club seems to be popular. I wish I'd known about it before.'

'They come to see the Boy. What can I say?' In his younger days, Leo had been known as 'Boy' De Souza. Although he'd long since sacrificed his boyish good looks to drink, he'd clung on to the name.

'Leo, why don't you go and mix with the customers? Let me catch up with Max and his friend.'

Leo stood. Before he left, he eyed Evelyn up and down, making no attempt to hide it. 'I hope we meet again soon, Dr Trevose.' His mouth twisted into a lascivious leer. Evelyn appeared oblivious to his attentions, but Betancourt suspected she was just sparing Ruby's feelings.

He'd expected Ruby to be annoyed, but she looked sad. 'I apologise for my husband.'

They made small talk and caught up on lost time: he promised to give her Theresa's address in Penang, and she promised him she'd write.

'Ruby, lovely though it is to see you again, I'm afraid we're here on police business 'I'm looking for anything you can tell me about this woman.' He handed her the copy of Akiko's photograph. 'I'm told her name was Akiko Sakai, and that she worked here.'

Ruby gazed at the picture. 'So, it's true. I'd heard rumours…' She handed him back the photograph. 'Poor Akiko.'

'So she did work here?'

Ruby nodded. 'It was a couple of years ago. Leo had got in with some bad types. He's so weak.' The latter remark seemed to be addressed to herself. 'One of these characters asked him to find her a job. We didn't need any more hostesses – things hadn't been going so well and I'd already cut some of the girls' hours. This man – his name was Chan or Ching or something like that – Chin, that was it, he insisted Leo find something for her. I could tell Leo was scared of him.'

'Was Chin Akiko's boyfriend?'

'I was never sure about that. He didn't act like her

boyfriend. He ordered her around like—' Ruby considered for a moment. 'It was like he owned her.'

'What did he look like?'

'Youngish, perhaps thirty. About the same height as you. Fancy dresser, always the latest European fashions.' It sounded very much like the man Belle had described.

'When did you last see him?'

'I don't remember. I don't pay Leo's friends any more attention than I have to, but he's been in here from time to time. Leo takes care of him. Gives him a private table in the corner and tells a couple of the girls to make sure they pay special attention to him and his guests. He never pays his bill. It's always on the house. But as long as there's no trouble in the bar, it's Leo's business if he wants to be seen with hoodlums.'

'So, you gave Akiko a job?'

Ruby nodded and picked up the photograph again. 'Well, Leo did. She was his type. Most of the women who come here looking for jobs are Leo's type. She soon had him wound around her little finger. He told me Akiko wanted to be a singer. I assumed he meant she wanted to try out for the backing group, so I told him she could come along and audition. But then he told me he wanted her to take my place. We had a huge row. I told him there was no way I was giving up my singing for his new floozy. He said it wasn't like that. He was under pressure from Chin. You know what, Max? I think I believed him. Or I wanted to believe him. I said she could take a few of the slots. As a trial. She was terrible.' Ruby laughed – a small, sad sound – and Betancourt laughed too, in sympathy.

'What happened then?'

'That's the strange thing. She sang for a few months and then she left, just like that. It's rare for one of our girls to leave. Of course, it happens sometimes – they meet a man and get married, or one of the other clubs offers them more money – but it's rare. You may think it can't be much of a life, waiting tables and being nice to men who've had too much to drink, but it's a lot better than some of the alternatives. Once they have a job here, they usually stay.'

Betancourt exchanged glances with Evelyn. He remembered the young women in her "hospital".

'You never heard from her again?

'No. Things sort of settled down between Leo and me, but it was never the way it was before. I told myself she was gone, and he wasn't seeing her anymore, but I don't think I ever really believed it. Poor Leo, he's such a fool. Maybe she really wanted to become a singer and thought he could help, but I think there was more to it than that. He thought she was in love with him, but a woman knows these things. She was just using him, the same way she used all the others.'

'There were others?'

'Akiko found it easy to attract men. I'm not even sure if Leo noticed that. He was so besotted with her, it probably never occurred to him he might not have an exclusive claim on her.'

'Can you remember if she was seeing anyone in particular, apart from this Chin character?'

Ruby thought for a moment. 'There was one man. An Englishman. A crony of the other one, Chin. They would often come in together. I saw her at his table often, drinking and laughing. He would try to paw her – I had to tell him to stop more than once – I don't allow behaviour like that in the club. He didn't take kindly to being told off, but those are the rules, take it or leave it.'

'Would you remember this man?'

'He still comes in occasionally, but not as often as when

Akiko worked here. He usually leaves with one of the other girls when we close.'

'Do you approve of that?'

Ruby shrugged. 'I can only pay them so much. Even with tips, some of them struggle. I tell them all to be careful, but I'm not their mother. What they do in their own time is their business.'

'You wouldn't know his name, would you?

She shook her head slowly and then seemed to remember something. 'Wait, he keeps a tab. Slow payer. I should have his bill somewhere.' She went to the bar and returned with a pile of dockets. 'One of the girls told me he boasted about being a bigwig at one of the shipping companies.' She pulled a sheet of paper from the pile. Pinned to it was a sheaf of bar bills. She handed it to Betancourt. Each of the bills was signed with a barely legible scrawl. *Guthrie.*

Evelyn raised her eyebrows. 'Euan Guthrie?'

Ruby thought about it. 'I think that was his name.'

A memory stirred in the back of Betancourt's mind. 'Napier's?'

Evelyn nodded. 'Archie Napier's nephew by marriage.'

'Is he a friend of yours?'

'Hardly. He tried it on with me once, at a dinner party. He's a nasty piece of work, that one.'

Betancourt turned back to Ruby. 'How about the other girls? Was Akiko particularly friendly with any of them?'

'She was friends with Hedy, the girl who served you. Not close or anything, but I used to see them chatting. Akiko could be a little... aloof. It was like she thought she was superior. She boasted about having friends in high places, whatever that meant.'

A shadow fell over Betancourt's shoulder. Leo picked up the photograph and a look of alarm crossed his face.

'What's going on?'

Betancourt didn't know for sure that the man Belle had seen in the *suteretsu* and the man who'd introduced Akiko to Leo were the same person, but he took a punt anyway. 'What can you tell me about this man Chin?' Judging by Leo's reaction, he'd backed a winner.

'Who the hell told you about that?' He turned to Ruby. 'Was it you? You stupid—' He lifted a hand, as though about to strike her. Betancourt gripped his wrist. There was a brief struggle, but Betancourt was younger and stronger, and Leo relented.

'Get out! Both of you.'

Betancourt helped Evelyn on with her shawl and they said goodnight to Ruby. When they reached the door, he turned to Leo. 'You know something? Ruby's the best thing you've got going for you. You might want to remember that.'

Leo gave a snide, disdainful laugh. 'I'll bear that in mind, Inspector Betancourt. But then I wonder if I should take marriage advice from a man who couldn't keep his own wife safe.'

Evelyn grabbed Betancourt's jacket and steered him away. It was probably just as well.

The night air was now cool. They'd walked no more than ten yards when a voice called from behind them. He turned to see the hostess, Hedy, running towards them.

'Inspector! You forgot your wallet.'

Betancourt instinctively felt for it in his pocket, but the woman pushed a scrap of paper into his hand. She gave an anxious glance in the direction of the doorman who was watching the exchange, and Betancourt gave her a small nod to let her know he'd twigged her ruse.

She dropped her voice. 'I have to be quick. If Leo knows

I've spoken to you, he'll throw me out. I saw the photograph. I need to talk to you. That's my address.'

'Tomorrow?'

She nodded. 'Not too early. I don't finish here until three o'clock and I need to get some sleep.'

She returned to the club, the heels of her shoes clattering. The guard never took his eyes off Betancourt.

'What do you suppose that was all about?'

'I've no idea, but hopefully I'll find out when I speak to her tomorrow. Let's go, we're still being watched.'

'May I see you home?'

'No, but you may walk me as far as Raffles, if you like. I'll be fine from there.'

Evelyn linked her arm with Betancourt's. The voice of guilt that never strayed far from the front of his mind told him this was wrong. He flinched. She drew away. 'I'm sorry, I didn't mean anything.'

'Don't. I'm the one who should apologise. You were just being sociable. Shall we try that again?' He extended his arm, she took it, and he relaxed and allowed himself to enjoy the companionable silence.

When they reached the lights of Beach Road, they turned south, past the market, now quiet but which in a few hours would be a hive of colour and noise. A few lights shone in the recesses of the local police station and she mocked him when he craned to see if anyone he knew was working this late. After the station, they stopped and gazed out at the sea. Schools of small fish caught in the moonlight appeared like luminescent clouds, flitting here and there, turning and diving as one, as though they had surrendered individual will to a more important whole.

'I enjoyed myself tonight.'

He was surprised. 'I thought you might have been bored.'

'Are you joking? I'll take that over grilled lamb chops with a starched-collar accountant any day of the week.'

He glanced slyly at her profile and with a sudden flash of realisation understood why he'd found himself so intrigued by her. In the sodium light of the streetlamp, it was uncanny how much she reminded him of Anna.

They said their goodnights outside the hotel. Betancourt considered taking a cab, but it was a fine night for a walk. He felt alive for the first time in months. He was surprised to find how investigating a case, a real case, had invigorated him. At least, he hoped that's what it was.

As he walked along Connaught Drive, past the green sward of the Padang and on towards a now-silent Empress Place, he went over what he knew about Akiko Sakai. Bonham had said that she was just a prostitute and Betancourt was to treat her death accordingly. Above all, he was to keep Napier's out of the spotlight. And now here he was, like some self-styled avenging angel, digging into the murder – for he was sure it was a murder – of a woman linked to both a secret society gang lord and to Archie Napier's nephew. This time yesterday, all he'd had to concern himself with were a few run-of-the-mill opium smugglers. When would he ever learn?

Chapter Ten

Dawn was only half-broken when Betancourt pointed Alex's nose north, up Hill Street and onto a still-sleepy Victoria Street. The words of George Elias's article in the *Straits Tribune* returned to him as he passed the *suteretsu*. A few sorry-looking customers stumbled from doorways, but things didn't seem any busier than he was used to seeing them. But it was early yet.

Tightly packed shophouses gave way to individual homes set back from the road, shielded from the eyes of curious onlookers by leafy gardens. Eventually, he turned off and followed the long driveway linking Dunearn Road with the expansive car park of the Bukit Timah Turf Club, now empty save for the few cars parked by early birds who'd come to observe the morning's activities. At the crest of the drive, he turned right into a gated access road and the watchman in the small hut gave him a gap-toothed smile and a wave of recognition as he raised the wooden barrier. Betancourt had been coming to the track since he was, as his Uncle Stanley used to say, knee high to a pisspot.

Stanley, his Aunt Theresa's brother, had owned a leg in a capricious grey gelding optimistically named Star of the East, bought sight unseen from an Adelaide dealer who'd sent over a shipload of griffins – raw, unbroken, unproven horses. A sorrier-looking piece of horseflesh you couldn't have found. There was more than a hint of the feral about the Star, the dealer had acknowledged, but he had been enthusiastic about the nag's potential, enthusiastic enough to convince Stanley and a few other members of the Recreation Club to shell out two thousand dollars for the privilege of paying to feed the brute. They'd placed the horse with a then little-known Australian trainer named Bill Allenby. Allenby was good, but there wasn't enough talent in the world to convince Star of the East to run fast enough to warm himself up. The only thing he showed any talent for was eating and eventually the syndicate had to admit defeat and the horse was pensioned off in disgrace to a riding school, where he spent the rest of his days taking great delight in depositing the sons and daughters of high society onto the dirt.

Stanley had convinced Theresa to let the young Betancourt accompany him when he went to watch track work in the mornings. Later, when he was old enough to go on his own, he'd cycle to the stables at dawn and help out wherever he could before school. Eventually, Allenby allowed him to ride a quiet old horse that was recuperating from an injury and Betancourt was smitten. He loved being around the horses and the stables became his haven.

There was no sign of Allenby in his stable block. Osman, the stable *mandor*, stopped brushing and leaned on his broom, taking advantage of the interruption to light a cigarette.

'Where's the boss?'

Osman blew smoke and gestured behind him.

'Out the back. New horse.'

Allenby had never been in the front ranks of the training profession and as his old owners had died or drifted away, the number of horses in his care had dropped. Winners for him were becoming a rarity. The dozen horses he was left with were past their best and Betancourt imagined a new stable inmate would be welcome.

He found Allenby leaning on the fence of a small paddock, watching a rangy bay horse being led round by a syce. The horse had a long, low, loping walk and a kind, knowing eye. Betancourt knew Allenby would ask if he wanted an opinion, so he was content to watch in silence as the horse took a few more turns around the paddock. The more he watched, the more interested he became. Despite the placid, almost docile disposition, there was something about this horse that promised athleticism.

'Victory Parade.'

Faint peals of recognition sounded but Betancourt couldn't place the name.

'By Blenheim, the Aga Khan's 'oss what won the Derby at Epsom. Owners had high hopes for him back in the old country.'

Owners' hopes for their charges invariably exceeded the horses' abilities. 'Where did you hear that?'

'Talked to Wally, didn't I?'

Wally Hood was Allenby's stable jockey. He'd been a decent enough rider in his day, good enough to land a retainer to ride for the Duke of Rochester in England. Like many before him, the triple temptations of alcohol, women and easy money had been too much for Wally and he'd been warned off by the Jockey Club for taking a pull on the favourite for the Ascot Gold Cup. The way Allenby told it, Wally had intended to make his way back to Australia, to start again. By the time they let him reapply for a licence, he'd got as far as Singapore, but he was yesterday's man and Allenby was the only trainer who'd give him a leg up.

'Rode him first time out at Newmarket, Wally did. Won like a good thing, he said. Went wrong after that. They kept running the 'oss on hard ground. Needs the soft, Wally says. 'Oss got sore shins and ended up out here. Tin miner name of Hale up Ipoh way bought him. Gave him to Artie Pender to train. Artie, God love him, couldn't train a rambling rose to grow up a wall. Still, they fancied the 'oss to win the Chairman's Plate three, four years back. Backed him off the boards, they did. 'Oss broke down coming round the home turn.'

Those peals of recognition were ringing louder now. Betancourt turned again to the big horse, this time looking harder. 'Mind if I have a look?'

'Be my guest.'

He stepped through the paddock rails and made soft, gentling noises as he approached the horse. He ran a hand down one dust-covered foreleg, along the cannon bone at the front, then around the back where the long tendon ran, and over the fetlock. He did the same with the other leg. Clean. The horse nickered and nudged Betancourt with his head, as if to say, *See? Sound as a pound.*

He brushed the dust from his hands. 'Can't feel a thing.'

'Funny story. After the 'oss had done his tendon, this Hale bloke took him back to his property up country. Gave him to the daughter for the pony club. Anyway, comes time for the girl to go back to England and Hale's looking for another home for the 'oss. Bloke lives next door, Major Melrose – had a few 'osses with me over the years – he remembers the story about the Chairman's Plate punt, so he goes and has a look. Can't see nothing wrong.

'"Thought the 'oss was crook?" he says to Hale.

'"Was," says Hale. "Ain't crook no more."

'Turns out Hale's property's full of abandoned tin mines. Fill up with water when the rains come. The daughter took to swimming the 'oss in the mines. Seems like whatever was in the water fixed him up like he was brand new.

'Now, the Major's not daft so he says he'll take the 'oss off Hale's hands for a hundred. Hale's happy. Saves him having to get his gun out.'

'And Melrose sent him to you?'

'Correct.'

Allenby explained he'd been training the horse in secret, out on the heath at the back of the Turf Club where there were no prying eyes to monitor his progress. To make doubly sure the horse wasn't spotted, he'd been waiting until ten o'clock when everyone else had finished for the morning and gone home. Victory Parade hadn't done any fast work yet, but Allenby had seen enough to convince him the horse was as good as ever.

'This Major Melrose. I take it he likes a bet?'

'"You get him onto a racecourse, Billy-boy," he says to me, "and we'll have one last punt. A good 'un, like the old days."' Allenby lowered his voice, even though there was no one within twenty paces of them. 'Need to keep this one tighter than a duck's arse.' A sly smile touched the normally dour, taciturn mouth. 'Hear you've been having a few money troubles of your own. Want in?'

It rankled that Allenby knew his business and wasn't shy about discussing it, but Betancourt lived and moved in a series of small, interconnected villages. If someone knew something about you in one circle, pretty soon the news spread to all the others. Today's IOU was tomorrow's gossip. Allenby's offer was tempting, a quick way out, but he'd still have to find a stake and if it went wrong, he'd be in even deeper.

'All right if I have a think about it?'

'Take your time. No hurry.'

Betancourt checked his watch. By the time he'd changed and driven back downtown it would be nine o'clock, time to call upon his hostile in-laws and estranged daughter.

'Any idea what to get a teenage girl as a peace offering?'

Allenby guffawed. 'You're speaking to the wrong bloke, mate.'

As the enormity of Anna's disappearance had taken hold, the Cléments' disbelief was replaced first by grief, then by anger, and finally by outright rancour towards her husband for what they saw as his part in the loss of their daughter. Lucia had become infected by their antipathy towards him and gradually he had seen less and less of her until they'd reached the point where they hardly communicated at all. And now Louis Clément had summoned him to the house on Nassim Hill to discuss Lucia as though she was his child and Betancourt just an interested party.

Louis had been one of the most well-respected, not to mention successful, timber exporters on the river until, three years previously, a parcel of timber, incorrectly secured, had fallen from a gantry and crushed his spine. At one point, his doctors had prepared the family for the possibility that he might be completely paralysed for life, but he'd applied the same determination to his recuperation as he had to his business affairs and gradually recovered first his speech and then the use of his arms. He was however forced to give up the day-to-day running of the business and had handed over the reins to his son, Pascal. Being restricted to a wheel-chair had affected Louis deeply and he'd become bitter and self-absorbed. Anna's disappearance had given him even greater reason to hate the world, and Betancourt in particular.

'I said nine o'clock. You're late.' Louis looked up from his chair with thinly disguised contempt.

'I'd something to take care of.'

'There's always something with you, isn't there? Always an excuse. Don't know the meaning of the word responsibility.'

There was no point in responding. Betancourt had heard it all before.

'In here.' Odette, Louis' long-suffering wife, took the handles of the chair and pushed her husband into his study. The tragedy of losing her daughter had taken its inevitable toll, -- the cascade of red hair that Anna and Lucia both shared was now tinged with grey – but Odette still looked every inch the *grand dame* of the family home. It also appeared that she continued to bear the brunt of Louis' bile and Betancourt felt for her.

There had been a time when Betancourt had loved this room. After dinner, Odette would insist the men "leave us womenfolk in peace" and would pack him and Louis and Anna's brother, Pascal, off to the study, where Louis would dispense brandies and cigars and tell them stories of deals won and deals lost, while Odette spent much-cherished time discussing matrilineal matters with her daughter and granddaughter.

Betancourt sat in the armchair that was once his favourite. He felt uneasy to be sitting here again, under these circumstances, and hoped the discussion would be short. 'You said you wanted to talk to me about Lucia. Where is she, incidentally?'

'I asked her to stay in her room while we talked.' Odette picked up a letter from a side table and handed it to him.

'What's this?'

'I'm afraid there's been some… trouble, Max. Lucia's been missing school. We had no idea.'

Betancourt read the letter, then read it again.

'How on earth can she miss school? I thought your driver took her to the front door?'

'He was supposed to. It seems she told him we'd said it was all right if he dropped her at the Cathay Cinema. She told him she was meeting her friends there, and they would walk up to Mount Sophia together. Louis got rid of him. It won't happen again. But that's not all. The school telephoned us.' She hesitated. 'There have been other incidents, too.'

Louis had had enough of his wife's measured description of events. 'Incidents? Fights! My granddaughter, fighting like a common street tramp.' A fleck of spittle flew from his mouth and he wiped his face roughly with his sleeve.

Odette laid a pacifying hand on her husband's shoulder. 'There was an argument with another girl, apparently. I tried to speak to Lucia about it, but all she would say was that she hated the nuns and she'd no friends. She said she wanted to leave the school.'

The nuns who ran the establishment were some of the kindest people Betancourt had ever met, and Lucia had so many friends there he'd lost track of who they all were. Her behaviour had always been exemplary. What had changed since she had come here to live here? He was both mystified and angered. 'Why wasn't I informed of any of this?'

'The school said they tried to contact you, but you didn't respond.' Odette sat down on a low stool in front of him, so she could look him in the eyes. 'Max, there's more. I went to the school and spoke to the Mother Superior. She said you haven't been paying the fees.'

Jesus Cristo. Why had he left them so long?

'I told the school I would speak to you. I said if you were having trouble, we'd take care of the account.'

He stopped her. 'It's fine. I'll take care of it. It was just an oversight.'

Odette twisted a long necklace of beads round her fingers, as if counting out a rosary. 'Max, Louis and I have been talking—'

Apparently, this conversation was again proving too civil for his father-in-law. 'For God's sake, woman, get to the bloody point! What she's trying to say is, we won't allow this to go on any longer. I've instructed my lawyers to apply to the courts. Lucia will become our legal ward.'

Betancourt was on his feet. 'Who the hell do you think you are? You don't get to decide what happens to her. I'm her father.'

'You're not fit to be her father!'

There was a cry from the stairwell. 'Stop it! All of you!' Lucia stood on the stairs, her face stained with tears. 'You're talking about me as if I'm something to be haggled over, like a fish at the market.'

Betancourt went to her. 'I'm sorry. You shouldn't have had to hear that.' He reached out, uncertainly, and tried to take her hand, but she recoiled as though his touch was venomous. 'Get away from me. I hate you. It's all your fault. I never want to see you again!'

He stood, unable to speak, unable even to move, his arm suspended in mid-air. He'd no idea what to say to his daughter. Perhaps she was right. Perhaps it had been his fault. The question was, what could he do to fix it?

Chapter Eleven

Throughout everything that happened after Anna's disappearance, Pascal Clément had remained the solitary voice of solidarity. He'd felt the loss of his sister as keenly as the rest of his family, but he'd never joined in their mass vilification of Betancourt. Whenever they'd met since, Pascal had gone out of his way to lend fraternal support. Or as much as he could under the circumstances. What's more, he doted on his niece, and Lucia, in return, idolised him.

Betancourt had never been comfortable with the idea of using Pascal as a conduit between him and the family and it was for precisely this reason that he'd avoided the Clément godown the other day. But right now, he needed an ally. Maybe Pascal could act as the voice of reason, the peacemaker, until Betancourt sorted things out.

Pascal preferred to work from the company's main godown on the Singapore River – it was closer to the many after-work attractions of the town – so Betancourt parked Alex at Empress Place and walked back along the riverfront. He strolled the length of the loading area, taking in the bustle.

The wharf-side was alive with the familiar clamour of activity. Lighters pulled up three and four deep, jockeying for position at the prime landing spots. That way they could discharge their cargoes as quickly as possible before loading up for the return trip to the straits offshore where expectant ships lay at rest, awaiting their next consignment. He'd stop occasionally and chat to one of the lightermen, asking what he was carrying, or what ships he'd collected from. To be seen to be paying attention was as important as the paying of the attention itself.

All was as it should be.

The godowns loomed above him. Though the materials used to fashion the buildings were commonplace – mostly wood and corrugated iron – these were some of the most important premises in the empire. The banners above the entrances read like a mercantile *Who's Who*. Harrisons & Crosfield nudged up against Jardine, Matheson; Boustead's jostled for space with Sime Darby; and at the end of the row, set back as though aloof from its nouveaux-riche neighbours, was the largest and grandest of them all: Napier & Campbell. Dotted here and there, finding what space they could, were the premises of dozens of smaller enterprises which, if not quite feeding off the scraps falling from the top table, were often dependent on their more prestigious neighbours, and whose owners knew their place.

The godown Betancourt found himself in front of was one of these. It was cavernous in its own right, but it was dwarfed by those on either side. A faded enamelled tin sign above the door declared the owners of the establishment to be *Clément et Fils*. He went in search of the *fils*.

Compared to the Napier's warehouse, the Clément godown was quiet. Two elderly coolies shuffled past, straining to carry a parcel of hardwood they'd collected from a lighter on the river. The timber they bore on their angular shoulders was a deep, dark red and to Betancourt's admittedly untutored eye it looked freshly milled. A whiff of fragrant resin filled the air briefly before being carried away with the wood. When they were still on speaking terms, Louis had taught him the names of the woods from the forests of Burma, Borneo, and the Dutch East Indies that made their way through the Port of Singapore, on their way to the four corners of the globe. This lot might be meranti, from Sumatra. Much prized by the furniture-making trade, it would carry a high premium.

He tried to recall when, exactly, he'd last spoken to Pascal. Two months ago? Three? He followed the coolies inside and called out.

'Pascal!'

There was no response, so he called again. He blinked several times, encouraging his eyes to focus. The godowns were designed so that the air inside remained still and dry – the optimum conditions for storing a valuable commodity like timber. There were no windows, and the few narrow beams of light that infiltrated the skin of the building were speckled with dancing motes of sawdust.

When his eyes adjusted to the gloom, he stopped in surprise. The godown was filled to the rafters with bundle upon bundle of wood. It went as far back as Betancourt could see in the dim light. The last time he'd been inside the warehouse it had been less than a quarter full. The secret to the timber trade, Louis had once told him during happier times, was speed.

'Get it in, sell it, and get it out again. That's all there is to it, my boy.'

My boy.

The less time the timber spent in the godown the better,

and it was unusual to see it lie for more than a week or two. Surely this much timber would take months to clear.

He searched the corridors between the stockpiles, in case Pascal was there checking inventory. Down one passageway, the natural mosaic formed by the different hues was abruptly broken by a mass of charcoal grey. He edged between the adjacent stacks. Loose splinters caught in the linen of his jacket and he soon looked as though he'd suffered a fusillade from a battalion of tiny porcupines. He smelled the latex before he was near enough to touch it. There was a lot more of it than he'd seen from the main passageway. Bale upon bale concealed along the rear wall of the godown. Rubber in the warehouse was unusual enough – Clément's had always been exclusively timber exporters – but what made him think it was being concealed?

At the far end of the building, a bare electric light bulb shone in the small room that served as an office. Pascal had company. Betancourt slid between two towering stacks of Burma teak from where he could watch without being seen.

Pascal sat behind his desk, deep in the throes of a heated conversation. He emphasised a point by grabbing a sheaf of papers with one hand and smacking it with the back of the other before throwing the papers back on to the desk. In front of him was a man, Japanese or possibly northern Chinese. The man was in his late twenties, dressed in a Western-style double-breasted suit and tie, and stood in silence, arms loosely by his sides. He looked more like the playboy son of a *towkay* than someone with whom Pascal would have serious business. A relaxed, almost impudent smile suggested the man was taking these remonstrations with good grace. Whatever was troubling Pascal was clearly having no effect on his visitor.

It could be merely a coincidence that he looked like the man called Chin both Belle and Ruby had described, but

Betancourt didn't believe in coincidences. What on earth had Pascal got himself involved in?

He waited for the one-sided argument to conclude. He'd intervene if he had to, but whatever was going on here, it was Pascal's business, not his. Then, as though an invisible signal had been given, the stranger turned and strolled out through the stacked timber to the riverfront beyond.

Betancourt gave Pascal a moment to compose himself before slipping out from his hiding place and leaning through the doorway.

'Bad time?'

'What?' Pascal stared at him, his face devoid of expression. At first, Betancourt thought he hadn't recognised him.

'I was passing and I thought I'd drop in. It's been a while.' He took a small step back, as though making to walk away. 'I could come back another time, if you'd prefer.'

Pascal pushed back his chair and stood, beckoning him impatiently. 'Come in then. Don't just stand there.' He crossed to a filing cabinet wedged into the corner among piles of furniture catalogues, account ledgers, and stacks of invoices and receipts. He yanked open a drawer and pulled out a bottle of whisky and a single glass. He poured a shot, took a long swallow and refilled the glass. He looked again at Betancourt, as though he'd forgotten he was there, and then back at the bottle. 'Want some?'

Betancourt shook his head. He was shocked by the change in his brother-in-law. The Pascal he knew was handsome and athletic, lean and fit, with a ready smile and an engaging wit that had proved irresistible to many a young socialite. Normally, he sported a healthy tennis court tan, but today his face had the blotchy sallowness resulting from too many days and nights spent indoors under artificial light. He'd lost weight and the shirt that clung to his bony frame needed a good laundering. His eyes were rimmed with red and beads of sweat dimpled his brow. When he reached for a cigarette, there was a faint but noticeable tremor in his hand. He drained his glass before refilling it. Betancourt suspected this wasn't his first drink of the day, and raised an eyebrow.

'Hair of the dog, eh? Everything all right?'

'Why wouldn't it be?'

'No reason. Just making conversation. I heard the news about you and Sophie. I'm sorry.' Until a few weeks before, Pascal had been engaged to Sophie Napier, Archie's grand-daughter. It dawned on Betancourt belatedly that meant she must also be related to Euan Guthrie, the man who had been seeing Akiko. Sophie and Pascal had enjoyed a stormy rela-tionship at the best of times, but Betancourt was surprised when he heard she had broken off the engagement.

'I'm better off without her.' But Pascal's words didn't carry any conviction. He slumped back in his chair. A few moments ago, he'd been puffed up with bristling indignation and self-importance. Now he deflated before Betancourt's eyes, like a tyre that has run over a nail.

'What is it, Pascal? What's going on?'

'It's all this.' He waved a hand at nothing in particular. He seemed to struggle to gather his thoughts. 'My father… They called him Lucky Louis. Had you heard that?'

Betancourt was aware of the soubriquet but had put it down to the usual petty jealousies that fuelled the world of trade.

'He had this way about him. Like he was everyone's friend and business was just a game played for pocket money. A bit of a laugh. But he was bloody good at it, Max, I can see that now. It wasn't luck. He had a real talent for all this. He always bought at just the right price and always knew the person who needed what he had to sell and was prepared to pay top dollar. Behind the playboy act, he was a brilliant businessman.'

He was silent for a moment and looked off to the side, as if reliving memories.

'Everything I've done here… it was all on my father's instructions. He told me what to buy and when. He made calls and sold things himself. It was as if I was just the office manager, doing the paperwork and keeping the accounts in order. I wanted to do something myself, something big and important. I wanted to show him he could trust me, that he could be proud of me.' Pascal laughed, a bitter, sardonic sound. 'Let's just say, while I may have inherited some of his personality, I received none of his talent.'

He finished the last of the whisky in a single draught and threw the glass across the room where it smashed off the corner of a crate of veneer samples, sending shards spinning across the floor in every direction.

'When did you last eat?'

Pascal placed his head in his hands and rubbed his face vigorously. When he reappeared, he looked confused.

'I don't remember.'

At the far end of the stretch of godowns a ramshackle collection of food stalls dispensed cheap sustenance to the wharf workers. Betancourt steered Pascal towards the clouds of steam erupting from cooking pots. The few rusty iron tables were all occupied but two coolies stood up in recognition and vacated their stools, their departure driven more by wariness than altruism.

Betancourt ordered a bowl of fish ball noodle soup from a man who ladled the broth, redolent with ginger and spring onion, from a vat strapped precariously to the rear of an ancient bicycle. At first, Pascal looked at his food as if he wasn't sure what to do with it, but once he remembered, he ate with relish. When he finished, Betancourt ordered him another bowl.

'You not eating?'

'I'll get something later.'

Betancourt swiped at a mosquito that had landed on his arm. 'Bloody things.'

Pascal laughed. 'You're the local. You should be immune to them. They never touch me.'

Anna had been the same, and so was Lucia. It must run in the family.

'Consider yourself lucky.'

The hawker cleared the table and Pascal lit a cigarette and relaxed, one elbow leaning on his crossed leg, watching the boats on the river with thoughtful eyes. Satisfied the food had helped return him to his more recognisable self, Betancourt decided it was time to broach what he'd seen earlier.

'The godown looks to be full of timber. You're carrying a lot of stock – business must be good.'

Pascal shrugged, an expansive Gallic gesture. 'Business is always difficult these days. The bloody British…' He spat out a piece of tobacco that had worked its way loose. The action seemed to be performed as much to punctuate his feelings about the colonial administration as to clear his tongue. 'The Japanese were buying so much timber. They pay quickly, too. I had forward orders for six months.'

'And then the embargo kicked in?'

Pascal nodded. 'Bastards.' His voice was soft, but the venom in it was unmistakable. 'They said we were supporting the Japanese imperial war effort. I thought they would at least let me ship the back orders, but no. I was going crazy, Max. The contracts were coming due and I didn't have the cash to pay the suppliers.'

'So, what did you do?'

Pascal lit another cigarette from the glowing stub of the previous one and inhaled deeply.

'Out of the blue, I got a tip. A broker approached me with a big deal. It was a life-saver. He said he had a contract to build a new hospital in Shanghai and they needed timber. Lots of it. It was a sure thing. The deal was worth over a hundred thousand dollars. Twenty thousand to the broker, sixty to the sawmill for the cost of the timber, and Clément's would pocket the rest. It was the deal I'd been dreaming of. I didn't want to touch the company's main cash flow – Louis's money – so I went to that banker Cluny. You know him?'

Betancourt nodded.

'The man's a ghoul. He said he'd give me a line of credit all right, but the rate of interest was extortionate. It would have wiped out most of my profit. It was too good to miss out on, so I spoke to the broker again – explained I needed a few more days. He said it was no problem. He'd stake me the money if I was short, and at a much better interest rate than Cluny.'

'This broker. Was he the man I saw earlier?'

Pascal's eyes widened and his skin turned sallow. 'What did you hear?'

'Nothing. I arrived just as he was leaving. Who is he?'

'Nobody special. Just a business associate.'

'Pascal, I can't help you if you won't let me.'

A gust of wind blew by and Pascal's earlier bad mood returned with a vengeance. 'Who the hell asked for your help? Not me. You just can't stop meddling, can you? Why did you come down here today anyway?'

Despite the souring atmosphere Betancourt still needed Pascal's help. He related the substance of his visit to the family home earlier. Pascal seemed to relax a little. Perhaps he'd just needed to blow off steam.

'You know what, Max? Maybe it's too late. Maybe if you hadn't been so obsessed with your damn' job, if you'd been there more, you'd still have your wife now. Maybe my parents would still have their daughter, and Lucia would still have her mother. Maybe it's for the best if my parents take care of their grandchild. You need to ask yourself if you're fit to be a father.'

Betancourt cursed himself for having come down here. He was furious and didn't trust himself to say anything remotely appropriate, so he said nothing, got to his feet and left. To hell with Pascal. Better to take care of things without him. Betancourt would sort things out with his daughter and make a clean break from the Cléments. What that might mean if he ever eventually found Anna, well, he'd cross that bridge when he had to.

Chapter Twelve

Betancourt dragged his mind back to the case and rummaged through the pockets of his suit until he found the screwed-up ball of paper that Hedy, the hostess, had pressed into his hand the previous evening. The address she'd given him was on Ann Siang Road, less than ten minutes from his own front door. He returned Alex to the shed and walked the rest of the way.

Number seventeen was in the middle of a row of black-and-white-stuccoed shophouses, typical of the area. The insides of the windows were plastered with pictures of the latest hairstyles. In front of the shop, an old woman swept the five-foot way. These covered walkways fronted all the buildings in downtown Singapore. They were wide enough for itinerant businesses to set up shop and along these passages the citizens could find cobblers, barbers, fortune tellers, letter writers, storytellers, and a host of others. Their design had been mandate by Raffles in his original town plan, and were one thing that he had got right, Betancourt thought.

He called to the woman. 'Hedy? I'm looking for Hedy.'

The woman gave him a blank look and carried on with her sweeping, so he entered the shop. The basins were all unoccupied and there were no hairdressers to be seen. Apparently, they weren't open for business yet. Chattering was audible behind a beaded curtain separating the salon from whatever lay beyond. He pushed the curtain aside. Half a dozen people from what must have been three generations sat around a Formica-covered table. Six pairs of chopsticks froze in mid-air and the babble of conversation ceased.

'Is Hedy here?'

No one spoke and none of them so much as blinked. It was as though time had been temporarily frozen.

'Hedy? I'm looking for Hedy.' It was now more in hope than anticipation.

The silence was interrupted by the distinctive *click-clack* of a pair of wooden-soled sandals on the treads of the stairway leading from the floor above. A few words of explanation to the group at the table and the spell was broken. Eyes swivelled back to the food, eating recommenced, and the jabbering of a family's mealtime conversation once more filled the air. The Serani was the girl's problem and could now be safely ignored.

Although he'd seen her only twelve hours ago, Hedy looked different from the girl he remembered. Her face was free from the heavy make-up she'd worn the previous evening and lines etched her face where there had been none before. In the electric light of the club, he'd have guessed her age at twenty-one or twenty-two, but here in the diffused daylight of the shophouse she looked older.

Two stools were tucked under a low glass-topped table upon which lay a packet of English cigarettes and a lighter together with a pile of Chinese hairstyling magazines. The sort of magazine the pictures in the front windows might have been cut from. She pulled out a stool and sat. No invitation appeared to be forthcoming, so Betancourt drew the other one for himself.

'Hedy, you said you needed to talk.'

She put a cigarette in her mouth and lit it. The lighter was one of those heavy metal ones favoured by American sailors. She took a deep draw and exhaled. 'My name isn't Hedy.'

This wasn't surprising. Many of the women working in the clubs and bars of the town took European names, either because they thought it might broaden their appeal, which in turn might lead to more tips, or because their employers insisted upon it. What was more interesting was she deemed it important that he knew. It would have been convenient for her to remain partially hidden behind her working name.

He held up his notebook for her to see. 'Do you mind if I take notes?' She shrugged as if she didn't care what he did. He glanced at the family sitting round the table. 'Friends of yours?'

'I rent a room from them. They're good people.'

'Are you comfortable speaking in front of them?'

Another shrug. 'They don't speak English.'

'But you do.'

'I studied it at school. I wanted to be a secretary. Besides, we get a lot of foreigners in the club and they expect us to speak to them in their language.'

'So, if your name isn't Hedy...'

'It's Mei. All the girls who work at the club have to take a European name. Leo keeps a list in the office of all the names he likes. Film stars and dancers. He gives each of us a name from the list and we're supposed to answer only to that.'

'And you don't like Hedy?'

'My name is Mei.' Her voice was firm and he took the hint.

'Very well. What is it I can do for you, Mei?'

She flicked the wheel of the lighter. The air was filled briefly with the perfume of naphtha.

'I asked Ruby. She said you were police. Is that right?'

He told her it was. He didn't see the point in elaborating.

'I saw you showing her the photograph.'

He produced the headshot of Akiko. 'This one?'

She looked at it and nodded.

'How did you come to know her?'

'Who said I knew her?'

'Ruby said the two of you were friends.'

'What did Leo say when you showed him the picture?'

They could go on for a while like this, batting questions back and forth without giving each other answers. He softened his voice. 'Before I can answer any of your questions, you need to tell me about Akiko. Can you do that?'

A tear welled in the corner of her eye. 'She called herself Kiki when she was working. It was funny.'

'Funny? How so?'

'Because she actually wanted to be a film star. She just didn't like anyone telling her what to do, so when Leo wanted her to use one of his film-star names, she refused. She was strong. Stronger than me.' Mei wiped her eye with the back of her hand and sniffled. A man seated at the table stood up and barked a question. She reassured him and he resumed his seat.

Betancourt pushed the photograph towards her and she picked it up. 'She looks different here. Her hair was shorter before and she used to dye it red, like some film star she'd seen.'

'You were friends?'

Mei thought about his question, as if she hadn't considered it before. 'I suppose so. She gave me the key to her apartment. Would you give someone your key if they weren't your friend?'

It was a good question. He realised he'd never considered entrusting anyone with a key to his own flat.

'You asked me what Leo said when I showed him the photograph. What did you mean by that?'

'Akiko and Leo were… you know… She never said anything, but we all knew. That's how she got away with not having to take one of his silly names. He'd do anything she said.'

He wondered if Ruby knew. Probably. Women were smarter than men that way.

'When did you first meet her?'

'She was already working at the club when I started. Two years ago. More, maybe. We got talking, and it turned out we were from neighbouring villages. We'd even gone to the same school. She was a couple of years younger than me. I didn't remember her.' Her eyes took on a vacant, distant look. 'Two little girls…'

'That's quite a coincidence.'

'Not really. My village is in Amakusa Province in the south. It's very poor. My family were farmers, but the soil is no good. Boy children can work but girls are a burden. In a way, we were lucky, Akiko and me. Our parents kept us alive. We would hear stories about baby girls being placed in caves and left for the tides to take them away. Then one day a stranger came to our village. Our fathers took all us girls to the village hall. The stranger took us into a room, one by one, and told me to take off my clothes. He prodded me and pinched me and looked down there, between my legs. Then he told my father I would do and told me to get into the back of a truck. About fifteen of us were chosen. I didn't understand, my father seemed happy but the fathers of the girls who were staying seemed sad. Thousands of Amakusa girls have been taken like that. To Hong Kong, Shanghai, Batavia. Here.'

Betancourt was silent for a moment. He'd heard the stories, but to hear an account like this, first-hand, touched him deeply. It redoubled his determination to find justice for Akiko.

Mei lit another cigarette and continued talking unprompted. 'At first, she was a hostess, like me. Serving drinks, fetching cigarettes, being nice to the customers... Then, after she and Leo got together, he let her sing.'

'Do you know if she'd been a singer before?'

'No, but that would never stop her. That was what she was like. She thought she could do anything. Be anything.'

'When did you last see her at work?'

Mei thought for a moment. 'At work? About a year ago. There were some American sailors in the club. On shore leave.' She glanced at the lighter and put it down. 'Americans always have plenty of money. They said they would take us out dancing when we finished our shift. We went to New World. Akiko seemed to know lots of people. I thought maybe she'd worked there before. She was in such a good mood. The sailors bought champagne and she had a lot to drink. That night was the most she had ever spoken to me. Maybe it was the champagne.'

'What did she say?'

'Just that she had a plan. She said soon she wouldn't have to work in places like the Blue Nightingale anymore.'

'And that was the last time you saw her?'

Mei shook her head. 'No. You asked when I last saw Akiko at work. I saw her again about a month ago. That's what I wanted to talk to you about. She left a message. Here at the salon, with one of the girls. She said she needed to meet me, so we met at a coffee house on Bencoolen Street. She'd changed.'

'In what way?'

'I don't know, just different. Quite the lady.'

'What did she want to see you about?'

'At first, she just asked me about the club, and how was I doing. Chit-chat like that. She was trying to act all casual, but I could tell something was bothering her. She kept looking around, like she was worried someone might be following her. We talked for a while and eventually she said she had some news. She told me her big plan was about to pay off. She said she wouldn't have to rely on men anymore. She wanted to go back to Japan, but first she had some business to take care of. I asked her what she meant and she just laughed. "Best you don't know, little Mei-Mei." That's what she used to call me. And then she gave me the key to her apartment. In case anything happened to her, she said. She was scaring me a bit, but she just said I was to keep the key safe and I wasn't to worry about her. That was the last time we spoke. And then I heard yesterday she was dead.'

'Did she tell you she was pregnant?'

Mei looked away, thoughtfully. 'No. Maybe that's what was different about her.'

The conversation was cut off by the sound of chairs being scraped across the wooden floor, and pots and pans being thrown into a tin basin.

'Do you still have the key?'

She reached inside the collar of her tunic and pulled out a length of string. Dangling from the end was a brass key, tarnished with streaks of bright blue-green verdigris brought on by the humidity and the sustained proximity to her skin.

'Could you show me Akiko's apartment?'

She thought about this, apparently torn. 'I suppose so, if

you think it will help.' She turned the key over in her hand and stared at it as though she might divine from the metal some insight into the cruel vagaries of life. 'Poor Akiko. She didn't deserve this.'

Akiko's apartment turned out to be a single room in a shop-house on Trengganu Street, a short walk from the salon. Betancourt gestured to Mei to go up the stairs ahead of him, so she'd be able to unlock the door first, but there was no need. The splintered remains of the door jamb lay on the floor and the door swung open at her touch. He placed a hand on her arm, signalling her to wait, and stepped over the threshold.

The room had been furnished simply, and the decor was unostentatious and mostly impersonal. The cushions from a cane sofa and chair had been ripped open and the kapok stuffing strewn across the floor. In the corner was a bed, the horsehair mattress treated the same way. Dresser drawers had been emptied and not replaced and clothes lay in a pile in front of the narrow teak wardrobe that had once housed them. Satisfied that no interlopers remained, he called to Mei to come in.

'Can you see anything obviously missing?'

Mei stood, hand over her mouth, unable to speak for a moment. 'I wouldn't know. I've never been in here before.'

Betancourt picked through the debris on the floor. There was little of interest, save for a framed photograph of a Marcel-waved Akiko, gazing away out of shot in the style of a Hollywood film-star's publicity still. The glass was shattered.

In a corner of the room by the bed a tall, narrow-necked, cloisonné vase lay on its side. He peered inside but the interior was too dark to reveal the contents. He thrust his hand in and withdrew it immediately with a yelp, sucking blood from a punctured finger. He tipped the vase upside down. The damage had been done by a sewing needle, still threaded with a length of coloured cotton. Homes everywhere had something like this vase – somewhere to keep all those bits and pieces that may come in useful one day. Anna's was a biscuit tin she'd kept in a kitchen drawer. He wondered what had happened to that tin.

He sorted through the rest of the contents of the vase: a tortoiseshell comb; several kirby grips, linked in a chain; an enamelled bangle; an old bus ticket; a Japanese pamphlet; a small steel key on a ring; a matchbook missing part of its cover. It was the kind of thing he did himself when he needed a piece of impromptu notepaper to give someone a telephone number or the like. He turned the matchbook over. It was from the Blue Nightingale. There was a number: 27392, written on the back above the striker. He passed it to Mei.

'It's recent.'

'How do you know?'

'When a customer buys a packet of cigarettes, we give them a matchbook. Ruby has them printed by a man on River Valley Road. They used to have a blue nightingale on a white background. Then, about three months ago she ordered a fresh batch, and the printer got the order wrong. He made them like this, with a white bird on a blue background. Ruby was furious, but we were running low, so she kept the new ones. So, this is three months old. Maybe less.'

'You didn't give Akiko this when you met her, did you?'

'No. I don't carry them.'

So, she must have been back to the Blue Nightingale recently, or have met someone who had.

'What about the number? Do you recognise it?'

Mei shook her head. 'A phone number, maybe?'

'Perhaps. I'll check it.' He pocketed the rest of the bric-à-brac and handed the pamphlet to Mei. 'What about this?'

She studied it and rolled her lower lip, puzzled. 'No idea. It's some sort of political circular.'

'What does it say?'

She looked perplexed again. 'It's difficult to explain. It's about loyalty to the Emperor and how one day Japan will rule all Asia. Japan is a tiger that is asleep. That sort of thing.'

Betancourt felt a tremor pass through him.

'What did you say?'

'It's about loyalty to Emp—'

'Not that bit, the last bit.'

She read aloud from the pamphlet. 'Japan is a sleeping tiger that will soon awaken.'

A sleeping tiger.

'What would Akiko be doing with something like this?'

Mei shrugged. 'How would I know?'

'Was she interested in politics?'

Mei seemed to find the idea highly amusing. 'Akiko? Politics? Dancing, and champagne, and men? Yes. Politics? No. Although…'

'Yes?'

'There was one thing. That day… the day she gave me her key. When I got home from work, there was a package wrapped in brown paper left outside my room. Inside was a note from Akiko. She said I had to look after it. I remember thinking how she didn't ask me to look after it, she told me. I just thought that was typical of her, but maybe she meant it was important. I unwrapped the package. It was a book. I think it might have been something to do with politics.'

'Where is the book now?'

'It's in my room. It looked boring, so I put it aside and forgot about it.'

'Can we go back and have a look at it?

She looked unsure. 'I suppose so. What time is it? I need to be ready for work by three o'clock.'

He glanced at his wristwatch. 'It's just after one. You'll have plenty of time.'

Mei's room was smaller than Akiko's and even more sparely furnished: a single wooden bed, separated from the rest of the room by a gauze curtain; a bedside cabinet with a jug and bowl for washing; a drop-leaf table and two unmatched chairs; a small shrine, crowded with burned out joss-sticks.

'Here it is.' The book lay on the table, beneath a pile of well-thumbed magazines.

'What's it called?'

She ran a finger along the text. 'Hmmm… In English? Something like *A Plan for Rebuilding of Japan*. No, wait. Not rebuilding, reorganisation. *A Plan for Reorganisation of Japan*.' She seemed pleased with herself and he thanked her.

The book hadn't been opened in a while and rifling through the musty pages irritated his nose. A flash of yellow stopped him. He leafed backwards until he found a sheet of heavy paper, folded into quarters. He handed the book to Mei and opened out the document. The corner had been torn off, leaving a ragged edge. Emblazoned across the top in an elaborate script was:

stered £5 per Cent. National War Bonds, 1938.

When he got back to the station, he'd check the fragment of parchment he'd found clutched in Akiko's hand, but he knew it would be a match. Regi. Not Regina: Registered.

While he'd been studying the bond, Mei had gone through the book again. 'Look.' She'd found a postcard. On the front was what looked a little like a ship's porthole: two black concentric circles bisected vertically and horizontally by a cross. The background to the piece was a crimson red rectangle. He turned it over. Pinned to the back of the card was a photograph, clipped from a newspaper, showing a distinguished-looking Japanese: middle-aged, tall and slim, with oiled hair and a toothbrush moustache. The man had posed for the picture in front of some sort of bureau. Underneath the picture was some *kanji* script and beneath that, written on the card in a scratchy copperplate hand, were the words: *When waking the Sleeping Tiger, carry a long stick.*

He showed it to Mei. 'How good was Akiko's English?'

'Better than mine.'

'So, good then. Which means she could have written this.'

Mei peered at the handwriting and nodded. 'Yes, it looks like her writing. She used to practise a lot when it was quiet in the club. She copied menus, brochures, magazines... anything she could get her hands on.'

When waking the Sleeping Tiger, carry a long stick. What was it that Belle had said? *I heard a name being mentioned, but you didn't get it from me. They call them the Sleeping Tigers.*

'Do you recognise the man in the photograph?'

Mei shook her head. 'Sorry, I've never seen him before.'

'What does the *kanji* say?'

She read. 'Nakano Seigō.'

'What does that mean?'

'It doesn't mean anything. It's the man's name.'

By the time they'd descended the stairs again, the salon was open and most of the seats were taken by women engaged in the various stages of primping and preening. The beauty business appeared to be in rude health. Again, the conversations stopped as Betancourt entered the room, but judging by the curious faces, his presence was, if not quite accepted, amiably tolerated.

A hand touched his head. Mei lifted the curls that half-covered his ears, as though checking to see nothing untoward was hidden beneath. She said something he didn't understand to one of the attendants. Whatever it was caused an outpouring of amused tittering from clientele and staff alike.

'You need a haircut. Come, sit.'

He felt a mild sense of panic and was filled with a pressing need to escape this alien environment. 'No, really, I must go. Perhaps another time.'

'I insist.' She clapped her hands and two of the attendants jumped to their feet and led him away, chattering gleefully the whole time. One removed his jacket while the other patted the chair, smiling winsomely and inveigling him to sit. Marjorie's chastisement about his slipping standards rang in his ears. He'd been meaning to visit the old man who cut hair for thirty cents from a stool on the five-foot way near his office, but seeing as he was here... Betancourt gave in and allowed expert hands to shampoo and cut his hair, wrap hot towels around his face, trim his nails, and massage his shoulders as he forgot about the world and all its evil for a delicious hour.

The early-afternoon sun had clambered its way over the red-tiled roofs. After the shade of the salon, the light dazzled him momentarily. Up ahead, Ann Siang Road jinked first right then left, like oxbows in the meandering river to the north. He turned into Club Street and found a table in a coffee shop which stood out from its neighbours because of its absence of customers. It probably meant the coffee wasn't much good, but he was prepared to sacrifice that for the comparative peace.

After he'd given the owner his order, and the man had wiped the surface of the table, Betancourt opened the book. It had that fetid smell that seemed eventually to infiltrate all paper in the tropics, and he flicked idly at specks of green mould while he turned the pages. Mostly, the book was dense with text but there was the odd map showing how the streets of some unknown town were laid out, and occasional photographs, mostly of severe-looking Japanese men, suited and moustachioed. Here and there too were occasional pictures of Europeans, bulky, bear-like, with a self-satisfied air their Japanese companions lacked.

His coffee arrived. It was thick and strong and smelled better than he'd expected. The owner hovered by his table.

'Policeman?'

'Guilty as charged.'

'Thought so. You look like a policeman.' Betancourt thought he looked nothing like any of the policemen he knew, but perhaps the man had some special vision that allowed him to gaze deep into his customers' souls. The man gestured to the cup of coffee. 'Are you going to pay? Policemen never pay.'

Betancourt found some coins and placed them on the table. Talon-like fingers swooped and the money was gone. Before the man escaped with his money, Betancourt called him back.

'Got any envelopes?'

'Envelopes? What would I need envelopes for?'

'Oh, I don't know. For sending off the application for your hawker licence, perhaps?' He made a show of glancing around the room. 'You do have a licence, don't you?

The latent threat had the desired effect, and the man stomped off, grumbling. Betancourt took a sip of his coffee. It was fine, and he decided it must be the ambience that put people off. When the man returned, he handed over two grease-marked brown paper bags – the type used to wrap bread for customers who wished to eat on the run.

'This is what you use for envelopes? No wonder your licence never arrived.'

Betancourt emptied his pockets and picked through Akiko's belongings. The comb, the hair grips, the bangle, and the bus ticket were all unremarkable and he deposited them in one of the bags. He placed the political pamphlet and the key in the other bag and sat for a while staring at the matchbook, willing it to divulge its secrets.

None of it made any sense. Why would a nightclub hostess conceal a British war bond inside a book on Japanese political theory? Why did she even have the bond? It's not like she would have purchased it as a safeguard against a rainy day. And as for this Nakano Seigō, what was he to her and what had he done to merit her keeping a clipping of him? He took out his notebook and made a list:

Ruby: matches
Quek: phone number
Cluny: bond
George: postcard
Evelyn

Evelyn what? He'd written her name without thinking.

He stood and called over the shop owner.

'I need to use your phone.'

'Ten cents.'

'It's police business.'

The man responded with the zeal of the self-righteous. 'See? Told you so. Policemen never pay.' He grumbled a bit more but placed the phone on the counter. 'One call only.'

Betancourt asked the operator to connect him to the Blue Nightingale. Ruby answered.

'It's me.'

'Nothing for years then I hear from you twice in two days. What have I done to deserve this?'

There were a lot of things he'd let slip, but no more. 'I know and I'm sorry. I promise it won't be so long next time. Listen, when did you last see Akiko?'

'Let me think… It must be well over a year ago. Why?'

'I was going through her things and I found a matchbook from the club. Mei told me it was one of the recent ones. I just wondered if she'd been in recently.'

'Not that I know of. I can ask the girls, if you like, but if anyone would know it would be Mei. Did you say you've been speaking to her?'

'She's helping me. I know I don't really have any right to ask favours, but I'd appreciate it if you wouldn't mention to Leo that she spoke to me.'

There was a pause as Ruby considered this. 'OK, I won't.'

'Thanks. There was a number written on the matchbook. 27392. Mean anything to you?'

'Nothing. Could it be a phone number? One of her gents?'

'Maybe, but it doesn't look right somehow.'

He thanked her and called the station. When the desk sergeant had located Quek, Betancourt read out the number.

'Call the telephone company and find out if it's one of their numbers. If it is, I want to know who it belongs to.'

He ticked off another item on his list.

Next, he called the Royal Edinburgh & Imperial Bank. A clerk answered, and he asked to be put through to Sir John Cluny. The banker's private secretary informed him that under no circumstances could Sir John be disturbed. If he'd care to come in later Sir John had fifteen minutes available at three o'clock, otherwise his diary was full. He took the appointment.

By this time the shop owner was waving his arms in an agitated manner. 'No more calls!' Betancourt turned his back on the man and asked for the offices of the *Straits Tribune*. He was in luck. George Elias was in the office and keen to speak to him.

'Got anything juicy I can use? I'm in dire need of a story – the old man's on my back again.'

From what Betancourt remembered, George's editor was rarely off his back. When he answered, he was careful to keep his voice non-committal. 'I could do with a bit of help with a case I'm working on. How about I drop round this afternoon and tell you about it then?' They agreed on four o'clock.

That just left Evelyn. He scored her name out. Later, perhaps.

Chapter Thirteen

I t was nearly half-past two when he left the coffee shop. He briefly considered stopping in at the station to see if Quek had made any progress with the phone number, but he didn't want to be late for his appointment at the bank. He cut along Cross Street, parallel to the river, and approached bustling Raffles Place from the southern end where he stopped outside his destination.

The headquarters of the Royal Edinburgh & Imperial Bank nestled between those of its larger, more illustrious neighbours, the Mercantile and the Banque de l'Indochine. Whatever else people might say about Sir John Cluny, he'd done well for himself.

The way the story had been told to Betancourt, the young Cluny had fled a poorhouse in his hometown and stowed away on a cargo freighter, jumping ship at the earliest safe opportunity. That opportunity was George Town, on the island of Penang, and the boy had quickly found himself a series of small jobs on plantations and tin mines in up-country Malaya where he'd worked hard, listened and watched, and conserved every cent that came his way. By the time he was eighteen he'd saved enough to buy a small section of land which he cleared by hand and planted with a stand of rubber trees. He tended the trees and tapped the rubber himself, still saving everything he made until, by the age of twenty-five, he'd amassed enough to be able to make loans to similarly minded entrepreneurial individuals at exorbitant rates of interest.

Hard work and a frugal existence had made him strong, and he found no trouble extracting the repayments. People still talked about the time a smallholder had lost his interest money playing cards in a nearby shanty town. The man was found the next day, naked, nailed to a rubber tree, and blinded by raw latex that dripped into his eyes from a tap cut into the stem. The authorities couldn't connect Cluny directly with the incident – the injured man himself was reduced to an insensible wreck by the assault – but none of Cluny's debtors ever missed a payment again.

By the age of thirty he'd established his bank, first in George Town and later in Singapore, where the real money was to be made. The trappings of society were important to Cluny, and even more so to his new wife, Maude. The "Royal" appellation was intended to confer the impression the bank enjoyed the patronage and support of the newly styled House of Windsor but was in fact a warrant assigned by a minor *tunku* in the state of Kedah in return for a debauched evening with a troupe of dancing girls, shipped over the Thai border at Cluny's expense.

Much the same applied to his own title for, when tired of waiting for recognition of his services in the name of the King Emperor, and with Maude becoming increasingly impatient, he'd done the pragmatic thing and purchased a hereditary peerage from a potless landowner who'd been evicted from his highland home in Sutherland after squandering his family's fortune in the cafes and nightclubs of Paris.

Betancourt had helped Cluny find his daughter, Victoria, after she'd run away with an Irish subaltern, six months shy of her eighteenth birthday, and Cluny had been duly grateful. Any time the inspector needed information on how money washed around the Singapore economy, Cluny provided it. Their relationship was cordial, but the banker's merciless reputation was never far from Betancourt's mind and he always remained wary.

A peon ushered Betancourt into Cluny's eyrie and he took a seat facing the great man. Even in these new-fashioned times, Cluny made no concession to modernity and kept a healthy set of mutton-chop whiskers above the traditional banker's uniform of stiffly starched winged collar and black serge frock-coat, buttoned to the neck. Smoke from a thin cigar wreathed his face.

'Inspector.' It had been two years since they'd last spoken, but Cluny was never one to waste half a dozen words when one would suffice.

'Sir John.' Betancourt pulled the torn bond from the inside pocket of his jacket, unfolded it, and smoothed it out before handing it across the desk. 'I came across this and was hoping you could tell me what it was.'

Cluny donned a pair of wire-rimmed spectacles and peered at the paper.

'It's a bearer bond. No use to anyone anymore, except perhaps as a spill, to light a candle. Damaged. See?' He held up the bond to illustrate his point.

Betancourt rummaged through his pockets until he located the scrap he'd found. He reached over and fitted it into the corner of the bond, like a piece in a jigsaw puzzle, and Cluny grunted his approval.

'What's it for?'

Cluny reclined in his wingback chair and drew a deep draught of cigar smoke. When he spoke, it was in the tone of a bored schoolmaster explaining a difficult subject to a particularly obtuse pupil. 'A bearer bond is a promissory note. The issuer, it could be a company, it could be a government – this one was issued by HMG – issues the bond in return for investment.'

He must have decided Betancourt wasn't following, so he leaned forward and positioned two desk ornaments in the centre of the table. 'Let us suppose this pipe stand needs money. And further let us suppose this paperweight has cash it needs to invest. The pipe stand issues a bond and sells it to the paperweight. The pipe stand then invests the cash it receives in more stock, more land, more guns, more people, more whatever, and every so often it is obliged to pay the paperweight, or whoever is now the bearer of the bond, a dividend – a share of the profits, if you will. Look here.' He pointed at the heading on the bond. '"Registered five pounds per Cent." So, every year, the bearer receives five pounds for every one hundred they hold in bonds.'

'And what if the paperweight needs its money back? Does the pipe stand have to buy the bond back?'

'Not at all. That's the beauty of these things. They're freely transferable. If the bearer wants his money back, he just sells it on the open market at whatever the prevailing price for the bond is at the time of sale. All completely untraceable.' His lips drew back in a grin, revealing a set of long, sharp teeth, stained with tobacco tar. He clearly found untraceable money an attractive concept.

'You said this one was issued by the government. Did you mean the colonial government, here?'

'No, not here. London. This is a war bond. People buy

them to support the war effort. It's like making a donation. A guinea apiece.'

A guinea? Betancourt was surer than ever that Akiko hadn't been holding the bond as savings for her retirement. A five percent premium on a guinea bond was 25 cents a year, give or take. He was convinced she hadn't left it in the book she gave to Mei for safekeeping. So, where had she got it and what had she meant Mei to do with it?

'How would I trace one of these things? Who bought it, who sold it, where it's been?'

'Can't be done. As I said, the market is anonymous. Unless you came across someone who had bought or sold some and was willing to tell you about it.'

'Does the Royal Edinburgh deal in bonds like this?'

'All the time.'

'Could you find out if any war bonds have come across the counter here?'

'I could, but whether or not I would want to is another matter.' The banker peered closely at him. 'What's all this about?'

'A woman was murdered. At least, I think she was. I want to find out if this bond had anything to do with her death.'

Cluny hummed and hawed for a moment and then rose from his chair. 'Give me the paper.' He marched off down the corridor towards the stairs leading to the main banking floor below.

He returned a few minutes later and handed the bond back. 'I spoke to our Chief Clerk. He doesn't recall any of our clientele asking for war bonds recently. It's unlikely they would, though. They tend to come to us for company bonds. If you want to buy a few of these the best place is the post office.' A calculating gleam in Cluny's eyes told Betancourt the story wasn't finished. 'Where did you say you found this?'

'I didn't. Why?'

'A few months ago, all the banks were sent a letter from Government House. We were told to watch out for any significant sell orders on war bonds. Attached to the letter was a list of serial numbers we were to look for.'

'And this number is on the list?'

'It's in the range.'

'But why would the colonial government be interested in a few war bonds?'

Cluny steepled his long slender fingers, more and more the headmaster with his pupil as each minute passed. 'More than a few, actually. With everything going on in Europe, people here naturally wanted to show their support and, as a result, demand for war bonds rose. The bonds are controlled by that shower up at Government House. They're supposed to keep them safe,' Cluny chuckled at this idea, 'and send them out to the post offices and smaller banks on demand. About a year ago, the jungle drums started beating. London was rattling the begging bowl and was planning to send a big batch of bonds over to be sold here. Our friends at GH were asked to do an audit of what they had left.'

'Don't tell me – the numbers didn't tally?'

Cluny gave Betancourt a stern look. 'All rumour and counter-rumour, you understand, but my contacts are rarely wrong. Government House was nigh on a hundred thousand short. Of course, no official charges were laid and the whole business was swept under the carpet. *An unfortunate oversight.* A head had to roll, for the sake of form, so a junior clerk, name of Johnston, is now working out his time at a water-treatment plant in the middle of a swamp in the Andaman Islands. As for the rest, not a blemish on their characters. If anything like that had happened in my bank...' He didn't need to finish.

'Do you still have the letter?'

Cluny reached for a leather-bound document file and flicked through the contents. He found what he was searching for and extracted the sheet. 'Never throw anything away, especially anything from Government House. You never know when you'll need it.'

Betancourt scanned the document. The text was dry and factual, and the content pretty much as Cluny had described it, but it was the signature that caught Betancourt's eye: *Raymond E. B. French, Assistant Secretary to the Treasury.*

He realised he'd never known what Ray French actually did at Government House. Was there any particular significance to his name being on the document? Blame or no blame, some scrutiny must have come his way, but if so, it didn't appear to have done him any lasting harm. Marjorie had never mentioned anything, but then there was no reason she would. The incident had happened a good nine months before their marriage. He wondered if French had even mentioned the affair to her.

'So, are you going to tell me where you got it? I'm supposed to report a sighting of any bond on that list.'

Betancourt gave him a brief sketch of the case, leaving the details deliberately vague. 'The bond turned up amongst some other knick-knacks. I'd appreciate it if you'd keep it between us, for now.'

Cluny continued to scrutinise Betancourt but said nothing. That was the closest he would come to giving his agreement. Betancourt presumed the meeting was over and stood to leave but there was something about the way Cluny remained seated, hands still crossed, gaze steady, that told him there was more to come. He sat down again.

'Was there something else?'

Cluny took a cheroot from a sandalwood box on his desk. He spun the wheel of a table lighter in the form of a horse's hoof. There was a spark but no flame. Betancourt struck a match from the Blue Nightingale matchbook he'd found at Akiko's flat and offered the light.

'Mind if I keep those? This damn thing's been playing up all day.'

Betancourt took a note of the number written on the inside cover and scribbled it in his notebook. He tossed the matchbook onto the desk.

When Cluny was satisfied that the cheroot was performing to his satisfaction, he opened a drawer and withdrew a large payment book, the sort used for bank drafts. 'Allow me to make you a loan, Inspector. It'll be strictly between us. I'll charge you a fair rate of interest. More than my regular clients, of course, but fair. Certainly fairer than your alternatives.' He unscrewed the cap of a fountain pen. 'A thousand do you?'

'I don't need a loan.' Betancourt added a belated 'thank you', so as not to appear ungrateful.

'Are you sure? I rather think this is an offer you should consider carefully.'

'I don't understand. What's going on?'

Cluny replaced the cap on the pen and sat back. 'I hear things. It's one of the necessities of being in my line of work. I hear lots of things about lots of people. Some of the things I hear might surprise you. It's a valuable commodity, knowledge. Don't you think?'

Betancourt had no idea what to make of all this. Cluny valued his time too much to spend it on idle chit-chat. What was he after?

'I know, for instance, you owe money to some rather dangerous men.'

Betancourt was on his feet. 'How the hell do you know who I owe money to?'

Cluny laughed, a dry humourless cackle. 'Oh, for God's sake, sit down, man, and stop taking yourself so seriously. I told you, I hear things. It's my business. You've run up debts all over town. Horses, is it? Or cards?' He shook his head and made no attempt to keep the derision from his voice. 'You know the house always wins, don't you?'

'Neither. It's none of your business who I owe money to.' God, how defensive did he sound? The same tone of voice he'd used when his school games master caught him taking a shortcut in the cross-country race. He dropped his register half an octave, to let Cluny know he wasn't to be trifled with. 'In any case, it's not much. I can pay it back.'

'I doubt that very much, Inspector, or you'd already have done so.' Cluny leaned forward over the desk, suddenly all business. 'What you may not know, Inspector, is the people you thought you owed the money to are no longer the people you actually owe it to.'

'What are you talking about?'

'Remember our little lesson about the bonds? Debt and bonds are not so unalike. Just as I can buy a bond from you and sell it to someone else without your knowledge and without requiring your permission, so too can the holder of an IOU sell his debt.'

'It was only small amounts, fifty dollars here, a hundred there. Why would anyone want to sell such trifling amounts?'

Cluny glanced at a note written on his desk blotter. 'With the interest, over a thousand dollars is what I'm told.' He looked up again. 'Not so trifling, really, I think you'll agree.'

'But not all to one person. Are you saying everyone I owed money to has sold my notes?'

'Precisely.'

'All at the same time? And all to same person? Seems like quite a coincidence.'

'It's no coincidence, I assure you. If I were you, rather than concerning myself with who's selling, I'd be focussing my attention on who's buying. As to who that is, I'm not exactly sure, but I'm led to believe it involves one of the secret societies. I'd suggest it would be worth your while finding out which one.'

Betancourt was sure he knew which one it was, and an involuntary spasm coursed through his bowels.

'As to the why, that's considerably more straightforward.' Cluny replaced the payment book in the drawer. 'Someone wants you in their grip, Inspector. Debt is power. If I were you, I'd start looking over my shoulder.'

Chapter Fourteen

George Elias, reporter and occasional scourge of Singapore's malfeasant classes, greeted Betancourt like a long-lost brother before ushering him into the press room and offering him a chair. He leaned forward and said something. A cacophony of telephone bells, typewriter keys and raised voices battered his eardrums and rendered Elias's words incomprehensible. The only reason Betancourt knew he'd said something was because he'd seen the reporter's lips move. He'd never understood how any work was done in here.

'What?'

'No need to shout, old thing.' Elias ran a pudgy hand over his scalp. 'I may have lost my luxuriant locks, but my hearing is still A1. I said, what's good?'

Elias knew Betancourt was close to Bill Allenby and was looking for tips. When, *if*, the Victory Parade coup was landed, Elias would assume that Betancourt was in on it and had deliberately excluded him, and he probably wouldn't speak to him for a few weeks, miffed at being left out. But he'd get over it.

'Haven't heard a thing. You?'

Elias shook his head resignedly. 'Me neither. My betting book's emptier than a nun's dance card.'

Dropping his voice wasn't an option in the press room, so Betancourt shuffled his chair forward and beckoned Elias closer. The reporter leaned in, always keen to join in on a bit of subterfuge.

'I need your help.' He showed Elias the newspaper cutting containing the photograph of the Japanese man, Seigō.

'Am I supposed to recognise him?'

Betancourt explained about Akiko's death and what he'd subsequently found out from Belle about the Sleeping Tigers. 'The dead woman had been seen around the *suteretsu*. I was going through her things and I found this. His name might be Nakano Seigō. That's all I know.'

Elias scratched his jaw. 'The dead woman... Japanese, you say?'

Betancourt nodded.

'*Karayuki-san*?'

'She'd been working as a hostess at the Blue Nightingale.'

'Same thing then. I did a piece about the number of tarts coming into the *suteretsu*. Did you see it?'

Betancourt nodded. 'That's why I thought you'd be able to help. Might be something, might be nothing, but it's worth a look.'

Elias looked at the clipping again. 'Looks like your typical Jap. Shifty. Tell you what I'll do – I'll let you use the archives. Have a root around. If you find anything interesting, I get first dibs on the story. Can't do fairer than that.'

The *Tribune's* archives were legendary. Betancourt didn't need Elias's permission to use them. He was investigating a suspicious death and that was enough to warrant access, but that way, he'd need to do the legwork himself and he'd hoped to talk Elias into doing the digging for him.

'I appreciate the offer, but it'll take forever if I try to look things up. You, on the other hand, know what you're doing.'

'I can do better than that, I'll introduce you to Daisy. She's a little… how can I put it? Unconventional. But she's bloody good. If anyone can find your Jap for you, it's Daisy. Come on, follow me.'

They climbed the central staircase to the fourth floor where Elias stopped to catch his breath. 'Wife signed me up for callisthenics classes at the Club. Now I'm knackered. Just one more.'

They climbed a final short flight of steps and entered through a low door what must at one time have been the attic of the building. It was surprisingly bright. The whole of the rear wall of the room was fitted with full-length windows. The blinds were raised and a bustling Raffles Place was evident below. Most of the rest of the room was filled with what looked like floor-to-ceiling wardrobes, each fitted with a large wheel. The wall to Betancourt's right was hidden by two rows of tall filing cabinets, containing dozens of small drawers. Labels in small brass holders identified the contents of each drawer. A young woman leaned on the furthest of the cabinets, apparently engrossed in reading a document.

Elias, still regaining his breath, waved a weary arm in introduction. 'Daisy Scott, this is Detective Inspector Betancourt. The inspector needs to avail himself of your inestimable skills in tracking down a cruel and bloodthirsty murderer.'

'I didn't say anything about—'

'Murder, eh? I'm partial to a good murder.'

Daisy was young, twenty-two or -three. Corn-yellow hair; lapis eyes; ample mouth painted the colour of ripe papaya; a small, dimpled chin. The rest of her was hidden by the filing cabinet.

'Right, I'll leave you two alone. Don't do anything I wouldn't do. Should leave you with plenty of scope.'

Betancourt crossed the room and shook her hand. The document in which she'd been immersed was a copy of *Hollywood Weekly*. A picture of a cheerful-looking woman with short copper-coloured hair smiled up at Betancourt from the cover. Daisy closed the magazine with an air of reluctance.

'Myrna Loy. Isn't she lovely? She had her hair done like that for *Double Wedding*. I was thinking of getting mine done the same. Do you think I'd suit it? It's either Myrna or Claudette Colbert.'

Betancourt suspected he was supposed to say something like "Your hair looks perfect as it is", but whenever he'd tried a similar approach before it'd landed him in hot water, so he kept quiet.

'Have you seen *Double Wedding*? No? Oh, you must.' She glanced down at his hand. 'Ah, married. That's a shame. Not to worry, it's never stopped me before. They're showing it at the Cathay next weekend. We can go together. Just tell your wife you're working late.' She gave a small conspiratorial giggle and her invitation was followed by a gravid pause, which he took advantage of to guide her back to the subject of his inquiry. He showed her the clipping.

'This man… George said you'd be able to help find out a bit about him. His name is Seigō, first name Nakano.'

'I know.'

'What? You mean, you recognise him?'

'Never forget a face. That's why they've got me working up here. Anyway, you've got it the wrong way around. Japanese do their names back to front. Funny lot. Nakano is his surname. If he were English, he'd be Seigō Nakano. You'll

find him over there: Ns are in cabinet four, Malacca to Pots-
dam. About halfway down.'

She returned to her magazine, her earlier effervescence
gone. He hoped it was because of the banality of his request
and not his rejection of her offer to accompany him to the
cinema.

Each drawer contained dozens of index cards. He flicked
through the first drawer, but the records only went as far as
Munich. He tried the next one down and about a quarter of
the way through found what he was looking for. The card had
the number 2519 inscribed in violet ink in the top left corner
and next to it, in neat handwriting, *Nakano, Seigō (12ᵗʰ Feb 1886
—) Japan. Politician.* Underneath this scant description was a
list of numbers in red, separated by commas, and another set
in green.

'Found it. Now what?'

Daisy rolled her eyes in an exaggerated fashion, as if to
say: *Do I have to do everything?* But she took the card from him.

'Blue card. That means nineteen thirty-five to the present
day. These numbers here in red are where you'll find him.'
She pointed to the tall cabinets with the steering wheels
attached. 'Come on, then.'

She grasped a wheel and, as it turned, the cabinet crept
away from its neighbour as though on invisible rails, until
there was a gap wide enough for Daisy to squeeze her narrow
frame into. She pulled out a yellowing newspaper and spread
it out on a table. It was a copy of the *South China Morning Post*
from Hong Kong, dated three years earlier. She showed him
the card again.

'See? 7374/12/4. 7374 is the copy.' She pointed to a label
stuck to the front of the newspaper, with the corresponding
number typewritten. 'Page twelve.' She turned to the page.
'And four is bottom-right.' Sure enough, there was an article

containing a picture of Nakano. The picture Akiko had kept must have been taken some time prior as the face of the newspaper Nakano was more lined and the hair a little greyer. The pose was like the one he'd found in Akiko's book, but in this one Nakano was seated. On a bookcase behind him was a small table flag in a holder. The design of the flag was the same as that on the postcard that had been pinned to Nakano's picture. The article carried the by-line of the Associated Press and had been written to mark an upcoming visit to the colony. Nakano was an ultra-nationalist politician, the founder of a political party known as the Tōhōkai, fiercely loyal to the Emperor.

'What are these other numbers?'

Daisy looked over his shoulder. 'Cross-references to other papers or magazines mentioning the same subject.' She took the card and turned another wheel.

An article in *The Times* carried a couple of column inches on a visit Nakano had made to Europe eighteen months previously. A photograph showed him shaking hands with a beaming Benito Mussolini. A copy of the *Herald Tribune* dated a few months later showed a similar image with Adolf Hitler. Other papers carried the same or similar stories, presumably all from the same news agencies.

The final paper Daisy pulled was a copy of the *Japan Times*. Betancourt turned to the page indicated where he found a picture of Nakano and a smiling young man cutting the ribbon at the opening of a building. The newspaper was dated two years earlier. The younger man wore his hair shorter than the last time Betancourt had seen him, and his suit was more conservative, but he was unmistakable. The caption read: *'Nakano Seigō, prominent politician, is accompanied by his son, Nakano Jin, at the opening of a new community centre'*. Belle's Manchurian gangster, Chin, was really Jin, son of a well-connected Japanese fascist. He was also a business associate of Betancourt's missing wife's brother.

'Could I take this?'

'Sorry, can't let anything leave this room. It'd be more than my job's worth.'

He didn't want to get Daisy into any trouble, but he had to have that clipping. 'It's warm in here. Any chance of a glass of water?'

She pouted. 'I'm an archivist, not your personal *pei pei* girl.' But she went off in search of water anyway, her thigh brushing his shoulder as she slid past him. He quickly removed the sheet containing the article and folded it away before slipping the remains of the newspaper into the pile on the desk.

When Daisy returned, he thanked her for the water and downed half the glass in one gulp. 'Where do you get all this information from?'

'I read the papers. That's my job: read the papers and cross-reference everything.'

Betancourt was genuinely impressed and told her so. She sidled closer. 'You quite sure about the cinema? Maybe there's something else you'd rather be doing?' She ran a painted nail down the lapel of his jacket.

He grinned. 'Not while on duty. Sorry.'

Chapter Fifteen

Betancourt's next call required finesse, so he waited until he was at home before making it. Ray French answered. Damn. Why hadn't he considered the man might answer the telephone in his own house? He identified himself and apologised for calling in the evening, asking if he could have a quick word with Marjorie? Just a trifling work matter. French gave a small sigh that Betancourt took to indicate exasperation, but the man was too polite not to pass on his request.

When Marjorie came to the phone, she sounded less than pleased to hear from him.

'You do know some people have dinner in the evening? With other people?'

'I'd heard that, but I'd no idea there was any truth in it.'

'Where have you been? Bonham is looking for you. He says you were supposed to deliver a report to him yesterday. You know what he's like when he doesn't get his own way. He's making my life absolute hell, so thank you very much for that.'

'Can you try to stall him for now? He'll get his report.' *Eventually*, he added under his breath.

'What did you call about, Max? And before you answer, it had better be good.'

'It's about Lucia.' He explained about his visit to the Cléments and his daughter's troubles at school.

'I can't believe it. She's an angel. She wouldn't behave like that. Something's wrong.'

'They grow up and change, I suppose.'

'Not Lucia. She misses her mother, that's all. And her father. Have you spoken to her?'

'I tried, but it was no good. Louis's talking about applying to the courts for permanent custody. They want to take her away from me, Marjorie. For good, I mean. I can't let them do that.'

'No, of course not. Oh, God, I'm so sorry, Max. What can I do?

'If they follow through on their threat, I'm going to need a lawyer.'

'My family have always used Cavan & Walshe and they're very good, but they're the same firm the Cléments use, so that wouldn't work. Let me ask around. Ray might be able to recommend someone.'

He thanked her and was about to hang up when he remembered something. 'Seeing as I have you on the line, may I ask a favour? Do you know anyone inside Napier's?'

There was a pointed silence before she spoke. 'Seriously, Max? Is there anywhere in colonial society where I don't know someone?' Marjorie took great pride in the breadth of her social network and, despite her stern tone, he suspected she was pleased to be able to show it off. 'Coralie Barker, Archie Napier's secretary, went to school with Anna and me. What's this about?'

'Euan Guthrie.'

'Archie's nephew?' Now she sounded wary. 'What about him?'

'I'd like to have a chat with him. Can you find me his address?' He quickly recapped his conversation with Ruby in the Blue Nightingale the previous evening. 'The dead woman —' He had to stop calling her that. She had a name. 'Miss Sakai knew Guthrie.'

'Knew in the biblical sense?'

'So I'm led to believe.'

There was a pause and when Marjorie spoke again, she sounded doubtful. 'Tricky one. Leave it with me and I'll see what I can do. No promises. But you owe me a favour in return. You must come to our party tomorrow.' He began to make his excuses, but she cut him off. 'I won't take no for an answer. No party, no address. One o'clock. Do we have a deal?'

'Deal.' Marjorie had won, as she usually did. He was about to thank her and ring off when she spoke again.

'Old friend or not, Coralie will mention to Archie that the police are asking about Euan. I thought Bonham told you to stay away from Napier's? They guard their privacy jealously. I hope you know what you're doing, Max.'

Did he know what he was doing? Maybe not, but it had never stopped him before. Old Man Napier would call Bonham and the latter would be straight on the warpath. As long as Betancourt stayed incommunicado, he should be able to avoid Bonham for long enough to do what he needed to do.

When he'd hung up, he sat at the window and let the sounds of the street wash over him. He tried to run through what he'd learned, but couldn't concentrate. He lifted the handset and then hesitated. Should he? What was the worst that could happen? He decided not to dwell on that and placed one last call.

He asked the operator for the number of Dr Trevose, Holloway Lane. No, he didn't have it. Yes, he'd hold. He hoped Evelyn hadn't asked to be ex-directory.

'The number is 7486. Would you like me to connect you?'

After what seemed like an eternity, the line crackled into life again with a familiar voice speaking. 'This is Dr Trevose.'

He wondered if she only used this number for professional calls, or if those were the only type she received.

'It's Betancourt. Are you busy?'

The club was about half-full and there was no sign of either Ruby or Leo. Mei greeted them and he asked her to find them a quiet table at the back. She treated them the same way she'd treat anyone who turned up looking for a table and gave no sign she'd spoken to Betancourt just a few hours before, let alone what they had discussed. When they were seated, Evelyn asked for whisky and water. A neon sign above the bar advertising Tiger beer winked at Betancourt and, perhaps answering its siren call without realising, he ordered one.

'Big bottle?'

'Why not?'

Mei returned with Evelyn's drink and a perspiring bottle of beer and a glass. 'Enjoy.'

There was no fan near the table and the air was close. He took a big swig of the beer and grimaced as the hoppy spume filled his mouth and gurgled up the back of his nose.

Evelyn seemed amused. 'You don't look as if you're enjoying that much.'

He shook his head. 'I've no idea why I ordered it. I don't even like beer.' He called to Mei and asked her to take it away again. 'I forgot. I'm allergic to beer. Makes me act unpredictably. I'll take a whisky as well.'

When his drink arrived, he told Evelyn about his meeting with Mei earlier that day.

'Bonham has warned me off from looking too deeply into Akiko's death and I don't have anyone at the Detective Branch that I can talk to anymore. I thought if I went through it with someone… Two heads are better than one, and all that.' Did he really believe that, or had he just wanted to see her again?

She looked at him curiously and he wondered if she was asking herself the same question, but when she spoke, it was with enthusiasm for the task. 'Excellent. I shall be Watson to your Holmes. I've always thought Watson's contribution was underestimated. Lead on, Sherlock. Tell me what you've got.'

That was a good question. What exactly did he have? He recited the facts as he knew them as systematically as he could, stopping only when she asked him to clarify the detail of some point or other.

'A woman is supposed to have committed suicide at the docks. Except she didn't take her own life – you found an underlying puncture wound in her neck and there was no blood left in the body after that. So, if she didn't die at the docks, she must have been killed elsewhere, and the body dumped where it was found. Everyone – Gemmill, the ship's crew, Bonham – dismissed her as a mere *karayuki-san* and not worth bothering about. But if she was just another unfortunate, why did Archie Napier, chairman of the most powerful trading company in the colony, put pressure on Bonham to have her death hushed up?

'And then there's the tattoo. I've never seen anything like it. My tame tattooist, Ah Ting, confirmed the quality of the work was too high to have been done by a local. What's more, it would have cost a lot of money. Whoever paid for it was making a statement. Akiko was valuable to him.'

'Belle said Akiko had worked in the *suteretsu*. Sometime afterwards, a Japanese gang known as the Sleeping Tigers moved in and are now believed to be trafficking large numbers of women into the area, reportedly to raise money for the Japanese war effort. Akiko was seen consorting with the head man.

'Then Ruby told us a man called Chin, who fitted Belle's description of the boss of the Sleeping Tigers, found her work here, at the Blue Nightingale, where she became involved with one of the regulars, Euan Guthrie, who just happens to be Archie Napier's nephew.'

'But why would a man like Chin put his girlfriend to work in a bar at all? Why didn't he just keep her at home?'

It was an excellent point. What was it Ruby had said? *He ordered her around like he owned her.*

'What if she hadn't just happened to meet Guthrie here? What if Akiko had been placed here *specifically* to meet him? Akiko told Mei she had a plan that was about to pay off. Could Akiko have planned the entire thing herself and been blackmailing Guthrie?'

'And then he killed her and now there's a cover-up going on?' Evelyn's eyes shone with investigative glee.

'Guthrie knew Akiko, so it must be a possibility, but why? What is there to cover up?'

Evelyn thought for a moment. 'Well, she was pregnant. It doesn't seem unreasonable to assume Guthrie was the father. Could that be it?'

'I wondered about that myself, but there must be more to it than that.'

He drained his glass and signalled for two more drinks.

When Mei had departed again, Evelyn shuffled a few inches closer. 'Do tell.'

'This is where it starts to get really interesting.' He pulled out the makeshift envelope containing the evidence he'd gathered and laid it out on the table. 'Akiko left a book with Mei for safekeeping. Tucked inside was this war bond ,which a banker acquaintance of mine confirmed was one of a batch stolen from Government House last year. Also hidden inside the book was this.' He handed her the photograph. 'His name is Nakano Seigō, and he's the founder of a fascist organisation known as the Tōhōkai, dedicated to bringing down the British Empire in Asia.' He omitted to mention Daisy's assistance in his discovery of this. 'And that's where the whole thing turns full circle. It seems that Chin, the *suteretsu* gangster, patron of Akiko and the man who introduced her to Euan Guthrie, is really Jin, son of this Nakano Seigō. The Sleeping Tigers and the Tōhōkai are linked, and Jin is the connection. Jin and Guthrie are also connected, but I haven't worked out how yet.'

Evelyn fell back in her seat. 'Wow!' was all she managed to say.

Wow, indeed.

He waved his hand in the air – the universal request for the bill – and when Mei brought it over, he handed her more than enough money to cover the drinks and the service. 'Keep the change.'

Evelyn looked at her watch. 'Oh, Lord, is that the time? I've a clinic first thing in the morning and then a friend's do in the afternoon. If I don't get my beauty sleep, I'll be no use for any of it. Walk me to the taxi rank?'

'Of course.' Betancourt stretched his neck. His head hurt and he was tired. And he hadn't mentioned the thing that bothered him most: he'd seen Jin for himself, first-hand, arguing with Pascal over a business transaction that very morning.

Chapter Sixteen

Betancourt rose early the next morning and put on a pan containing yesterday's coffee to heat. Normally, he couldn't stand reheated coffee, but his craving wouldn't wait until a fresh batch was made.

His conversation with the Cléments about Lucia was still raw and while he waited for the coffee to come to the boil, he took out the notices from the school that he'd secreted away in the drawer. He'd assumed they were all late-payment demands, but sure enough, near the bottom of the pile, was a letter from the Mother Superior, informing him of Lucia's unsatisfactory conduct.

He washed and dressed quickly and rode north, crossing the river at Coleman Bridge. Skirting Holloway Lane and the *suteretsu*, he made his way along Middle Road before eventually pulling up at the gates of St Seraphima's School for Girls.

The imposing building on Mount Sophia had once been the residence of a trader named McLennan who'd made his fortune in palm oil and had settled there with his young bride, a *pei pei* girl he'd been introduced to in one of the many gentlemen's private clubs he frequented. In his later years, so the story went, McLennan was visited by a host of seraphim as he lay delirious during a bout of malaria. When he recovered, he took the visitation to be a heavenly warning and promptly made over the house and land to the holy sisterhood, who now ran their school there while he lived in retirement in a more modest establishment on the east coast of the island.

An elderly Tamil *kebun* was tending to the gardens, sweeping up leaves and other debris, his cane rake creaking as he dragged it through the coarse grass. No sooner had he gathered the leaves into a rough pile than a gust blew them apart again, but the man didn't seem to mind and methodically started raking again. A long-forgotten school lesson jumped into Betancourt's head. An image of Old Jeyaratnam, a teacher God had intended for better things, trying to teach a class of unruly, uninterested fourteen-year-old boys about the myth of Sisyphus and his never-ending struggle to roll a rock up a hill.

The school was closed for the holidays, but he'd taken the chance that Lucia's headmistress would be on the premises anyway. He was right. He was met at the top of the grand stone stairway by a familiar figure.

Sister Mary Michael was a round woman: round of body and round of face. She was one of those people that a bit of extra weight seemed to suit, having the effect of smoothing out the wrinkles, but it made her difficult to age.

'It's been too long, Inspector. We've missed you.' Soft grey eyes that matched the colour of her habit belied the impression of sternness she was aiming for.

'You know how it is, Mother Superior. Too much evil in the world. It's been keeping me busy.'

She led him down a long corridor lined with a series of

stout doors. The floor was damp, and the air smelled of disinfectant. A novitiate wrung out a mop over a steel bucket.

'You've missed a spot, Sister Catherine.'

The young woman hung her head and replied with a whispered, 'Yes, Mother Superior. Sorry, Mother Superior.' She caught Betancourt's eye briefly. There was something familiar about her, the shape of her face or her eyes, but he couldn't think what it was and quickly dismissed her from his mind.

The Mother Superior pushed open the door of a room leading off a side corridor and stood back to allow Betancourt to enter. She made a small but firm gesture with her hand, indicating he should take a seat. Though appearing to be an invitation, it was, in fact, a command. He understood how she exerted control over a roomful of adolescents. She herself sat behind a large ornately carved wooden desk and shuffled a few papers before returning them to where they had been in the first place. The manoeuvre reminded him of the tic-tac-toe hustlers he used to lift for, fleecing the tourists down on Raffles Quay. *Watch the lady, lady.*

He'd decided on the drive up that the best form of defence was attack. 'It's about my daughter Lucia.' The nun sat quietly. Of course it was. What else would it be about? 'I spoke with her grandparents. They told me my daughter has been having... some challenges.'

'These unfortunate incidents happen when they're that age. I had to discipline Lucia. You understand my position, don't you?'

'Incidents? You mean this happened more than once?'

'I'm afraid so. Don't get me wrong, Inspector, Lucia is a lovely girl and we're all most fond of her, but since her mother... well, she's just not been the same. We tried to write to you, to make you aware and to enlist your help, but when we received no response, we had no choice other than to contact her grandparents.'

There was nothing to say. He'd let his daughter down. He hadn't been there when she'd needed him, and he was ashamed.

The Mother Superior tilted her head, watching him. When she spoke, her voice was gentle and filled with compassion.

'Forgive me, Inspector, but there's something else we need to discuss. About the school fees. It's been several months now since you paid them. We've written to you. Perhaps we have the wrong address?' She lifted a pair of tiny spectacles, attached to her habit by a thin gold chain, and placed them on the end of her nose. She read from a typewritten sheet that she took from the top of one of the piles. 'Number 16A, Duxton Hill?'

They both knew she had the right address.

'My post is delivered to my landlord. He may have overlooked the letter. I'll check when I get home.'

'Letters, Inspector. We've written several times.'

Betancourt looked out of the window at the windblown leaves on the lawn and said nothing.

'The account now stands at four hundred and eighty dollars.' She paused, as though broaching a particularly delicate subject. 'If you're having difficulties…'

'I'm not having difficulties.' He was angry and it showed. He forced himself to regain his composure. 'I've been busy. I'll sort it out.'

She picked up another letter. She seemed genuinely uncomfortable about relaying its contents. 'There's something else, Inspector. I received this.' She handed it to him.

There was no signature. The note was short and headed by the title *A List of Debts Owed by Det. Insp. M. Betancourt,* followed by an itemised list of his IOUs, with the names of the people he owed. He sat there, frozen. Who the hell knew about those IOUs? Apart from the people he'd borrowed from, nobody had the whole picture. Who would do something like this? His stomach sank as he remembered the conversation with Cluny. The banker's words thundered in his head. *Debt is power. If I were you, I'd start looking over my shoulder.* He knew his affairs weren't the secret he might wish, but contacting Lucia's school? That was something else again. If whoever had sent this letter had meant to rattle his cage, they'd succeeded.

'You understand how this looks, Inspector? What the trustees will think if it is brought to their attention? Perhaps if you were to make a payment on account – a cheque for a hundred dollars, say? That would keep the bursar happy.' She gave him a small smile. A happy bursar made for a happy Mother Superior, it seemed.

He went through the motions of patting his pockets. 'I would, but... cheque book... wallet... I'll forget my head one of these days.'

The smile receded from the Mother Superior's face and was replaced by a look of sadness. 'I'm sorry, Inspector, but we really have to do something. Your wife's family, perhaps—'

'No!' He was on his feet. 'I forbid you to approach them. I won't allow it. I've said I'll take care of it and I will.'

The nun watched him for a moment and then she too stood, with an air of finality. 'Very well, Inspector, but as soon as you can, please. The trustees meet next week. After that it will be out of my hands. Needless to say, I won't mention anything about our conversation to Lucia.'

He thanked her. If the Cléments got wind of this, he could kiss goodbye to any chance of holding on to custody of his daughter. He'd get the money. He had to. It was all or nothing now.

'How much?'

Allenby turned and gazed at Betancourt, looking him up and down, as though seeing him for the first time.

'And a very good morning to you too, Inspector.'

'You asked me if I wanted in on your coup. So, how much?'

Allenby took out a pouch and rolled himself a cigarette, thin as a twig, more paper than tobacco. He placed one booted foot on the lower rail of the paddock and the cigarette in his mouth, and looked off into the distance, as if considering Betancourt's question. He wasn't really considering it. He'd already have everything planned down to the finest detail. He'd know exactly how much he wanted out of this thing, and how much he'd need to put in to get it.

'Had a few lean years. Got the missus nipping me ear about wanting to go back home. See the grandkids. Maybe time to think about cashin' in me chips. One last big 'un'll see me right.' Betancourt wasn't sure if Allenby was talking to him or to himself. Maybe a bit of both.

A tweed-jacketed figure emerged from the margins of the shade offered by a nearby tree. An unremarkable-looking man, short, with a marked stoop, thinning sandy hair, and a smile that looked more like a permanent fixture than an indication of any particular emotion. A man many would be tempted to dismiss, but something about him told Betancourt that to do so would likely be a mistake. He guessed this was the man Melrose that Allenby had mentioned the last time they'd spoken.

'Young Betancourt here's wanting in. Reckon five thou should do it. What do you think, Major?'

Melrose said nothing. Silent acquiescence. Betancourt's shoulders sagged. He'd nothing like that. A few hundred in the bank, maybe, and Cluny had offered him another thousand. Maybe he could scrape up two grand at the outside, but not five. And even if could raise additional money, he already owed two thousand. He shook his head.

Allenby scratched his stubbled chin. 'Mind you, we're getting ahead of ourselves a bit. Might not be anything to have a bet on.'

'What do you mean? The horse looks as fit as a fiddle.'

'Fit for swimming around in ponds, maybe. Racing's a different thing. I've done a bit of pace work with him, but that's it. 'Oss hasn't had a proper gallop in three years. I'm not risking a cent without seeing if he can still run.' He ground out the remains of the cigarette, slowly and deliberately. 'Come on, then. No time like the present. You can help me saddle him up.'

When they'd put on the saddle and bridle, they walked Victory Parade out to the heath track. A young jockey awaited them, clad in khaki jodhpurs and polished brown ankle-length boots. Wally Hood couldn't be any older than twenty-five but the rigours of wasting, not helped, Betancourt suspected, by too many late nights in clubs and bars, had taken its toll and the young man's face was drawn and lined beyond its years.

Allenby legged him up into the saddle and gave him his instructions. 'Trot him once round, then take him down the bottom and let him go. Ground's wet so don't try and pull him up too quick. Don't want him slipping and doing himself a nasty.'

When the jockey had ridden the big horse away, Betancourt raised a quizzical eyebrow at Allenby.

'He's a good lad. Bit simple, but he's learned his lesson. Knows how to keep his mouth shut.'

Hood jogged the horse slowly once around the heath to loosen his muscles. By the time he returned to his starting point, Betancourt, Melrose, and Allenby had taken up position on a low knoll, half-hidden by a stand of trees. Allenby held a stopwatch, his finger on the button. Melrose's eyes were obscured by a giant pair of military-issue binoculars.

A troop of monkeys, knowing from experience what was about to happen, scattered from the track in front of them, chattering their displeasure. Hood gathered up the reins and gave Victory Parade a kick in the ribs. The reaction was electric. The horse flattened out and settled into an even gallop and his rider settled with him, crouching low. Betancourt could see he had good hands. He tuned in to the rhythm of the hoofbeats and started to pace the workout the way Stanley had taught him, counting off the seconds in his head. *One Mississippi, two Mississippi, three Mississippi*. A torrent of exhilaration surged through his veins as he watched man and animal in perfect harmony, and for those precious few moments his cares dissolved like waves on a seashore.

Horse and rider reached the rising ground at the top of the heath and Hood stood up and let the reins slip out through his fingers. The well-schooled Victory Parade slowed himself and the pair jogged back to where the hopeful connections stood before gradually coming to rest. Betancourt looked at the horse's flanks. He was barely out of breath.

Allenby consulted the stopwatch and his face twisted into a lop-sided leathery grin. 'I can't bloody believe it! Thirty-five seconds for three furlongs. Uphill. In the soft. And look at him. He wouldn't blow out a candle.'

Wally Hood beamed. 'Told you he was a good 'un, didn't I?'

He was right. It was a phenomenal time on rain-softened ground like this. The big horse could run. If he could transfer that form to the racecourse, he'd be a certainty.

Hood slipped the reins over the big horse's head and led him back to the stable. Behind him, Allenby and Melrose walked together deep in a conspiratorial conversation. Betancourt followed. When they reached the yard, Allenby gave the syce instructions, clapped the horse on the rump, and turned to Betancourt.

'Well? You've seen what the 'oss can do. You in or out?'

'Can you give me a minute?' He needed to think. He walked away, round to the back of the stables where his only company was a lone cicada. He could borrow more. How much he wasn't sure, but it would mean staving off Lucia's school for a few more weeks. The horse had travelled like a winner, but what if something went wrong? What if he borrowed again then lost the money? The Cléments would use it as further evidence of his unfitness as a father. He went back to where Allenby and Melrose were continuing their planning.

'I appreciate the offer, but it's too rich for my blood right now. Maybe another time. But if you need a decoy, I'd be happy to act as your stool pigeon. You can trust me.'

'I know.' Allenby looked thoughtful. 'Funny you should say that. Me and the Major here, we've been having a chin-wag. Reckon there's a way you can come in, no money down.'

Allenby was pulling his leg, surely. But he looked serious enough and Melrose still wore his serene smile. Whatever plan they'd cooked up between them, they both seemed happy with the outcome.

'The Major here's got himself a bit of a reputation over

the years. Been a bit lucky, you might say.' Melrose's eyes gleamed. 'Bookies won't touch a bet from him these days. If this thing's going to work, we'll need to do it on the course and timing'll be crucial if we're going to hold the price up. We need someone the professionals won't suspect to place the bets.'

'I'm no use to you. They all know me – I've arrested most of them at one time or other.'

'No, not you. Well, leastways not exactly.'

Allenby outlined the plan, Melrose nodding enthusiastically the whole time.

'So, you in?'

'Just try to keep me out!'

The major leaned forward. 'Excellent. From now on, it's codename Triumphus.'

'Pardon?'

'That's what we're calling it. A *triumphus* was a Roman procession, you see, held to celebrate a military success. A victory parade, if you will. Knew my schoolboy Latin would come in handy one day.'

Melrose could call it whatever he liked. It was an unbelievable offer. Betancourt thought back to the speed and the power the big horse had shown earlier, and he couldn't believe his luck.

Chapter Seventeen

The first thing to greet Betancourt the next morning was a note from Marjorie. She'd tracked down Guthrie's address. She was a marvel. He wondered if Bonham recognised the talent right under his nose. He doubted it. Of course, having access to the upper echelons of society helped. His marriage to Anna had granted him occasional admittance to the inner circles of Singapore, but those doors were closing as memories of her faded. In any case, as a Eurasian, there were some avenues that never were and never would be open to him. Marjorie met with no such barriers and she exploited her position to great effect.

The address she had left was in the Arab Quarter, not far from the Blue Nightingale. A thirty-minute walk might be tolerable at this time of the morning, but it wouldn't be later on. He called the carpool and asked for a car and driver to be sent round.

He'd enjoyed, if that was the right term, only a few hours' fitful sleep, disturbed by dreams of giant red letters, a banker with the head of a shark, and a Mother Superior sitting like a high priestess on a throne, judging his every action and finding him guilty. Now his head ached, and he hoped for one of those perfect drivers for whom the words "Where to, sir?" were the limit of their engagement. He was in luck. It was his old friend Awang who turned up. Betancourt handed over a scrap of paper on which he'd scribbled the address and Awang pulled out into traffic. Both men understood that no further conversation was required or welcome until they reached their destination.

It wasn't yet eight o'clock but the last of the morning freshness was disappearing as the sun poked its head over the parapets of Sultan Gate, the busy little street that connected the seafront at Beach Road with the Istana Kampong Glam, the palace of the original Sultans of Singapore. Betancourt stuck his head out of the window, took one look, and told Awang to stop. 'It'll take all day to drive through this lot. Wait for me here. I shouldn't be long.' He climbed out and set off in search of Euan Guthrie's digs.

It was slow going at first. He pushed his way through gaggles of merchants unloading bales of brightly hued cotton, early-morning bargain hunters haggling over all manner of fruit and vegetables, and the general stream of humanity weaving its way up and down the street while somehow avoiding colliding into each other, like a trail of well-ordered ants guided by an invisible hand. A large sack of yellow split peas left by its owner blocked the five-foot way and Betancourt had to step off the pavement to avoid it, causing him to trip over an earthenware pot filled with flowers. A Javanese woman hunkered down beside the pot to pick up the scattered blooms, scolding him with language he was more used to hearing at the docks.

Eventually the crowd thinned, and he found himself looking up at a neat, whitewashed building set back from the street. A fat, orange-turbaned Sikh *jaga* lay snoring on a gaudily coloured charpoy outside the gate. Betancourt roused him with a rough shake of the shoulder. The man squinted through sleep-gummed eyes. When Betancourt's warrant card came into focus, he rolled his prodigious belly off the side of the bed and stumbled to his feet.

'What's your name?'

'Balwinder Singh, sir.' The *jaga* gave a makeshift salute.

'Which one is Tuan Guthrie's residence?'

'Tuan Guthrie?' The man stroked his beard. It appeared Betancourt had posed him a perplexing problem, one that required a good deal of thought. 'Tuan Guthrie. Ah, yes! He is an Englishman.' He smiled broadly, baring a set of large, perfectly straight white teeth, like the keys of a xylophone.

'I know what he is. I'd like to speak to him. Police business.'

The *jaga* took a set of keys from a hook on the leg of the bed and opened a bronze gate that led to a dappled bougainvillea-lined courtyard. He pointed to a door on the first floor of the building. 'Tuan Guthrie.'

Betancourt climbed the wrought-iron stairs and rapped on the door.

'Who is it?' The voice sounded edgy and suspicious.

'My name is Betancourt. Marine Police. I'd like a word.'

'What about?'

'Just a few questions. It won't take long. Can you open the door?'

A bolt was pulled, and a lock turned, and a face poked around the frame of the door. Betancourt had seen that face before, at the docks, on the day of the hostilities. It was the young Englishman he'd spoken to outside the godown, the one who'd threatened to report him to Bonham. Guthrie's clothes were dishevelled and the black rings under his eyes suggested a lack of sleep while the bristly shadow on his face suggested he was yet to make his ablutions that morning. His bloodshot eyes widened in recognition.

'You.' He looked up and down the verandah that ran the length of the building. 'What the hell do you want?'

'Mind if I come in?'

'Were you followed?'

'Followed, Mr Guthrie? I'm a police officer. Why would anyone be following me?'

'No reason, I suppose.' He stood aside, admitting Betancourt into a small hallway. The sweet- sour aroma of stale whisky hung in the air. Guthrie checked the passageway again before closing and bolting the door.

'What's this about?'

'I'm investigating a death. May we go inside?' Betancourt didn't wait for permission.

He took a few seconds to orient himself. The room was divided informally in two. On the left a rattan settee and two lounge chairs, cushions covered in mildewed chintz, were arranged around a small, chipped glass coffee table, forming a living area. The other half of the room looked as if it was missing a dining table and chairs. Instead, a warped teak bookcase occupied the wall, its shelves empty except for a few paperback books and a photograph of Guthrie with a young woman, laughing, outside a grand stone building that looked older than Singapore itself. Dotted around the floor were tea chests containing more books and other personal effects, and on the scuffed parquet floor lay a small steamer trunk, battered and much used, from which clothes spilled. A label tied to the handle showed a stylised image of a ship, front-on, and the words *Batavian Princess*.

'Recently arrived, Mr Guthrie?'

The man shook his head quickly, as though trying to

clear his thoughts. 'What? No. Over a year.' He followed the direction of Betancourt's gaze as though seeing the chests for the first time. 'I was staying in a hotel. Not long moved here.'

He filled a tumbler from a bottle of whisky standing on the windowsill. 'Drink?' He raised the glass, by way of example.

'Bit early for me.'

'Don't mind if I do, then?' It wasn't really a question. '*Cin-cin*.' He downed half the contents of the tumbler and grimaced. 'Damn cheap local gut rot.'

He lit a cigarette and pushed the box across the table. Betancourt took one.

'Turkish.'

'What?'

'Your tobacco. It's Turkish. Been there recently?'

'What the hell would I be doing in bloody Turkey? Bought them from a fellow on the boat coming back from Shanghai. Don't know why I smoke them. Coffin nails.' He sat on the arm of the cane settee and took another draw of the acrid smoke.

'I see from your trunk you travelled on the *Batavian Princess*.'

'Yes, that's right.'

'When was that?'

Guthrie appeared to give the question some thought. 'A month or so ago. I forget.'

'So, not in the last week, then?'

'No.'

Had he noticed a flash of fear in Guthrie's eyes?

'Shanghai.'

'What about it?'

'You said you were there. Was it a long visit?'

'God, no. Horrible bloody place. A week, no more. That was plenty.'

'I see. And what took you there?'

'What's that got to do with you?'

'Just answer the question, Mr Guthrie.'

'Company business. You know the sort of thing.' Guthrie took another pull on his cigarette and waved it in the air, as though eddies of smoke would explain the inner secrets of "company business".

'No, Mr Guthrie, I don't know "the sort of thing". Please humour me.'

'Very well. I delivered a package.' His eyes darted away. Either he was lying or there was more to his trip than he was letting on.

'Is that what you do at Napier & Campbell? Run errands?' Betancourt was aware that he was goading the Englishman now, and it was working. Guthrie's face flushed with anger.

'How do you know I work for Napier's?'

Betancourt didn't reply. His dart had hit its target and he had Guthrie's full attention. When he'd introduced himself, he'd mentioned he was here investigating a death. Guthrie was yet to ask him whose death, or what it had to with him. Time to give him a prod. He took out a photograph of Akiko and placed it on the table. No brushed hair and make-up this time. The picture showed her death stare and the wounds to her neck that had killed her. He wanted Guthrie to see her as she was in death, not remember her as she was in life.

Guthrie blanched and his shoulders sagged, as though he had been punched in the solar plexus. The room was perfectly still, save for the chirping of a golden oriole sitting on the window ledge, peering in on the unfolding drama. Betancourt waited, allowing the full impact of the image to sink in.

'This woman was killed and her body found near to the *Batavian Princess*, shortly after she docked last Monday. The same day we met at the docks.'

Guthrie looked as if he were going be sick. That's better, Betancourt thought. Now he was getting a reaction.

'Perhaps you'd like a glass of water?' Guthrie shook his head, so Betancourt continued. 'Her name is Akiko Sakai. Do you recognise her?'

'No.'

'Are you sure, Mr Guthrie? She worked as a hostess at a night-club. The Blue Nightingale.'

'I've heard of it.'

Betancourt weighed up Guthrie's reactions. It was time to get tough. 'I know you have. In fact, I know you're a regular customer. You even have a large unpaid bar bill there. I also know you and Miss Sakai were – how shall I put it? – on friendly terms.'

'The place is full of tarts. It's difficult to tell them apart sometimes.'

Betancourt had no intention of allowing Akiko's status to be reduced to that of a piece of flesh, indistinguishable from so many others. He'd keep using her name until Guthrie relented and acknowledged she was a person he knew intimately.

'How did you and Miss Sakai meet?'

'Meet? You don't meet women like that. She was just there. She came on to me. Practically threw herself at me. She was prettier than the others, so I wasn't going to say no, was I?

'Then you weren't introduced by a mutual friend? A man named Chin?'

That stopped Guthrie in his tracks. He dropped the glass onto the table, spilling whisky over the photograph.

'I don't know what you're talking about.'

A year or two back, a professor from the university had come into the Hill Street station to give a talk to the division. He'd taught his audience how much could be gleaned from watching a suspect's eyes. When Betancourt had mentioned Chin, Guthrie's eyes had darted up and to the right. He was lying again, and now he was scared too.

'Were you still seeing Miss Sakai?'

'I was never "seeing her", as you put it. I told you, she was just a tart. I finished with her months ago. Passed her on to one of the chaps. I forget who, before you ask.'

Betancourt felt the anger well up inside him. Passed her on? He was tempted to hit that smug face, to knock a bit of respect into this young pup, but he told himself to stay calm. He was onto something here. Chin had introduced Guthrie to Akiko and now she was dead. He reached into his pocket for his notebook and as he did so, his fingers brushed against a piece of paper. The bond. He unfolded it and held it up so Guthrie could see it. 'I came across this amongst Miss Sakai's effects. Do you know what it is?'

This time there was no disguising the panic. Guthrie lunged forward and tried to snatch the bond, but Betancourt was too quick and held it out of his reach. This only angered the young Englishman more. 'It's a war bond. Do you have any idea what Miss Sakai might have been doing with it?'

'No idea. She probably stole it. You know what they're like.'

'They?'

Guthrie fumed in silence.

'Tell me, Mr Guthrie, do you hold bonds like this yourself?'

'Of course, I do. Everyone has them. There's a war on. One does one's bit where one can.' His lip curled into a sneer.

'Everyone who's loyal to the King that is. I expect that counts the likes of you out.'

'I'd like to see your bonds, Mr Guthrie.' If the numbers on Guthrie's bonds were in the same range as the one Betancourt had shown to Cluny, he'd know he was definitely onto something.

'Do you really think I'd be so stupid as to keep them here?'

'Where do you keep them?'

'In a box at the Royal Edinburgh Bank. Good enough for you? Now, I've had enough of this. Get out, or I'll have the *jaga* throw you out.'

Betancourt smiled to himself at the thought of the portly nightwatchman stirring himself to an act of aggression. Still, it was probably time to go. He had enough for now and he remembered Marjorie's warning. For all he despised Guthrie and everything he stood for, any further provocation could backfire on him. He picked up the photograph of Akiko from the table and replaced it with a business card. 'In case you think of anything.'

When he heard the bolt being shot behind him, he paused for a minute, deciding what to do next. He heard Guthrie's raised voice from inside the apartment, so edged along the verandah to the window where the golden oriole still sat watching. Peeking through a crack in the shutters, Betancourt looked on as Guthrie stabbed repeatedly at the receiver of the telephone. 'Hello? Hello? Answer, damn you!' Eventually he spat out a number.

'I've just had a policeman here, asking about... the woman. He had a bond. I think it was one of ours. I told you it was a mistake! You said everything would be taken care of.' There was silence as he listened. Then, eventually, 'He calls himself Betancourt. I've got his card here. It's one of those damned Eurasian names. I'd better spell it for you.' But apparently there was no need for him to spell out Betancourt's name. Whoever Guthrie had been talking to seemed to know who he was. 'Well, you'd bloody well better take care of it, and properly this time, or you won't be making any further use of my ships.'

<hr>

Betancourt closed the door to his office behind him and leafed quickly through his messages. Most were trivial, but the last one in the pile caught his eye. It was from Bonham: *Where the hell are you? Call me as soon as you get this.* If he called, Bonham would be incensed to find he was still investigating the Sakai case, and would have an apoplexy if he learned Betancourt had been to Guthrie's flat. He tore up the slip and let the pieces flutter into the waste basket. He couldn't act on what he'd never received.

One advantage of keeping his office door locked and not leaving a key at the front desk was that the cleaners couldn't get in, which meant his desk was never tidied, which meant things were easy to find. He pulled the ship's passenger manifest from its envelope and scanned the names. No Euan Guthrie. There was a chance Guthrie could have been telling the truth, that he hadn't arrived on the recently embarked *Batavian Princess*, but even the slovenliest bachelor wouldn't leave a trunk full of clothes lying on his living-room floor for a month. Guthrie had been on that vessel when she'd arrived last Monday, Betancourt was sure of it. Someone had removed his name from the manifest.

He rang through to Customs where an adenoidal voice announced itself as belonging to a Sub Inspector Purvis. Betancourt put on his best "one of the chaps" accents.

'Inspector Betancourt here. I'm calling about the *Batavian Princess*. She docked last Monday. Can you dig out the landing cards? I need to check up on some passengers who disembarked.'

'Anyone specific?'

He didn't know this Purvis or where his primary allegiance lay, and he didn't want anyone connected with Napier's being alerted to the fact that he was paying special attention to Guthrie's presence on the ship. That went double for Bonham. He picked up the manifest and read out some names at random. 'Beatty, Fisher, McNally, Thomas, and Wishart.'

'When do you need this by?'

'It's just a routine check, but as soon as you can would be good. Oh, wait, there's one more. Guthrie.'

'Right, got it. It'll be a couple of days.'

Betancourt thanked the man and rang off. He checked his watch. Half-past two. Damn. Marjorie's party. He was late.

Chapter Eighteen

Swiss Club Road was a quiet, affluent street off Dunearn Road, home to bankers, ambassadors, and wealthier European merchants. A bird's-eye view would show it was a stone's throw from the Bukit Timah Turf Club, but the thrower of the stone would need a strong arm as a lush copse of mahogany trees protected the privacy of the street's inhabitants.

A leafy driveway led to a low bungalow, enwrapped by a verandah for shade. It might not have been as grand as Marjorie's family home next door to the Cléments' on Nassim Hill, but it was impressive nonetheless. Cars parked one behind the other, down the drive and out into the street, their white-liveried syces gathered in small groups, smoking and chatting and sharing the news of the day. Betancourt raised a hand in greeting and they nodded back. One of the men inclined his head and muttered something to the other drivers. Apparently, Betancourt's face was known. For his part, he didn't recognise any of the men or, therefore, who they drove for.

A colonial service-type – young, thin, greasy pasty skin – met him at the threshold. He planted his feet shoulder-width apart, blocking Betancourt's passage, challenging him.

'Staff entrance is round the side. Get a move on. You're late.'

'I read somewhere it was fashionable to be late.'

The man took a half step forward. Close enough for Betancourt to smell his cheap cologne. 'You heard me. Less of the lip and get to work.'

Betancourt considered what he might say to put the young fool down, to embarrass him, but it wasn't worth the effort. He placed a hand on the man's shoulder and pushed him firmly to one side. 'Friend of the family.'

It was a mixed crowd. A turbaned Sikh chatted to a Chinese man in Army dress uniform while an olive-skinned woman wearing a large hat, as if dressed for the races, nodded in feigned interest as a loud American expounded his theories on Japan's designs on the orient. Mostly, though, the guests were Europeans, men in cream linen suits and women in party frocks. On the patio, a four-piece band in oversized white dinner jackets played a subdued version of "Summertime". It was all very civilised.

Betancourt stopped a Malay houseboy and took a glass of lime juice from a tray as he enquired, 'Mem French?'

'Over there. With the *tuan*.' The man pointed to the far side of the garden, near an aviary populated by a host of vividly coloured birds. Betancourt scanned the faces and found Marjorie's. Next to her stood Ray French, a tall, slender, slack-shouldered man with a shock of untamed grey hair. They were deep in animated conversation with a young couple. French continually glanced from his guests to Marjorie, laughing at every remark that left her mouth and smiling proudly. He looked devoted. Betancourt studied the other couple. The woman was

Sophie Napier, granddaughter of Archie and, until recently, fiancée of Pascal. He didn't recognise the man she was with.

The breeze shifted direction and carried with it a whiff of perfume. *Joy*. The scent that Anna used to wear when she socialised. He turned, curious to know the source of the perfume. It was Evelyn, her arm linked through that of a grey-looking man in a double-breasted suit. Betancourt wondered if this was the one whose company she'd passed over in favour of a visit to the Blue Nightingale.

'Inspector. What a pleasant surprise.'

'Dr Trevose. Likewise.'

'Let me introduce you. Alistair, this is Inspector Betancourt. He's a *policeman*.' The way she said it made it sound as though being a policeman was akin to being a secret agent. 'Alistair's an accountant. He can do things with numbers that would make your head spin. I know mine often does.' Alistair beamed, seemingly oblivious to his escort's gentle mockery.

Betancourt extended his hand. 'An accountant, eh?' He couldn't think of anything more to say. Close up he could see that the man's suit was made of a worsted material, far too heavy for the conditions, and as a result he was perspiring heavily. He blotted his forehead with a handkerchief and Betancourt casually withdrew his hand again, before Alistair had a chance to shake it.

'You interested in numbers, B—. Sorry, I'm not very good with these foreign names. What was it again?'

'It's Betancourt, and no, I have to admit, I'm more interested in people than numbers.'

Evelyn disentangled herself from Alistair and gestured to a small group huddled near the bandstand. 'Oh, look. Isn't that the Kirks? Would you be a love and say hello to them from me? I'd like to have a word with Inspector Betancourt.'

Alistair trotted off, seemingly happy to carry out any command given to him by the lady doctor.

'So that's the "starched-collar accountant"?'

'Behave.'

He smiled to himself, pleased to have got the upper hand with her for once. 'I can't say I expected to see you at an affair like this.'

'And what sort of affair *would* you expect to see me at?'

'That came out wrong.'

His advantage had been short-lived, and she laughed at his discomfiture.

'You look lost so allow me to be your guide. Besides, I need to mingle. There are a few cases of gout and at least one communicable disease here that pay for my clinic. Let's mingle.' He protested, but she dragged him by the arm. 'Come on. It's what people do, you know, at affairs like this.'

As she introduced him to the great and the good of Singapore society, he was struck by how popular she seemed to be and how unaffected by that popularity. When she said he was a policeman, he was given the odd lecture on exactly what the police should be doing, and how they ought to be doing it better, faster, and with far greater regularity. Occasionally, someone would recognise his name. 'Betancourt, did you say? Anna Betancourt's husband? Terrible business.' Usually followed by an accusing stare. But mostly there were only speculative glances aimed towards Evelyn. *Why is this man here and why did you introduce him to us?*

Eventually, they met up with the group Marjorie was entertaining. She embraced him and then greeted Evelyn. 'I didn't know you two knew each other.'

'Dr Trevose is helping me with the Sakai case.'

Marjorie raised an eyebrow at Evelyn, who shrugged, as if

to say *Don't ask me*, before their hostess made some introductions.

'Finally, you and Ray meet in person.'

French extended his hand. 'Delighted you could make it, Max.' Betancourt was slightly wrong-footed by the warmth of the welcome.

'And Sophie you know, of course.'

She gave him a quick peck on the cheek. 'It's good to see you, Max. It's been too long. And this is my... friend, Robert Fullerton. Robert works for my grandfather.' She took just long enough over the pause before the word *friend* to make it clear she hadn't decided what Fullerton's status was yet, and the young man's aggrieved look suggested he'd noticed.

Evelyn deposited her glass on a passing tray. 'I'd better find Alistair.'

Marjorie turned to her husband. 'Well, in that case, Ray, why don't you and Max go and have a chat – get to know each other better – while I introduce Sophie and Robert to some people their own age?'

'Of course.' And then to Betancourt, 'Shall we go inside?'

French switched on the electric fan. 'That's better. Warm out there. You'd think I'd be used to it by now. Been in the East for nearly twenty years.'

The study was a revelation. Betancourt had expected bland and functional, like he'd imagined its owner, but besides row upon row of books on the orient, the cases contained an array of artefacts. These were no ordinary tourist souvenirs, purchased from gift shops. He reached out and touched an extravagant purple silk headdress, intricately accented with silver thread.

'Beautiful, isn't it? It was given to me by the wife of a Hmong clan chief.' French lifted a reed and cane lute, painted a vivid turquoise blue. 'The Karen make these for ceremonial use. I settled a land dispute and this was a thank you gift from the elders. And this one's a model of a Dayak canoe. They bury them with their dead, so they'll be able to paddle from this world to the next.' He studied the model. 'Not sure they quite got the scale right.'

'Marjorie never mentioned you were so well travelled.'

'This was all in my younger days. I've settled down now.'

French poured generous whiskies, added soda, and handed one to Betancourt. 'Cigar?' Betancourt shook his head. French took one from the box on a sideboard. When he had the fat tube of tobacco burning to his satisfaction, he sank back into a rattan chair and beckoned Betancourt to do the same.

'How are you finding married life?' he asked.

French smiled with what appeared to be genuine content-ment. 'I'm a very lucky man.'

'To be honest with you, I was surprised when I heard Marjorie had married. I think we all were.'

A lesser man might have taken Betancourt's comment as a veiled judgement, but French seemed to take no offence. 'It was as much of a surprise to me as to anyone. Marriage wasn't something I gave much thought to when I was a young man. I had my work, the travel, and then, suddenly, there I was, hurtling towards fifty and for the first time in my life I was lonely. Marjorie and I met at a dinner at a mutual friend's house in London. I was enchanted. We fell in love, I proposed, and we married as soon as we could get a licence.'

Betancourt put down his drink on a side table, next to a silver-framed photograph showing a young-looking French with a familiar figure. 'Is that who I think it is?'

French looked across. 'Yes, that's Gandhi. The "Indian Saint" as an acquaintance of mine likes to refer to him. I was paymaster to Lord Lytton when he was Governor of Bengal. Gandhi was holding a private conference – up country, at a place called Kadda. Lytton was invited but couldn't go, so he sent me instead. Interesting character, the Mahatma. Wasn't a fan of the Empire, I can tell you. Still isn't by all accounts.'

'Who are the other two?'

'Pass it here.' Betancourt handed over the picture and French studied it. 'Chap with the turban – Chatterjee, I think his name was – he owned the house. As for the other fellow, I forget. A house guest, probably. It was a long time ago.'

'And is that what you do now – act as paymaster?'

'Amongst other things. I'm just the Governor's dogsbody.' French gave a self-deprecating laugh.

'Only I was speaking with Sir John Cluny, the banker, the other day, and he mentioned some war bonds had gone missing. Did you ever track them down?'

'No, we never did. Hidden away in a shoebox under a bed somewhere, I shouldn't doubt.' French looked more serious. 'Are you asking in a professional capacity?'

'Force of habit. Apologies. Just something I'm working on.' He sketched out brief details of Akiko's death. 'I found a war bond among her effects. I showed it to Sir John, and he confirmed the serial number was on the list circulated to the banks.'

French sat up. 'That's excellent news. Does Anthony Bonham know?'

'Not yet. I only found it yesterday.'

'And this woman was Japanese, you say? I spent a bit of time in Japan after I left India. I still keep an eye on what the Japs are up to. Particularly now, with everything that's going on in China. I have a few contacts at the embassy there. Let me know if there's anything I can help with.'

'In that case, there is something.' Betancourt repeated what Belle had told him about the Japanese women being brought in to raise money for Japan's war effort. 'Would that make sense?'

French pursed his lip. 'Sounds a tad fanciful to me. Can't see how it would be worth their while. Let me ask around, though, and I'll let you know if I hear anything useful.'

'I'd appreciate it.'

'Don't mention it, and if there's anything else I or my department can do, just shout. And let me know how you get on with tracing that bond. Just between you and me, the entire affair was a bit of an embarrassment. Anything I can give Sir Shenton by way of a progress report would be most welcome.'

'There you are. I've been looking all over for you.' Marjorie stood in the doorway.

How long had she been listening? French seemed unconcerned about anything she might have overheard.

'We were talking about you. All bad, I'm afraid.'

'Then I'll just have to see what I can do to get back into the good books of my two favourite men.' Marjorie kissed French's head. A pang of guilt gnawed at Betancourt. His earlier mistrust had been irrational, born out of a self-imposed duty of care towards Marjorie. She was fine, she could look after herself.

She reached out and took Betancourt's hand. 'Come on, there's someone who's been asking to speak to you.'

People had enough trouble pronouncing Betancourt correctly. God only knows what they made of René Henry de Solminihac Onraet.

Betancourt had only met the magnificently named Inspector General of Police once before, when he was offered the position at the Marine Branch. The Onraets were friendly with Marjorie's family and when she heard on the grapevine that the Inspector General was looking to set up a new anti-smuggling division, she'd recommended Betancourt. Even then, the two men hadn't exchanged more than a few dozen words but today Onraet greeted him like a long-lost friend, leading him away with a paternal arm around the shoulders to a quiet spot where Betancourt found the Inspector General to be in a solicitous mood.

'I never had a proper chance to say how sorry I was to hear about your wife.'

'Thank you. And I never thanked you properly for the job.'

'Not at all. You came highly recommended. Now tell me, what's good at this weekend's races? I hear you're the man with all the inside information.'

It was common knowledge that Onraet was a keen polo player and they spoke for a while about horses. Onraet had written a book on feeding in the tropics and was keen to hear Betancourt's thoughts. The conversation was easy and unhurried, and he was genuinely interested to hear some of Onraet's ideas. But the Inspector General had a reputation for shrewdness and cunning, and Betancourt was sure he wouldn't have interrupted a social engagement to single out a pariah ex-detective just to talk about the relative merits of American and Canadian oats. Sure enough, eventually the discussion took a different turn.

'A little bird tells me you're keen to get back to detective work.' He'd need to have a word with that little bird once her hostessing duties were complete. 'So, tell me, what's keeping you busy?'

Betancourt told him about Akiko, and what he'd discovered in the days following her death. When he arrived at the finding of the photograph of Nakano Seigō, Onraet was suddenly on the alert.

'Nakano. You're sure that was the name?'

'I'm certain. I checked it against old newspaper records. Is he familiar to you?'

'Nakano Seigō…' Onraet frowned and didn't answer, seemingly absorbed in some internal conflict. After a few moments, he emerged from his contemplation. 'Carry on digging. Make sure you leave no stone unturned and keep me updated on what you find.'

Betancourt considered whether he should mention Bonham's orders to bury the case as quickly as possible. He had precious little respect for the man, but equally had no particular desire to insult him by going over his head. But this was the Inspector General he was speaking to. 'I might be challenged to manage that. The AC wants the case wrapped up and I'm under strict instructions not to involve Napier's.'

'And what particular challenge does that present you with?'

Betancourt explained about his visit to Guthrie's flat earlier that morning. 'He was involved with Miss Sakai, and I'm sure he was on that ship. Not to mention, he got very touchy when I showed him the bond.'

'Are you telling me you suspect the nephew of Sir Archibald Napier of being involved in the death of this woman?'

'I'm afraid, sir, that it's more than a suspicion. I'm convinced he's involved. I'm just not sure how yet.'

Onraet had a faraway look in his eyes, as if pondering something. 'Very well. Leave Bonham to me. Now, my wife will be wondering where I've got to. Good day, Inspector. This has been a most interesting chat.'

When Betancourt returned to the party, he found Evelyn on her own and preparing to leave.

'Had enough?'

'Yes, duty done for another day.'

'No Alistair?'

'I left him discussing long-term amortisation schedules. There's only so much excitement a girl can take in one day.'

He was overtaken by an impulse. 'What are you doing now?'

'I hadn't decided. Why, did you have something in mind?'

'I'm going to see a man about a horse. Would you care to join me?'

She eyed him curiously. 'Well, aren't you just full of surprises?'

Chapter Nineteen

B etancourt realised he hadn't thought this through.

'If you think I'm getting on that thing wearing *this*, you're dafter than you look.' She was right. Party frocks probably weren't the most suitable attire for perching on the back of a motorcycle.

'We could walk, but it would mean going through the trees.'

She lifted one sandal-clad foot. 'Again, not prepared. Come on, we'll take my car.'

They climbed into a red Austin 10 that had seen better days and he gave her directions. Evelyn drove skilfully and confidently – a little too confidently for his liking. He occasionally found himself pumping imaginary brakes as she crossed intersections without so much as slowing up.

'Turn right here.'

The watchman emerged from his security box, one arm raised, but when he saw Betancourt in the passenger seat, he waved them through.

She parked the car where he indicated, in the shade of a

yellow Chinese flame tree. As they walked past rows of loose boxes, heads emerged, curious to see who had come to visit and, more importantly, whether they'd brought food. Betancourt reeled off the names of the horses and gave her a potted summary of each inmate.

'That's Marengo. He's a morning glory. He can beat anything in training but won't do a tap on race day, he just comes home in his own time. And this one's Palmyra Court. She's a sweet old thing. She's getting on a bit now but there's still a race in her somewhere.'

'I have some mints. Do you think she'd like one?'

'She'll be your friend for life.'

Evelyn stroked the mare's head and offered her the sweet, which was enthusiastically accepted.

'Next to her is Bintang Emas. Best not to get too close. He bites. He could be decent, if Wally Hood can get him to settle.'

Evelyn stood still and gazed at Betancourt with a look of wonderment on her face. 'How on earth do you know all this?'

He told her about his uncle and about his pre-school visits to watch track work. About how Allenby had taught him to ride and how came here most mornings. About how this place was his escape.

'You really do continue to surprise me, Inspector.' This time the mockery had disappeared from Evelyn's voice and she seemed genuinely interested.

Victory Parade's usual paddock was empty. Betancourt asked a syce where Allenby was.

'Back stables. Horse is sick.'

'Sick how?'

The man shook his head sadly. 'Sick in the leg.'

They found Allenby and Melrose and Osman the *mandor*

huddled outside a box in the middle of an otherwise empty row. Inside stood Victory Parade, his front legs swathed in thick blue bandages from which layers of protective cotton protruded.

Allenby acknowledged Betancourt's presence without taking his eyes off the horse. Betancourt introduced Evelyn to the glum-looking trio.

'What happened?'

'Leg's gone again. Hopping lame. Must have done something when he galloped yesterday.'

'I could swear he never put a foot wrong the whole way.'

'Happens like that sometimes. Sound as a bell last night. Took him out this morning and he could hardly put a foot to the ground. Tried everything. Had a hose on it for an hour. Packed it in ice. Poulticed it. Did everything short of calling out the witchdoctor. Too late, damage is done.'

Melrose sighed. 'No Operation Triumphus, then?'

'No, Major, no Operation Triumphus. Not unless you can come up with a miracle between now and next weekend.'

The sense of disappointment radiating from the three men was palpable. Betancourt picked up a stone and threw it against the fence in frustration. He realised how much hope he'd been pinning on Allenby's coup to get him out of trouble. What would he say now if the Cléments followed through on their threat to go to court? How could he show he was fit to look after his daughter if all he had to show was a pile of bills? He stroked the horse's neck. 'Pity. If he was back up in Ipoh, you could have tried swimming him in the tin mines again. It seemed to do the trick last time.'

Allenby gave a small laugh. 'Reckon I'd try anything about now, but ten hours standing on the back of a float would finish the 'oss for good.'

They stood watching Victory Parade, as if the power of

concentrated gloom would somehow reverse the damage. Eventually they broke up and Betancourt and Evelyn returned to the car.

'That poor horse. Such a shame. But why is everyone in such a black mood? He'll get better, won't he?'

'Hard to say. Hope so. Allenby and Melrose thought they'd got him right. They were going for a touch. Been planning it for weeks.'

'And you were in on this touch, were you?'

'The truth is, I could do with the money.' He watched her eyes for signs of disapproval, or at the very least disappointment, but to his surprise and relief, all he saw was excitement.

'Life around you is nothing if not interesting, Inspector. Did I hear Mr Allenby say the horse had been injured before?'

'Yes, he hurt himself racing.' He told her the story of Hale and his pony-clubbing daughter and the flooded tin mines. 'Sounds far-fetched, doesn't it?'

'Not at all. I was reading an article the other day about the efficacy of mineral salts on the treatment of injuries. A hospital in Australia has built a mineral pool where they're treating patients with arthritis, with great success. I imagine those mines were chock-full of minerals.'

'That must have been it. Anyway, it's done now. That's horses for you. Build you up one day and break your heart the next.' He opened the door of the car for her but Evelyn remained standing, apparently deep in thought, showing no sign of wanting to take her seat.

'We should get back. Are you coming?'

'Not so fast. I think I might have an idea... Wait here, I need to speak to Mr Allenby.'

It was nearly dark when they finally set off back down Bukit Timah Road towards the city.

'What was all that about?'

'You'll just have to wait and see.'

'Am I at least allowed to ask where we're going?'

'Home.'

It wasn't until she turned the car to follow the Rochor Canal that realisation of where "home" was for her dawned on him. It was then no surprise when she stopped the car behind the clinic on Holloway Lane. He hesitated at the foot of the wooden staircase.

'Come on then. You're perfectly safe – I don't bite. Well, not usually.'

He wasn't sure how to take this, but followed her anyway. As they reached the first-floor landing, a timid face peeped out. Evelyn stopped to give the girl a few quiet words of reassurance and the door closed again. He followed her up to the second floor and into her apartment where she invited him to take a seat. She removed her shawl and draped it over the back of the sofa. Wanting to maintain a decorous distance, he opted for the armchair.

'Whisky all right?' She headed towards what he presumed was the kitchen, not waiting for a reply.

The apartment must have taken up the whole of the top floor of the building. She had furnished the place simply but elegantly. All the furniture was oriental but bore the stamp of quality. The pictures adorning the walls were mostly of pastoral scenes, bringing a touch of the cool European countryside into the heart of hot, steamy Asia. Rows of books filled the shelves of a mahogany dresser and a set of silver-framed photographs arranged in a sweeping crescent took pride of place on a heavy sideboard. Through the blinds he could see into the windows of the other shophouses with their basic utilitarian furnishings. Evelyn's flat seemed opulent by comparison.

She returned and handed him a tumbler containing a generous measure. She clinked her glass against his. 'Cheers.'

He wasn't sure what to say next. It had been a long time since he had been alone with a woman like this. Fortunately, she broke the silence.

'So, tell me more about the mysterious Inspector Betancourt.'

'Mysterious? I'm the least mysterious person there is.'

'I disagree. A person can never hide their eyes. You affect this world-weary outlook but those eyes of yours never stop moving. They take in everything.'

'Just naturally curious, I suppose.'

And so it began, hesitantly at first, but the more he told her, the more he wanted to tell her, until he found himself pouring out his past to this woman he hardly knew but whom he found strangely beguiling. It was as though he could finally remove his finger from a dam, the pressure of which he had been resisting for too long. He told her about his upbringing. About Theresa and how she'd stepped in when his mother had left in search of her trumpeter; about how pleased she'd been when he'd earned a scholarship to attend St Joseph's Institution, the best Catholic school in the city; and about how she'd hoped he'd become an engineer and join the Public Works Department; about how he could tell she was disappointed when he'd announced he'd signed up to join the Police Force but had a put a brave face on it. But mostly, he spoke about Anna – how they'd met, their life together, the little house at Pearl's Hill, and their precious Lucia.

'And then she was gone.' He was quiet for a moment. 'She came into the station one morning. She worried I didn't eat properly, so she often stopped by with food. Lucia had a dance lesson, out Katong way. Anna said they would take the bus. I had a car. I said she should take that. It was lying idle and Manniam, the driver, would be glad of the activity. That would be perfect, she said. She had something she needed to take care of while Lucia practised. A couple of hours later, the dance teacher called the station, asking when someone would be coming to collect Lucia. I said Anna must have been delayed and would be along shortly. Then word came through there had been an accident – a car had left the highway on Keppel Road. I didn't put the two things together at first; it was miles from the church hall in Katong where she'd left Lucia.'

He paused and looked away, trying once again to make sense of what had happened.

'The car had been smashed in down one side. Something had hit them hard enough to cause the vehicle to cross the verge and end up in the sea. Manniam's fingers were still gripped around the steering wheel. He must have been killed instantly.

'And Anna?' Evelyn's voice was soft.

'There was no trace of her.'

A lemon-coloured gecko watched them from its gravity-defying viewpoint on the ceiling. They said nothing for a while. There didn't seem to be anything to say.

He took another swallow of whisky. 'It was my fault.'

'You can't blame yourself for letting your wife use the car.'

'It's not that.' He told her about the secret society and the warning Anna had received. 'If I'd heeded them, my daughter would still have her mother.'

'Oh, God, Max. Perhaps there was some other explanation. You can't go through life thinking you were to blame. These people, they're unpredictable. I know, I have some experience of them myself.'

He thought of the girls sleeping on cots on the floor below, and the risk Evelyn took by harbouring them. 'I'm sure you do.'

He peered into the bottom of his glass. 'Sorry. I didn't intend for all that to come out. I should be going.'

'No, stay,' she said. She pinched a pleat of her dress between finger and thumb and lifted it an inch. 'I'm not used to wearing such frippery so, if you don't mind fixing yourself another drink, I'd like to change. Get one for me too. I've left the whisky on the sideboard. The ice has probably melted. You'll find more in the refrigerator.'

When she'd disappeared, he picked up the glasses and went to the sideboard to find the whisky. He gazed at the row of photographs. Most were of Evelyn with one or more women taken at picnics or trips to the beach. One woman in particular appeared in two or three of the pictures. Her face was vaguely familiar. The backgrounds were all rolling fields and distant cliffs. England, he presumed. He moved from the sideboard to the bookcase and took down a newish-looking volume, opening it at the bookplate. An inscription read: *To my darling E, Happy Birthday from your loving K.* It was dated June of that year.

Evelyn took the book from his hand. 'My sister. That's her.' She pointed to the familiar-looking face in the photograph.

She'd changed into a red brocade pyjama suit and her feet were bare, which explained why he hadn't heard her approach. She sat down again on the sofa and this time he sat next to her.

'She's much younger than me. She fell in with a bad crowd. The usual thing – naïve girl meets charismatic man. He promises her the earth, she believes him.' Evelyn paused and looked him in the eye. 'Have you heard of the white slave trade?'

He studied her for signs she might be joking, but there were none. 'I've heard of it, of course, mostly in films, but I always thought it a myth.'

'Think again. This man – his name was Hooper – convinced Kitty to run away with him. I had no idea she was planning it. He took her on a boat to Shanghai where he handed her over to a powerful man called Kanai. Hooper was a professional procurer. Kanai liked young European women, especially young English women, and Kitty was just his type. When I discovered what had happened, I travelled to Shanghai and found her. I demanded Kanai let Kitty go. He told me she was his property and he had no intention of giving her up. *His property!*' Evelyn's face flushed with anger at the recollection. 'I said I wanted to see her, so he had one of his bodyguards take me. She had her own chamber – silk cushions, tapestries on the walls – she was obviously a favourite. When I found her, she was deeply asleep. I begged the man to leave us, just for a few minutes. I managed to wake her, but she didn't recognise me. I'd treated enough addicts to know the signs. She was stupefied with opium. When I returned, Kanai said he'd reconsidered and that we might be able to come to an arrangement, after all.'

'He wanted to take you as a concubine, too?'

'What?' She stared at him, her brows knitted in puzzlement. 'Good God, no. I would have been far too old for him. He needed a doctor to look after the women in his brothels.'

'I wouldn't have thought men like that would care about the welfare of their women.'

'They were little more than livestock to him, but just as a farmer looks after his animals, Kanai knew a healthy woman was a productive one.'

'So, you set up a practice there in Shanghai, like the one here?'

She nodded. 'And in return, he allowed Kitty to come with me. A local convent helped me take care of her. The nuns had treated lots of women in her position. Gradually, she grew stronger, and when I judged she was ready to leave the sisters' care, I asked Kanai to let us both leave Shanghai. I didn't think there was the remotest chance of him agreeing, but to my surprise, he said he would consider my request. It took all my savings, but he agreed to let us go.'

'That was when you came here?'

'I knew some people already and Kitty wasn't ready to go back to England.'

'And now?'

'Now Kitty is settled here, and besides, I really care about these girls − sometimes I'm all they have. I feel like I'm doing something genuinely good.'

'Where is Kitty now?'

'She missed life in the convent. The nuns had a profound effect on her, so I asked one of the sisters in Shanghai to write her a reference. With that, I found a position for her here. She's safe and healthy and happy... or at least as happy as she will ever be.'

They talked and talked. He'd forgotten how it felt, just being with someone like this, the intimacy of hearing another person sharing their hopes and dreams. He was also more than a little drunk.

After a while he rose to his feet uncertainly. 'It's late. I really have to go.'

She stood too and they faced each other, close enough for him to feel the whisper of her breath on his face.

'Must you?'

He looked into her eyes, feeling torn. Then he pushed her away, harder than he'd intended. 'I'm sorry. I can't do this.'

He fled the apartment, accidentally knocking into a side table and smashing a cut-glass flower vase. He'd apologise later. If there was a later. Halfway down the stairs, he missed a step, lost his balance and ricocheted off the timber wall as he attempted to steady himself. Evelyn's voice called out after him, but he carried on. When he reached the floor below, an anxious face appeared from behind the door. The girl pulled her sheet tight about her when she saw who it was, to protect her modesty. He didn't have time to dwell on the irony of her actions given what she did for a living, but continued to descend the steps until he was outside.

The door slammed behind him, alerting the street to his departure. Chinks of light appeared as blinds were pulled aside and inquisitive eyes tracked his progress. He slowed down when he reached Victoria Street and stood for a moment, unsure what to do next. A rickshaw coolie, eager for a fare, spotted him and pulled his machine round in a wide arc across the road, drawing an irate chorus of horns. Betancourt climbed in without thinking.

'Where to?'

'Just go.'

He sat back in the ancient seat, shifting to avoid the springs that pressed into his legs through the worn covering. He willed the coolie to put as much distance between them and Holloway Lane as he could, as quickly as possible.

They reached the junction with Bras Basah Road, a stone's throw from Raffles Hotel where he'd met Evelyn just two nights previously. It now felt like another lifetime. The rickshaw coolie turned to him and awaited further directions. Betancourt gave him the address. When they reached home, he climbed from the carriage and handed the man a banknote. The coolie, used to receiving coins for his effort, thanked Betancourt for his generosity with a delighted grin, and padded off.

Duxton Hill was quiet. The shutters that fronted Mr Tan's *kopi tiam* were secured and bolted. Lights still burned in the *pei pei* house next door, but business was done for the evening. The girls crowded around a felt-topped table, shrieking and cursing at the turn of the cards as they gambled away their wages. The only place that was still open was the bar opposite, its illuminated Tiger sign twinkling a forlorn welcome.

His reaction to Evelyn's advance had shocked and confused him, and God only knows what she'd made of his reaction. He needed to rest.

He unlocked the door and was about to push it open when a sixth sense made him stop. Something was wrong. Then he spotted it. The piece of cotton he'd planted between the hinge of the door and the jamb lay coiled on the floor. Someone had been into his flat. Might still be in there. Mr Tan had a key for emergencies, but in all the time Betancourt had rented the place, he'd never known his landlord use it. He put his ear to the door but couldn't hear anything. Turning the handle as slowly and as quietly as he could, he opened the door and slipped inside. He stopped again and listened. Still nothing. The door to the living room was open. There was enough light from the street outside for him to make out the furniture. He watched, looking for movement. Bedroom next. It was pitch dark here, at the back of the house, so he reached for the light. Holding his breath, he flipped the switch. Nothing untoward in there either.

He began to relax. Perhaps the cotton had simply become

dislodged. He was distracted and had assumed the worst. He'd check the kitchen, just to make sure. The door was slightly ajar, so he pushed it open and took a step forward. Before he could set foot inside the room, the door rebounded back towards him and caught him full in the face. He staggered back into the hallway, yelping at the pain. A figure dressed from head to foot in black barged past him and sprinted for the stairs. Betancourt gave chase but by the time he reached the street, his assailant had disappeared.

He trudged back up the staircase, blood streaming from his nose. He checked to see if it was broken, but it seemed intact. He put on all the lights and the flat seemed instantly less threatening.

Envelopes lay strewn across the kitchen floor. He must have interrupted the intruder rifling through the drawer where he kept the bills. He was welcome to them. But then he remembered, too late, there had been more than just bills in the drawer. When he'd come home to change for Marjorie's garden party, he'd stowed the bond at the bottom of the drawer, under the bills, intending to take it into the station when he was next in. He searched through the few letters that remained in the drawer and then the ones that had been cast onto the floor. The bond was gone.

By itself, the bond was worth very little. But this hadn't been a simple robbery. Someone had been very keen to get hold of that bond for reasons other than its intrinsic value, and Betancourt knew who. When he'd shown it to Guthrie that morning, he'd been desperate to get his hands on it. It wouldn't have been Guthrie himself who'd broken in, it would have been one of Jin's goons. It must have been Jin whom Guthrie had been speaking to on the telephone while he'd listened at the door.

He cursed himself for his stupidity. Now all he had was

what he'd written in his notebook. He could only imagine what Bonham would say to him when he broke the news of this latest development.

He uncoupled the telephone receiver from the base unit and draped a blanket over the whole thing. He was exhausted and needed sleep, and he didn't want to be woken. If anyone wanted him, they'd have to wait until the morning.

Chapter Twenty

A black-liveried bus stood waiting on Empress Place, smoke belching from its exhaust. When Betancourt entered the foyer, the desk sergeant was handing out small round riot shields to a queue of nervous-looking constables.

'What's going on?'

'More trouble at the docks. It's getting ugly.'

'Last time I checked, I was still in charge. Why wasn't I told?'

'I tried calling you, but the operator couldn't get through.'

Damn. He'd forgotten to put the receiver back on the hook. 'There must be a problem with the line. I'll get it checked. How many men have you rounded up?'

'Six here, and another six already down there on customs duty. I rang and told them to stop what they were doing and meet us at the entrance.'

'Better put another box of shields and truncheons on the bus. The men down there won't have anything. How bad does it sound?'

'Worst it's been, apparently.'

'I'll go down myself. Tell the bus to wait for me.' Betancourt went to his room. He rarely carried a gun – he loathed the things – but if the situation was bad enough to warrant riot gear being issued, it might be prudent if he was armed, too. He retrieved his Webley pistol from the cupboard in which it was stored. He checked it, filled it with ammunition, and went to join the waiting transport.

Traffic queued back along the approach ways to the docks and the drivers were out of their trucks, remonstrating with the protesters. The angry dissonance of horns filled the air. Normally, the demonstrations were noisy but peaceful; today there was a palpable air of menace. The main group of protesters, usually fifty or so strong, had swelled to several hundred, and they blocked the gangways, waving their placards. Like last time, a second group had formed, but unlike the previous encounter, this was no group of building-site coolies brought in for nuisance value. This lot looked like professionals, mean and menacing, and they were armed. Wooden staves, broken on an angle to reveal wicked points; lengths of angle iron; the odd broken beer bottle; a machete or two. A few yards back from the line of confrontation, standing on a crate, was the conductor orchestrating the ugliness. It was Jin: Sleeping Tiger and now *agent provocateur*.

His eyes met Betancourt's. Jin gave urgent instructions to one of his lieutenants, who waded into the group of agitators, shouting and cajoling the men to press forward. If they got much more hostile, Betancourt's small posse would struggle to keep the peace. Scanning the crowd, he spotted Sergeant Quek. He ran over and pointed to the godowns. 'Find a phone. Call Headquarters. Tell them we need backup. Immediately!'

Betancourt looked back to where Jin had stood just moments before. He was gone. Two of his men were lugging the crate he'd been standing on. The box looked to be heavy, the men struggling to keep it clear of the ground. One of them, unable to hold onto the rope handle any longer, stumbled and dropped his end of the box. Liquid seeped out onto the hot tarmac from between the wooden slats. What the hell were they carrying?

Skirmishes broke out. Betancourt shouted to his men to form a line between the two factions and they linked arms, riot shields and truncheons raised. But these were customs officers. Usually they checked shipping documents and, judging by the looks of fear on many of the faces, he wasn't sure how long they would last if this turned into a full-blown riot. It would take at least fifteen minutes for reinforcements from Central to be mustered and dispatched. If he could keep the protesters apart that long, he might defuse this without too much bloodshed.

Yells rang out from behind him and people spilled from the godowns. He saw now what the two men had been carrying. One of them yanked bottles from the crate as fast he could while the other brandished a cigarette lighter. The bottles were filled with a pale liquid and long cotton wicks hung from the necks. Petrol bombs. They hurled salvo after salvo towards the godowns, apparently without favour, seemingly intent on doing as much random damage as they could. Fortunately, their aim was poor and most of the bombs fell short of their targets. Betancourt pulled out his revolver and yelled at them to stop. He loosed off two air-shots, and the arsonists abandoned their deadly stash and scampered away.

At least one bottle had found its target. Tongues of flame licked the doorframe of a godown, and thick plumes of viscous black smoke spewed out into the sky from somewhere in the roof. The sound of bells drew nearer. The fire engines would be here soon, and police reinforcements wouldn't be far behind. The only small chink of light was that the fires had caused the protests to disperse. He redeployed his small force to shepherd the crowds away to safety.

The building that was on fire was the Clément godown. Where else would it have been?

'You stink.'

He sniffed the sleeve of his jacket. 'Smoke.' He told Marjorie about the disturbance at the dock.

'That doesn't sound good. Was anyone hurt?'

'Only in the pocket. The Cléments' godown suffered a fair bit of damage.'

Pascal had turned up before Betancourt had left. He'd expected to see anger in his brother-in-law, possibly to hear demands for reprisals, but Pascal had seemed almost bereft. Betancourt couldn't understand it at first. No one had been hurt and the damage to the building itself was less severe than might at first have been imagined. It was only the contents that had been lost and those would be covered by insurance. He pointed all that out, but it had done nothing to lighten Pascal's mood. Then it had dawned on him: the cargo hadn't been insured. It had been due to leave on the first ship out, in a few days from now, and Pascal must have skimped on the premiums. He liked his brother-in-law, but he was a fool – a boy playing a man's game, and none too successfully, it seemed.

'Is Bonham in? I have to bite the bullet sometime.'

'No, he's up at Government House. Meeting Ray, as it happens. The Governor is looking for an update on the bond you found. He said I was to make sure you checked it into the evidence room when you were next in. He wants it tested for fingerprints.'

'Ah. Small problem there. I don't have it.' He explained about his midnight intruder.

'You are in the wars, aren't you? Are you all right?'

'I'm fine. I need to go home and get cleaned up. Tell Bonham I'll be back in later to file my report on this morning. And probably best if you don't mention the bond thing. Don't want to get his blood pressure up any more than it already is.'

———

He washed and changed and was thinking about stopping in at Mr Tan's for sustenance when the phone rang. It was Evelyn.

'They're burying Akiko this afternoon. Two o'clock at the Japanese Cemetery.'

'But her death hasn't been signed off by the coroner.'

'Apparently it has. Anyway, I haven't got all day. I assumed you'd want to know.'

'Listen, I want to—'

The line was dead. She'd hung up. If she'd sounded frosty, he could hardly blame her.

Chapter Twenty-One

The rumbling roar from Alex's engine, normally so noticeable as it cannoned off the walls of the city buildings, settled into a deep hum as Betancourt left the metropolis behind. He drove northwards on Serangoon Road and soon the rows of shophouses and offices gave way to stands of rubber trees interspersed with the occasional fishpond. A coolie on an ancient bicycle rang his bell and waved. In the field opposite, a buffalo raised its great grey head to see what was going on. Betancourt was a city man at heart. He preferred the anonymity of the noise and the bustle and the multi-coloured mass of humanity. No one paid him any attention in the city; at least not when he was off duty. Out here in the countryside everyone seemed to notice him.

A towering tembusu tree kept silent watch over the gates to the graveyard. The only shady spot was taken by a battered old flat-bed truck bearing the name of the cemetery. A man wearing a simple uniform of black tunic and grey trousers sorted spades and forks and coils of ropes strewn across the bed of the truck. A gravedigger. Betancourt pulled Alex onto her stand in a small square of residual shade offered by the truck. The man smiled and nodded, and Betancourt raised a hand in acknowledgement.

Inside the gardens, elaborate tombs styled with slender fluted columns and replicas of Japanese deities paid homage to the lives of wealthy entrepreneurs and other men of high social standing. A small crowd had gathered on the far side of the cemetery where the monuments gave way to simple stone markers. He followed the maze of paths until he reached them. Judging by the names on the adjacent plots, this area of the cemetery was dedicated to women. A bare patch of ground, still too raw to have been covered by the thick carpet of couch grass growing elsewhere, showed where one of Akiko's sisters had recently been interred.

Mei, looking more like a schoolmistress than a nightclub hostess in a severe black jacket and skirt, stood close to the graveside, weeping silently into a small, embroidered handkerchief. Ruby patted her arm, a gesture of comfort and solidarity. Belle spoke quietly to the priest. Behind her were three women dressed in *mofuku* – black funeral kimonos – workers from the *suteretsu*, he guessed. For one so popular in life, Akiko had precious few friends in death. She might not have led a blameless life, but she hadn't deserved what happened to her. She'd died alone on his watch and her death had touched him. That her life had touched these other people too was somehow comforting.

To Mei's left stood Evelyn. He had to speak to her – he owed her that after his behaviour the night before. He moved towards her. They both stood staring ahead, refusing to be the first to look the other in the eye. She broke first and jabbed him in the ribs with her elbow. It hurt, and he turned to express his displeasure. She gave him a malevolent look, a simultaneous contortion of her mouth and eyebrows.

'What was that for?'

'Your helmet.'

'What about it?'

'Take it off.'

He hastily removed the offending headgear.

'Why didn't you tell me?'

'I just did.'

'Evelyn, about last night—'

'Shut up. It's starting.'

The priest adjusted his robes, cleared his throat, and censured the pair of them with a grim look. Apparently satisfied their conversation was complete, he began to chant a *sutra*, a prayer for Akiko's soul.

It was the first Japanese burial Betancourt had attended and he'd no idea what was expected of him as an observer. His experience of funerals had been limited to the theatrical protocols of the Roman Catholic church interspersed with the odd service for a departed colleague involving the peculiar brand of hellfire and brimstone the Church of Scotland seemed to revel in. Although he didn't understand a word the priest said, he negotiated the rest of the service without putting his foot in anything.

When it was over and Akiko's remains had been consigned to the damp earth, the group of mourners fell into little groups. Handkerchiefs were passed around, consoling hands were placed on shoulders, and quiet words of shared sorrow were passed.

He sensed a presence at his elbow. It was Belle. 'I tried to call you earlier at the station, but they said you were away on police business. Does attending the burial of a *karayuki-san* count as official business now?'

'I came to pay my respects. What was it you wanted?'

'The other day – I told you about those Japanese girls coming into the *suteretsu*.'

'I remember.'

'A new shipment arrived this morning. A lot of girls.'

Damn. How were they slipping these women in right under his nose? He'd redoubled the checks on ships. Today was unfortunate timing. All his men had been called to the disturbances at the yard.

'Let me know if you hear anything else.'

'And you'll remember your part of the bargain, won't you, Inspector?'

She meant protection. He refrained from mentioning he hadn't actually promised anything, now wasn't the time, and limited his response to a non-committal grunt.

At the cemetery gate, he found Evelyn and Mei waiting for the others to join them.

'Can I have a word?'

Evelyn handed her parasol to Mei and told her, to wait outside. 'I'll see you at the bus stop.'

When the other woman had gone, Evelyn folded her arms across her chest and looked at Betancourt. 'Well?'

'If I'd known you were coming, I'd have suggested joining you.'

'If I'd known you were coming, I'd have told you not to bother.'

'Evelyn, what the hell is going on?'

She stared at him. 'I beg your pardon? You storm off without having the decency to tell me why, and now you're demanding to know what's wrong? You have some cheek.'

'What? No, I don't mean that. I mean this. The funeral. How can she be buried without an inquest?'

'I've no idea. Although I admit I was surprised when I heard that it had all been signed off.'

'But there's been no inquiry. Who dealt with it?'

'Ferguson, the chief coroner. Apparently, he decided an inquiry wasn't required. The verdict was suicide. I saw the paperwork. An undertaker came for the body and I had no choice but to release it. I assumed you were aware of all this.'

To sign off the death of a prostitute without an inquiry was in direct contravention of the law. As the massed forces of the establishment had insisted that Akiko was a *karayuki-san*, there should have been an inquest. But Ferguson was old school. If someone wanted things pushed through quickly with no questions asked, he was as good a choice as any.

'Did the undertaker say who'd arranged the funeral?'

'He didn't offer the information, and I didn't think to ask. Now, if you'll excuse me.'

Something stank, but it was clear Evelyn was as much in the dark as he was. He'd speak to Bonham about Ferguson when he returned to the city.

'It's peaceful here, don't you think?'

He started. It was the priest speaking to him. Betancourt introduced himself and the priest bowed.

'My name is Zenzo. Let us walk. Do you know the history of this garden, Inspector-san? Some forty years ago, three brothel owners secured this part of the cemetery from the colonial administration. They wanted to provide a place of rest for the *karayuki-san*.'

Betancourt realised he knew little about the cemetery and nothing of its origins. It was just one of those places that had always been there.

'A question, Zenzo-san. Who pays for the burial of someone like Miss Sakai?'

'The plots are paid for, but we rely on donations to pay for the funeral ceremonies and the upkeep of the graves. Our funds are limited, so I was pleased a benefactor could cover the costs for Miss Sakai's funeral.'

'That was most generous. May I ask the name of this benefactor?'

'I don't deal with that side of things myself, but I believe the donation was anonymous. Is it important?'

'It could be.'

'Then I will try to find out and let you know.'

He took the card Betancourt offered him.

'If you don't mind my saying so, you surprise me, Inspector. It isn't often a British policeman pays much attention to the fate of a *karayuki-san*.' He held up a hand to stay Betancourt's protest. 'Even one who is not a Britisher himself. I wish you good fortune in finding justice for the death of our sister.'

Betancourt trudged off to recover Alex from where he'd left her. The truck that had earlier provided a scrap of shade was nowhere to be seen and he had to ease himself gently into the saddle as the heat from the leather burned through the thin fabric of his suit. He kicked the starter pedal until the engine roared into life and turned the wheel towards Yio Chu Kang Road and the silhouette of the Downtown Core beyond.

The group of mourners had converged by the side of the road, awaiting the city-bound bus. Evelyn glared at him as he sped past. He didn't look back. Tomorrow, he'd track her down and try to make peace with her. Fleeting images of green fields and tree-lined properties sped into his vision and just as quickly disappeared again. He settled in to enjoy the rest of the drive.

A tooting horn interrupted his brooding. Glancing over his shoulder, he caught sight of the truck from the cemetery.

He was in no hurry and wasn't in the mood to speed up, so he stuck out an arm and waved at the vehicle to overtake. The noise of the truck's engine grew louder. There was nothing ahead of them on either side of the road; if the driver was in such a hurry, why didn't he pass? Betancourt waved again, this time with more emphasis, but the truck sat resolutely on his rear wheel. He pulled in as close as he could to the grass verge separating the road from the storm ditch and waved a third time. A rush of hot air engulfed him as the truck pulled alongside. He eased back on the throttle to let the gravedigger pass and readied himself to launch a tirade, but before he had a chance to form the words, the man wrenched the wheel to his left. There was a screech of metal on metal and Alex left the road, engine howling as the wheels lost traction, and hurtled towards the ditch.

He lifted his head and tried to make sense of where he was. His sight was blurred, but he detected the tangled mesh of metal that had been the motorcycle twenty yards behind him. A wet warmth crept up his arm. He touched his sleeve tentatively and was relieved to find it was just muddy water. He ran a hand along each of his limbs in turn. Everything that had been there before appeared still to be there now. He attempted to stand, but a searing stab of pain shot up his right leg and he fell back into the rivulet of swampy sludge at the bottom of the drain.

Up ahead, the truck had pulled off the road, and he made out the figure of the truck driver as he approached. The time for recriminations would come later. For now, he just needed to get back up to the roadside. He extended an arm towards the man. 'Help me.'

The man bent over until his face was close enough that even with his befogged vision Betancourt could discern his features. 'Take this as a warning, Inspector. Stay away from the *suteretsu*. There is nothing there for you. Forget what you have learned, if you know what's good for you. You already lost your wife. It would be a shame if you were to lose your daughter as well.'

Enraged, Betancourt tried to grab at the man's leg, but his reactions were dulled and he clawed at thin air. His assailant's face slipped out of focus as a wave of nausea engulfed him and his head slumped back into the mud. The last thing he remembered was the man's boot, crashing into his face.

Chapter Twenty-Two

The smell of TCP conjured up images of playground fights and skinned knees. He twisted, but something held him in place. His fingers touched crisply starched linen, and he realised his restraints were nothing more than bedsheets, tucked in so tightly he couldn't move.

The face of a young nurse swam into view. According to her badge, her name was Vanda. She leaned over him.

'Good. You're awake.'

He raised a hand to his face and winced as he pressed the swollen flesh. He tried to speak, but his mouth was bone dry and the thick words were unintelligible. Vanda lifted a glass with a drinking straw in it to his mouth.

'Try to sip some water.'

He drank half a glass, and the words came easier. 'What happened?'

'We were hoping you might tell us.'

Memories drifted back: the motorcycle, the truck, the fake gravedigger and his boot...

'How did I get here?'

'In an ambulance. We think you must have hit a stone or something and left the road. You were very lucky. The damage from the crash isn't too bad, mostly bruising, but you could have drowned in the ditch.'

Betancourt tried to shake his head. He wanted to explain he hadn't hit a stone, or anything else for that matter, but it would have to wait, the pain was too great. His head fell back onto the pillow.

Vanda had said "we".

'Who are *we*? How do you know all this?'

'Dr Trevose told me.'

'Evelyn's here?'

Vanda shook her head. 'Gone.'

'Gone where?'

She shrugged. 'Maybe home? She said you'd be safe now, so she left.' Vanda smiled. 'I think she likes you.'

Betancourt tried to speak again, but the nurse hushed him and fussed with his pillows. 'Plenty of time to talk later. Now you must sleep.' She took a syringe from a bowl on a pedestal next to the bed and he felt a prick in his arm. A blissful curtain descended over his brain, and he surrendered.

When he opened his eyes again, the sun was streaming in through the blinds. The clock on the wall said 8.30. He'd been asleep for over twelve hours. He ran a hand gingerly over the stubble on his chin. God only knew what he must look like. He noticed movement at the edge of his vision, so he raised himself onto his elbows and tried to focus. He had a visitor. 'How long have you been here?'

'All night. I wanted to make sure you were all right.' Evelyn said this as though it were the most natural thing in the world.

'The nurse said you brought me in.'

'We were on the bus. Ruby spotted your motorcycle lying on the verge. I told the bus driver to pull in. He didn't want to because there was no stop, but I said I was a doctor and this was an emergency. Belle went to find the nearest farm and call for an ambulance. I accompanied you here and made sure you were settled in and then I went home to clean up.'

'Thank you.'

'I'm a doctor. It's what I do.'

'Sit up with patients all night?'

A faint blush coloured her cheeks. 'It doesn't mean I'm not still mad as hell with you.'

'Any chance we can call a temporary truce?'

She didn't say yes, but she didn't say no either.

Something was niggling away at the back of his mind. Something she'd said. What was it?

'Tell me again. You were on the bus.'

'Oh, for God's sake. Is your ego so fragile that you need to hear tales of women flocking to your rescue?'

It wasn't an unpleasant thought... 'No, it's not that. Something you said made me remember a dream I had last night and now it's gone again.'

Evelyn recapped. 'Bus... Ruby... motorcycle – death-trap, while we're on the subject – bus driver... Belle... ambulance—'

'Belle! Belle said something to me after the funeral.' What the hell was it? Something about the girls... He had it. He pulled back the sheets and dragged his legs over the side of the bed.

'What do you think you're doing?'

'What does it look like? I'm getting up. Give me a hand.'

'You've had a bang on the head. You may have concussion. Speaking as your doctor—'

'Stop fussing and hand me my clothes.'

Evelyn retrieved them from the locker where they'd been placed the night before. 'It would be a courtesy at least to let the nursing staff know you're leaving.' He started to protest. 'Don't worry, I'll do it. I presume you're capable of dressing yourself?'

He winced as he pulled the hospital gown over his head. His ribs had been strapped and an angry damson bruise spread outwards from the margins of the bandage. He struggled into shirt, trousers, socks and shoes, and set off in search of the exit.

'I told him he should stay longer.' Evelyn gave the nurse-in-charge on the reception desk a *what-can-you-do?* look.

'I'll be fine. Just give me some aspirin.' Betancourt's eyes cast about the desk. Surely the hospital had supplies of freely available painkillers for departing patients to take handfuls of.

'At least wait until the resident has seen you.'

The argument continued for a few more minutes until Evelyn convinced the nurse to let him leave if he agreed to absolve the hospital of responsibility for any consequences.

They stood by the entrance, waiting for the nurse to return with the paperwork.

'So, what was this eureka moment you had earlier?'

'Belle told me there had been a new shipment of Japanese women yesterday. My men might have caught it, if they hadn't all been down at the dockyard breaking up a disturbance. There was a similar protest a couple of weeks ago, the same day the previous shipment of women arrived.'

'Coincidence?'

Reluctantly, he had to admit she may have a point, and felt his earlier enthusiasm evaporate. 'But there have been more and more of these disturbances in the last six months. If I can find out when the shipments of Japanese women arrived, I can compare them to the dates on which the disturbances took place and find out if there's a clear pattern.'

'And if there is, what then?'

She had another good point. What indeed? 'Do you have a pen and something to write on?' He scribbled a few words on the back of the envelope she gave him.

'How did you get here?'

'I caught the bus.'

'Let's try to find a taxi.'

Just then, a long black car pulled up outside the entrance to the hospital and two men stepped out. They wore nondescript suits, not unlike Betancourt's own. One of them was young, with a shock of red hair. Betancourt knew him from his detective days; his name was Henderson. He'd moved to Special Branch. He didn't recognise the other man who was older and an altogether nastier-looking specimen. He had a wall-eye and a squint, and when he spoke to Betancourt, he appeared to be addressing someone off in the distance.

'Come with me, Inspector.' He took Betancourt firmly by the arm, causing him to wince with pain.

Betancourt tried to wrest himself free, but in his current state he was no match for the man's iron grip.

'What the hell is going on?' Evelyn tried to remonstrate but she was brushed aside.

Wall-eye held open the rear door of the car, staring straight ahead, or at least his own personal approximation of straight ahead. 'Get in.'

Betancourt turned to Evelyn. 'It doesn't appear as though I have much choice.'

'I'll call Bonham.'

'There's no point.' He guessed that Special Branch wouldn't have forcibly detained him without having at least communicated their intent first, so Bonham would already be aware. If it came to a choice between Betancourt and Special Branch, he knew which side the kow-towing Bonham would choose. He folded the piece of paper and pressed it into her hand. 'Take this to Belle. Number twenty-four Bugis Street. Red door. You can't miss it. Get her to give you the dates on which the other Japanese women arrived. When I've got rid of this lot, I'll compare her dates with our records.' He caught the concern in her eyes. 'Don't worry, I've dealt with worse than this before and survived.'

He'd lost count of the number of times he'd been inside police headquarters, but he'd never had reason to visit the top floor where the Inspector General's office was located. His erstwhile guardians accompanied him as far as a wood-panelled reception area before leaving him with a young sub-inspector, whom he took to be Onraet's private assistant. The man looked at him askance. Betancourt didn't blame him. He'd caught a quick look at his face in the bathroom mirror earlier that morning, and with the bruises, swelling, and his generally unkempt appearance, he'd have excused the man for thinking he was some vagrant a watchman had found outside, in the bushes, sizing up the building. After scrutinising Betancourt's warrant card and double-checking a desk diary to corroborate the name, the man opened the door behind him and announced the visitor.

The room into which he was admitted was smaller than he'd imagined. The modern blondwood furnishings and paintings of polo ponies were neither arrestingly striking nor offensively bland, and the overall impression was one of function rather than form. An office that could have belonged to the manager of a middle-ranking import and export firm.

Onraet himself sat behind a metal-and-glass desk. He had the decency to stand when Betancourt entered the room.

'Ah, Inspector. My apologies for all the drama. They tell me you've been in the wars and now I can see the evidence for myself.'

Onraet had company. In the visitor's chair sat Ray French. 'Raymond is here representing Government House.' French greeted him with a terse nod and averted his eyes. Further conversation was apparently unwelcome. Whatever Betancourt had been brought here for it wasn't a social call.

Occupying a low armchair opposite French was a short, spare man with a mane of fair wavy hair, swept to one side. He was casually dressed in cotton shirt and baggy flannels as though he'd been ready for an afternoon's cricket at the Padang and had been diverted. Onraet introduced the man simply as Montgomerie.

Betancourt took the remaining seat.

'Refreshment, Inspector? Tea, perhaps? Although, judging by your bruises, perhaps something stronger wouldn't go amiss.'

'Tea is fine. And painkillers, if you have them.' The assistant didn't need the order to be reconfirmed and scuttled off in search of a tea caddy and the first-aid box. 'What wouldn't go amiss is an explanation of why you've brought me here.'

When tea had been served and codeine swallowed, Onraet got down to business. 'I hope I don't have to overemphasise this, but anything you hear today must remain strictly – how do our friends in the legal profession put it? – *sub rosa*.'

Betancourt assumed that meant secret and nodded to show he understood.

Onraet continued. 'The other day, at the French residence, you told me what you'd uncovered about the death of the Japanese woman.'

'Miss Sakai.'

Onraet acknowledged his point. 'About the death of Miss Sakai. I'd like you to repeat to Mr Montgomerie what you told me. Speak freely, there are no secrets here.'

When Onraet said the words "no secrets", he stared directly into Betancourt's eyes. He was trying to pass on a message. Whatever was going on here, Onraet didn't appear to be a wholly willing participant and Ray's muted presence suggested that Government House might not be entirely happy either. There were very few people who could exert the kind of power that allowed them to use the Inspector General of the Straits Settlements Police as a go-between, which meant that Montgomerie had to be secret service. Betancourt quickly weighed up what he should say and what he should omit. Keeping it simple and telling the truth usually worked. Though not necessarily all the truth.

'Last week, a dockworker found the body of a Japanese woman at the docks. I attended the scene. The body had been arranged to make it look like suicide.'

When Montgomerie spoke, it was in an authoritative tone that gave the lie to his foppish appearance. It was that of someone used to commanding, not being commanded. 'If the evidence suggested suicide, why did you continue to investigate?'

'I said, "the body had been arranged to make it look like suicide".'

'Very well, what made you decide it wasn't in fact a suicide?'

'The post-mortem established the wounds were inconsistent with self-inflicted ones. That, and the absence of blood, led me to conclude Miss Sakai had been killed, and afterwards the body placed where it was found.'

'You're referring to the findings of Dr Trevose, the locum police surgeon?'

Montgomerie had been well briefed. Extreme caution was required here. 'My first task was to identify the victim. She had a distinctive tattoo. I showed a picture of this to a local artist, but he didn't recognise the work, so I tried the *suteretsu* – that's the Japanese red-light district.'

'I'm perfectly well aware of what it is. Go on.'

'One of my contacts there recognised Miss Sakai from her photograph. She also told me a new gang was working the area, and that it was trafficking women. Miss Sakai had been seen in the presence of one of the gang leaders.'

'The Sleeping Tigers.'

'That was the name that was mentioned to me, yes.'

There was a lull in the conversation as Montgomerie pondered something. 'Tell me, Inspector, during your investigation, did anyone mention the Gen'yōsha to you? Also known as the Dark Ocean Society?'

Betancourt frowned and shook his head. 'Another gang?'

Montgomerie tilted his head from side to side as if weighing up this interpretation. 'Yes and no. In their early days, perhaps, but they changed direction, at least publicly, to devote themselves to honouring and protecting the Emperor and his empire. In private, they were a group of high-ranking ex-army officers dedicated to military expansion and, ultimately, Japanese rule of all Asia. They primarily had designs on China and Korea and established a presence in both countries, helping dissidents and providing arms and training for terrorist attacks.'

Betancourt had heard rumours about such ultranationalist groups but as their reach didn't extend to Singapore, and they weren't involved in smuggling or trafficking or any of the other matters that filled his days, he'd paid scant attention to the stories. 'If their business is in China and Korea, what do these Dark Ocean characters have to do with us?'

'We're not sure. Perhaps nothing, but one of their *modi operandi* is to establish networks of brothels. As well as raising money, these are also used as rendezvous points for agents and to gather information for blackmail. The women they recruit are highly trained. There's even talk of a special academy where they're taught not only the art of seduction but how to extract secrets as well.'

'And you think the Sleeping Tigers are related to this Dark Ocean Society?'

'Before I heard your story, I'd have said no. There's no record of them operating this far south. Also, having a separate faction to do their dirty work doesn't fit the pattern, but who knows? Times change. Everything else you said sounds right: the brothels, the trafficking... If it is them, they'll be using a local agent and we need to find him.'

Should he mention Guthrie? As if reading his thoughts, Onraet gave a tiny shake of the head.

'I still don't understand. What is it you want me to do?'

'Do, Inspector? I want you to *do* precisely nothing. Special Branch, under my personal supervision, will pick up the investigation from here.'

Betancourt had vowed to find justice for Akiko. This was his case and there was no way he was letting some government agent take it away. He turned to Onraet, but the Inspector General's expression was inscrutable. If Montgomerie's interference was a slap in the face, he seemed to be taking it well. Betancourt made a mental note never to play cards with the man.

'That will be all, Inspector. I'll brief Assistant Commissioner Bonham and let him know you're being relieved of responsibility. As far as you're concerned, this case never happened. Are we clear?'

There was that look again. Onraet's words said one thing but his eyes said another. He was known to be a shrewd operator and Betancourt trusted him, so he simply nodded and left the room.

Chapter Twenty-Three

Betancourt barged open the doors to Bonham's office. The Assistant Commissioner and Marjorie were hunched over the desk, checking a list of figures.

'I need to talk to you. Now.'

'I don't doubt it.' Judging by his smug grin, Bonham seemed to be relishing the situation. He dismissed Marjorie, who gave Betancourt an anxious glance on her way past. 'I've just had the Inspector General on the phone.'

Onraet had wasted no time.

'What did he say?'

'That you'd been relieved of your duties regarding the murder of the Japanese woman, effective immediately.'

'And you're all right with that?'

'If you mean, am I happy to see cases being taken by Special Branch, then, no, I'm not all right with it, and neither is the Inspector General, but this man Montgomerie seems to be pulling the strings now. If you'd done as I instructed in the first place, then none of this would have happened.'

'Since when did Special Branch start giving the orders?'

'Montgomerie isn't Special Branch. He's Military Intelligence, works out of Shanghai. He's a ghost – comes and goes as he pleases. Anyway, none of that is your concern any longer. The question is, what do we do with you next?' Bonham wasn't mulling over the question on his own account; he was perfectly capable of coming up with ways to keep Betancourt busy. He wanted Betancourt to come up with a plan, so he'd have sufficient plausible deniability.

The riots and the trafficking had to be linked. It was as good a place as any to keep looking and Bonham would be none the wiser. 'If I'm off the murder, I need to devote all my attention to getting on top of the disturbances at the docks. If anyone asks, I'll tell them those were my orders.'

'Consider yourself so ordered. I'll call the Inspector General and let him know. In the meantime, what have you got on this afternoon?'

'Nothing in particular. Why?'

'Get yourself cleaned up and report to the Victoria Hall. I intend to ensure that Mr Mosley's visit goes off without incident and we don't give the press anything else to write about.'

A substantial crowd had gathered outside the Victoria Memorial Hall. A few distributed leaflets, and others carried hand-painted signs bearing messages like *Blackshirts Go Home* and *No to Tyrants*. The placards were waved feebly, accompanied by half-hearted boos, as if it really wasn't the done thing to be seen exhibiting such sentiments in public.

A phalanx of men identically dressed in black tunics, black trousers, and black belts fastened with broad square silver buckles, guarded the entrance to the theatre. These must be the infamous blackshirts Betancourt had read about.

They were a mixed bunch. The man closest to Betancourt looked to be about fifty. With a protuberant gut and a rasping asthmatic wheeze, he appeared patently unfit for any form of action. The one behind him was well over six feet, but probably didn't weigh more than his paunchy comrade, and his stick-thin limbs looked like they might snap if asked to cope with anything more than a stiffish breeze. If this was the pride of British Teutonia, perhaps the free world didn't have so much to fear after all.

A queue had formed and the audience was filing in. Betancourt stood at the side and waited until the final stragglers were being admitted before he moved forward. The corpulent little blackshirt took a half-step to his left, blocking his path. He stood on the bottom step of the entranceway, about six inches up, but was still unable to look Betancourt in the eye.

'British people only.'

Betancourt tried a placatory smile, but he was sure it came out as more of a grimace. 'That's fine, I'm a British subject.'

The man didn't blink. He was like a fat lizard, sitting on a rock, watching for insects. 'I meant *real* British people. Now hop it.' A few of his comrades shuffled their feet and puffed out their chests, presumably trying to look menacing, but failing miserably. Betancourt held his warrant card close to the man's face. 'Read, can we? Police.'

Another blackshirt had come over to join the party, and this one looked like he could handle himself. 'Don't make no difference. You're chinky police, not proper police.'

An unmistakable mop of red hair appeared between the lizard-man and Betancourt. It was Henderson, the Special Branch detective. 'Detective-Inspector Betancourt is here on official business. Let him past or I'll arrest the lot of you.'

Mosley's vigilantes grumbled amongst themselves before standing back with bad grace to allow Betancourt to enter.

'I could have handled that myself, but thanks anyway.'

Henderson nodded. 'I know. Bonham saw what was going on – sent me out. He told me to make sure you weren't causing trouble.'

It sounded like something Bonham would say. With allies like him, who needed enemies?

Betancourt stood with Henderson as the guest of honour's cavalcade pulled up outside the hall. Three long, sleek, black-liveried Bentleys, polished until they shone. The gold lettering on the doors proclaimed the cars were the property of the ironically named Everlasting Life Funeral Parlour, more used to ferrying funeral-goers than foreign dignitaries of dubious distinction.

He took up his place in the rear corner of the hall where he had a good view of the audience, if not of the dais itself. As Mosley took to the stage, there was a chorus of subdued booing, but Betancourt was surprised to hear ripples of applause and the odd cheer of approval as well.

There was no welcome, no thanking the audience for attending, no introduction of any sort. Mosley launched straight into his speech. He started slowly, almost ponderously, as though having difficulty framing a cogent argument for a difficult subject. It was all clearly an act he'd practised and it didn't take long for him to build a tempo and, with it, rapport with his audience. He spoke of how, though the miles separated them, the British were still one people; of the need for unity in the face of common enemies; of their shared struggle. Betancourt had come prepared to dismiss the man as a crank, but he was as charismatic a speaker as the newspapers had made him out to be. The speech, although calculated to appeal to the emotions, was carefully constructed, its effects cunningly orchestrated. The earlier heckling had disappeared, and the room had become quiet save for Mosley's stentorian monologue. The more he spoke, the more beguiled the audience became. It was no longer a talk; it was a dramatic performance.

As he spoke, he waved his arms wildly, pointing for emphasis and challenging an unseen opponent. There was a palpable sense that a grand crescendo was near. Finally, Mosley paused and hung his head, as though spent by his efforts. He looked out across the sea of enraptured faces one last time. His voice cracked, as though he was on the verge of tears.

'My friends, my countrymen, join me. Together we will hold high the head of England; lift strong the voice of Empire. Let us, to Europe and to the world, proclaim that the heart of this great people is undaunted and invincible. This flag still challenges the winds of destiny. This flame still burns. This glory shall not die. The soul of Empire is alive, and together we will make England great again.'

The crowd rose to its feet, and the hall filled with applause. Where before there had been cries of *shame!* the theatre now rang with *bravos!* and *hear hears!* Betancourt shook his head. It was frightening how quickly a crowd could be turned into a mob.

Mosley stood for a few moments, upright, proud, a half-smile showing he considered the adulation no more than he was used to and deserved. Then, as quickly as it had begun, it was over. Flanked by his henchmen, he descended the steps from the stage and they strode up the aisle in single file, five pairs of heels hitting the wooden boards in perfect unison, the staccato rhythm of their steps providing a chilling coda to the performance. Betancourt felt sure the effect was just as calculated as the rest of the show.

Pockets of protesters who had been forbidden entrance to the main event had spilled out onto Empress Place and surrounded the cars containing Mosley and his henchmen. A blackshirt leaned out of the window and struck out with a billy-club, raining blows on the obstructors. Some of Mosley's newly converted zealots ran from the hall to join in the scuffles. A photographer crouched down, his flashbulb popping, recording the scenes for posterity. Betancourt turned to find Bonham at his shoulder.

'Bloody idiots. I was worried this might happen. Well, don't just stand there, man, do something. I can't have this in the papers.' His priorities, as ever, were clear.

Betancourt took stock and barked a series of instructions. Two ranks of constables peeled off and inserted themselves between the groups of adversaries. A semblance of order returned as the antagonists backed away from each other. A few looked embarrassed to have let their excitement get the better of them. How typical, he thought. It wasn't the fact that the young Chinese policemen represented the voice of authority that had calmed the situation; it was that, above all else, these people were British, and it didn't do to parade one's dirty laundry in front of the locals.

Empress Place had cleared sufficiently to allow the procession of black cars to exit. Mosley sat in the rear seat of the middle vehicle. As the car swept past, he appeared to look straight at Betancourt, who turned and glanced behind him. He could see no one. The fascist couldn't have been looking at him, surely. Of what interest could he possibly be? He studied Mosley's profile as the car sped away. Under the glare of the electric lights in the hall, and standing so far back, he hadn't had a clear view of the politician's features. Whether it was a simple case of *déjà vu*, he wasn't sure, but there was something familiar about that face.

Chapter Twenty-Four

When he arrived back at his flat, the telephone was ringing. It was Lucia and she sounded as if she was crying.

'You have to come!'

'What's wrong? Has something happened?'

'There were two men. They tried to make me get into their car...'

'What? Where? Are you all right?'

'Outside the house. I was walking home and a car pulled up. One of the men grabbed my arm and tried to push me into the car. I bit him. He squealed. I hope it hurt. I ran off through the hedge. I'm scared!'

'Where are you now?'

'In the house. Upstairs.'

'Are your grandparents there?'

'They've gone out. To the theatre, I think.'

'Is there anyone else there?

'Ah Lin.'

Louis and Odette were so concerned for Lucia's well-being they'd left her in the care of an octogenarian *amah*? But he was being unreasonable and he knew it. There was no way they could have foreseen something like this. It was down to him, not them.

'Find Ah Lin and go to your room. Wait for me there.'

'I'm scared.'

'I'll be there in fifteen minutes, I promise. Now go.'

'Are you hungry?'

'Famished. Can we have *mee goreng*? Grandma won't let me eat hawker food. She says you never know what's in it.'

When he returned with food from Mr Tan's, he found his daughter on the sofa, feet tucked under her, leafing through a dog-eared copy of *True Stars* magazine that she must have brought with her.

Despite his efforts to appear outwardly calm and in control, he'd been barely able to control his anger. Everything that had happened to him before this – sending the list of his IOUs to the Mother Superior, the attack here at the flat, the fake gravedigger pushing him into the ditch – was all between him and Guthrie and Jin. This was different. They'd made a very serious mistake by involving Lucia.

'Father, we need to talk. I've been thinking and I've come to a decision.' She continued to flick through the pages of the magazine, refusing to meet his eyes. He winced at the awkwardly formal *Father*. What had happened to the little girl who would leap from the sofa when he came in, wrap her arms around him, kiss him, and call him Papa?

'Oh, yes?'

Lucia cast the magazine aside. 'I've decided to leave.'

'Leave what, exactly?'

She gave him a look of exasperation, as though he was a dullard – a little slow on the uptake. 'School, naturally. Tomorrow, I'll write a letter to Sister Mary Michael, so she knows not to expect me back for Spring term.'

'I see.' He didn't, but it seemed wise to humour her. 'And what do you intend to do instead?'

'I'll come and live here, with you. I'll take care of everything while you're at work. It'll be just like when Mum was still alive.'

When Mum was still alive? So Lucia thought Anna was dead. Was he the only one who was still clinging to the hope she was alive? Was it time for him to let go?

'And what about your grandparents?'

'They'll miss me terribly, of course, but I'll visit them regularly.' Lucia was doing her best to maintain an air of insouciance, but he could hear the tremor in her voice. As she spoke, she turned a ring over and over, around her finger. It was her mother's engagement ring. A constable had found it near the abandoned car and returned it to Betancourt. By now, her face was wet with tears and he held her until her sobbing subsided.

She sat up and wiped her eyes with the sleeve of her cardigan. He offered her his handkerchief, but she waved it away. She fingered the ring again. When she spoke, her voice had dropped almost to a whisper. 'I'm sorry, I found this in your kitchen drawer. I wasn't prying, honestly. I knew you had it somewhere.'

'Keep it. It looks beautiful on you.'

'But what about—'

'It's what she'd have wanted.' He covered her hand with his and gave it a squeeze of reassurance.

After they'd eaten, they sat by the window in quiet companionship, listening to the bullfrogs' plaintive lament.

Eventually, Lucia turned to him and when she spoke again, her voice was hesitant, as though she was about to broach a subject she'd rather not. 'Is everything, you know, all right?'

'It will be. I'll sort this out. Those men won't come near you again, I promise.' He'd spent the last half-an-hour trying to work out exactly how he'd keep that promise.

'No, I didn't mean that.' She reached into the small grip she'd brought with her and her hand emerged clutching a handful of envelopes, the uppermost stamped with FINAL in red ink. 'I found these.'

He tore the envelopes from her hand. 'Those are private!'

She shrank back. 'I didn't read them. I saw the letters when I was looking for the ring. I was worried. Are we having —' She searched for the right word. 'Problems?'

All the problems were his, and he'd no right to bring her into any of it.

'No, no problems. I've been busy, and I've let things slip a little, that's all. I'll sort it out. There's nothing for you to worry about.'

'It's just… the last time I went to the bursar to get my pocket money, he said there was no more left. Pocket money, I mean. He said he'd written to you about it.'

'I heard. I've sorted it all out with the Mother Superior. It was just a misunderstanding.'

Lucia watched him the way Anna used to. As though if she held his gaze for long enough, she'd be able to divine an alternative truth from his eyes. He broke the spell.

'What's this I'm hearing about fights?'

'Oh, that. It was Angela Shaw.' She said it as though mere mention of the girl's name was explanation enough. *It was Angela Shaw – what more could you expect?*

'And what did she say that was so bad it was worth fighting over?'

'She told everyone that her father said you don't pay your bills. She said I was only allowed into the school because of the charity of the nuns.'

'That's nonsense. What did you say?'

'I told her she was a buffalo.'

Whatever else he'd expected to hear, it wasn't that his daughter had taken to referring to her classmates as wild oxen. 'A what?'

'I said, if we were discussing charity, she would do well to leave some of the teatime cakes for the other girls instead of eating them all herself because she was beginning to look like the buffaloes that pull carts to market. Then she pulled my hair, and that's how it started.'

He knew he ought to administer a rebuke for this personal attack on the Shaw girl, but he couldn't stop himself from laughing, and when he laughed, Lucia laughed too, and the tension was broken. Was it too soon to hope it was broken for good?

After he bade her goodnight, he took sheets from the hall cupboard and made a makeshift bed for himself on the sofa. He tossed and turned for a long time until finally drifting off into an uneasy sleep, the stack of overdue bills still gripped tightly in his hand.

Lucia's resolve to move in and become mistress of the manor had hardened overnight, and he woke to find her surveying the kitchen – looking in cupboards and underneath counter-tops. After each examination, she shook her head and added a note to a list. Betancourt looked over her shoulder. The list already covered three-quarters of a page.

'I suppose it could do with a bit of a tidy up.'

'A tidy up? I hardly know where to start.'

'It's not that bad, is it?' He ran a hand along a shelf. His fingertips came up black. Mr Tan's wife had offered to come in and clean for him. Perhaps he ought to take her up on it. 'Get dressed. I'll have breakfast sent up.'

While she was dressing, he called Marjorie. 'I know it's a lot to ask, but I need to know she's safe.'

'Don't even mention it. I can't wait to see her again.'

'What about Ray? Will he be all right with having a teenage house guest?'

'There's some flap on at his work. It's keeping him busy. He'll be happy for me to have the company. Anyway, I've some leave due. I'll take a few days off. We'll have a wonderful time together.'

He'd left a note for the Cléments the previous evening, when he'd collected Lucia. He should probably have called them last night, when they'd have returned from the theatre, but he couldn't face the inevitable arguments. He couldn't put it off any longer. Louis still seemed shocked and put up only a token protest. Betancourt gave him Marjorie's number. 'You can call Lucia every day. When this is over, we'll talk again.'

When he told his daughter about the plan, there were tears at first.

'It's for your protection. I have to see this case through, and I can't risk a repeat of what happened yesterday.'

'But I don't want protection. I want to stay with you.'

'I know.' He understood now. He'd been thinking a lot about her behaviour and her animosity towards him this last few months. Finally, he got it. Yes, she blamed him for the situation that led to Anna's disappearance. But she hadn't rejected him at all. In his daughter's eyes, it was he who'd rejected her. Throughout the devastation of losing her mother, the one person she'd needed to be with her had deserted her too. He'd make it up to her, but right now, he needed to know she was safe.

Lucia perked up a bit when Awang arrived. Having the use of a police car as her personal transport appealed to her. She even asked if she could do a tour of her friends' houses, to show it off.

'Perhaps another time.' He gave Awang Marjorie's address. 'Go straight there. Don't stop for anyone or anything.'

The last thing Betancourt remembered before falling asleep the previous night was giving a silent prayer to a god he didn't believe in that Allenby would somehow perform a miracle and cure Victory Parade of his lameness. He was considering whether he had time to stop by the stables when the phone rang. It was Evelyn.

'You need to get up here. There's something you should see.'

'Where's "here"?'

'Mr Allenby's.'

'What are you doing at Allenby's?'

'Stop asking questions and get up here.'

When he arrived, the little red Austin was sitting outside the gates of the stables but there was no sign of its owner or of anyone else. Morning was normally the busiest time around the yard. Horses should have been coming and going and syces should have been busy saddling them up before they went out, or scraping the sweat off them after they came back, but the place was dead and the only welcome he received was a subdued whinny from an inmate, looking out for a piece of sugar. He checked the feed room, where he'd have expected to find Osman, the *mandor*, measuring out the morning oats. The floor was strewn with iron buckets, waiting to be filled, but there was no sign of life. He tried the converted box next door that Allenby used when making the entries or paying bills, but that, too, was empty.

A noise that might have been laughter came from the back of the yard where Allenby had stabled Victory Parade after the injury. When Betancourt turned the corner, he found his way blocked by the rear end of a rusted truck. On closer inspection he could see the vehicle was a makeshift fire tender. Had there been a fire? Surely, Allenby would never have evacuated the stables, leaving the horses to fend for themselves. A hose led from a tank on the bed of the truck towards the small paddock where he'd first seen the horse. He picked his way through a mosaic of puddles that had formed where rents in the hose had caused it to spill its contents. At the end of the hose, he found the source of the laughter he'd heard earlier: Allenby, Melrose, Osman, and the half-dozen syces who worked in the stables formed a human ring around the paddock. In the middle of the group was Evelyn, looking pleased with herself.

'What's going on?''

Allenby made space for him next to the fence. 'Have a look for yourself.'

A trough about twelve feet long and three feet deep had been dug out of the red earth and sealed with a tarpaulin. In this makeshift pool stood Victory Parade, splashing about knee-deep in muddy water, enjoying himself immensely.

'Remember you said it was a pity we couldn't take the horse back up to Ipoh and swim him in the mines, seeing as how the magic water had fixed him last time?'

'And you said he wouldn't be able to take the journey.'

'Well, your lady friend came up with an idea.'

'She's not my—'

'She's a star, that's what she is. You tell him, Doc.'

'It was that clinic I told you about, the one in Australia where they were treating arthritis patients with mineral baths. They bring water in from a spring. I thought, if you can't take a horse to water, why not take the water to the horse?'

'The fire truck. You had water from the mines shipped down here?'

'Well, it was my idea, but the Major claims credit for that part of it.'

Melrose beamed. 'I'm a warden in the ARP. Not much for me to do really except get the volunteers together on a Monday evening and practise the odd drill. We were done for the week and no one would miss the truck for a few days, so when Dr Trevose suggested her plan, I got Siew, my second-in-command, to drive to Ipoh and fill her up.'

Allenby took up the story. 'Osman got the syces to dig a hole. Ever tried to shift that much dirt? Took them all night. By the time they were finished, Siew was back with the water. 'Oss's been in there night and day since. Took to it like a duck.'

'And did it work?'

'See for yourself.'

Osman led the dripping horse out of the makeshift pool and trotted him up the path and back. There was no tell-tale nod of the horse's head as he put down his foot that would have showed he was feeling pain. His gait was even and straight. He was completely sound.

'Real battler, this 'oss. Give him a couple of days off and he can be ridden again. Nothing fast, though. Just need to keep him ticking over now – that's the go, I reckon.'

Betancourt turned too quickly and a spasm of pain shot down his side. His hand went involuntarily to his ribs.

'Didn't like to ask. Wouldn't want to see the state of the other bloke.' Allenby lowered his voice in deference to Evelyn's presence. 'Woman trouble?'

'In a manner of speaking.'

'Well, you can stop being such a gutless wonder. Need you fit and well. If the 'oss can recover in time, reckon you can too. Come on, look lively! You, me and the Major got us a bit of planning to do. And not forgetting the doc.'

Chapter Twenty-Five

A pink slip lay in the centre of Betancourt's desk, fluttering weakly in the breeze from the fan, like a harpooned fish that had accepted its fate. He read the words scribbled on it. Purvis in Customs had phoned to say he had the information on the arrivals records Betancourt was looking for. He called the number and a voice said Purvis was on his tea break.

'Wouldn't want to interrupt that, would we? Get him to call me as soon as he returns.'

Purvis called back fifteen minutes later. 'Those passengers you asked about. They all disembarked from the *Batavian Princess* on the day in question.'

'You're sure? Including Guthrie?'

'Quite sure. I have the log here, and there's a note of Mr Guthrie's passport number. It matches the papers used on the other dates he travelled.'

'What other dates?'

'Mr Guthrie is a regular traveller. According to our records, he made around a dozen trips in the last year.'

'Do you have a list of where he travelled to?'

'Not exactly, we don't record that, but I can tell you where he was travelling *from* when he disembarked. Let me see… Yes, all on the *Batavian Princess* and all showing Shanghai as point of embarkation.'

'Hold on.' Betancourt found his pencil stub. 'Give me those dates.'

He jotted down the information and hung up. The passenger manifest on the ship had been altered and Guthrie's name removed. Someone wanted his presence on the *Batavian Princess* covered up. Question was, had they wanted it covered up before Akiko was found dead or because she was?

He placed another call.

'Are you sure you have the right address?' The operator sounded unused to being asked to connect calls to residents of the *suteretsu* and, what's more, seemed to view the task with some distaste.

'I'm sure.'

'In that case, I'm putting you through now.' He hadn't imagined it – there was a definite hint of censure in the haughty response, as though she thought she might catch something, just by being a party to the call.

A Japanese voice answered and he asked for Belle. There was a giggle, and then the sound of chattering in the background as the phone was passed over. Another voice came on. He repeated his request, this time adding the word 'Police', for additional motivation.

'You stay. I look.'

Finally, Belle came to the phone. 'On the mend, I hope.'

'Couple of bruised ribs and a bang on the head, that's all.'

Reassured he'd suffered no lasting damage, she resorted to her usual deprecating tone of voice. 'So, you have your lady friend running errands for you now? That didn't take long.'

'I told you, she's not my—' What was the point? 'Dr Trevose is helping me with inquiries.'

'Can't say I've heard it called *that* before.'

'Did you get the dates I asked for?'

There was a sigh. 'What a bore you are, Inspector. Wait a minute.' There was a rustle of paper and Belle read out the list of dates.

Betancourt scribbled them down, interrupting occasionally to check he'd picked her up correctly. 'How accurate do you think these are?'

'It was the best I could do. I'm not guaranteeing they're all correct or there aren't any missing. People in the *suteretsu* can be a bit absent-minded, you understand?'

He did. If you didn't give away information in the first place, no one could come back later and try to hold you to it.

He thanked her and she rang off. He placed Purvis's list of dates showing when Guthrie had travelled next to Belle's list of when shipments of women had arrived, and compared them. There were one or two matches, but nothing suggesting a regular sequence. What was he missing? He needed to speak to Newton about the doctored manifest.

<hr />

It was shortly after eleven o'clock when he ascended the gangway that connected the baking tarmacadam of the dockyard to the peacefully slumbering *Batavian Princess*. He had yet to shake off the concussion fully; it still felt as though someone with a large hammer was striking away at the inside of his skull. The sensation wasn't helped by the noise of chaotic activity as bands of stevedores loaded boats in readiness for the first departures of the new year.

As Newton had said when they'd spoken that first day,

there was only a skeleton crew left on board over the holiday. A few labourers scrubbed the teak walkways while others applied touches of white gloss paint to fittings. Betancourt stopped a painter and asked if the captain was on board. The man shook his head. Either he didn't understand or he was pretending he didn't.

A large tow-headed engineer clad in overalls that might once have been blue but were now streaked with black, emerged from a hatch. What skin Betancourt could see was ingrained with grime. The man was attempting to remove a thick coating of oil from his hands with a scrap of filthy rag. He regarded Betancourt with curiosity.

'Help you?'

Betancourt showed his warrant card and repeated his question about Newton's whereabouts.

'Not seen him since the day we docked. You could try the charge. He should be on the bridge. Don't know how much sense you'll get out of him, though. They seem to get younger every year. Or maybe it's me who's getting older, eh, Inspector?' He laughed and waved a massive oily paw in Betancourt's direction before heading off towards the stern of the ship.

He climbed the stair to the ship's superstructure and pushed open the door of the bridge. When he saw who the charge officer was, he understood the engineer's misgivings. The young cadet, Stevens, sat with his feet propped up on the instrument deck. He was engrossed in an American pulp novel with a lurid cover depicting a scantily clad young woman in the grip of a man with a raincoat, a trilby hat, and a gun. It wasn't clear from the artwork whether the woman was being abducted or saved.

Stevens appeared to be unaware he had company and Betancourt cleared his throat noisily to attract his attention.

After they'd exchanged pleasantries, he explained he needed to speak to the captain. Stevens shrugged. 'Can't help you, I'm afraid. Could be anywhere. He's on shore leave, see?'

'Is that normal? What if you need to get hold of him in case of an emergency?'

'Emergency? You mean, if someone knocks over a tin of paint or trips over a mop?'

The cadet was clearly pleased with himself and gave a series of chuckles that sounded like the panting of an overly warm dog. Betancourt ignored the attempt at wit. 'I've no idea. You're the one who works here. Didn't he leave contact details?'

'If I need anything, I contact the shipping agency, but as you can see, Inspector, it's quiet as the grave here.'

Given the events of earlier in the week, Betancourt wasn't sure if this was an attempt at gallows humour or just a crass remark, but he let that slide, too. 'Which agency do you use?'

'Owen's.'

Betancourt knew Owen well. He could usually be relied upon to come up with a decent bit of information for the price of a glass of something.

'If you hear from Captain Newton, tell him I'm looking for him.' But Stevens had returned to his novel and showed no sign of having heard.

Owen's office – little more than a tin shed – sat on the northern side of the docks, a few hundred yards from where the *Batavian Princess* was moored. Betancourt knocked on the rusty door and entered. The interior was like the inside of a brick oven and he recoiled from the blast of heat that greeted him.

Owen was a thirty-year veteran of the waters of South-East Asia and only retired from active service when he decided being at sea meant having to survive for too long between the delights of the waterfront bars he considered his second home. A bulbous nose that stood out from a face criss-crossed with spidery purple veins bore testament to his new regime. The man's predilection for strong drink should have rendered the heat even more oppressive, but he appeared oblivious to the furnace-like atmosphere.

'Jesus, what happened to you?

Betancourt waved away the enquiry. 'Difference of opinion with a gravedigger.'

Owen touched a fat finger to his nose. 'Ask no questions and you'll be told no lies, as my old mum used to say. What can I do for you?' He gestured towards the *Batavian Princess*. 'That's the last one in, and I won't have anything else for you to look at until next week.'

'That's not what I'm after. Did you hear we had a death the other day?'

'Nothing gets by old Owen. I hear everything.'

Betancourt looked questioningly at the pile of documentation on the desk. 'Busy?'

'Not especially. What did you have in mind?'

'Can we get out of here before I cook from the inside out?'

'You on the bell?'

'Aren't I always?'

Owen scampered to his feet, energised by the promise of free drink. 'Let me find my keys and I'll be right behind you.'

They found an empty table in Leilani's. Owen ordered a Tiger beer with a whisky chaser. 'Make it a large one, love.' He placed one palm above the other to indicate a measure that looked to Betancourt more like a pint than a double tot.

'Coffee.'

Mama Leilani winked and went to fetch the drinks.

'You do the manifests for the Napier's boats, don't you?'

'Ships. We call them ships. Sometimes. It depends. They've got their own people who take care of all that. If they're busy, they throw work my way. Or like now, when they're all off gallivanting.'

Betancourt showed Owen the passenger list Newton had given him. 'When you prepare an official passenger list, you wouldn't write it out by hand like that, would you?'

'No chance. Not these days. Me and a few of the other blokes, we club together to pay a young thing to type them all up for us. Miss Ho, they call her. To her face, anyway. The companies give us headed paper to use.' He picked up the paper and held it up to the light. 'This one looks like some-one's copied the list out on milady's best correspondence stationery.'

'Why would someone hand write a passenger list like this?'

'No idea. Even if they'd lost the original, they'd still have a spare copy.'

'A spare?'

'When the lovely Miss Ho does the typing, she makes copies. Carbon paper. I keep a copy for my records, a copy goes to Customs, and two copies go to the ship. One for the captain and one for the chief steward who looks after the passengers. So, if the steward drops his copy in the mulli-gatawny soup, there'll always be another one.'

'How would I find out which names were on the original?'

'Which ship did you say this was from?'

'I didn't, but it's that one, the *Batavian Princess*.'

Owen frowned. 'It's not like Napier's. They're usually squeaky clean when it comes to paperwork. She came in from Shanghai, didn't she? The harbourmaster there should have a copy. Want me to ask a few questions? It'll be easier for me to do than you.'

'I was hoping you'd offer.'

'It'll be thirsty work, mind you.' Owen drained the last of his drink and Betancourt called to Leilani for refills.

He gave Owen the list of dates Guthrie had travelled on. 'Have a look for anything unusual on or around these dates.'

'What counts as unusual?'

'I'm not sure. Just look for any patterns, would you?'

On the off chance, he took a photograph of Akiko from his jacket pocket. 'Can you remember seeing this woman around the docks?'

'That her what copped it?' Owen looked at the picture for a few seconds and shook his head. 'Can't say I have.'

Leilani returned with the drinks. She stooped to run a cloth over the pool of water left by the sweating glasses and picked up the photograph.

'Is this the poor girl who was killed?'

'Yes. Have you seen her around?'

'Hmmm… maybe.' Leilani studied the picture and then nodded. 'Yes, I think I know her. Her hair was shorter then, but it looks like the same girl. She used to come in here sometimes. Late, after work. With a *mat saleh*.'

'This *mat saleh*, would you recognise him again?'

'Sorry, dear, you know how it is, they all look alike to me.'

Betancourt described Guthrie but Leilani looked doubtful. 'No, doesn't sound like the same man. I remember this one was dark.'

'But you're sure it's the same woman?'

'I'm sure.'

She collected the empty glasses and sashayed away.

Owen said he had to get back to his shed and would be in touch when he heard something. He warned Betancourt not to expect anything quickly. Even though most of the dock-workers didn't celebrate the Western New Year, their bosses did, which gave an excellent excuse to down tools for a few days, safe in the knowledge that no one would be around to check on them.

Chapter Twenty-Six

'What have you got?'

When he'd returned to his office, there was a message from Owen. He'd made quicker progress than he'd expected and had something Betancourt needed to see right away. Rather than use the phone, he returned to the dockyard.

'You'd better sit down.'

Betancourt had assumed the agent would want to repair to a nearby watering hole and, on this occasion, had hoped he would. Instead, Owen pointed to a chair that might have graced someone's dining room at one time but was now fit for little more than firewood.

Sweat ran down the back of Betancourt's neck and he swiped at a mosquito that tried to land on his face. He spotted a small electric fan tucked under Owen's desk. 'That thing work?'

Owen pulled out the fan. 'You warm, then? I'm used to it. Don't even notice it anymore.' He weighed down the papers on his desk with staplers and hole-punches and plugged in the fan. It turned slowly at first, like an aeroplane when it was started up, but before long it picked up speed and was soon spinning away, carving a gentle breeze from the torpid air.

'How's that?

Betancourt nodded 'Come on then. This better be good.'

Owen gave him a sharp look. 'Can I just remind you I'm doing you a favour here? Not that you'll be thanking me when you hear what I've got to tell you.'

He unlocked the door of a battered cupboard and withdrew a folder. It contained several sheets of foolscap paper, covered with handwritten notes. Betancourt tried to squint at the papers to see if he could make anything out, but the writing wasn't sufficiently legible. Owen clasped his hands together and rested his arms on the folder, obscuring the document, and regarded Betancourt with lugubrious solemnity, like a clergyman about to deliver a sermon on the ancestral sinfulness of man.

'Those dates you gave me, where did you get them from?'

'I can't say. Not yet. Why?'

'I charter ships for Napier & Campbell. If there is anything, how shall I put it, untoward going on, you'd let me know, wouldn't you?'

Betancourt's heart leaped. Owen must have uncovered a connection with Napier's. He prayed that connection included Guthrie. 'I'll look after you, you know that. Now, what have you got?'

'Cost me an arm and a leg in drinks, all this. I trust you're paying expenses.'

'Let's see what you've got first, and then I'll decide how much it's worth.'

Owen opened the folder and ran a finger down a column of figures, as though confirming he hadn't misremembered anything. 'I checked the comings and goings on each of the dates you gave me. On average there were around a dozen arrivals and departures each day. Multiply that by the twenty-four dates and you've around three hundred individual ship movements. I didn't think there was any chance of noticing any patterns, but it was actually easier than I expected. Several ships on the list were chartered by Napier's. I even arranged a few of them myself, hence my earlier question. But there was one name kept coming up that I didn't recognise: the *Taiyou-maru*.'

'Japanese?'

'Yes and no. I'll come to that. I asked around. Old Norrie Minto – him what works for Jardine's – he said he knew her. She did the Dutch East Indies run: Sumatra, Batavia, Sulawesi, Borneo, the usual. Norrie reckons she was a right old rust-bucket, mostly used for under-the-table stuff – not the type Napier's would normally touch with a barge-pole – but he'd heard nothing about her doing the Japan run.'

There was a whole fleet of ships that fitted that description, mostly used to transport cash cargoes around the Java Sea or north to the Gulf of Thailand. Smuggling ships like the *Taiyou-maru* were Betancourt's bread and butter.

'When I found out Napier's might be leasing ships without going through me, my nose was out of joint. It's a competitive business and every charter counts. At first, I told myself to leave it, but things had been quiet, and I couldn't afford to lose any more of Napier's business, so I called Mr Guthrie, just to make sure there was nothing he was unhappy about.'

'Wait. Euan Guthrie?'

'The same. Why?'

'Never mind. Go on. What did he say?'

'He said it was nothing to do with me, and how the hell did I even know about it? I fobbed him off with some story about dockside scuttlebutt. I apologised for bothering him and he said if I wanted to do business with Napier & Campbell in the future, I'd do well to forget all about it.'

'But you didn't? Forget about it, I mean.'

'I might have done, but I take exception to threats, especially ones from young upstarts like Guthrie, no matter how well-connected they are. I'd gone to all this trouble, so I thought I might as well see it through. On the QT, of course. I didn't want it getting back to Napier's. Now, get this, it turns out the *Taiyou-maru* was leased to Napier's just the week before she sailed for Japan for the first time.'

'Leased from whom?'

'Some holding company registered in Panama. Flag of convenience.'

It had always intrigued Betancourt to see the variety of home ports on the stern of ships that dotted the harbour and he'd come to recognise all the flags of the ports of registration. Flags of convenience were a popular tactic with traders who'd rather avoid a visit from him and his men.

'You didn't find out who owned the holding company, did you?' It was a longshot, but on this occasion, he hit the bullseye.

'As it happens, Inspector, I did. A mate of mine, name of Fish, looks after the Shanghai route. Once upon a long time ago, Fishy did his clerkship at Lloyd's Shipping Registry in London. He still keeps in touch with a few of his old muckers there, so I got him to send off a wire. See what he could find out. He came up trumps. The company has one director—a Nip.'

Owen turned the page around and pushed it towards Betancourt, so he could see the name for himself.

The name of the company meant nothing: Suimin Tora – postal address in Nagasaki. Probably an accommodation address but he copied down the details anyway. When he read the director's name, he was gripped by an old familiar feeling: that dawning sensation of the clues starting to connect and point in the same direction. He felt a visceral quake that, until now, he would have thought himself incapable of feeling again. The director of the company that had leased the ship to Napier's was Nakano Jin.

'You've done well.'

'Mean something to you, does it? Good. Keep that happy thought, because you won't like what's coming next. When I realised the same names were coming up in both lists, arrivals and departures, it became obvious there were pairs of dates: voyages out and voyages back. So, I looked for patterns. I started with the arrivals and I immediately noticed something.'

'What?'

'The ships in question were all carrying just what you'd expect: rice, silk, paper, tea. Standard stuff you see coming in from China, so nothing particularly interesting in *what* they were carrying…'

'Why do I have the impression there's a *but* coming?'

'Because there is. The but is that none of them carried full loads.'

'None of them?'

Owen shook his head. 'That's definitely not the Napier way. If they've got space on one of their ships, they get me to find a cargo from someone else, to fill the holds. Archie Napier didn't make his money sailing half-empty.'

'Wait a minute.' The heat had made Betancourt's headache worse, and he was struggling to keep this story straight. He pulled out his notebook and found a blank page. 'Give me all this again.'

Owen patiently recited the dates, shipping movements, cargoes and quantities. 'And there's more.' He paused, as though he was sorting out his thoughts and choosing the right words to convey them.

'Finally, I checked on the outbound cargoes. All the Napier charters had sailed with full loads of rubber for Shanghai, but there was no paperwork for the Shanghai to Kobe leg for any of the voyages. Now, that can happen. Sometimes cargoes are arranged at short notice, but it was strange that every sailing on the dates you gave me only had cargo as far as Shanghai.'

'That is odd. Any way of tracing what the ships carried up to Kobe?'

'Already done. I gave Fish the names of the ships and the dates.'

'And? What did he find?'

'Before I say anything more, you need to give me your word you'll keep me out of all this. I don't understand what's going on, but whatever it is, I know it's not good.'

'You have my word.'

Owen drew a deep breath and paused to compose himself before he spoke. 'When Fish laid his hands on copies of the bills of lading, he discovered none of the rubber had been offloaded for distribution in Shanghai.'

'What?' That made no sense at all. The rules governing the export of embargoed goods were clear.

'The whole lot – every single shipment – was reshipped to Japan under French shipping documents.'

This was dynamite. The embargo only applied to goods shipped from British territories, like Singapore. The Shanghai International Settlement was jointly administered by Britain and the United States, but the French concession was self-governing and not subject to British rules. Napier's was shipping embargoed goods to Shanghai, and those goods were being immediately re-exported to Japan under French cover.

Guthrie had travelled on each of those voyages. He was up to his neck in this. But what part had Akiko played, and why had Guthrie killed her? Betancourt intended to find out.

'Did your man say who issued the re-export licences?'

Owen's demeanour grew sombre and he looked away, as though unable or unwilling to meet Betancourt's eyes. He pulled an official-looking document from the bottom of his pile of paper and pushed it across the desk.

'For each of those journeys, the *Taiyou-maru* was chartered on behalf of Napier's by Clément et Fils. The export licences were authorised by Pascal Clément.'

Chapter Twenty-Seven

Betancourt's head spun and he slouched in his chair, immobilised by Owen's revelation. Now the visit from Jin to Pascal's godown made sense. Jin wasn't just a broker who'd offered Pascal a lifeline; there was something much bigger going on here. But there was the dilemma. If Pascal had any information about what Jin and Guthrie were up to that might help to solve the mystery of Akiko's death, Betancourt had to find out what it was. But he couldn't afford to alienate the Cléments any more than he had done already, and questioning their son about his connection with a suspected gangster was a very good way of doing exactly that.

One step at a time.

'Can I borrow your phone?' Betancourt called the *Straits Tribune* and asked to be put through to Daisy.

'You changed your mind about the film then? Turns out *Double Wedding's* finished but *Too Hot to Handle's* on at the NAAFI, if you fancy it?'

'Another time, perhaps. Daisy, listen, I need your help. It's urgent. Could you look something up for me?' He gave her the query.

'That's easy. Don't even need to look it up.'

And he didn't need to write down her answer. He'd known before he asked. He thanked her and promised to think about *Too Hot to Handle*.

'Can I take your notes?'

'They're yours, if you can read my writing.' Owen handed over the folder. 'Fancy a drink? If you don't mind my saying, you look like you could use one.'

'Not now. But tell Leilani to put your tab on my account.'

Inside the godown, everything appeared the same as it had the last time he'd been in. The electric light in the office at the back burned dimly. Behind the grimy glass, Pascal berated a man dressed in the de facto clerical uniform of the river – white short-sleeved cotton shirt and black trousers.

Betancourt stood in the doorway and addressed the clerk.

'Leave us.'

The clerk was clearly confused by the order and Betancourt could see the options playing out in his head. Should he stay and continue taking a browbeating from his employer or do as this stranger bade him?

'Now.'

The man took one last uncertain look at Pascal before turning and scurrying past Betancourt, who stood aside to let him pass. Pascal leaped to his feet.

'What the hell do you think you're playing at? This is my business, and you don't—'

'Shut up.'

During all the time the two men had known each other, Betancourt couldn't remember so much as raising his voice in Pascal's company. The effect of his swiftly delivered order was instantaneous and punctured his brother-in-law's bravado like a thorn pricking a bubble. Pascal cowered back in his chair as Betancourt stood before him, gripping the edge of the desk so hard his knuckles shone white.

'When I was in here last week, you told me that man Chin had just turned up here. "Out of the blue" were the exact words you used. But that isn't true, is it, Pascal?'

'I don't know what you're talking about. Are you saying I lied?' It was a token effort at re-establishing his position as the aggrieved party, but his voice rang hollow with fear.

'You know exactly what I'm talking about. You've known Chin for a lot longer than you claimed and you didn't meet by chance. How about you start telling me the truth?'

'Or else?'

'That depends. There was no timber contract, was there? Why don't I call Louis and you can tell him how you pilfered the company's money to get into bed with a bunch of gangsters and then tried to cover it up? Who knows – he might even think you showed initiative, but somehow I doubt it. And after that, I'll arrest you for flagrant contravention of the embargo on shipping strategic goods to Japan.'

'You're bluffing.'

'So you don't deny it?'

Pascal wrapped his arms around himself, as though afraid he might disintegrate at any moment. When he spoke, his voice was thick with emotion. 'What is it you think you know?'

Betancourt ticked off the items on his fingers. 'One: you seem to have diversified lately. I noticed that as well as timber, you now have large quantities of rubber in your godowns. Or at least you did, before the fire. I thought that was a strange choice as rubber is embargoed and you need a special licence to export it.

'Two: a ship – the *Taiyou-maru* – sailed from Singapore to Kobe on the fourteenth of October. She was carrying rubber as far as Shanghai. So what? you might say. Nothing wrong with that.

'Three: the *Taiyou-maru* was leased from a holding company named Suimin Tora. That name meant nothing to me at first, so I called my friend Daisy. Bright young lady is Daisy – knows pretty much everything. I asked her to look it up for me. Do you know what Suimin Tora translates as, Pascal? No? Oh, come on, try a bit harder. All right then, I'll tell you. *Tora* means tiger and *suimin* means sleeping. Suimin Tora: Sleeping Tiger.'

Betancourt watched as the colour drained from his brother-in-law's face. A deathly hush fell over the small office. Even the coolies on the wharf outside seemed to have downed tools. The faint ticking of a wall clock provided a metronomic backdrop to the scene, and it seemed to Betancourt to be keeping perfect time with his heartbeat.

'You know Owen the agent, don't you?' Pascal's head barely moved. Betancourt's catalogue of evidence had rendered him dumb. 'I got him to do some digging for me. That rubber never left the ship. It was immediately re-exported to Japan, in direct contravention of the embargo. The paperwork was submitted by Clément's. The name on the export licence is yours. Need I go on?'

He broke his stare and gazed around the office before resting his eyes again on Pascal. 'I know most of what happened. By the time I leave here, I'll know everything. Let's start with how you know Chin. Or should we call him by his real name: Nakano Jin? And I want the truth this time.'

Pascal tried to speak, but the words stuck in his throat. He coughed. 'I need a drink.' He stood up to walk to the filing cabinet where he kept his bottle.

'Too bad. Sit down.'

Pascal obediently sat. He ran a hand through his lank hair. 'Have you got any cigarettes?'

Betancourt ignored the request. 'Jin. How long have you known him?'

Pascal's eyes were now dull and his expression vacant. When he spoke, his words were an incoherent mumble.

'Speak up.'

'About a year, maybe more.'

'How did you meet?'

'How does anyone meet anyone in this city?'

'You owed money?'

'Very good, Detective.' It was said with an attempt at a sneer but just about devoid of any real venom.

'How much were you into him for?'

Pascal shrugged. 'Him? Nothing. Not then. Sure, I owed money here and there, but it was all right, I could manage it. I was just having a bad run.'

Why did all habitual losers think their luck was about to change?

'Then a friend introduced us. Jin said he would take care of things. His terms were very generous. Better than the money lenders'. Better even than Cluny the banker's.'

'Let me guess what happened next. Jin waived the repayments. Told you to pay when you were able. Meanwhile the interest was mounting up.' It was an old trick the gambling hall bosses used. Getting them hooked was one thing. Keeping them on the hook was the real art. 'And then one day, "out of the blue", he called in your markers. Am I close?'

A sullen glare confirmed he was on track.

'But by then you were past the point of no return. You knew the people you were dealing with would never let you pay off the money you owed, even if you could find it. So you were stuck, and you were desperate.'

Pascal sat slack-jawed, either disbelieving what he was hearing or shocked that Betancourt had seen through his lies.

'This "friend" who made the introduction... it wouldn't have been Euan Guthrie by any chance, would it?'

Pascal's eyes darted from side to side, as though looking for an escape. 'For Christ's sake, Max! I can't...'

'Guthrie. Yes or no?'

'All right! Yes, it was Euan. He's Sophie's cousin. He was as good as family. I trusted him. It was all Euan's idea. I just went along with it.'

'Why was Akiko killed?'

Pascal crumbled before his eyes.

'You know about Akiko?'

'What happened?'

'She was Euan's girlfriend. He said he didn't mind if I... She and I started seeing each other. Compared to Sophie, she was... She let me do things... It was only supposed to be a bit of fun. A few weeks ago, she came to me. Said she was pregnant and wanted to return to Japan with the child. She wanted money. I told her I didn't even know if the child was mine, but she said it was, and if I didn't help her, she'd expose me. I'd be ruined.'

Guthrie said he'd passed on Akiko to a friend. The friend was Pascal.

'You paid her?'

'I said I'd give her the money for her passage, but she said she didn't want my money. She had bigger plans. She wanted a copy of the export licences. I guessed she was going to try and blackmail Euan or Jin. I warned her about them, but she wouldn't listen. Said she had it all worked out. I thought if I could find her enough money, she'd forget about the blackmail idea. I tried to borrow from Euan. He said he would take care of things. I thought he meant he'd have a word with her. Scare her off.'

Akiko had told Mei she had business to attend to before she went back to Japan. Business that meant she wouldn't have to rely on men anymore. Her plan had got back to Guthrie, and she'd paid for it with her life.

'It was you who paid for Akiko's funeral, wasn't it?'

'I was devastated when I heard she was dead. You have to believe me.'

'When did all this start?'

'About a year ago. I thought Euan was doing me a favour, but then he asked me to falsify some shipping documents. I was shocked. When I refused, he threatened to tell Sophie. You've no idea what she's like. She'd have thrown me out like yesterday's rubbish.'

Betancourt didn't blame her one iota. 'So, you fixed the documents?'

'It was supposed to be a one-off, but that's when Euan introduced me to Jin. He offered me a share of the profits. The money was too good. I could finally show my father that I was making a success of Clément's. All I had to do was provide the shipping documents. Euan took care of the actual shipping.'

'Illegal rubber out, illegal women in.'

'At first it was only the rubber. The women came later. It was Jin's idea. That bloody ship, the Japanese one, it was barely seaworthy and the holds were hellholes. I told them to use one of Napier's own boats, but Euan wouldn't have it. He went crazy when I suggested it. Said we'd be asking to be caught.'

'What about the bond?'

'What bond?'

'Among Akiko's things. I found a war bond. It had been stolen a year ago.'

Pascal seemed genuinely shocked by this revelation. He held his head in his hands. 'Oh, Christ. She must have taken it. A few months ago, I took a packet of bonds to Shanghai. Bonds are what they use to pay for the girls. Easy to exchange and untraceable. No cash ever changes hands. Euan usually did the payment runs but he had some family thing to attend, so he told me to go in his place. I was to take the steamer to Shanghai where I was to meet with some friend of Jin's and deliver a bunch of papers. Seemed straightforward enough and I was glad to have something to do. It meant a week or two out of the office and I was bored, so I thought :"Why not?" I took Akiko. I thought she might enjoy it.'

'What happened when you got there?'

'Euan gave me instructions to visit a bar called the Club Rouge, on the Bund. I was to take a booth in the farthest corner from the door and wait until someone found me. A booth had been reserved in my name, so I ordered a drink and settled in. I didn't have long to wait. A Japanese appeared and took the package. Never said a word.'

'And then?'

Pascal shrugged. 'And then nothing. I went back to the hotel where Akiko was waiting. We returned home the next day. They'll kill me if they find out what happened. I need a cigarette. Please.' Betancourt gave him one and held out his lighter. Pascal cupped his hands around the flame. He was shaking violently. He took a deep draw. 'When we were at sea,

274

on the way up to Shanghai, I opened the packet of bonds and showed them to her. I thought she might be impressed. She must have taken one from my trunk when I wasn't looking.'

No wonder Pascal was so desperate. He now looked visibly weaker and when he spoke, he slurred his words. At times he had trouble stringing sentences together. Betancourt would have to stop soon and get him into custody. Stealing Government bonds, breaking the embargo, trafficking women; he had enough to put Guthrie and Jin away for a long time. But he didn't want to stop until he had the evidence that would see Guthrie hang for the murder of Akiko.

Betancourt realised Pascal had started speaking again, but it was as if he was now talking to himself. 'There were two women. On the boat. They suffocated and died. They just threw the bodies overboard for the sharks.' He frowned, like a little boy confused at encountering a problem for the first time. It was time to stop.

'Come on. I need to get you down to the station. You can tell me the rest when we get there.'

Pascal continued as if Betancourt hadn't spoken. His voice had taken on a trance-like quality, as though he was taking part in a seance, acting as a medium between this world and the next. 'I couldn't have that. Not that. It was too much. I told Jin – no more, I was finished. He laughed at me. Said I'd be finished when he said so. And then she disappeared.' Pascal seemed to be oblivious even to Betancourt's presence now. 'They took her away. Jin said if I wanted to see her again, I'd do what they told me.'

What was he talking about? No one had mentioned Akiko disappearing before. Clearly, Betancourt wasn't going to get any more sense out of Pascal. He put his hand on the phone to call for a car. Then he froze. *They took her away.* It felt as if he'd been shot through the heart. He put down the phone and spoke, slowly and deliberately. He had to hold himself together for a few minutes more. 'Pascal. Who disappeared? Who did they take away?'

There was no answer. Betancourt looked into his brother-in-law's dull eyes. 'Pascal, listen to me. Was it Anna? Did Jin take Anna?'

Again, there was no response. Betancourt shook Pascal and screamed in his face. '*DID JIN TAKE ANNA?*'

Pascal nodded slowly.

'Where? Where did they take her? Is she still alive?'

'I don't know. They said they would keep her safe, but I don't know. I'm so sorry.' Tears streamed down Pascal's face and he shuddered as though in the grip of some sort of spasm. He was completely broken.

Nothing in his life had prepared Betancourt for this. He grabbed at the desk to stop himself from falling over. Everything he'd been through, everything that had happened to him since, to Lucia, to Anna's family, to her friends. He'd lost his job, his house, the respect of everyone he knew, and the whole time he'd thought he was responsible for everything that had happened. But it was because of Pascal, and he had known it all the time. Pascal, the shining star of the Clément family; Pascal, of whom Louis wouldn't hear a bad word said; Pascal, the younger brother Anna had adored and the uncle her daughter still revered. Betancourt couldn't contain himself any longer. He lashed out at Pascal with both fists and didn't stop hitting until his hands hurt so much that he could hit no more.

He picked up the phone. 'Ambulance and police.' He gave the address. When the operator asked for his name, he hung up.

He took one last look at the bloody face before him and

turned to leave. He couldn't stand being near Pascal another moment. As he crossed the room, his eyes fell upon a box containing a length of coiled rope. He picked up the rope and threw it onto the desk. 'There's always another way. Trouble is, you're too much of a coward to do the decent thing.'

Chapter Twenty-Eight

'Oh, God, Max, I can't tell you how sorry I am.'

Evelyn handed him a pill and a glass of water. 'This will help with the pain.' Betancourt flexed his fingers. Everything seemed to be working.

Once he'd got over the initial shock of Pascal's revelation, he'd become more sanguine about the possibility of Anna being found safe. It had been seven months now since she went missing. If the Sleeping Tigers still had her in captivity, then as long as they remained unaware that he knew they'd taken her, they were unlikely to do anything. By now, Pascal would be safely locked away at Police HQ, so he couldn't tip them off and, outside of the duty officers at headquarters, no one other than Betancourt, and now Evelyn, knew. If, on the other hand, his wife had been dead all this time, there was nothing more to be done anyway. He needed to focus all his energy on bringing down the gang.

'I was right. Guthrie's up to his neck in this. He's in league with the Sleeping Tigers. Together, they're shipping embargoed goods out and trafficking women in. Pascal is the proof.

Guthrie provides the transport and Jin supplies the women. They used Pascal's relationship with Akiko to blackmail him into falsifying shipping documents. Akiko gathered evidence of the smuggling and was planning to blackmail them. Word got back to Guthrie, and he either killed her or had her killed.'

'Who do you think is running the show, Guthrie or Jin?'

'If I had to bet on it, I'd say Jin, but the truth is, I still don't know.

'What do we do next?'

We? He couldn't help but smile. 'You've done enough for now. The first thing I need to do is arrest Guthrie. Once I've got him alone in a cell, I'll make him fill in the gaps. Then I'll go after the Tigers. It sticks in my throat a bit, but I may have to involve Montgomerie and his Special Branch thugs.'

'They'll probably take any credit that's going anyway, though I'm not sure credit's the right word to use to describe any of this. The fact that it's been going on all this time doesn't exactly paint the colony in a good light.'

'I'll call Onraet, then I'll call Ray French and let him know so he can brief the Governor. Sir Shenton will want it hushed up, but it's probably too late for that now.'

'You know, Max, it might not seem like it right now, but if you get the Sleeping Tigers off the streets, it'll mean fewer girls facing lives of servitude, so some good might yet come out of all this.'

Betancourt scoured the station for reinforcements. The place was dead. Eventually, he found Sergeant Quek in the typing pool, perched on the edge of a desk belonging to a young stenographer, the pair of them studying the pages of a newspaper showing a list of films on offer at the various picture houses around the town.

'Come on, Romeo, you're with me. Call for a car and meet me out the front.'

He'd taken a liking to Quek, but he'd feel better if he had additional support. The only other person he could find was a constable who'd been tasked with cataloguing the boxes in the evidence room. Betancourt told the startled rookie to come with him.

Awang had the engine running, and Quek jumped into the front seat.

'Out. That's my seat. In the back with— What did you say your name was?'

'Aroozoo, sir.'

'In the back with Aroozoo.'

Betancourt gave Awang instructions. 'Sultan Gate, quick as you can.'

'You going to the same place as last time?' Betancourt nodded. 'OK, this time I go the back way: North Bridge Road, Kandahar Street, Baghdad Street. Quicker. Not so much crowds. Want me to put on the siren?'

Betancourt stared at him. It was the most he'd ever heard Awang say in one uninterrupted burst. 'No. I don't want to announce we're coming.'

Balwinder the *jaga* lay snoring on his charpoy. Betancourt shook him awake.

'I remember you.' The watchman beamed. 'You are also policeman.' He noticed Quek and Aroozoo. 'More policemen. Many policemen.'

'What do you mean, *more* policeman? Have other policemen been here today?'

'Yes, *tuan*. Other policemen. Come to see Tuan Guthrie. He is very important, yes no?'

'What time was this?'

'Not long. Half-hour maybe.'

'These other policemen, what did they look like?'

Balwinder thought about it. 'Something like Chinese.'

Something like? It must have been Jin. Betancourt ran towards the stairs.

The *jaga* called after him. 'You want keys, *tuan*? Other policemen ask for keys.'

Somehow, Betancourt didn't think he'd need them. He doubted Jin and his goons would have bothered about locking up after themselves.

'Quek, you come with me. Aroozoo, you stay here and if you see anything at all, scream your lungs out.'

Sure enough, the door to Guthrie's apartment was swinging open. Betancourt pushed it back and called out: 'Police! I'm coming in.'

He caught the sickly-sweet smell of blood before he saw the body. In the space where the dining furniture should have been was a single chair. Guthrie had been run through with a long, curved samurai sword. It had entered his body just below the ribcage and been driven upward. It would have gone straight through his heart. They had dressed him in a silk kimono and tied him to the chair with sisal rope. His head lolled forward, revealing the back of the kimono. It was embroidered with an image of a tiger, identical to Akiko's tattoo, and the point of the sword protruded from his back just beneath the animal's paw. Like Akiko's, Guthrie's death had been staged as a suicide.

He told Quek to call for an ambulance. 'That phone was working last time I was here.'

How long ago was that? Was it really only three days? So much had happened since.

When he'd listened outside the apartment then, he'd heard Guthrie tell someone to take care of things. Well, Jin had taken care of him. Betancourt wondered if he'd ever know the truth of what had happened. Had this been a simple falling out between thieves? It was unlikely. The staging of Guthrie's death suggested a planned execution. Now what? He'd been so sure Guthrie had killed Akiko. Instead, not only was his main suspect dead, but for the first time he questioned if he'd got things wrong all along.

He ran through his interview with Guthrie again. For the most part, the Englishman had been sullen and belligerent. Until Betancourt produced the bond. That's when he'd become animated. And when he'd listened in at the window, Guthrie had said, "He had a bond. I think it was one of ours."

One of ours?

Quek had finished with the telephone and Betancourt grabbed it. When the operator answered, he asked for Owen's office.

'There's no answer from that extension.' He gave the woman another number. Leilani answered.

'Is Owen there?'

'Yes, he's been here all morning. He said you'd settle his bill.'

'Don't worry, I'm good for it.'

'Of course you are.' She didn't attempt to conceal her disbelief. 'He's here somewhere. Let me have a look.'

Trays of glasses dropped onto the countertop; orders were called and confirmed; an argument raged about whether someone called George Allison was the right man to lead the Arsenal to the title again. The sounds of a busy bar echoed down the wire as he waited. Come on, come on!

'Owen here.' The voice that greeted him was thick and slow. His source sounded as if he'd taken full advantage of the free tab.

'The ship that Napier's chartered, the *Taiyou-maru*. I need you to find out who paid for the lease and how it was financed. Can you do that?'

'Depends. If it was cash, it might not be possible. People have a habit of forgetting cash deals. I'll have a look tomorrow. Come down and have a drink.'

'Tomorrow's no good – I need it now.'

Owen swore. 'Give me half an hour, then call me back.'

A peon led Betancourt up the curving staircase to Cluny's eyrie.

'What is it now, Inspector? I have a bank to run, you know.' He used a grumbling tone but Cluny's eyes betrayed a keen interest in the reason for this visit.

'If I wanted to know whether a certain person had accessed their safe-deposit box recently, could you find out?'

'We're a bank. We keep records. I assume you haven't disturbed me in the middle of the day just to pose hypothetical questions. Which person are we talking about?'

'Euan Guthrie.'

Cluny's discreetly lowered lids all but shrouded his eyes. He watched Betancourt like a hawk watches a mouse. Eventually, he reached for his telephone and gave instructions. 'Dates and times the box was opened. Deposits and withdrawals.' He covered the mouthpiece of the receiver with his hand. 'Going back how far?'

Betancourt thought about it. Pascal said the racket had been going on for about a year. 'At least twelve months?'

'You'd better make it two years.' Cluny hung up. He tore a match from a book and lit a cheroot, balancing the matchbook on edge in front of him. It was the one Betancourt had given him the last time he'd been in this office – the one he'd found in the vase in Akiko's room.

'Have you thought any more about my offer? It's still open.'

'Thanks, but I've come up with an alternative plan.'

'As you wish, but when your alternative goes down the toilet and you need even more money, you may not find me so generous with my terms.'

'I'll take my chances.'

The peon knocked and presented Cluny with a sheet of paper. He donned his spectacles and scanned the list.

'Mr Guthrie might have opened the box on a few more occasions than is the average, but I can't see anything untoward.' He tossed the sheet across the table. 'Are you going to tell me what it this is about?'

Betancourt took out his notebook and went through the list, date by date, comparing it with the trips Guthrie had made to Shanghai. There were too many matches for it to be coincidence.

'I need to look inside this box.'

'Certainly. Just as soon as you can convince a magistrate to issue a warrant.'

'That would take days. I need access now. I'll call Inspector General Onraet. It might take half an hour, but I'll get access to that box today.'

Cluny seemed amused by the combative response and gestured to the telephone handset. 'Be my guest.'

Betancourt mentally crossed his fingers, hoping Onraet wouldn't ask for too much in the way of justification. He gave a sigh of relief when the Inspector General gave his reply.

'Tell Mr Cluny he'll be contacted in fifteen minutes.'

Betancourt passed on the message. Cluny nodded and picked up the discarded matchbook. He turned it over and appeared to study it. 'You left this. You noticed it has a number written on it, I take it?'

'I thought at first it might be a telephone number, but I had it checked. Wrong number range, apparently.'

Cluny chuckled, pleased with himself about something. 'I noticed it this morning. If you'd asked, I could have told you it wasn't a telephone number.'

'Really? My man had to call the telephone company to find that out.'

'It was all this talk of safe-deposit boxes that reminded me. Unless I'm very much mistaken, this is a box number. Or, more correctly, the serial number of a key that fits a safe-deposit box. One of our boxes, as it happens.'

Betancourt's chest thumped. He stared at Cluny.

'I thought that might get your interest. You don't have the key to go with the number, do you?'

He remembered the key he'd taken from the vase in Akiko's flat and rummaged in his pocket until he found it. 'This any good?'

Cluny examined it and made a non-committal noise. 'Could be. It's the right sort.' He compared the number engraved on the barrel of the key with the number on the matchbook. 'And the numbers match.' He returned the key to Betancourt.

'Do I need to call the Inspector General back for another warrant?'

'No. Whoever presents the key is entitled to open the box.'

They were interrupted by the ringing of the telephone. After exchanging pleasantries, Cluny listened carefully, confirmed he was satisfied and put the phone down. 'I'm impressed. That was the Governor himself. There aren't too many people can get him on the phone at fifteen minutes' notice. It seems I'm to provide you with every assistance, Inspector.'

Betancourt had never been inside a strong room before and the space was smaller than he'd imagined. Four steel safes bearing the Chubb logo took up one end of the room. The other three walls were lined from floor to ceiling with doors of varying sizes.

'These boxes are the same specification as that used to guard the Koh-i-Noor diamond. Shall we open the box your key belongs to first?' Cluny invited Betancourt to insert his key in the lock of a door measuring about six inches by four. There was a loud click as the tumbler disengaged. The clerk used a second key from a large ring of similar-looking ones and the door swung open. Cluny gestured. 'It's all yours.'

Behind the door was a slim metal box. Betancourt slid this out and carried it to a table in the centre of the room. It was light. Whatever Akiko had hidden inside had no great substance to it. He opened the lid. On top were several shagreen-covered cases. He opened them. Jewellery, mostly earrings and necklaces. The cases bore the names of local Chinese dealers. Good quality but not the highest. Gifts, presumably, from a lover.

Beneath the jewellery cases was a rolled-up piece of oilskin, bound with ribbon. He untied this, revealing a sheaf of papers, which he separated and laid out on the table. The papers were all annotated with the spidery scrawl he'd seen on the clipping about Nakano Seigō. The first document was another bond, identical to the one he'd found hidden in the book at Mei's flat. On it was written a date: *14th October '39*. He'd check later, but knew he'd find the date corresponded to that of Pascal's trip to Shanghai, the one he'd taken Akiko on. Next were copies of export licences. He recognised one or two from Owen's investigations. Akiko had underlined the quantities of rubber shipped and Pascal's signatures. After the licences were manifests and shipping schedules. A tiny cloth-bound diary contained dates of sailings with destinations. Some of the entries were marked with an arrow and the letter N. Forward shipments to Nippon? The last document was an envelope, secured with a wax seal. He broke this open. Inside was a single sheet of lined paper, the kind you'd find in a school jotter. It was covered on both sides with more of the scratchy handwriting. As Mei had said, Akiko's English was good, although there were passages where her proficiency deserted her and she'd resorted to writing Japanese *kana*, but there was sufficient there for him to understand. It was a complete history of the smuggling operation, with details of everyone involved and their roles. This was what Akiko had meant when she told Pascal she'd something much more valuable than the cost of a ticket home.

'Interesting?' Cluny's stock in trade was information, but he'd have to wait a little longer before learning the contents of Akiko's journal.

'You could say that. We can open the other box now, but I know what we'll find.'

The clerk opened the door and withdrew the second box and laid it on the table. This time it was Cluny who opened it. The box was almost full. On top was the usual documentation for someone of Guthrie's status: a will, a roll of banknotes, an insurance policy, a sheaf of letters written on lavender paper in a feminine hand. But taking up the bulk of the space in the box were the stolen bonds, or what remained of them. No wonder they hadn't turned up in the intervening year. They'd been sitting right here in the vault of Cluny's bank. The missing bonds and the evidence that would bring down the person who took them had been lying just feet apart all this time.

Cluny, normally the picture of inscrutability, looked shocked. 'If those are what I think they are, we have a problem.' He dismissed the clerk and pushed the vault door closed. 'You asked me to open Guthrie's box.'

Betancourt looked at him, confused. 'Yes, that's right. And now we have the bonds. Guthrie stole them and hid them here. We have the proof.'

'No, you don't understand. You said: "Guthrie's box". The report showed when Guthrie accessed the box. I told you, whoever presents the key is entitled to open the box. Guthrie had the key to this box, so he was free to open it.'

Realisation dawned. 'You're saying it wasn't his box?'

Cluny stared at the paper in his hand, as if hoping to find there had been some mistake. 'This box was rented by Raymond French. I have his signature here.'

Chapter Twenty-Nine

Betancourt pushed at the front door. It was open. He called out and Marjorie emerged from one of the bedrooms. She wore a housecoat and was pinning her hair back.

'Max. You've caught me at a bad time – I was just about to take a bath. What on earth are you doing here?'

'I was looking for Ray, actually. Is he around?'

'You've just missed him. He was here earlier. He'd planned to work from his study – he gets more done that way, he says – but he received a phone call and had to return to the office. Why?'

Betancourt tried to force a smile, to put her at ease. 'I need to speak to him about those bonds that went missing. I've got a lead. All right if I have a look in the study?'

She looked uncertain. 'I suppose so, if it's really necessary.'

The study looked exactly the same as it had when he'd last been here. There were a few assorted papers on French's desk. He had a quick look through them. Run-of-the-mill accounting statements. Whatever had taken him away, it wasn't this.

Betancourt kept his voice light. 'Did he mention who the call was from?'

Marjorie shook her head. 'No, but it was someone he knew, I think. From Government House, I assume. I didn't ask.' Her brow furrowed and she showed the first signs of concern. 'Whatever it was, it put him in a bit of a flap. He said I shouldn't wait up for him as he didn't expect to be home. I offered to pack him a bag, but he said not to worry, he'd do it himself.'

Betancourt took one more look around the room. His eyes alighted on the picture French had shown him last time. He picked it up. Gandhi, French, the owner of the house, Chatterjee, and the mystery man. He'd been right. He had seen that face before. He showed the photograph to Marjorie.

'Do you recognise this man?'

'Of course, that's Oswald Mosley. Ray and he are friends. Sort of. Ray is terribly proud of that picture. They met when the photograph was taken, and they've kept in touch over the years. I met Mosley the other evening, as it happens. Ray brought him here, after the talk at the Victoria Hall. He's one of those characters you know you really ought to dislike, but somehow can't. He's incredibly charming.' She laughed. 'Don't tell him I told you this, but I think Ray holds a bit of a torch for him.'

Raymond French and the bonds – Oswald Mosley and the fascists – Nagano Seigō and the Tōhōkai – Jin, Guthrie and the Sleeping Tigers – Pascal and Akiko. Finally, Betancourt had all the pieces of the jigsaw.

He stopped and listened hard. Something wasn't right here. The house was too quiet. 'Marjorie, where's Lucia?'

'Oh, she's gone.'

'What do you mean, gone?'

'She's been pestering Ray to let her see the inside of the Governor's Istana. He said he might as well take her as he was going in. I said she should go another time as Ray had this brouhaha on, but he didn't seem to mind. In fact, he insisted. I expect he'll send her back later with the driver.'

An icy hand clutched Betancourt's heart.

'Do you have a copy of today's paper?'

Marjorie handed him the *Straits Tribune*. He leafed through the pages until he found the Comings and Goings. Four o'clock. He had less than an hour.

'When did he leave?'

'About twenty minutes ago. He should be at the Istana by now. Max, you're starting to scare me. What is it? What's going on?'

'I'm sorry, Marjorie, but you'd better get dressed. And I must use your phone.'

He called Onraet. 'I need blockades put in place at the train station and the airport. I'll cover the docks. Send back-up.' He hung up and placed another call. 'I need you to pick her up. I'll explain later.'

Awang got him to the docks in record time. When they pulled up at the side of the wharf, smoke was surging from the twin funnels of the *Batavian Princess*, which was making ready to leave. Betancourt waved frantically at a crew member standing by a hawser, ready to cast off, but the man was oblivious to his calls over the sound of the ship's engines.

He spotted a familiar face. Dwarfed by the ship, Abu Bakar stood waving instructions to the last of the coolies as they trooped down the gangplanks. He put a hand to his ear and shook his head. He couldn't hear what Betancourt was saying. Betancourt cupped his hands and yelled into his ear: 'A European with a young girl?'

Abu Bakar nodded and smiled, pleased at finally under-standing. He pointed at the ship. 'Already on board.'

'Send the coolies back onto the ship. Don't let them off again until I tell you.'

Betancourt ran up the gangplank, leaving Abu Bakar pointing at the smoke emanating from the funnels and shout-ing, 'Too late!'

The first person Betancourt saw on board was Stevens. The deck cadet raised a hand. 'Whoa! You can't board, we're just about to depart.'

'Which way to the passenger cabins?'

Stevens pointed. 'That way, but you can't go down there.'

'Are they all taken?'

Stevens nodded. 'We're full. Except for the one we keep for the sick bay. That never gets used.'

'Which one's that?'

'Last one on the port side. Red cross on the door. But you can't—'

'Find the captain. Tell him to shut down the engines.' Betancourt unclipped his gun and waved it at the steps leading to the bridge above. 'Move!' Stevens looked at him as if he'd taken leave of his senses, then took off like a scalded cat.

Betancourt edged up to the sick-bay porthole. The curtains were closed. He checked his gun and clicked off the safety catch. He took a step back and raised his foot. The door flew back in a hail of splinters. French stood with his back to the wall holding Lucia, wide-eyed with terror, in front of him. Close to her neck, a lethal-looking curved dagger ensured Betancourt wouldn't try anything. A thin line of blood had already formed where French had pressed too hard.

'That's far enough, Max. Losing your wife was careless. To lose your daughter as well would be plain stupid.'

'If anything happens to her, you're a dead man, you know that, don't you?' He waved the revolver threateningly.

'Then we appear to have reached an impasse.'

Betancourt raised his free hand slowly, keeping his eyes locked on Lucia's the whole time. 'It's going to be all right. You just have to trust me. You trust me, don't you?'

Lucia blinked.

'Remember when that man tried to grab you outside your grandmother's house? How brave you were?' He caught a glint of understanding in her eye. He prayed she understood what he wanted her to do. 'I need you to be brave like that now.'

French looked from one to the other, confused, before he ordered, 'Shut up!' Lucia took advantage of his momentary inattention and sank her teeth into the fleshy part of his hand. She'd taken him completely off guard. He shrieked and grabbed at the place her teeth had caught him. She squirmed out of his grasp, threw herself across the cabin and clutched at Betancourt, who held her tight to him while he kept the gun trained on French.

Stevens had returned and brought Harvey, the first officer, with him. 'What's going on?' He saw the gun and backed off. Betancourt extricated himself from Lucia's grasp and nudged her towards what remained of the door. 'These men will look after you. I'll be with you soon, I promise.'

French watched him with a fevered stare. His face was mottled and flushed, lips pulled back and teeth bared. A cocoon of sputum had gathered at one corner of his mouth. He was unrecognisable from the convivial host and loving husband Betancourt had seen at the garden party. Whether this change resulted from pain, or from sick, blind rage, or whether this was the real Ray French he was seeing, he neither knew nor cared.

'The others told me you wouldn't be a problem, but you always concerned me. If anyone was going to catch me, I worried it might be you. Marjorie was forever going on about how much everyone underrated you. About how clever you were. That was why I made it my business to stay close to what you were up to.' French's face twisted into a cruel smile. 'Fortunately, Marjorie gave me everything I needed to know. She's prone to pillow talk, did you know that? Why else do you think I married her? You didn't really think it was for love, did you? I needed someone close to the police and, believe me, making love to a silly besotted woman is cheaper and more reliable than bribery.'

Betancourt knew that no good would come of it, but he couldn't resist. He cracked French across the jaw with the butt of the revolver, set Harvey and Stevens on guard, and went outside onto the walkway to wait for his backup.

Chapter Thirty

A row of cane chairs lined the tiled lobby of the Central Police Station. They were intended for use by citizens wishing to report a transgression or seeking news of a recently arrested friend or family member incarcerated in the cells below. Today, only two of the chairs were occupied, and neither for their predetermined purpose. Lucia clung to Betancourt's arm like her life depended on it. He told her, as gently as he was capable, about Pascal's role in Anna's disappearance.

'So it wasn't your fault? I knew – deep down, I mean – that it wasn't you to blame. Grandfather was so sure, but I knew it couldn't have been.' His daughter shook her head over and over, as though struggling to process this seismic shift in things she'd hitherto held to be immutable. It would take a while for the wounds to heal, but he would be there with her this time. The sound of a car horn interrupted his murmurs of reassurance.

'Go with Awang. I'll call as soon as I'm finished here. I won't be long.' He'd expected her to protest when he'd suggested she go and stay with Evelyn, but she hadn't even asked who Evelyn was. Just nodded silently. His daughter had had to grow up a lot today. Too much. He saw her into the car and gave Awang his instructions. Holloway Lane. Awang raised an eyebrow but sped off to fulfil his task.

In twenty years on the force Betancourt had never once stepped inside the Inspector General's office. Now, here he was, twice in a week. The attitude of Onraet's aide-de-camp was markedly deferential compared to the last time. No scrutiny, no protracted checking of identification. The man held open the door and gave a polite nod. 'Inspector. They're waiting for you.'

Behind his desk, Onraet puffed away on a pipeful of foul-smelling tobacco. To his right, in the seat Montgomerie had occupied two days previously, sat a tired-looking Sir Shenton Thomas. The only other time Betancourt had seen the Governor, he'd been wearing dress uniform and standing on a dais. In this more down-to-earth setting and wearing a less than showy tweed suit, he appeared frailer and more world weary than Betancourt remembered. The other seats were taken by a glowering Bonham, a taciturn Montgomerie, and French, who, if he was feeling any emotion at all, wasn't giving it away.

Onraet made the introductions. 'Obviously, this is still Montgomerie's show, but I asked Assistant Commissioner Bonham along as I know he'd like to congratulate you in person.' Onraet didn't bat an eyelid as he said this and Bonham looked even more thunderous, if that were possible.

Betancourt had called Daisy earlier to fill in the last few remaining gaps and he ticked off the points of his story. 'The

Tōhōkai was an offshoot of Mr Montgomerie's Gen'yōsha but unlike its parent, the new group had significant political ambitions. Nakano Seigō, the founder, was obsessed by the idea of an Asian corridor linking South-East Asia directly with Nazi Germany. The Emperor liked the idea, so Nakano used some of the methods the Gen'yōsha had perfected. He sent his son Jin to Singapore, to establish a trade pipeline with Japan that would break the British embargo and provide much-needed supplies for the Japanese war effort. To do that, he needed someone on the inside. Nakano spoke to his fascist ally, Oswald Mosley, and he in turn suggested his acolyte, French. Nakano put Jin in touch with French and the planning began.

'French needed funds to get the enterprise moving. Fortunately for him, he'd just the thing close at hand. He took the war bonds he was entrusted with keeping safe. No one was asking for them at that time, so the chances of his being found out were negligible. Then things escalated in Europe, and people wanted to buy bonds again. It made them think they were doing their bit from thousands of miles away. The Colonial Office agreed to send out additional supplies of bonds, but they wanted an audit done first. French "discovered" the discrepancy and reported the old bonds stolen.

'If French was going to send the illegal rubber to Japan, he needed shipping he could control. Jin knew Euan Guthrie from the Blue Nightingale. As an employee of Napier's, Guthrie had access to ships. Recruiting him was a simple task. Jin just had to tempt Guthrie with the promise of beautiful women and lots of cash. But for the embargo-breaking to work, the gang needed a stooge to forge the export licences for them. That required a genuine trader – someone with access to the right documentation. Guthrie hooked Pascal Clément, using his girlfriend, Miss Sakai, as bait.

'The women came later. It was Jin who saw the potential in the *suteretsu*. Setting up a chain of brothels and siphoning back the money was an old Gen'yōsha trick. He already had ships sailing to Japan, so why not bring women back on the return trips? He could purchase young girls from brokers in Shanghai for a fraction of their potential earning power. Put a team of heavies into the *suteretsu* and the rest would take care of itself. He shared his plan with Guthrie and the Sleeping Tigers were born.

'But then Guthrie made a mistake, one that was to prove fatal. He was entrusted with running bonds up to Shanghai to pay for the shipments of women. On one such occasion he had a clash in his social diary, so he got Pascal to do the run. Pascal showed the bonds to Miss Sakai, who stole some. She knew about the smuggling from having been first with Guthrie, then with Pascal. She documented the entire thing and planned to use the evidence to blackmail someone into giving her enough money to return to Japan with her unborn child. But who? Not Pascal – he tried his best to talk her out of it. He even offered her money. Guthrie? He was a low-life, involved in every facet of the smuggling, and for a while, I had him down as the prime suspect. But then he was killed, and things no longer added up. I thought I must have got something wrong. If it wasn't Guthrie, then who else could it have been? Jin and his Sleeping Tiger thugs? Possibly, but Akiko feared Jin. She told her friend Mei that she had to complete the transaction before Jin found out. Why would she say that if she was planning to blackmail Jin himself? And would he have even cared? No, she'd intended to threaten the person who stood to lose the most if the bonds came to light again. Raymond French.'

He turned to face French.

'You killed Miss Sakai to stop her talking. Then you had

the Sleeping Tigers clear up your mess for you. They faked her suicide. But you didn't count on Dr Trevose spotting the two sets of wounds. You still might have got away with it all, if hadn't been for Pascal's attempt to impress a lady by taking her with him to Shanghai.'

The room was deathly quiet. Eventually, Sir Shenton spoke. 'Is all this true?'

French smirked. 'More or less. You can't stop us, you know. I alerted Jin. He'll be long gone now, but he'll be back one day. Seigō and Oswald are talking weekly. Seigō is impressing upon the Emperor the need to establish a formal alliance with Herr Hitler and Signor Mussolini. Soon Japan will control Asia and Germany will control Europe, and your effete little dominion of colonies will be finished.'

Onraet shook his head, apparently in disgust. 'Will you give us a minute, Inspector?'

Betancourt nodded. 'I need to check on my daughter.' He looked at French. 'I'll charge him and take his statement when I get back.'

'Before you go, Inspector, a question, if I may.' It was the ghost, Montgomerie. 'I've had a dozen men following the Gen'yōsha for two years. How did you put all this together on your own?'

'It was the demonstrations at the docks that set me off on the right track. Someone was trying to foment ill-feeling between the dockworkers, but in political terms, that made no sense. Then I discovered the demonstrations coincided with shipments of women into the *suteretsu* and I had my first concrete link. The protests were being staged to divert the attentions of my men away from the incoming vessels. Guthrie was my prime suspect, so I checked the dates on which he travelled to Shanghai and those too coincided with shipments of women. Everything came together. Pascal filled in most of the missing details for me. As for the rest, I suggest you tell your men I recommend they start cultivating Daisies.'

Betancourt lit a cigarette and asked the desk sergeant for the phone. He gave the operator Evelyn's number.

'How is Lucia doing?'

'As well as can be expected. She's through the back, helping Martha at the moment. She seems, I don't know… at peace. Does that seem odd to you?

'No.'

'She said you saved her life. What happened?'

'I'll explain later.'

'All right. When will we see you?'

'I don't know. Tell Lucia I called, will you?'

'She's safe here. I promise.'

He was about to hang up when a confusion of emotions engulfed him. Absolution? Redemption? Vindication? All of these. And above all gratitude. 'Evelyn.'

'Yes?'

'Thank you.'

When he got back, the aide had disappeared and the door, usually so jealously guarded, had been left ajar. The mood in the room was sombre. French was gone, presumably to the cells below.

'Is there anything else? I want to charge him and start on his statement as soon as possible.' He noticed there was another empty seat – Montgomerie was missing, too. 'What's going on?'

Bonham looked at Onraet, and they both looked at Sir Shenton Thomas. Onraet shuffled uncomfortably. 'Sit down, Inspector.'

'I'll stand. I said, what is going on?' He looked again at the empty seats and a sickening dread gripped him. Even before the question left his mouth, he knew the answer. 'Where's French?'

The Governor checked his wristwatch and provided the confirmation. 'He'll be arriving at Seletar airport in about twenty minutes. From there he'll be escorted to London where he'll be dealt with appropriately.'

Montgomerie had taken him.

'He couldn't remain here. You understand that? It would never have done for an official of his seniority or standing to be seen to have acted in such an unbecoming fashion. We couldn't allow him to be prosecuted like a common criminal. What sort of message would that have sent to the locals?'

Betancourt felt the blood rush to his head. 'Unbecoming fashion? *Unbecoming fashion?* What the hell is wrong with you people? He didn't just wear the wrong dinner jacket at the mess dinner. Or forget to pay his bar bill at the club.' By now, Betancourt was well past the stage of being in control of his anger, and didn't care. 'French betrayed *your* country, the one you claim to hold so dear. He illegally raised money to help the war effort of your sworn enemies. And make no mistake: eventually Japan will use that money to invade Singapore. He was involved in the enslavement of hundreds of young women, and with his own hand murdered one of them so he wouldn't be found out. *For God's sake, they took my wife, my daughter's mother, and you're worried about how things might look?*'

Onraet was on his feet, his voice low. 'You'd do well to remember to whom you are speaking, Inspector. I was deeply sorry to hear the news about your wife – we all were – and I know I speak for everyone in this room when I say that, as long as there remains a chance she is still alive, no matter how slim, no stone will be left unturned in our efforts to find her.'

He resumed his seat. When he spoke again, his tone was milder and more conciliatory. 'We live in uncertain times, Inspector, and Singapore needs to be ready for whatever challenges it faces. The Police Force is key to that and Sir Shenton and I are in agreement that changes need to be made. There will be ample opportunities ahead for the right people, for people who understand the rules of the game.'

Betancourt remembered what Bonham had said to him that day in his office. It seemed like a lifetime ago. *Learn to play the bloody game.* He eyed each of them in turn. Rules of the game? He was sick to the stomach of their bloody games. And he was sick of them.

A white-hot mist of anger wrapped itself around him. He stumbled out onto the street and turned, unthinkingly, northwards. He needed fresh air. Even the smell of the Singapore River would be sweet compared to the putrid stench of colonial corruption and entitlement he'd just witnessed. What was the point? What was any of this for? They said Singapore wasn't like the other colonies, that it was a decent place, a just place, a place where everyone was respected equally. Hollow lies. Where was the justice in what had just happened? For Akiko? For the women who had died on that ship? For Anna?

A voice called out behind him. It was Bonham. What the hell did he want? He couldn't talk to any of these people. Not now. He walked away but was stopped by a hand on his shoulder. He shook it off.

'Whatever it is, get some other fool to do it. I've had a gutful of all this.'

There was an uncharacteristic hesitancy in Bonham's voice and for the first time, Betancourt saw something approaching compassion in the man's eyes. 'It's Pascal Clément. I'm very sorry to tell you this. He's dead. '

By the time Betancourt returned to the station, Sergeant Quek was waiting for him. Pascal had been taken down and lain on the cot in the cell. Someone had closed his eyes. One final act of decency, at least. The marks around his neck where the ligature had tightened were already a vivid purple.

'How did it happen?'

'When they locked him up, he told the guard he was allergic to insect bites.' In the cell's corner a mosquito net lay, coiled up like a diaphanous beehive.

You're the local. You should be immune to them. They never touch me.

'He was only left alone for fifteen minutes. The guard came back with a cup of tea…' Quek pointed to a length of steel conduit that ran across the ceiling of the holding cell.

'Did you see him?'

Quek nodded. 'There's nothing more you can do here. I can take care of this. Go home. Get some rest. I'll send someone to break the news to the family.'

Betancourt shook his head. He needed to finish this himself.

Chapter Thirty-One

To avoid any chance of being spotted, Betancourt had told the others to meet him at midday at a coffee shop beside the Old Bukit Timah railway station. There were no trains due and the place was quiet. He handed each of them a stack of notes, with instructions.

'Five hundred each. Remember what we discussed. I'll be in the betting hall, near the entrance. Make sure you get there in plenty of time, so you know where I'm standing. Wait, and watch for my signal. On no account are you to talk to me or even acknowledge my presence. Understood?'

Ten heads nodded.

'When I give the signal, start placing the bets. Small amounts – twenties and fifties. When you're done at one window, walk away, give it a minute, and then go to another window and place another bet. You need to be finished and out of the hall no later than five minutes before the start. Got all that?' He looked around the table at them. Some of the faces looked nervous, some excited, one or two gave nothing away.

He turned to the last of his punters and handed over a much larger wad of notes. 'Five thousand. Just stick to what we discussed. You won't need it, but good luck anyway.' He hoped he sounded more confident than he felt.

Victory Parade whinnied and fretted as Allenby tacked him up. Betancourt hadn't seen the horse like this before. The occasion was getting to him. Lucia was in the box, eyes alight as Allenby showed her how to put the saddle on. Marjorie watched from the side of the parade ring, godmotherly concern etched on her face.

'Is she all right, do you think? That horse is huge.'

'What were you like at that age? I bet they couldn't have dragged you out.' He kissed her on the cheek. 'How are you?'

She gave a wan smile. 'I'll be fine. I've decided men don't suit me. It's the single life for me now.'

Allenby led the big horse out of the stable and Lucia came running back. 'I've decided. I will learn to ride, and you will teach me.' If there was one thing Lucia hadn't inherited from her mother, it was circumspection.

'I'd like that.' He tousled her hair affectionately.

Marjorie placed an arm around her. 'The Onraets have a table. Lucia and I will watch the race from there. Why don't you join us?'

He muttered something about needing to place a bet for a friend.

Marjorie waved at someone over his shoulder. 'Over here!'

He turned to see who she was calling to. It was Evelyn. He scanned the crowd in front of him, looking for an exit path that wouldn't involve bumping into her. A plump matron with a parasol was regaling her companion, a bored-looking young man bearing a family resemblance, with her assessment of the chances of the favourite. Betancourt ducked between them, causing the woman to rock back and place her foot in a deposit left by a runner in a previous race. He shouted a fleeting apology.

Taking up position next to the first betting window, he scanned the room. Everyone was in place. One of his punters made as if to wave but Betancourt stayed him with a stern look and a small shake of the head. The Tannoy crackled into life and he jumped. He hadn't noticed he was standing directly underneath.

'Fifteen minutes to post time.'

The public had finished appraising the horses in the paddock and the betting hall was filling up quickly. If he left it any longer, the windows would be too busy, and they wouldn't have enough time to get all the bets on. He folded his newspaper and fanned himself. His punters caught the signal and sprang into action. The indicator board was showing Victory Parade at 30–1 as, one by one, they placed their bets. He kept a running total in his head of how much he thought had been placed, watching the odds all the time. As more bets went on, the price would come down. The trick was to place the bets at a slower rate than everyone else was betting on the rest of the field. Slowly, Victory Parade's price ticked down. 25–1, 20–1, 16–1. The board settled at 12–1. All the bets were on. Act one was complete: five thousand on, five thousand to go. His crew trickled out of the hall to await the finale and when they were all gone, Betancourt followed them out.

'The horses are coming out onto the track for race six: The Queen's Prize for four year olds and up. Weight for age. Fillies and mares allowed five pounds. Leading them out is Happy Wanderer, owned by Mr Archibald Napier and ridden by champion jockey Harry Dunman,

winner of this race last year and odds on to make it a double. Next out is Seven Bells, the four-to-one second favourite, Arthur Hartley up...'

Betancourt blocked out the voice of the commentator and watched as Osman led out Victory Parade. When the horse caught sight of the crowd leaning over the rails, shouting and pointing, he took fright and baulked and swung round. Osman stumbled and fell to his knees but refused to let go of the lead rope. The horse dragged him along the turf for a few strides before coming to a standstill, quivering, and turning his head from side to side, like a sparrow watching for a hawk.

'The outsider Victory Parade is playing up on the way to the start. Wally Hood doing well to stay in the plate there.'

Damn! The horse was so relaxed at home that none of them had considered he might get strung up after being off the track for so long. Too late now. Wally stroked the horse's neck and whispered in his ear and Victory Parade relaxed. Osman unclipped the lead and Wally settled the horse into a steady canter away from the crowds and down the straight towards where the starter had stretched an elasticated rope across the track. Crisis averted, for now.

Betancourt checked the board again. The last bets had gone on about five minutes ago, but in the meantime the money had kept coming for the other horses. Victory Parade's price crept slowly up again: 13–1, 14–1, 15–1.

'The horses are at the start and the starter's assistant is checking the girths. Not long to go now.'

He returned to the betting hall. The last big bet had to go on two minutes before post time and it had to go on all at once. Any sooner and the professionals would have time to react and lay off their bets, bringing the price crashing down. Any later and they risked being stuck in the queue and missing the punt altogether. He checked the windows again. Come on, come on. Where are you?

Finally, his punter entered the hall and stood in line. Three people in front. They might just make it.

'Checks are complete, and the starter is calling the field into line.'

Two still in front... Hurry, for God's sake!

'Bit of a ragged line and the starter has told the jockeys to take a turn and come back in.'

Just one more – an elderly European who looked as though he'd waited until he'd reached the front of the queue before making his selection. The man took off his glasses and propped them on his head, and turned his newspaper over, as though hoping he might find more inspiration on the other side.

'That looks like it. An even line. They're under starter's orders...'

No, not now! Not when they were so close.

'Wait! Hood has turned Victory Parade. They'll have to line up again.'

God love you, Wally Hood.

The crowd were pouring out of the betting hall, bets placed, back to the stand to find a square of space to watch the race from, and Betancourt had to push his way through the oncoming tide of people. He placed a hand on the old man's arm and showed him his warrant card. 'You need to come with me, sir. We've had reports of counterfeit currency circulating.'

'But my wife wanted me to place a bet for her and now I can't remember which blessed horse she wanted.'

'It won't take a minute.' He led the bewildered old man away to a corner where he checked his five-dollar note and pronounced it genuine. He thanked the man for his help and wished him luck for the rest of the afternoon.

'Late money for the outsider, Victory Parade'

He couldn't see the board. Had they managed to get the whole lot on?

'*The starter's calling them in again... And this time they're off! An even break but Victory Parade is a little slow to find his stride.*'

The hall had emptied, and Betancourt was left on his own. He made his way out into the sunshine and found a spot by the rails, close to the furlong pole where the crowds were sparse. The Totalisator board in the infield had cleared. If they'd managed to get the second five thousand on, what had it done to the price?

'*Passing the grandstand for the first time, it's Burmese Ruby who settles down in the lead. Persephone on her outside, and Tanah Merah runs third. Dunman has Happy Wanderer relaxed in midfield ahead of Seven Bells and Joi de Vivre. Mata Hari is second last and Victory Parade is the whipper-in.*'

The drumbeat of hooves filled the air as the horses thundered past. Wally had settled Victory Parade into a good rhythm. The horse's eyes shone with the thrill of the chase. He was doing what he was born to do: running.

'*Into the back straight they go, six furlongs left to travel, and it's still the hare, Burmese Ruby, taking them along. Persephone is close up in second, and Happy Wanderer now moves into a menacing third. Mata Hari makes up a place or two and Victory Parade, who came here after a long spell out, still trails the field.*'

He couldn't watch this on his own. After everything that had happened, win or lose, he needed to be near the people he loved.

'*Rounding the turn for the final time. Burmese Ruby has run her race and Persephone pays the price for trying to go with her. Mata Hari and Seven Bells take it up with the favourite Happy Wanderer in the box seat running third. Joi De Vivre isn't finding much, and Victory Parade is running on past tired horses.*'

He climbed the steps to the grandstand and stood with his back to the unfolding drama of the race. It was as if he was watching a frozen tableau. There was Lucia, face obscured by a pair of binoculars, jumping up and down on the spot. Behind her Marjorie, looking anxious, gripping the girl's narrow shoulders.

'Into the straight and Dunman sets sail for home on Happy Wanderer. He's gone two lengths clear, and he's showing no sign of stopping. Mata Hari's done for and Seven Bells is finding nothing for Hartley. Victory Parade is best of the rest.'

A row in front, Evelyn, bright-eyed, cheered and waved a betting slip. Alistair, her accountant friend, looked on disapprovingly, seemingly unhappy at such public displays of emotion.

'Inside the final furlong and it's Happy Wanderer's race to lose, but he's shortening stride. Hood is getting a tune out of the rag, Victory Parade, and he's closing. Happy Wanderer is out on his feet. He's rolling about like a drunken sailor. Will the post come in time for the favourite?'

In the far corner of the stand, on his own, stood Major Melrose, looking inscrutable. He'd seen it all before. Whatever the result, he'd take it with equanimity.

'They're neck and neck. It's Happy Wanderer and Victory Parade, Victory Parade and Happy Wanderer. There's nothing in it...'

The roar of the crowd rose to a crescendo as the two horses battled to the line, eyes wide, nostrils flaring. And then it was done.

'Photograph, photograph! Please hold on to your tickets until the judge announces the result.'

The two horses circled in front of the stand, flanks heaving, every ounce of effort and determination spent. Allenby descended the steps leading from the small trainers' stand to the winner's circle, ready to meet his charge. He shrugged as someone tapped him on the shoulder, asking the question everyone wanted the answer to. Who won? Betancourt read his lips. 'On the nod.' The horse that had dipped his head as they flashed across the line would get the verdict. A stride before or a stride later might have meant a different result, but that didn't matter now. The crowd hushed as it waited for the judge's decision.

'Here is the result of the photograph...'

Betancourt turned and left.

Chapter Thirty-Two

Outside the Blue Nightingale a sign read: *Closed. Private Function.* Inside, Betancourt was slightly drunk.

Allenby sat at the head of a long table, a benign buddha of the betting ring, dispensing big-hearted munificence to all. At his right hand, Wally Hood and Major Melrose, his familiar beaming smile firmly back in place, discussed past coups won and lost. Allenby called Betancourt over. 'The biggest punt ever landed in the history of Malayan racing. That's what they're saying.' Thanks to Betancourt's counterfeit money check, they'd got the final five thousand on by the skin of their teeth. The price had dropped to 11–1 at the off, but they'd still made over a hundred thousand dollars.

'How's the horse?'

'Right as rain. Told you he was a good 'oss. Did I say he was a good 'oss or did I not?

'You did.'

'So, is that it?'

'What you on about?'

'That day, at the stables, when you let me in on all this. You were talking about packing it in.'

Allenby laughed. A great, deep, booming belly laugh. 'Don't you worry about me. Only way they're getting me away from me 'osses is in a pine box. Anyway, I was just saying to the Major here how we couldn't have done it without you. You and your gang. Can I be honest with you? I didn't fancy our chances when you told me the plan, but you came through. You're bloody diamonds, the lot of you.' Allenby pulled a battered holdall from beneath the table. 'Time to divvy up the spoils. You do it, son. They're your people.'

Betancourt went around the table, distributing the envelopes, and when they were opened, the noise ratcheted up several levels and the champagne flowed even more freely. Abu Bakar, wreathed in clove-scented smoke, was being taught the words to a risqué shanty by Leilani; Belle and Mei caught up on old friends and village gossip; Mr Tan and Ruby exchanged tips on how to extract maximum profitability from the hospitality business; Daisy and Martha shared their mutual passion for Cary Grant; George Elias gave Owen a stride-by-stride replay of the race, complete with actions. Yes, they were his people. They'd trusted him and they'd done everything he'd asked of them without question. And they'd kept their mouths shut. Betancourt gazed at his impromptu crew with fondness and with pride. Bloody diamonds was right.

One diamond was missing. He slipped the last envelope into his pocket.

He climbed the spiral staircase to the mezzanine above and stepped out onto the verandah. He looked out over the lights of the city: a city bound by greed; greed for money and greed for power. Still, it was his city, and it wasn't such a bad place for all that.

The breeze picked up a whiff of scent and blew it in his direction.

'You'll never make a spy if you wear that stuff.'

'Don't you like it?'

'I like it very much indeed.'

Evelyn stood next to him. He was unsure what to do. She saved him further anxiety by leaning across and kissing him gently on the cheek. She linked an arm through his and this time he didn't shy away.

'I've got something that belongs to you.' He handed her the envelope.

She opened it and looked inside. 'I can't take this. I only did it for a bit of fun.'

'Take it. It's yours. Use it for the clinic. You earned it. For a moment there, I didn't think you'd make it.'

'That poor old man. The look on his face when you dragged him away. Counterfeit money! Where did that come from?'

'I needed to get him out of the way, and it was the first thing that came into my head.' He looked around. 'Where's Lucia?'

'Downstairs. Learning everything there is to know about the manifold attractions of Mr Cary Grant.'

'Another few days and I'll be able to bring her home. Thank you for looking after her.'

'It's a pleasure. I think she's enjoying herself. The girls love her. Yesterday, a few of them took her off for the afternoon.'

'Took her where?'

'Relax. Fifteen-year-old girls are worldlier than their fathers realise. Besides, she had a wonderful time. The girls dressed her in a kimono. It suited her.'

What kind of father would condone *karayuki-san* dressing his daughter in their working clothes? And yet, he felt for the first time since Anna had disappeared that he could properly care for her again.

'I thought I'd lost her. It seems wrong that it took all this to get her back.'

'Give her time. She's a very special young lady. What about the Cléments? They must be devastated. First Anna, and now Pascal.'

'Odette's taking it badly, but Louis's now claiming he always had his doubts about Pascal. He's had enough of the business. He's selling up. To Napier & Campbell, would you believe? How's that for irony? He wants to use some of the money to buy a house for Lucia and me.'

'That's a generous offer. Did you accept it?'

'I said I'd think about it.'

'Oh, God, Max. What an awful business this has been. At least you and Lucia are back together, so something positive has come out of it. I have some news of my own. Kitty is coming to stay with me for a while. The nuns feel it would help her rehabilitation. I thought we might take a holiday. The Cameron Highlands or perhaps Penang – somewhere like that. I think she'd like it.'

Nuns.

'St Seraphima's... There was a young nun there. I thought there was something familiar about her. It was her eyes. She had your eyes. Sister Catherine. Kitty.'

'She told me she'd seen you. She asked the Mother Superior who you were then asked me if I knew you.'

'And what did you say?'

'I told her the truth. I said I did, and I thought you seemed like trouble.'

He leaned into her. For the moment, he was content.

'There you are. We thought we'd lost you.' It was Ruby.

Betancourt embraced her. 'No Leo?'

'Leo's gone. I should have done it years ago, but you cling on, hoping things will change, don't you? I'm thinking of selling this place. Too many memories. I still have family in Malacca. It might be time to spend some time with them.'

Evelyn touched Ruby's arm. 'You'll be missed.' Her face took on a speculative expression. 'Maybe I should buy the club. Do you think I'd make a good nightclub hostess?'

'I'm sure you'd make a wonderful nightclub hostess. But not as good as you are a doctor. Come on, let's rejoin the party.'

There was an empty seat next to George Elias and Betancourt took it. 'How's the story coming along?'

'I can only write what's made public and Government House is playing its cards close to its chest. Praise all round for young Guthrie. Died bravely thwarting a plot by the dastardly Japs. French has a new posting in Blighty. The good folk of Singapore are safe once again, but they need to remain extra-vigilant as Japan is upping the stakes in Asia. The usual rubbish.'

'That it?'

'Unless you've got something else?'

'You know what, George? I think we can do a bit better than that. Bring your glass. Let's find somewhere quiet. But remember…'

Elias grinned. 'A good journalist never reveals his sources. You know that, Inspector.'

Chapter Thirty-Three

Betancourt watched as a car stopped to let a snaking line of uniformed children, hands linked, two by two, cross the road that divided the waterfront from the coffee shop outside which he sat. On the table in front of him a copy of that morning's *Straits Tribune* fluttered lazily in the breeze. The wind that had disturbed the pages of the newspaper had stirred up low, fat waves that melted away to effervescent clouds as they kissed the foreshore.

A small boy, six or seven years old, clad in a torn singlet and an oversized pair of football shorts, stood in the wash at the edge of the sea, a few feet from the spot Betancourt had come to visit. No school for this little man. He had to bring home food for his family. He watched with reminiscent curiosity as the boy reached into a rusted tin bucket and extracted a prawn, which he expertly affixed to a fishing hook. The sun caused tiny rainbow sparks to fly from the shell of the crustacean as the animal wriggled and squirmed in protest. Perfect bait. This boy's family wouldn't go hungry. He whirled his length of twine in an ever-increasing circle and when he judged the bait had reached terminal velocity – the point at which the prawn would become detached and fly off into the sea by itself – he let go, and the lead weight the boy had fastened to his line carried the bait out beyond the breakers. For a moment, a pang for the simple pleasures of childhood gripped Betancourt, and he wondered if Lucia might be interested in going fishing with him. They could rent a boat at Jardine Steps, go out the Sister Islands, take a picnic.

Evelyn walked slowly towards him. 'Is this seat taken?'

'Seeing as it's you… How did you know where I'd be?'

'I bumped into Marjorie. She said I might find you here.' She picked up the newspaper. 'George Elias got his scoop, I see. That was a good bit of detective work. None of the other papers have anything like this much. You'd almost think he had a contact on the inside.'

'Resourceful fellow, George.'

They sat in silence for a while, watching the waves.

'Is this where it happened?'

'Over there.' He pointed to a patch of sea grass, beyond where the boy was now wrestling with an indignant fish. 'I come down here sometimes and just watch. It's stupid. It won't bring Anna back.'

Evelyn shook her head, and when she spoke her tone was soft and intimate. 'It's not stupid. So, what happens next? Will you keep looking for Anna?'

He looked away, out to sea. 'Pascal didn't know what Jin and his men had done with her. Until I know for sure, I won't be able to rest.'

She reached across and touched his hand. 'When you're ready, you know where I'll be.'

They said their goodbyes, and he watched as she disappeared into the distance. When she was no more than a dot, he turned up his collar against the first specks of rain and walked away, back towards the Singapore River.

Note from the author

This book is a work of fiction. That said, I was keen to represent the Singapore of the 1930s as closely as I could, and the street names and other placenames are as correct as my research would allow. I'm particularly grateful to OneMap, a website produced by the Singapore Land Authority, for their historical maps, and to the National Archives of Singapore for making available their wealth of historical material. There are a few caveats to this factual approach. Most notably there was no morgue named The Crypt, or anything else that I am aware of, beneath the Singapore River. Nor were there a Royal Edinburgh & Imperial Bank, a *Straits Tribune*, a St Seraphima's School for Girls, or a Blue Nightingale jazz bar.

Conversely, the characters in the book are nearly all products of my imagination. The exceptions are René Henry de Solminihac Onraet, Inspector-General of the Straits Settlements Police prior to the Second World War; Sir Shenton Thomas, the last Governor of the Straits Settlements; and Oswald Mosley, leader of the British Union of Fascists in the latter part of the decade. His visit to Singapore, on the other hand, requires the granting of a little authorial licence.

When I started writing this book, I was surprised to find how little social history existed that adequately described the lives of the non-colonial immigrants who formed the majority of the residents of Singapore in the 1930s. To that end I am indebted to Professor James Francis Warren's excellent books *Rickshaw Coolie: A People's History of Singapore*, and *Ah Ku and Karayuki-san: Prostitution in Singapore 1870 to 1940*. It was the latter book in particular which alerted me to the *suteretsu* and the lives of the women who worked there.

Glossary

bumboat — small craft used to ferry goods and people

charpoy — traditional Asian bed consisting of a wooden frame strung with webbing

char kuay teow — popular dish of stir-fried flat rice noodles with other ingredients

cheongsam — high-necked close-fitting dress originating in Shanghai

coolie — unskilled labourer

copra — dried coconut kernels (a source of coconut oil)

gweilo — Cantonese epithet for Europeans (literally *'ghost man'*)

hai — affirmative in several Chinese dialects

horishi — master tattooist

irezumi — highly-decorative, intricate tattoos applied by hand

jaga — watchman or guard

kampong — traditional Malay village

kanji — Chinese characters used in Japanese script

karayuki-san — Japanese prostitute (literally 'Miss Gone Abroad')

kaya — sweet coconut egg jam

Glossary

kebun — gardener

kopi tiam — traditional coffee shop, often serving food

kretek — Indonesian cigarettes containing tobacco and cloves

long sai — day labourers, often women, employed to clean the hulls of ships (corruption of 'alongside')

mama-san — brothel manager

mandor — foreman

mem — lady (showing respect)

padang — playing field

rotan — stiff bamboo cane, used to administer punishment

seppuku — ritual suicide

Serani — Eurasian (of people) (from the Malay approximation of *Nazarene*, meaning 'Christian')

Suteretsu — Japanese red-light district (pronounced *suh-tret-suh*, an Amakusa dialect transliteration of the English word 'streets')

syce — groom (also, a chauffeur or driver)

topi — hat, especially one for protection from the sun

tuan — sir

tunku — a member of the Malay nobility

Acknowledgments

My heartfelt thanks to the many people who have helped and supported me through the writing of this story as it has developed from the merest twinkle of an idea to the book you now hold in your hand.

To my agent, Euan Thorneycroft, whose belief in the book and in me sustained me through more than one bout of self-doubt. Thanks also to the rest of the great team at AM Heath.

To Rebecca Collins and Adrian Hobart at Hobeck Books, first for taking a chance on me, and then for working so hard to bring the book into the world.

To my editors, Rob Dinsdale, Sam Boyce, and Lynn Curtis, whose expert eyes helped shape, craft, and polish the manuscript. Thanks also to Jem Butcher whose cover design captures the essence of the book so well.

To my tutors at the Universities of Edinburgh and East Anglia – Allyson Stack, Jane McKie, Robert Alan Jamieson, Tracey Emerson, Henry Sutton, Tom Benn, Laura Joyce, and

Bill Ryan, without whose masterful guidance I would still be stuck writing dreadful short stories.

To the friends I met during my stints at university. From Edinburgh (by way of Monterey, CA), Lori Sheirich, who has read every draft of the book through its many iterations, and who approached each new read as though it was the first. From East Anglia, Niamh O'Connor, whose enthusiasm for the book was both constant and infectious, and to my fellow Waffle Press-ers, Natalie Marlow, Roe Lane, and Denise Beardon for their cheer, their humour, and the occasional shoulder to cry on. Waffles are on me.

To Abir Mukherjee, a gentleman and a damn fine writer whose book *A Rising Man* convinced me there were, after all, people who wanted to read the kind of thing I was writing. Later, for being kind enough to read the finished story, and even kinder to write the recommendation you find on the cover.

To my family, with special thanks to my mother, Alison, who has never stopped believing in me, despite me having given her many reasons to do so over the years.

To Rudi, the black Labrador, for selflessly making himself available to receive snacks, whatever the time of day or night.

Most of all to Lillian, for her love and support, her encouragement when my own courage deserted me, and her belief when mine waned. (And for all the tea.)

And finally, I couldn't end this without a word for my muse, Singapore herself. She got under my skin as soon as we met and has never left. Without her, this book would never have happened.

About the Author

Mark Wightman was born in Edinburgh before growing up in the Far East, first in Hong Kong before spending most of his formative years in Singapore, which he found a fascinating, complex place. The idea of writing a novel set there had lain, sown but ungerminated, for a long time. He particularly wanted to explore the elements of history that lay at the margins, where the recorded facts have either faded or been hidden.

After a successful career in media technology, Mark took time out to complete master's degrees in Creative Writing, first at the University of Edinburgh, and then at the University of East Anglia, where he received a distinction for his debut novel Waking the Tiger.

Mark was the winner of the Pitch Perfect event at the Bloody Scotland Crime Festival in 2017, also for Waking the Tiger, and was selected to be one of the seventeen UNESCO City of Literature Story Shop emerging writers at the 2017 Edinburgh International Book Festival.

To find out more about Mark and his writing please visit his website: **www.markwightmanauthor.com**.

Hobeck Books - the home of great stories

Hobeck Books is an independent publisher of crime, thrillers and suspense fiction and we have one aim – to bring you the books you want to read.

For more details about our books, our authors, including Mark Wightman and our plans, plus the chance to download free novellas, sign up for our newsletter at **www.hobeck.net**.

You can also find us on Twitter **@hobeckbooks** or on Facebook **www.facebook.com/hobeckbooks10**.

Hobeck Books also presents a weekly podcast, the Hobcast, where founders Adrian Hobart and Rebecca Collins discuss all things book related, key issues from each week, including the ups and downs of running a creative business. Each episode includes an interview with one of the people who make Hobeck possible: the editors, the authors, the cover designers. These are the people who help Hobeck bring great stories to life. Without them, Hobeck wouldn't exist. The Hobcast can be listened to from all the usual platforms but it can also be found on the Hobeck website: **www. hobeck.net/hobcast**.

Finally, if you enjoyed this book, please also leave a review on the site you bought it from and spread the word. Reviews are hugely important to writers and they help other readers also.

Lightning Source UK Ltd.
Milton Keynes UK
UKHW020631200621
385805UK00010B/795